To Ann & Ralph.
Thank you both for
your hospitality and
good humour.

Crystal Vision

Crystal Vision is a 'time slip' novel set in
two periods – 1845–1855 and 2007–2016.

Best wishes,
Hope you enjoy the book,

by

Alan Young

Alan Young

GW00691482

Grosvenor
Publishing

Alan M Young is hereby identified as author of this
work in accordance with Section 77 of the Copyright, Designs
and Patents Act 1988

The book cover, map of Expedition and 'Ditty Box' photograph
are copyright to Alan M Young

This book is a work of fiction and, except in the case of historical fact, any
resemblance to actual persons living or dead, is purely coincidental.

This book is published by
Grosvenor House Publishing Ltd
Link House
140 The Broadway, Tolworth, Surrey, KT6 7HT.
www.grosvenorhousepublishing.co.uk

A CIP record for this book
is available from the British Library

ISBN 978-1-78623-057-7

Dedication

This book is dedicated to my late Dad, David 'Davy' Young

My late Mum, Muriel, who encouraged and inspired me to write this novel and to my late Aunt Mary, who encouraged me to finish it.

My son, Stephen David Young

For my Nottingham and T. S. Mercury friends, who died while in their late teens in the same road accident, Malcolm Eley and Phil (Soapy) Hudson – 'I remember them well'

Lastly and respectfully, for all the crew members aboard HMSS Erebus and HMSS Terror, whose well-documented fate tragically outlived their mortal souls

'To minds that can soar, that will rise and not be discouraged by obstacles or difficulties that will chance and dare for what they love and know to be right' Beatrice Fry (1862–1946)

Wife of Commander C. B. Fry, Training Ship, Mercury (1912–1946)

Personal Acknowledgements

To my wife, Tarn, who initially bought me two books on how to write a novel, then read them herself first, producing two novels of her own. She's now on her third. I grudgingly put pen to paper 'literally' some considerable time afterward. However, without her expertise in sourcing information from the internet, her enthusiasm and encouragement throughout and her ability in transferring the written word to the computer, I may have failed miserably. Her collage of photos gave birth to the cover of Crystal Vision, reconfigured and improved by my nephew, Christopher Hill, to obtain the right format for publication.

To my lifelong friend, Colin Fryer, who I have known since we were 'knee high to grasshoppers', who patiently and diligently read the draft chapters prior to publication, offering genuine, 'I'm not pulling any punches' honest advice; essential for any 'novice' writer.

Thanks also to my two other readers, Rob Ellis, my cousin in Colchester and Jeff Sale, my cousin Elaine's husband in Nottingham. Your comments were greatly appreciated.

Also, to the Davies's in Vancouver and the Cayer's in Quebec, who exemplified Canadian hospitality by taking an interest in a fledgling British Merchant Seaman, in the late sixties, welcoming me into their lives and homes. A belated thank you!

Lastly, thanks to Ann and Andrew, librarians at Mapperley Library Nottingham – my other information source.

Acknowledgements

Books: 'Across the top of the World: the quest for the North West Passage' – Author: James P. Delgado

'Ice Blink: the tragic fate of Sir John Franklin's lost Polar Expedition' – Author: Scott Cookman

'Sir John Franklin's last Arctic expedition: a chapter in the history of the Royal Navy' – Muster Rolls of H.M.SS. 'Erebus' and 'Terror' (Collated with the original rolls, Public Record Office, London) Author: Richard J. Cyriax

'Frozen in Time' – Authors: John Geiger, Owen Beattie

'The History of the Hudson Bay Company 1670–1870' Author: E. E. Rich

'The Honourable Company' –
Author: Douglas McKay

'Nicholls's Seamanship and Nautical Knowledge' (1961) –
Authors: Brown, Son and Ferguson

'Meteorology' (1961) –
Authors: Kemp and Young

'The Encyclopaedia of Ships' –
General Editor: Tony Gibbons

'Great Classic Sailing Ships' –
Author: Kenneth Giggal

'The World's Great Sailing Ships' –
Author: Olivier Puget

'The Royal Marines 1664 to Present' –
Author: Richard Brooks

'National Geographic Magazine'

'The Indomitable Beatie' –
Author: Ronald Morris

'Lady Franklin's Lament' –
Origin unknown, circa 1850

'The Yarn of the Nancy Bell' –
Sir William Schwenck Gilbert 1866

'Sir John Franklin' (Epitaph) –
Alfred Lord Tennyson

Other information obtained from:
Internet sources

PART ONE
THE EXPEDITION

'......And then we murdered the Bo'sun tight,
And he much resembled pig;
Then we wittled free, did the cook and me,
On the crew of the captain's gig...'

William Schwenck Gilbert (1836–1911)

CHAPTER ONE

'Desperation'
Near 'Whale Cove' (Tikirarjuaq)
Hudson Bay – 1849

The deck knife's blade glistened in the reflected light from the pack ice as the sun shone brilliantly over the near Arctic's magnificence.

With deft strokes, Tom, the bosun severed the last remaining strands of meat from the thigh bone...there was no blood...all life had departed from the carcass weeks before, in stark contrast to his own gnarled and calloused hand. He laughed...a laugh bordering on the hysterical as he contemplated the seemingly inevitable end to their plight. He would never give up on his shipmates, but even he had to admit that their position was desperate.

'Eat Davy...eat,' encouraged the bosun, 'got to keep your strength up.'

Davy stared vacantly through bloodshot eyes, but did as he was told.

Rob, Tom's lifelong friend, watched nervously before casting a meaningful glance in the Bosun's direction. His innermost thoughts were in turmoil; who would have thought that it would come to this, as he too chewed fatalistically on a strip of cold flesh.

❧

The bosun, formerly a butcher's apprentice at Smithfield before his seafaring days, was a burley, craggy faced, barrel chested cockney, with a dour sense of humour and a heart of gold. He stood six foot three in his stockinged feet, a veritable mountain of a man. Tom was also Davy's uncle and mentor who'd taken the bright young boy seaman under his wing when Davy's feet first trod the quarterdeck of the ship at Chatham docks. That particular event now seemed a lifetime ago, but it focused his mind. He'd promised his sister to look out for her son and he fully intended to keep that promise. Their situation might be bleak, but he was determined to succeed, despite the odds, which, horrifyingly were stacked against them.

❧

The three bedraggled and half starved men were huddled in the lee of their upturned boat on the rocky shore near Whale Cove. It afforded them minimal protection from the chill arctic wind that had sprung up moments before, but they were glad of it nevertheless.

Their trek from King William Island across vast frozen tracts of spectacular but perilous land and seascapes had been daunting in the extreme and they were becoming noticeably weaker by the day. Fort York[1] beckoned,

---

1 Fort York – Hudson Bay Company (near modern day 'Churchill')

bewilderingly close but still a monumental 250 miles to the south, over formidable terrain.

'Let's move on now before we freeze to death,' stated Tom, matter-of-factly. Although his confidence levels were at an all time low, he winked wryly at his shipmates, before he cajoled them into another massive effort. 'Well, what are you waiting for...a horse and cart?'

Rob raised an eyebrow and looked at Davy and then they both laughed, humour reviving their spirits once more.

Ditty Box Contents

CHAPTER TWO

A Curious Collection
Nottingham and London –
April 2007

Thoughts of my father invaded my conscience as I approached the heavily porticoed entrance to 'Hudson Eley' in the refurbished part of Nottingham's historic lace-market.

On entering, I was greeted by a distinguished looking female solicitor in her early thirties. She was expecting me and smiled in welcome. She ushered me into a not insubstantial traditional office which boasted several oil paintings and a large antique oak desk on which sat a small rustic and well used 'ditty box'. I was intrigued, but no more so than the solicitor, Jane Eley. She eyed me speculatively, obviously expecting me to provide answers to the many questions she'd been guarding since my father, David Young, had lodged his Last Will and Testament with the firm, along with the auspicious box.

'Now Mr Young, I've requested your presence to discuss the contents of your father's Will and to hand over this box and its contents...my condolences by the way. I must admit to being extremely curious about the contents, of which I'm aware and hope, therefore, that you will be able to enlighten me. Of course, I do realise that my curiosity must remain unsatisfied if you so wish, but an explanation of such a strange collection of objects would be wonderful, although, fundamentally, I do not wish to pry and it does sound somewhat unprofessional of me.'

I responded cautiously, 'Well, as I am unaware of the contents myself, you have me at a disadvantage. Perhaps we should open it and see?'

Jane produced a small key, which she gave to me, sliding the box in my direction.

I inserted the key into the lock and lifted the lid to reveal several items contained in small canvas pouches, each with a drawstring. I opened the first to find three iron-forged keys of variable size. The second pouch contained, what appeared to be an item of 'scrimshaw'[2], etched on a whale's tooth, depicting or perhaps charting, an area near the Arctic Circle... intriguing to say the least. The third contained a wood handled and exceedingly sharp knife in a copper sheath. A fourth, contained a hand brass compass with an inscription on the base – 'To Tom, may you always find your way back to me, Love forever, Marie'. The final pouch contained an exquisite gold ring, which incorporated a sapphire, flanked by two large diamonds.

'I'm totally perplexed myself,' I said. 'I haven't any idea who Tom or indeed Marie might be, what these items mean or where they came from, so I'm sorry to disappoint...I haven't an explanation to enlighten you.'

Jane was, however, plainly disappointed having 'guarded' the contents for several years. She sighed, 'Oh well, perhaps if you find out what information they hold, do please let me

---

2 A carved or engraved article, especially of whale ivory, whalebone, walrus tusks, or the like, made by seamen as a leisure occupation.

know.' With that she proceeded with the more mundane aspects of finalising the Will.

I left 'Hudson Eley' later that misty morning; excitement and, dare I say, a slight unease enveloped me, which I couldn't explain. The prospect of again examining the contents of the box, preoccupied my mind.

∞§∞

Several hours later, I took out the artefacts once more and chuckled to myself. Dad enjoyed mysteries and it was so in keeping that the contents of the box were bereft of any explanation but probably akin to a plot in a 'Jeffrey Farnol' novel, for which he had a fondness.

The piece of scrimshaw seemed to offer more information than the other items. The engraved map portrayed an area annotated 'King William Land' and another area named the 'Great Fish River'. Routes and markings criss-crossed the surface with the letters 'E' and 'T' figuring prominently on an area west of the island, along with the date, 24th May 1847.

My mind foggily reacted to these dates. I recalled an article in National Geographic, re-kindling latent memories of the ill-fated expedition of one Sir John Franklin in the search for the North West Passage. Could this be an artefact from that expedition? I determined to find out more and immediately began researching the expedition in my spare time. My mission gained pace with the appropriation of some background information and a detailed account of the expedition, prior to the crew's disappearance and apparent demise. I also obtained a crew list of the ships' involved, one for the *Erebus* and one for the *Terror* and was stunned to encounter the name of one sailor on the *Erebus*...David

Young, an eighteen year old ship's boy...could we have possibly been related?

By now, I was really enthusiastic to find out more!

A search of the family tree, of which I had prior knowledge (having previously investigated the line), produced some remarkable coincidences. Apparently, my great, great grandfather, James, who just happened to be a marine store dealer or ship chandler in the London area around Whitechapel at the turn of the 19th century, fathered three sons in 1816, 1818 and 1826. The last boy was named David, born in June of that particular year. The name was apparently resurrected for my father on his birth in 1915. Significantly, as I recall, my dad remembered 'his' father retelling a tale of tragedy in the family that occurred many years before and he was named David after that relation.

I decided to visit London and within days found myself standing in front of Sir John Franklin's statue and monument in Waterloo Place, off Pall Mall. A plaque confirmed the list of lost souls who'd met their fate during the voyage to locate the North West Passage. David Young's name stood out dramatically and this sent a distinct shiver down my spine, the personal consequence of which left me in no doubt that I should pursue the mystery of the contents of the 'ditty box'.

I booked into a convenient hotel and planned my next move, having taken leave of absence for an undetermined period from my work in Nottingham.

CHAPTER THREE

A Meaningful Contract
Admiralty Buildings London –
1st April 1845

Stephan Goldner was ecstatic. He strutted jauntily away from the Admiralty, where he had just been awarded a victualling contract for storing the *Erebus* and *Terror* with canned goods. He smiled to himself...it was, after all, 'All Fools Day'... He recalled the faintly humorous scene as the contract was signed in one of the instantly forgettable and dreary meeting rooms at the rear of the impressive building alongside the Thames.

The stuffy bespectacled rear admiral displaying a haughty attitude and an abundance of gold braid, had imperiously declared that the contract was his, with the proviso that all provisions were to be delivered from 137 Houndsditch Road in Whitechapel (Goldner's own factory) by May 12th.

Obsequious and scheming as Goldner was, he had sufficient business acumen to convey a glowing presentation of the attributes of canned provisions, at present in its infancy, for expeditions such as the search for the North West Passage.

He reflected on the fact that these cans, some several thousand, constituted approximately one third of the total food supply to be delivered to the ships. Consequently, he did have a problem. He knew that his canning process factory could not produce the 8,000 cans in the time-frame submitted, so he would have to cut corners, firstly in the preparation of the food and secondly in the can production process. For a fleeting instant, he considered several possible scenarios of his greed, but salved his conscience by remembering the large profit. After all, he was the lowest bidder and the Admiralty were notorious for choosing the cheaper tender.

By the time the expedition, (scheduled to last at least three years, possibly more), were consuming the contents of the cans and other provisions, he would be able to disclaim responsibility…natural spoilage came to mind. He made a mental note to discuss this in detail with Mr Ritchie, his personal secretary. The samples previously supplied to the Admiralty in support of the tender were, of course, of good quality and specification, how else could he have competed with the likes of 'Gamble', 'Hogarth' and 'Cooper and Aves', also on the Admiralty victualling lists. He chuckled once more to think that the 'braids'[3] hadn't smelt a rat when he tendered his bid. It was in total, half that of the other bidders and promised 'immediate delivery' as the 'coup de grace' with no charge for delivery; a masterful stroke no less.

---

3 Gold Braid – used on uniforms to denote rank

CHAPTER FOUR

'Misgivings'
London – 25th April 1845

Sir John Franklin sat opposite his wife, Jane, in the small teashop adjacent to the Admiralty buildings where he'd been finalising preparations for the forthcoming expedition. Her countenance betrayed her true feelings. She wished her husband, now nearly sixty years old, would forego his passion and ultimate goal of finding the North West Passage and retire gracefully instead.

She vented her feelings in one last vain attempt to prevent him from pursuing what she regarded as 'a lost cause'. 'John, this expedition is madness...you're too old! Isn't it enough that during the Back Expedition of 1836, the *Terror* was badly damaged and only just survived that Arctic fiasco? Since then, the *Terror* and the *Erebus* have been to Antarctica with John Clark Ross and Francis Crozier...another four years of extreme conditions, when the ships also suffered considerable damage. Both vessels are older now and so are you. Why don't you step down? I've a strange feeling of foreboding about this voyage and I can't rid myself of some awful visions.'

'Calm yourself my dear, I'm not in the least bit concerned. This will be the best led and best equipped expedition ever proposed by the Admiralty...and the rewards...should we succeed and find the North West Passage to the Pacific, will be great indeed, for our nation and for ourselves. The trade possibilities are endless, please do not concern yourself, as it will be my last voyage...I promise! I do have experience of the area already. Granted it will be harsh, but I have every confidence in the crews of the *Erebus* and the *Terror*, some of whom I have sailed with previously...have no fear!'

The pair drifted into pleasantries, which gave Franklin time to re-assess the refitting of both vessels.

Erebus and *Terror* were fitted with 'Copperknob'[4] 20 horsepower steam engines, designed by Edward Bury and built by Robert Stephenson & Company, capable of propelling the vessels at four knots. They were relatively light at 24 tons and used a bar framed construction. His one concern was that the modifications inherently weakened the structural integrity of each ship at the bow, (although they had been reinforced with iron plates) but, significantly, at the stern. The ship's sides, of course, had been strengthened to withstand the pressures of sea ice, but he had to admit to certain misgivings concerning the bow and stern areas. *I'll keep **that** to myself,* he thought.

---

4 Copperknob Engines –Terror – Planet Type 0-4-0 – Developed and built by Robert Stephenson & Co. and Designed by Edward Bury. Used on the London to Birmingham Railway as a contractors engine until 1845, when sold to the Royal Navy. Erebus – Planet Type 2-2-0 – A copy of Robert Stephenson and Company's and Designer Edward Bury's engine, built in 1836 by Marshalls of Wednesbury. Previously used on London and Greenwich Railway and sold to the Royal Navy in 1845. Note 1 – Both engines were essentially old rolling stock and 'second-hand', having engaged in ten years of service, prior to their purchase. Note 2 – An example of a Copperknob engine can currently be viewed at the York Railway Museum.

Two hours previously, he'd witnessed the screw[5] being repositioned, alongside other dignitaries and several Lordships associated with the expedition. If necessary, the propeller could be taken on deck to facilitate repairs at sea, using a system of tackles and chains. He noted that this fact and a report would be included in tomorrow's edition of 'The Times' newspaper.

His thoughts were abruptly interrupted when his wife tapped his hand encouragingly.

'John, time to leave, we've an appointment to keep at home.'

He dutifully obeyed. A small price to pay for his earlier steadfast rebuttal of her earnest suggestion, to stay at home. Worryingly, however, he couldn't help contemplating a recurring thought whenever he observed the ship's name – Erebus – a place of darkness in the Underworld, on the way to Hades! Sobering indeed!

He was preparing to leave the premises when a uniformed officer entered and handed him an official note from James Fitzjames, commander of the Erebus. It read—

'Regret to inform you that we sustained our first casualty whilst securing the propeller. The weight of which caused the crew to lose control of the double purchase on the swinging derrick[6], which was catastrophic. In that the propeller collided with the side of the hatch coaming. Unfortunately, James Stanley, ship's boy was on deck at the time and was

---

5 Smith Patent Propellers could be lifted out of the water so that ships could proceed under sail alone, reducing drag.
6 A Swinging Derrick usually positioned over the ship's centreline and moved using a double purchase block and tackle systems

crushed to death by the impact. His next of kin have been informed and arrangements made for his funeral. I will endeavour to find a replacement for the voyage. J.F.

Franklin crumpled the missive in the palm of his hand before shoving it into his greatcoat pocket.

'What is it dear?' asked his wife.

'Oh nothing to concern yourself with...just details,' he responded, dejectedly contemplating a letter to the parents. He also determined that the accident should not be reported in the next edition of 'The Times' along with some inevitable journalistic nonsense of a jinx on the expedition. He knew J.F. would write up the incident in the ship's log book, an important point of reference with respect to anything which occurs on board, providing valuable evidence for an enquiry, should one be deemed necessary. Nonetheless, he was concerned and his worried frown confirmed his inner emotional turmoil.

CHAPTER FIVE

A Nagging Problem
London – 26th April 1845

Sir John arrived early at his temporary office in the Admiralty buildings. He still felt uneasy after the events of the previous day, but concentrated his attention on the task in hand.

The installation of the auxiliary engines to both *Erebus* and *Terror* presented a unique challenge to himself and a successful outcome to the voyage. He was acutely aware of the possible pitfalls associated with such an undertaking for two or possibly three reasons.

Firstly, the engines were not new, having completed a decade or so on their respective railways.

Secondly, they had been adapted for use aboard the two ships, which also needed extensive alterations to accommodate them. This affected quite dramatically, the structure and, more importantly, the stability of the vessels. Lastly, there was the question of the expertise required to run the engines in auxiliary mode and operate the lead lined heating and water systems.

Four stokers had been engaged to facilitate the hard graft necessary to run the boilers and now the only outstanding problem, which needed solving was to employ someone with the essential operating knowledge.

With this in mind, he had arranged to meet with an experienced engineer from the East Midlands, who had previously worked with Edward Bury, in Robert Stephenson's engineering works. He was to meet with the gentleman this morning at 8 o'clock sharp and was relieved to note that the engineer had already arrived prior to his arrival and was waiting in an annex. The Admiral's intention was to instigate a comprehensive interview to determine and review the extent of the possible problems that they may encounter on the voyage. He conceded that his knowledge of such things was negligible; quite a forthright criticism of himself, but he was confident of presenting the advantages of the expedition to this man, in positive terms.

∽✺∾

Sir John stepped out of his office to instruct his secretary to show in the engineer. The secretary acknowledged Sir John, 'Certainly, Sir, would you care for refreshments to be brought?'

'Yes, but not immediately; give me half an hour with him to assess his credentials and calibre before we're disturbed,' responded Sir John.

The secretary nodded his acknowledgment, then proceeded to the waiting room. He entered. 'Please come this way Mr Fryer, the Admiral is expecting you.' The engineer followed the secretary into an impressive office displaying an abundance of naval history, especially with respect to the oak panelled walls on which hung several large oil paintings depicting seascapes and ships in full sail.

'Mr Ernest Fryer,' announced the secretary.

'Do please sit down Mr Fryer.' Sir John waved him to a leather upholstered chair adjacent to his desk.

'Thank you, sir,' responded the engineer with cautious optimism. He'd never met a man of such importance, with a reputation to match before, but was determined not to be overawed by the occasion.

Sir John sensed this in the man and became more relaxed himself. He needed an insight into the man's knowledge and experience and an acknowledgement of mutual respect was essential from the onset. He needn't have worried unduly, because from the moment Mr Fryer introduced himself, an understanding existed between them.

'I'm Sir John Franklin and I'm very pleased that you were able to accept my request to attend here this morning. No doubt you're a very busy man yourself?'

'Yes, I'm always busy sir,' replied the engineer, 'but I'm also intrigued by your summons, as I feel somewhat insignificant in your presence.'

'Nonsense,' laughed Sir John. 'I'm sure your experience of your own field is as good as mine is in other areas. I need your opinion and knowledge of engineering to help strengthen my endeavours to discover a route through the Arctic. Will you help me Ernest? I hope you don't mind me addressing you informally by the way?'

'Not at all,' replied the engineer, 'but I'm usually known by my middle name amongst my peers...reputation you see.' He smiled, then continued, 'My friends and associates call me Colin...'Cautious Col', actually, because I take time to assess the risks in my work before putting them into practice. It's paid dividends in the past when undertaking complex engineering problems.'

'Col it is then!' chuckled Sir John. 'Right then, let me brief you on my plans to determine how you can be of help to the expedition, now that the 'ice has been broken.'

Nothing like a dose of 'black' humour, thought Sir John as he proceeded to enlighten the engineer.

The secretary made several visits with refreshments during the course of many hours of intense conversation between the Admiral and the engineer. He'd never seen Sir John quite so animated and enamoured with anyone for quite some time.

Innovation of any kind and a clear understanding of that knowledge was something Sir John enjoyed immensely, so it was something of a surprise to find that they had been talking and discussing issues for most of the day.

It was now three in the afternoon and apparent to the Admiral that he had a stark decision to make. There was no question that this man, 'Cautious Col' would be an essential component in ensuring the success of the enterprise. He could not and would not sail without him, despite the fact that he was a civilian, had no experience of seafaring, especially in Arctic conditions and had little knowledge of the workings of the Royal Navy. What he did have, however, was overwhelming knowledge and experience in the intricacies of the two recently installed engines. Consequently, he presented his most persuasive argument to secure the engineer's services.

'I've certainly learnt a great deal in the last few hours,' enthused Sir John, 'which leaves me in no doubt whatsoever, that I don't know enough and never will,' he laughed. 'I'd be extremely grateful if you'd consider joining the expedition. If we're to have any success at all in our endeavours, your experience would undoubtedly be invaluable!'

The Admiral scrutinised the engineer, raising his eyebrows in expectation.

'Col' for his part was surprised at the unexpected proposal because he'd assumed he'd been called in only to give expert advice. A berth on the *Erebus* was the last thing he expected and it did quite shock him.

'Don't give me an answer straight away,' enthused the Admiral. 'Think about it and come back tomorrow. I'll arrange for you to stay in London and send you a complete résumé of my offer, which I hope you'll find acceptable...it will be an offer you can't refuse. I'm sure you'll derive a great deal of enjoyment and satisfaction in accepting an invitation to an adventure of a lifetime, whilst essentially operating in your own environment, of course.'

The engineer didn't actually have to think more than momentarily. During the course of their discussions, the Admiral had inspired and convinced him that this search for the North West Passage was exceedingly worthwhile. Col was delighted to have been asked to join the expedition. He hadn't any matrimonial ties or immediate family to prevent him joining the expedition and the company for whom he worked would give him leave of absence on a secondment for the three or more years required.

The invitation was too much to resist, with a consequence that he rose immediately from his chair, surprisingly throwing caution to the wind, to offer the Admiral his hand. 'No need to think about it Sir, I'm your man!'

Sir John grasped Col's hand and shook it enthusiastically. 'Excellent! I'd a feeling in my bones that you'd make the right decision...and thank you again because I doubt we'd have got very far without you along to oversee the running of the engines, an important part of this expedition...Oh, one last thing, you'll need some form of status aboard ship, consequently, I propose an appointment as 'Lieutenant'. Of course you'll appreciate that this is almost unprecedented, but the men respect a position of authority, prior to respecting the man himself, but I'm sure you'll not have a problem on that issue!' The Admiral chuckled at his own erudite observation of the engineer before clapping him enthusiastically on the back.

'Thank you, Sir John,' responded Col. 'I'll not let you down!'

'Oh, almost forgot,' said Sir John nonchalantly, as an afterthought. 'We need a another engineer for the *Terror*... can you recommend someone?'

Col, though mystified at Sir John's apparent lack of memory on such an important subject of 'an engineer for the *Terror*,' responded positively. 'As a matter of fact I can, he's an experienced engineer who I've worked with on combustion problems with the 'Copperknob' before commissioning on the railways...James Thompson, by name. He might be available and I know he's looking for a new challenge.'

'Excellent,' guffawed Sir John. 'Let me know by the end of this week at the latest. Then I'll be able to organise his appointment or arrange an alternative.' With that, Sir John shook Col's hand enthusiastically before turning on his heel to return to other pressing tasks that needed finalising prior to departure on the 19th May.

With the Admiral's recommendation ringing in his ears, Col exited the office and made his way to the heavily porticoed entrance to the building.

Sir John Franklin returned to his wife that evening in a rejuvenated mood, far removed from his melancholia of the previous day. His optimistic smile had returned, while his countenance fully betrayed his elation. Jane too was pleased with the obvious change in his demeanour, as she welcomed his return, although she knew full well that the time for his departure was drawing ever closer.

CHAPTER SIX

An Illuminating Meeting
London – 19th November 2007, 5.30 p.m.

Dusk had fallen and the street lamps cast eerie shadows on the almost deserted stretch of Houndsditch Road in the commercial district of Whitechapel. From a stranger's perspective, I could be forgiven for believing that the area hadn't changed much since the nineteenth century. If it wasn't for the bright red Ferrari parked adjacent a small warehouse entrance, displaying a vivid crimson sign indicating 'Internal Solutions', one would think that time travel was indeed possible. A tabby cat was taking advantage of the still warm bonnet and stirred momentarily as I approached, seemingly reluctant to vacate its chosen spot, unless provoked.

I stroked underneath his chin, as I checked my bearings and he mewed appreciatively. If I was not mistaken, Goldner's original cannery and warehouse facilities lay beyond the massive oak double arched doors, displaying a weatherworn sign.

'Copperknob' Nautical Museum
and Ship Chandlers'
137 Houndsditch Road

(suppliers of chain, rope, canvass, blocks, tackles and all associated equipment required by the seafarer)

A brass post box had been inserted into the Judas gate, which formed part of the large formidable entrance. The gate was secure, so I pressed the illuminated bell push, only half expecting a response, as it was already past five thirty. However, my luck was in when a satisfactory clunk of a large key turning in an even larger lock indicated a positive presence.

The gate swung inwards to reveal an elderly silver haired gentleman. 'Can I 'elp yer son?' enquired the man as he peered over his rimless spectacles.

'Sorry to bother you at this late hour, but I have some questions that you may be able to help me with.'

'Not the law are you?' he queried suspiciously.

'No,' I replied, slightly amused at his assumption.

'Well then, better come in to the yard and we'll go through to the office, then you can ask away.'

He led me to a room, which although relatively spacious in size, was cluttered with an abundance of bric-a-brac with several dusty columns of long forgotten filing stacked in corners. He offered me the visitor's chair, before seating himself in a leather Captain's chair behind the desk whilst observing me closely over an elaborate Victorian inkwell.

'I'm Seth Terry, curator of the museum. What can I do fer yer, Mr...Mr?'

'Young,' I said. 'I was hoping you could provide me with some information regarding the Goldner Canning Operations during the nineteenth century.'

'Well now, you do, do you?...well you've come to the right place sure enough, although the old factory and warehouse has changed considerably since those times. I've been here for nigh on sixty years, so ask away.'

'Good, I hope your knowledge will be invaluable then, as I've some strange requests and questions.'

'Hold on,' interrupted Seth, 'it looks like you're here for the duration, so I'll put the kettle on. Sugar and milk?'

'Just milk thanks,' I replied, warming to the old man and his quirky mannerisms.

Seth placed a steaming mug of tea on an old dog-eared copy of 'Notices to Mariners' in front of me. 'Now then, 'ow can I 'elp?' he offered, raising a quizzical eyebrow in anticipation.

'Well, I'd better start at the beginning, otherwise you might find my tale confusing...how much time have you?'

Seth considered my question before responding. 'Time is about the only valuable asset I still possess, but one I'm willing to share. I'm an old man now, nearly eighty, but I'm intrigued. I've a feeling that listening to you may prove rewarding...go ahead, I'm all ears!'

I began my tale with the death of my father and the reading of his will, with its surprise element...the ditty box and its contents. 'My curiosity took over and I was determined to find answers to the strange collection of items,' I explained. 'That led me to London, which gave me an insight into the last voyage of Sir John Franklin and his expedition to find a North West Passage to the Pacific.

'You may well ask how these contents led me to the conclusion that the 'starting point' was *that* particular expedition. Well, two things really...one, the item of scrimshaw in the box and, two the name of my father, which coincidentally is the same as a crewmember aboard the *Erebus*, Franklin's ship. Here, let me show you, I've brought them with me.' I retrieved the 'ditty' box from my rucksack and took out the contents, laying them side-by-side on the old oak desk. 'Look, there's a map engraved on the surface of the scrimshaw. I'm fairly certain it depicts an area in which Franklin was acutely interested, so there's not much doubt that there's a connection and a possible significance. I don't think I'm making too much of a leap, in that the letters, 'E' and 'T'...see there, to the west of the island, may have some actual relevance to the ships *Erebus* and *Terror*.'

Seth eyed me curiously, not so much to infer that I was jumping to conclusions, but to indicate a certain understanding between us. His gaze had wandered from the scrimshaw to the brass compass, which he picked up to examine. 'An interesting artefact,' he observed. 'Circa 1820 and well made.' He turned it over and read the inscription on the base—

'To Tom,
May you always find your way back to me
– Love forever Marie'

Seth paled and a rheumy tear filled the corner of his left eye. Seconds passed until he realised I was staring at him, then he cleared his throat to speak. 'I'm astounded,' he whispered. 'If I'm not mistaken, this compass was given by my great, great grandmother to my great, great grandfather. His name was Thomas Terry and him and Marie were walking out in 1845, before his ship sailed. How do I know, you may ask...well, I'm also interested in genealogy and I know that for a fact...I also know,' and now it was my turn to be stunned, 'that Tom Terry sailed as boatswain with Franklin on the *Erebus* in 1845!'

I stared at him for almost a minute, completely dumbfounded. 'How...how and why would my father have the compass in his possession, if what you say is true?'

'Not so strange I think,' Seth replied in an excited state, or as excited as a near eighty year old is ever likely to be. 'You did say your name was 'Young' and that your father had the same name as a crew member of the *Erebus*? Well, it's not much of a leap in assuming they were shipmates on that expedition. One thing eludes me, however...which you've already put your finger on...how did your father come by it and indeed, the scrimshaw?'

I shrugged, a little perplexed, but I did want to pursue my investigation, so started to speak, but Seth immediately interjected once again.

'Wait a minute...what else have you here?' he exclaimed, picking up the keys with interest. 'Old Mortise lock keys... three of 'em. Funny, they seem vaguely familiar.'

I raised my eyebrows questioningly and started to smile, as intrigue and enthusiasm invaded Seth's countenance.

CHAPTER SEVEN

The Jolly Sailor
Whitechapel – 27th April 1845

Tom contemplated his half empty tankard of ale in sombre mood as he recalled the horrifying recent event aboard the *Erebus*. The loss of young James Stanley, crushed to death before his life had barely begun was a decidedly sobering thought. His companion in the 'Jolly Sailor' in Ratcliffe Highway that day was his shipmate and lifelong friend Rob Ellis, carpenter aboard the *Erebus*.

The 'Jolly Sailor', their preferred venue, was in essence a tavern by day and a theatre gaff by night, one of many which had sprung up in recent years, not only to accommodate budding amateurs in the acting profession, but also the abundance of drinkers and smokers who wanted entertainment or possibly more. It was no coincidence that predatory prostitutes, pickpockets, thieves and other ne'er-do-wells also frequented these establishments, but, for the moment, the tavern was quiet.

Rob, a very experienced carpenter supplemented his wages aboard ship by helping build the stage structure extension to the tavern along with a balcony on the upper floor, which incongruously had to be reached using a rickety ladder. Consequently, his ale was free, a favour extended to Tom who'd also mucked in on occasion.

'What do you make of the accident Rob?' queried Tom.
'Could have been avoided,' replied Rob.

'Maybe so,' Tom continued, 'but that derrick should have been secured properly. Inexperience or incompetence, I'm not sure, but there's bound to be an inquiry.'

Rob sipped his own ale before commenting, 'Let's hope the lad's replacement knows what he's letting himself in for.'

'I'll drink to that,' said Tom, glancing in the direction of the bar! 'Two more please Marie.' He smiled his request at the not unattractive landlady, Marie Harding, who had a real soft spot for the *Erebus's* Bosun.

'I suppose you'll be wanting some of that pork pie on the side as well eh Tom?'

'Well if you're offering Marie, how could I refuse such an offer from a lovely lady?'

She giggled in response, before adding, 'I'll cut a piece for you too Rob...you do most of the work while he delivers the flattery.'

Rob and Tom laughed in unison at her good humour, before continuing their conversation.

'The replacement lad's name is David Young. He's expected tomorrow,' said Tom. Let's hope he's not got wind of the accident or he'll be heading in the opposite direction.'

'Shouldn't think so, it wasn't reported in the papers,' mused Rob. 'Anyway, I'm sure you'll make him welcome.'

'Actually, yes I will,' said Tom. 'He's my elder sister, Eve's son and she's asked me to look after him...or there'll be trouble! Of course, she doesn't mean it really, but she is genuinely concerned for him as it's his first voyage.'

'Well he's in safe hands then and I'll keep my eye on him too.'

'Thanks Rob...I know you will and I appreciate your help as always.'

Tom wasn't under any false illusions as to the task ahead as he had sailed with Sir John Franklin previously and with another commander, James Clark Ross on his voyage to the Antarctic in 1839, so was well aware of the perils of polar expeditions. However, this did not deter him from signing on once again with the *'Explorer'* and *'Adventurer'*, whose reputation was legendary.

He'd also noted that whilst Franklin would command the expedition to locate the North West Passage on the *Erebus*, that Francis Crozier, also vastly experienced, would Captain the *Terror*.

Not long afterward they left the tavern and returned to the ship before the evening's entertainment got in to full swing and attracted the attention of 'H' Division[7] at Stepney.

---

7 The Metropolitan Police Act of 1829 defined the original Metropolitan Police District as an area of about seven miles radius from Charing Cross. Within the next year, seventeen police divisions were set up including Stepney/H Division and Greenwich/R Division.

CHAPTER EIGHT

'Signing On'
Woolwich – 1st May 1845

David Young stood on the dock and gazed in dumbstruck awe at the amazing spectacle of the hitherto bomb vessel, now converted into a ship modified for Arctic exploration. It was only eight in the morning but the activity aboard was alarming to the uninitiated, which included himself. Men were scurrying about with determination and intent, to ready the ship on its voyage of discovery to determine the North West Passage.

The dock also accommodated the *Terror*, alongside, but further down the quay. She too was in the final stages of refurbishment. Carpenters, caulkers, rope and rigging workers moved around like bees in a hive, all with their own specific tasks to accomplish.

It wasn't long before Tom spotted his nephew rooted to the spot on the quayside. He shouted, 'Davy Young, get yourself up that gangplank and say hello to the *Erebus*.'

Davy was relieved to hear a familiar and welcoming voice and waved in response.

Tom helped the young lad aboard, slapped him on the back then immediately gave him a warning. 'Say nowt, except 'yes sir', do as you're told, keep your nose clean and follow my lead and you'll be ok...got that?'

'Yes, Uncle Tom...sorry Bosun. Oh, I've got something for you from mam.' He produced a package from his kit and handed it to Tom. 'Mam says you enjoy a slice of this.'

'I do indeed,' said Tom, who knew what it would be before he even opened it. Eve always knew how to bake and she hadn't forgotten his favourite...Madeira cake.

'Come below and I'll show you your berth,' said Tom.

Tom escorted the boy seaman to the lower deck amidst all the hustle and bustle of voyage preparation. Davy was immediately overwhelmed by the seemingly claustrophobic atmosphere below decks. He could not have imagined its impact prior to joining.

Men were vying for the best spots to sling their hammocks. Usually the experienced sailors had the advantage and picked the centre of the gantline[8] to lessen the 'swing' when the ship rolled. Most of them used spreaders across the nettles[9] of the hammock to make them wider and more comfortable. The Royal Marines, seven in total and seconded to the vessel were quartered below the poop deck, led by and including, Sergeant David Bryant. His counterpart on the *Terror*, Solomon Tozer led a similar contingent, but all were experienced and presented a formidable force. Most were relieved that the total complement of fourteen, exceeded the number thirteen, which would have given the superstitious among them cause for contemplation.

---

8 Gantlines: Wire ropes fixed across the beam of ship on accommodation decks under tension, several feet apart. Hammocks are 'slung' between them in a fore and aft configuration.

9 Nettles: Thin rope in fan formation attached to metal eyes in canvas on head and foot of hammock. Longer ones in the middle, shorter ones at the side where 'spreaders' (a piece of wood or dowelling) are fixed.

Davy, although inexperienced, was astute enough to realise that order existed beneath the apparent chaos – A fact to be confirmed a few days later when everyone had found their feet and all was 'shipshape and Bristol fashion[10] below decks, as indeed were topside.

Most of the essential work was now complete, including the strengthening of the vessel itself. Stores were still to be loaded, not least the provisions expected from Goldner's canning factory...already behind schedule. None-the-less, a state of readiness was approaching quite speedily, much to the satisfaction of Franklin and Francis Crozier, Captain of the *Terror*, whose experience and knowledge would be invaluable on a voyage of such importance.

Later that evening a weary but excited Davy spent his first night in a hammock and actually slept soundly.

While Davy slept, Franklin, Crozier and Ross in an advisory capacity, were discussing the forthcoming voyage. They had adjourned to the Captain's quarters on the *Erebus* and over a glass of Lisbon's finest, expressed their numerous concerns to one another. The oil lamp cast a somewhat eerie glow on their features as they grappled with the many practical and other potential problems, likely to be encountered.

Ross was the first to comment. 'You will be aware gentlemen, that the *Terror,* whilst engaged on the 'Back Expedition' in 1836/7, sustained substantial damage when imprisoned in the pack ice. George Back reported that, at

---

10 'Ship-shape and Bristol fashion' is actually two phrases merged into one. Ship-shape came first and has been used since the 17th century. Bristol fashion was added later and is first seen in print during Bristol's heyday as a trading port, in the early 19th century.

one point, she was pushed forty feet or more up a cliff before the ice released her, but not before the sternpost shattered, displacing it out of true. They applied tensioned chains around the hull, essentially to hold the *Terror* together, but it still leaked like a sieve. Apparently, they were extremely fortunate to make the Irish coast, where she was beached, having manned the pumps all the way across the Atlantic.

It was quite remarkable that the Admiralty managed to salvage her and effect the repairs for my voyage to the Antarctic, when both the *Terror* and the *Erebus* were under my command. I won't say that the *Terror* is unlucky, but she does seem to have her share of bad luck, along with the *Erebus*. We didn't come out unscathed from that expedition either. Both ships rudders were wrecked by ice in a gale and *Erebus* even lost the copper sheeting from her hull—not to mention our frightening encounter with two icebergs after *Erebus* and *Terror* collided. That caused *Terror* to lose her bowsprit and *Erebus's* topmast being carried away, which made manoeuvring difficult.'

'Yes, yes', said Franklin tetchily, 'but you were under sail alone and now both ships have auxiliary engines, so a recurrence of that particular situation is extremely unlikely! Anyway, I'm sure the repairs to both vessels have been substantial…why, they've been virtually rebuilt!'

At this point, Crozier interjected as he was in reflective mood and did not feel placated by Franklin's assurance, on a virtual rebuild. 'Maybe we do have cause to worry, as the naval architects have revised their plans. Both vessels have the same modification now, in that their sternposts have been cut in two to accommodate the new propeller shafts. The sternpost of each is strengthened by iron 'H'-shaped bands, but what concerns me is the possibility that these modifications aren't as strong as the original one piece sternpost.'

'Actually, I reciprocate your unease, despite my last comment,' added Franklin, 'not least since I spoke to Lang, who is in overall control of the dockyard here at Woolwich. Controversially, whilst speaking to their Lordships at the Admiralty, they confirmed that Lang had not given any assurance as to the overall strength of the sternposts. In fact, he went to great lengths to explain that in some respects the sternposts were probably weaker! When pressed on the subject, he gave an opinion that the modifications were robust and probably adequate for the voyage. However, his half-hearted assurance to the Admiralty doesn't fill me with overwhelming confidence, when assessing the risk. I am, of course, aware of this potential problem, but providing we monitor the sternposts at regular intervals for any signs of failure, we'll control the situation. I suggest we appoint a crewmember on each vessel to make regular checks on the status of the sternposts.'

'Agreed,' mumbled Crozier and Ross in unison.

A number of minor matters were discussed before they wound up the meeting, but not before Goldner's name was mentioned in non-complimentary terms, although, at this particular time, the supplier was one of their lesser concerns.

CHAPTER NINE

Good Times
Woolwich and Whitechapel –
9th May 1845

The *Erebus* and *Terror* were almost in a complete state of readiness except for the delivery of Goldner's canned goods. Despite the Admiralty's insistence on prompt delivery and several factory visits, the shipment was still pending.

In exasperation, a contingent consisting of the ship's purser, Charles Osmer, Richard Wall, the ship's cook and William Bell, quartermaster, were sent to investigate.

They came back with a promise, but not much to substantiate it and a tale of chaos at the cannery. They commented that the labour left a lot to be desired, in that the lead soldering technique appeared not to have been mastered, albeit a good proportion of the cans had originated in Hungary and had just recently arrived.

However, the crews of the two ships having completed almost all the storing were in jovial mood.

Shore leave was granted to many of them and only a handful remained on board the ships.

Tom and Rob accompanied by Davy, on a promise of a real entertaining night out, made tracks for the 'Jolly Sailor'. Davy was introduced to Marie, who immediately took a shine to him!

They sat on stools next to a table made from a hogshead barrel cut in two and upturned. It served its purpose well, accommodating their three, full to brimming, tankards with room to spare for three huge pieces of pork pie on a platter.

'Now don't go leading this lad astray,' warned Marie in good humour. 'I know you two too well and don't give him too much to drink. Them ships are dangerous places, especially after a night on the town. You need to have your wits about you.'

Rob spluttered his laughing response into his raised tankard, 'Of course we will, won't we Tom?'

'Definitely,' agreed Tom before adding, 'We might take him on to 'Paddy's Goose' later for a surprise!'

'Oh no you won't,' retorted an irate Marie. 'The 'ladies' in that establishment leave a lot to be desired, if you get my meaning. If you go, he stays here with me...I've someone I want to introduce him to.'

Rob and Tom laughed uncontrollably at her concern, but considered a retreat was in order. 'All right Marie, we'll go on alone and leave him in your capable hands, but not just yet, we've still more ale to sup,' placated Tom.

Davy was, if the truth be told, extremely grateful to Marie for rescuing him from what he considered an awkward and probably embarrassing position. He didn't believe he was a man of the world in any sense, so didn't relish meeting any ladies of ill repute, having listened to some of Rob and Tom's hair raising tales of the 'fairer' sex, whilst aboard the *Erebus*. Stick with me tonight Davy,' said Marie. 'I'll look after you... they'll be incapable!'

The third act on the makeshift stage, introduced as the 'sweetest voice in Whitechapel' had them all applauding and calling for more. Her name was Catherine Knight and Davy was transfixed from the first moment she appeared. This didn't go unnoticed by Tom and Rob, who winked knowingly to each other.

Davy was indeed mesmerised and couldn't believe his luck when shortly afterward, Marie introduced Catherine to her party of friends. 'Catherine, this is Rob, Tom and Davy. Davy, this is who I wanted to introduce you to.'

Catherine nodded, acknowledging the three with a smile before offering each her hand in turn. When it came to Davy, much the same age as herself, she blushed and lingered whilst holding his hand.

'I knew they'd get on,' whispered Marie to Tom, to which Tom replied.

'You had that in mind ever since I told you we were coming tonight...crafty soul, but I love you for it!'

'Oh do you now Tom Terry, perhaps I've got something to say about that!'

Rob and Tom stayed at the 'Jolly Sailor' and caught a couple more acts before leaving for 'Paddy's Goose'. Davy stayed, enjoying the company of Catherine and Marie.

The night wore on and was going remarkably well for all three shipmates, albeit in two separate locations. Tom and Rob were in controlled inebriated states at 'Paddy's Goose' and Davy was in 'walking on air' euphoria at the 'Jolly Sailor'. His evening with Catherine had been wonderful and she'd agreed to see him again prior to the 19th when the *Erebus* was due to sail.

Davy wasn't the only one in an ecstatic state of well being that morning. After several drinks, Tom considered leaving Rob to his own devices, but not before assuring him of his intention of proposing to Marie.

He'd been thinking of it for some time now and was pretty sure she'd say yes...all the signs were there: the flirtatious smile, an occasional coy look over her shoulder, her hand resting on his longer than necessary when she brought drinks over. All were clear indications of her affection. Perhaps he was slow in putting two and two together, but Rob was more pointed in his appraisal.

'Could have told you that myself a couple of months back. She's 'ad eyes on you for ages...pity she'll 'ave to settle for second best...could have 'ad me!' laughed Rob, until his sides split, because he couldn't resist the temptation to pull his mate's leg. 'Daft sod,' responded Tom good-humouredly. 'You might be a brilliant carpenter, but you've a lot to learn when it comes to understanding the fairer sex. Anyway, I'm off, she'll have finished work by now and I've delayed too long already if she's to say 'yes' before the *Erebus* sails.'

Rob threw up his arms in exasperation, but smiled his approval. 'Oh, I do like a good wedding,' he chuckled. 'You can't see her refusing then?' he laughed again at his second attempt to wind up his shipmate and good friend.

Tom squinted at Rob then raised a questioning eyebrow, but laughed with him anyway. 'Oh course she'll say yes, I'm a good catch,' then added, 'Now don't go falling in the dock on your way back, you know you lose your sea legs without my help.'

'Look who's talking,' countered Rob unconvincingly.

With that, Tom left on his mission, without knowing exactly what he was going to say, or indeed the best way of saying it...

He arrived at the 'Jolly Sailor' to find it in darkness, except for one candle illuminating Marie's upstairs window. He glanced around for a handful of grit and small pebbles to toss at the glass, but could only find a rough edged, not altogether small stone. *Oh well,* thought Tom, *in for a penny*.

He heaved the stone at the window and was mortified when it crashed through a small bull's-eye pane.

'Marie...are you all right?' Tom's voice combined an apology with concern, but he was not prepared for the response, which emanated from the now open window.

'Tom Terry...what the 'ell do you think you're on with? If it wasn't you, I'd be callin' H-Division at the top of my voice.' She sighed her disapproval before adding, 'you're probably drunk and what do you want anyway?'

'I'm definitely not,' responded Tom, somewhat aggrieved. 'I thought you'd be pleased,' he smiled, unfortunately forgetting to mention the most important part of his mission.

'Pleased about what? No one appreciates their window broken at 3 o'clock in the morning.'

'Oh, sorry,' mumbled a contrite Tom, momentarily lost for words, but suddenly remembering why he'd come. 'Ah, well now,' ventured Tom in his most conciliatory voice. 'I was hoping you'd agree to marry me!'

A palpable silence ensued. *Did she hear me?* thought Tom...*I'd better ask again*...but before he could, Marie leant out, rested her chin on her folded arms and observed him closely through sparkling eyes.

She spoke after a long pause for consideration, which left Tom feeling strangely uncomfortable. 'If you're not drunk and you really mean it, then of course I will.'

Tom smiled and engaged his own eyes with hers. *Lucky bugger, that's me* he thought and hastened to the barred door for her to let him in.

Unfortunately for him, he could not stay as long as he wished, but he made the most of it anyway. At 5 o'clock he bid Marie a very reluctant farewell, which left him just sufficient time to be back aboard by half six...not that he particularly cared, as he too was walking on air!

CHAPTER TEN

A Gift
'Jolly Sailor Inn'
Whitechapel, 11th May 1845

Since Davy met Catherine for the first time, they'd managed two evenings together and some snatched hours in the afternoons. In this brief spell, their destinies became entwined forever. Catherine was slightly younger by a few weeks, but it was of little importance, they were truly in love and had been since the moment their eyes met.

Marie and Tom on the other hand were acquaintances of long standing and had known each other for some years. Their relationship had grown from acknowledgement to friendship to affection and now, love. Marie always harboured an inkling that Tom might be for her, but waited patiently for him to make the first move, as she knew he would.

Trust him to ask for her hand only a couple of weeks before he was due to sail on the *Erebus* on a voyage expected to last for three years or more. No matter, she knew she loved him and would wait for him. They couldn't marry before he left as it was too short notice. Banns had to be read in their church for three Sundays prior to a wedding and they couldn't afford the ten shillings 'special licence' to marry sooner.

However, that didn't prevent them spending as much time as possible together! Tom pulled a few strings with the

Erebus's officers, several of whom owed him favours. This gave him the all important and essential time away from the ship. His standing with the officers and men had always been first class and consequently, he was well respected. He'd also made an impression on the marines who'd boarded several days earlier. They too had benefited from his knowledge and expertise.

The sounds of the city could be heard through the window, which still displayed the broken glass, as Marie and Tom lay together on the small double bed in the upstairs room.

They had made love for the second time in the last hour and were now snuggled together in a blissful state that only true love can achieve.

She whispered in his ear. 'I've a present for you.'

'Oh, I thought I'd just had one,' he answered.

She giggled. 'No, not that, I've a present under the pillow.'

'Ok, let's have a look see, I'm not used to being given presents.' He fondled her breasts as she reached under the pillow, so she kissed him in response, before retrieving the item.

'Do you want this or not, or do you want to make love again before you see it?'

'I don't mind either way,' laughed Tom. 'Might there be time for both?'

'Tom Terry you're terrible, but I might be convinced!' She presented him with a small package which intrigued him somewhat and was pleasantly surprised at its content...a small compact hand compass in a neat hand-crafted gimbal. It bore an inscription on the base from Marie.

'A token of my love.' she explained.

'I'm really touched. I'll treasure it always,' responded Tom.

'I obtained it from a Dutch Sea Captain. He stayed for a couple of nights at the inn and only had guilders for payment. We eventually agreed on a barter arrangement. He came up with the compass and a pair of silk gloves, which I've already sold...that paid for his two night's stay. So the compass...and it's a quality one, is a bonus.'

'I quite agree and I'm very pleased you've given it to me.'

'Good!' she eyed him mischievously, 'now make love to me again!'

Catherine and Davy were not experienced and had not made love with each other or for that matter anyone else prior to their meeting.

Their intimate meetings were restricted to kisses and fondling, usually out of eye or earshot to avoid any embarrassment and to restrict any ribald comments, which undoubtedly would have come their way. They'd agreed to wait until Davy's return. It wasn't that they weren't totally sure of their future together, but an unplanned baby, however, much they wanted to make love, couldn't be considered. It did seem a long time but they were complicit in their commitment to each other.

Catherine, however, did have a surprise for Davy. She'd been asking around the ship's crew and was surprised to find that the *Erebus* did not have a ship's cat. The old resident 'Tomcat' had died whilst the refitting was being carried out. He'd been a good 'ratter'. As luck would have it, Marie's Dutch Captain mentioned a litter of kittens, born to their female cat aboard the *Van Diemen*, a schooner rigged Aak barge, whilst loading at Delfzijl near Rotterdam. The kittens were now eight weeks old, so Catherine accompanied the Captain to pick one out. She came back with two! They already had names, which suited, so there was no point in changing them.

'Davy, I'd like you to meet two friends of mine,' Catherine stated enigmatically.

Davy turned around, expectantly, but only encountered a rough-hewn wooden box. 'Small people are they?' he intimated pointing to the box.

'Oh very small,' countered Catherine, smiling as she continued, 'why don't you open the lid?'

He did her bidding and eased off the lid before peering inside. The two kittens blinked affectionately, if a little apprehensively at another stranger. 'I'd like to introduce you to 'Mitzi' and 'Fritz'.'

'They're beautiful,' commented Davy.

'I know!' said Catherine. 'They'll be your companions aboard the *Erebus*. Commander James Fitzjames has already given permission. He was quite enthusiastic about a replacement for 'Drake' and was delighted when I said there were two and one with a name similar to his own – 'Fritz'.

'Thank you so much Catherine,' said Davy, then kissed her passionately. 'I'll look after them well, as part of my duties will be to distribute food to the crew and assist the ship's cook. The small amount they'll eat won't be missed I'm sure.'

CHAPTER ELEVEN

Goodbyes
Greenhithe, Kent – 17*th*/18th May 1845

In the early morning of the 17th May, both ships were moved downriver to Greenhithe from their berths in Woolwich. The move was accomplished without mishap and the officers were pleased with the efforts of their respective crews.

Whilst the *Erebus* and *Terror* were engaged in moving location, Marie and Catherine took the opportunity to lodge at Catherine's aunt's cottage, two miles away from the docks, but within easy walking distance of the ships.

The two kittens, Mitzi and Fritz were snuggled together in an old box, covered by some calico, just inside the hallway, unaware of their impending voyage.

Catherine was in half a mind to keep them, but she'd promised Davy and also Commander Fitzjames, so felt obliged to honour her word. She'd have Davy take them aboard when they said their goodbyes.

The kittens mewed softly when they heard a knock at the door that afternoon, which was opened by Marie. Davy and Tom stood outside and conveyed a mixture of happiness and sadness to the two ladies in the hallway. The men were happy to be there but sad at the same time, as this would be their last visit before the *Erebus* and *Terror* sailed.

Marie and Catherine noticed the contradiction in their demeanours immediately, but could do nothing to mask their own sadness and indeed, apprehension for the possible dangers their men would undoubtedly encounter. However, both couples were determined to make the most of the available time left to them. The women had organised a farewell meal in the kitchen, prior to some special time when each couple would be on their own.

The time flew by in a whirlwind of emotions; laughter tinged with the bittersweet sensation of leaving a loved one preoccupied their whole beings, all too soon it was time to leave.

Marie and Catherine walked with their men back to the ships. The men carried kitbags, each containing a gift of a woollen garment from their respective girls and one or two edible treats. Catherine and Marie took turns in carrying the small box containing the kittens.

They arrived at the *Erebus* to find Tom's sister, Eve, Davy's mother, standing on the quay. She gave each a huge hug before turning to wink at Catherine. 'Now, remember what I asked you to do Tom Terry.' She admonished him good-humouredly, 'Don't let him get into any mischief!'

'I won't,' Tom insisted, 'but now there's two of you expecting me to look out for him.'

'Make sure you do,' said Catherine with a smile.

The two couples said their goodbyes as meaningfully as possible. They embraced and kissed passionately before the men strode purposefully to the gangway.

The three women, each with their private thoughts, waved them goodbye. They watched Tom and Davy ascend the gangway, Tom with his heavy kitbag and Davy precariously holding the kittens and his own, not insubstantial kitbag. They would, of course, see them off from the quay on the

19th May when the ships sail on the 9 o'clock tide, but would be unable to touch them again to convey their innermost feelings. At that moment, three years seemed a very long time indeed.

CHAPTER TWELVE

Eleventh Hour Delivery
Greenhithe Kent – 18th May 1845

A commotion on the quayside heralded the long overdue arrival of the canned provisions. A number of heavily laden wagons, accompanied by none other than Stephan Goldner himself, made their presence felt. They drew up alongside the two moored vessels.

Goldner knew he had left the delivery exceptionally late. This was partly intentional and also partly due to his ineptitude and inexperience in administering such a large contract. However, it did have one distinct advantage, the stowage of the canned provisions would take some considerable time to accomplish. Consequently, Goldner gambled that not enough time would be available for the crew to check the quality of the cans, the contents, or, for that matter the quantity. In actual fact, Goldner was some one hundred and fifty cans short of the total order but he had crated them in such a way as to be near impossible to check. He'd gambled on his late delivery and the crew's haste to stow them aboard, prior to sailing on the following morning's tide, to go in his favour. All he required was a signature on the documentation to prove the delivery was accomplished, albeit not on time.

He suspected that Commander Fitzjames would have other, more important issues to consider, prior to departure and one signature was neither here nor there in the whole process. This proved to be the case, although not without incident, as it transpired.

Goldner made his way to the top of the gangway, clutching his documents case, a highly flattering, leather embossed article bearing the initials 'S.G.' He imperiously announced his presence to a junior officer by demanding his own immediate priority of being escorted to the commanding officer's cabin.

A little overawed, the officer did as he was bidden and led Goldner to Commander Fitzjames quarters. He knocked hesitantly as Goldner breathed stale tobacco breath down his collar in the close confines of the alleyway.

'Enter!' The strong command emanated from inside and the junior officer opened the door to allow his visitor access.

'Mr Goldner, Sir,' announced the officer.

'Ah, Goldner!' exclaimed Fitzjames. 'I'd almost given you up as a lost cause. Nevertheless, do take a seat, as your presence means we can conclude the transaction. I trust all the canned provisions are in the wagons I've observed on the quay?'

'Yes indeed Commander,' answered Goldner graciously, as he didn't want to upset the applecart at this late stage. He knew his delivery was late in the extreme, so he continued. 'I must apologise once again for our eleventh hour delivery commander. Our crate suppliers let my good self down and what with other issues, such as the poor quality of meat delivered, which we returned, might I emphasise, we were inevitably delayed. However, I can assure you that all is well and the meat used was eventually of the best quality!'

'I'm pleased to hear it,' confirmed the commander, 'but as I have many duties to perform today, I'd be obliged if we could dispense with formalities and sign the necessary papers. I am, of course, able to offer you a glass of port, whilst we engage ourselves with the inkwell.' The commander laughed a little too heartily and a trifle longer than necessary at his own joke, unlike Goldner who frowned. He wanted to be gone as soon as possible and hardly felt a glass of port would help his disposition. He was still conscious of the missing cans in the order. Fortunately for him, his fears were unfounded, as Charles Osmer, the purser, reported to the commander, in his presence that the cans were aboard, stowed and tallied. His 'crating' tactic had obviously paid off.

Goldner smiled nonchalantly, but with some relief as he signed alongside the commander's own signature, before downing his glass of port in one gulp. 'Thank you Commander,' said Goldner. 'Now I must take my leave, as I appreciate we are both busy men. All that remains is to wish you a successful voyage and a speedy return. Good day, Sir.'

Fitzjames escorted Goldner to the gangway before Goldner, in one last passing comment, ingratiated himself pointedly to the commander. 'There's some extra special cans for the officers in two crates marked with yellow paint. I hope you enjoy them when celebrating any successes you may achieve.'

'That's extremely generous of you, Mr Goldner,' responded the commander. 'I'm sure we will, we're obliged.'

Once on the quay, Goldner chuckled, slapped his thigh, stuffed the documents in the leather case and boarded the wagon. He then placed them under his seat and instructed the driver to proceed back to London. Another successful day, he concluded, his conscience not in the least bit troubled by the manner of the transaction.

CHAPTER THIRTEEN

Departure
Greenhithe, Kent and the Orkney Islands
19th May 1845

A palpable sense of excitement could be felt by all aboard the ships. Their imminent departure on the tide was tinged with sadness and apprehension for those being left behind, who hid behind false smiles and frantically waved scarves.

Both ships were 'singled up'. *Erebus* would proceed ahead of the *Terror*. The last but one rope was released by the men on the quay and hauled aboard by the ship's crew, only the spring hawser remained, which would allow the bow to move off the quay.

Col's auxiliary engine sprung into life and the ship moved slowly off. The 'spring' was let go and hauled aboard amidst cheers and shouts from those aboard and ashore. 'God Speed' and 'Good Luck' could be heard, proclaiming their departure, in addition to the more personal messages of love and devotion from family and friends, not least those from Catherine and Marie. Their tributes mingled with their tears and the anguish of their impending separation, but they still tried to hide their emotions, as they took one last look at Davy and Tom, who waved from the stern. Then they were gone, lost from sight.

Terror followed in the wake of the *Erebus* at a comfortable distance. Both ships were using their auxiliary engine until they reached a position at the mouth of the Thames, where they would anchor and retrieve the Smith patent propeller before proceeding north along the east coast under sail alone.

Franklin's orders were to proceed along the east coast of England and Scotland and then anchor off the Orkney Islands to replenish water and other supplies before continuing their passage across the north coast of Scotland, passing south of Iceland. Navigation would be relatively straightforward at this stage of the voyage, as they would follow the 59th parallel of latitude, using the North Star and Sun sights to determine their position accurately. They expected to sight Cape Farewell without any problems, but if they encountered fog south of Greenland, they would proceed with caution after estimating their position by 'dead reckoning'.

The experienced navigators aboard the vessels usually had a canny knack for accurately estimating their position to within a few nautical miles of the actual position. Good-humoured arguments as to 'who was right' in their 'guesstimates' was always considered a worthwhile pastime when determining the daily noon position. However, inclement weather conditions were not expected during the latter part of May and early June, so a 'fix' on Cape Farewell was probable.

The passage to the Orkneys was uneventful. Davy was busy learning his duties, while Tom and Rob were engaged with the crew on essential duties commensurate with their positions of Bosun and Carpenter. Rob's duties included the sounding of ballast and fresh water compartments on a daily basis. This duty was also important should the ship run aground unexpectedly, whilst exploring uncharted areas, a not uncommon occurrence in itself.

On reaching the Orkney's the two ships anchored in a sheltered bay to the east of Stromness and the crew stood down with the exception of an officer and lookout on watch.

Dusk was approaching so the loading of provisions and fresh water would begin the following morning.

Tom beckoned to Rob to meet him below deck. 'We'd better make the most of the evening eh, Rob...fancy a game of cards?'

'Sounds like a good idea to me,' replied Rob. 'I'll see if Davy's finished his duties and ask him to join us, along with Col the engineer. He reckons he's up for a game or two... used to play in the guard's wagon on the Birmingham to London railway, before he joined us seafaring types. Mind, he's been sick as a dog since we left the Thames behind, perhaps the cards will take his mind off puking and give him something else to think about.'

'Reckon you're right,' laughed Tom. 'He's been tinkering around with that engine most days, but he's still green lookin!'

Rob made his way aft, past a line of hammocks and found Davy in the galley feeding the two cats. Only a few days had passed since the ships sailed, but their feline friends knew where the food was cooked.

'Look at you Davy,' joked Rob. Them two treat you like their mother. What do they say, happiness is being owned by a cat!'

Davy glared at Rob then got a dig in himself. 'You'll not be laughing when the rats are nibbling your toes in your hammock. 'I'll look after Mitzi and Fritz and they'll look after me!'

'It'll take more than a rat to frighten me,' said Rob. 'Anyway, are you up for a game of cards tonight?'

'Why not,' responded Davy. 'Uncle Tom taught me to play a game or two from when I was a nipper, so you might be in for a thrashing.

'We'll see...we'll see,' hedged Rob. 'There's plenty more games to be had on this voyage, win or lose tonight.'

As it happened, neither of them managed to latch on to a winning streak and the honours that evening were shared between Tom and Col, who proved he wasn't green when it came to concealing a good hand, unlike his seagoing pallor, which was decidedly transparent.

⁓

Whilst the crew played cards, Franklin and Crozier were engaged in a meeting aboard *H.M.S. Rattler*, also at anchor in the bay off Stromness. Captain Henry Smith of the *Rattler* and Captain Owen Stanley of *H.M.S. Blazer* had orders along with Captain Edward Griffiths of the supply/transport ship, *Barretto Junior* to escort and possibly tow, if required, *Erebus* and *Terror* as far as Greenland.

Extra supplies were to be off loaded from the *Barretto Junior* when they reached Whitefish Bay on Disko Island, on the West coast of Greenland.

'We'll transfer the extra tons of coal the *Barretto* is carrying, in the shelter of Whitefish Bay,' Franklin stated matter of factly. 'I believe that the water there is relatively calm, consequently, I don't anticipate any problems with *Barretto* coming alongside each vessel to discharge the coal and the other cargo,'

'Fairly straight forward I should think,' confirmed Captain Smith. 'In my experience, the sea thereabouts resembles the aura of a millpond for the most part...if you can find it in the first place!' he laughed at his own joke. 'Damn fog sometimes restricts visibility you see.'

'Better *Rattler* leads the way then,' interjected Crozier wryly. 'The young leading the old; built in '43 wasn't she, with an engine designed by Isambard Kingdom Brunel no less!'

'You're well informed Captain Crozier,' he acknowledged. 'We've been engaged in propeller trials as recently as March and April this year and tested over thirty different types. The Admiralty used us as a floating test bed, but thankfully we've settled on one, not dissimilar to yours on the *Terror* actually.'

'Is that so?' commented Franklin and Crozier simultaneously.

'Yes and this escort duty is as much an expedition as yours in a way,' explained Captain Smith.

'Well, if our propeller performs as well as yours did against the *H.M.S. Alecto* in that tug o' war then we'll be well satisfied,' said Franklin with sincerity. 'That paddle steamer had an equal power rating to your ship, if I remember correctly, suffice it to say I'm impressed.'

The Captain of the Rattler *was* suitably impressed. To be congratulated by such a personage as Sir John Franklin, was indeed an honour. 'Thank you, Sir,' he mumbled, slightly embarrassed. If our business is finished, I'd like to propose a toast to your success in finding the Passage.' He broke off to instruct his steward to charge everyone's glass before standing formally to present the toast.

The following morning all hands were on deck, including the marines who worked the same 'watches' as the crew. Their duties included rigging, cleaning, provisioning and storing of armaments as required. Loading the extra provisions kept everyone occupied.

Time flew by and at noon their task was complete. The anchor was hauled in under the guidance of the mate. One seaman operated the steam windlass, a far cry from the old capstan[11] and the bars of the 'swifter'[12]. With the anchor aweigh, both ships resumed their passage and by

---

11 'Capstan' – an older system of retrieving an anchor.
12 'Swifter' – A rope passed horizontally through notches in the outer ends of the capstan bars, drawn very tight. This steadies the men if the ship rolls, when heaving in the anchor.

late afternoon were well clear of the islands, heading towards the setting sun, escorted by *Rattler, Blazer* and *Barretto.*

Several days later, the flotilla rounded Cape Farewell, the southernmost tip of Greenland, on passage to their rendez-vous point at Whitefish Bay.

Unfortunately, the premonition of fog around Disko Island became a reality. Bearings along the coast were few and far between and consequently the *Rattler*, as lead vessel, misjudged the location of Whitefish Bay by several miles. This resulted in the ships having to backtrack before anchoring in the bay, which proved embarrassing for its Captain.

Fitzjames observed Franklin muttering under his breath, obviously alluding to another almost forgotten tragedy, until the latter surfaced from his revelry when he detected Fitzjames obviously studying him intently. 'Oh, sorry Fitzjames, I'm not mad...yet, just reminiscing on a bygone era. Let me explain—'

'I'm all ears,' encouraged Fitzjames.

'Well you may have heard of Sir Cloudesley Shovell's catastrophe when several of his fleet wrecked themselves on the Scilly Isles. All down to an error in longitude[13] and

---

13 The British government established the Board of Longitude in 1714: "The Discovery of the Longitude is of such consequence to Great Britain for the safety of the Navy and Merchant Ships as well as for the improvement of trade that for want thereof many ships have been retarded in their voyages, and many lost..." (and there will be a Longitude Prize) 'for such person or persons as shall discover the Longitude.' The task was taken up by many and eventually a method based on a chronometer built by John Harrison, a Yorkshire carpenter, with his marine chronometer; that timepiece was later known as H-4, which did get its sea trial and satisfied all the requirements for the

inclement weather! Anyway, it inspired the Admiralty to offer a substantial reward for anyone accurately determining a way of predicting longitude and one John Harrison, succeeded. He eventually claimed the elusive prize after many, many years of perfecting his timepiece. Longitude by Chronometer was born out of his and the endeavours of others,' confirmed Franklin with enthusiasm. 'However, even Harrison or any of his contemporaries for that matter, who improved the design of the nautical chronometer can claim that their timepieces will disperse fog!' he added jokingly.

Fortunately, the *Rattlers* embarrassment was short lived, compensated by the efficient manoeuvring of the vessels in coming alongside stem to stern. The transfer of the coal and stores, which included several recently butchered oxen, was also achieved in seamanlike fashion. This pleased Franklin, who praised the Captains of the *Rattler*, *Blazer* and *Barretto* in his log entry, making only scant reference to the error in navigation.

Two days later the *Terror* and *Erebus* bid farewell to their escort, but not before five crewmembers were medically discharged by Surgeon Stanley. Three of the crew were suffering with extremely violent stomach cramps with none

---

Longitude Prize. However, he was not awarded the prize and was forced to fight for his reward.

Though the British Parliament rewarded John Harrison for his marine chronometer in 1773, his chronometers were not to become standard. Chronometers such as those by Thomas Earnshaw were suitable for general nautical use by the end of the 18th century. However, they remained very expensive and the lunar distance method continued to be used for some decades.

specific causation and one with a broken arm. The last seaman to be taken over to the escort vessels was stretchered aboard with severe lacerations to his left leg. He would need constant attention to avoid the wound becoming gangrenous; consequently, Stanley considered it was in the seaman's best interest to send him home on the *Rattler*.

'Well Stanley,' boomed Franklin good humouredly, 'That's five less to worry about, but that's not to say I'm complacent, or not concerned why the three were suffering violent cramps.'

'Indeed, Sir,' agreed Stanley.

'Anyway, that leaves us with a manageable total complement of one hundred and twenty nine souls now. Let's not lose any more, especially to stomach complaints, eh Stanley?'

'No, Sir, I'll have a word with the cooks, Wall and Diggle on the *Terror* to see if we can shed some light on the problem.'

'Thank you, Stanley, I'm sure you'll come up with something,' encouraged Franklin.

CHAPTER FOURTEEN

An Exchange in Baffin Bay
26th July 1845

'Whaling ship, two points on the starboard bow,' shouted the lookout from his lofty perch in the crow's nest.

'How far?' queried the officer of the watch, Lieutenant Graham Gore.

'About five or maybe six miles, sir,' answered Able Seaman, John Strickland, who always kept a 'sharp eye' on the horizon.

'Alter course to intercept,' ordered the lieutenant to the helmsman. 'Nor' Nor' West' should do it! – Able Seaman, Hartnell, inform Commander Fitzjames that we're coming up on a whaling ship, we may be able to purchase some oil and possibly other supplies from them to supplement our own stores.'

'Aye, aye Sir,' responded Hartnell.

Shortly after, Fitzjames joined Gore and issued instructions for the sail captains to prepare a 'whaler[14]' and have crew on standby. 'Signal the *Terror* to follow our lead,' ordered Fitzjames as he placed a telescope to his right eye, steadying himself against a mast stay as the ship rolled slightly.

---

14 Whaler – small ship's small boat NOT a whaling ship

The ships closed quickly and it wasn't long before he was able to ascertain that there was not one but two ships. They too altered course toward the *Erebus* and *Terror* and were engaged in reducing canvas to a minimum, just enough to maintain steerage.

The ships soon came within hailing distance and 'hove-to'[15] in the slight choppy sea and low swell.

'Ahoy there,' bellowed *Erebus's* mate, Edward Crouch. 'What ships and where bound?'

Enterprise and *Prince of Wales*,' came the response. 'Outward bound from Baffin Island. Now on passage to Leith with our cargo before the winter sets in.'

'We're sending a boat across with some mail and a few requests,' continued the mate.

'Bring some of that Navy rum and you're welcome,' explained a jovial voice, emanating from an even jollier bearded whale hunter.

The whaler was duly lowered from the davits, one of nine different types of boat aboard both *Erebus* and *Terror* and crewed by eight men and a coxswain. The eight had been vying for crew duties to relieve the monotony of the voyage, by 'escaping' for an hour or two.

Rob, Tom and Davy were among the lucky few and took with them hastily written notes, because time was of the essence from the moment the whaling ships were sighted.

Official correspondence (some already written on the off chance of meeting a homeward bound vessel) by Sir John and other officers, accompanied their own meagre offerings.

The whaler was soon clunking alongside the *Prince of Wales*, rope fenders protecting the side of their small craft.

---

15 'Hove to' – not underway, or making way and not anchored.

Lines were put aboard and a rope ladder lowered. Two men were left tending the boat whilst the rest boarded, to be greeted by Captain Dannet and a pungent odour of blubber and 'big fish'.

'Welcome aboard,' boomed the captain, whose magnificent presence filled the immediate deck area. His bulk loomed over those in Fitzjames's party, but he was most welcoming.

He invited the commander to his quarters to discuss a transaction, whilst the *Erebus* crew swapped stories and 'bartered' with the whale ship's crew.

Rob instigated a conversation with a sailor known as 'Wild Man Eric' to his shipmates. Apparently, he survived fourteen days in an open boat after his ship capsized, before being picked up as the only survivor. He'd never been quite right since but always kept 'stum' about what he 'ate' during that time. However, this didn't deter Rob and he took the opportunity to purchase three whale teeth of varying size to transform into ornate works of scrimshaw, when the expected dark nights of an arctic winter drew in.

Others in the party had the same idea and soon, many such items were being lowered into the boat, along with official items purchased, mainly oil for the lamps and some whale meat, rope tallow and canvas, not needed by the crew of the *Enterprise*, as they were homeward bound.

Some two hours later, the party pulled away from the *Enterprise*. 'Give way together,' ordered the coxswain and four banks of oars cleaved the water in unison.

The sea was relatively calm and consequently they made rapid progress toward the *Erebus*, despite the extra load they were now carrying. Ten minutes later, the order *'oars'* quickly followed by *'Toss your oars'* was shouted by the coxswain. A heaving line was thrown to the crew aboard, attached to a heavy rope to secure the boat alongside, before eight able seamen hauled on the block and tackle falls to efficiently lift the boat from the water. The davits were swung inboard and the 'spoils' of their brief encounter with the *Enterprise* stowed away.

Col was on deck to welcome the returning party and commented to Tom, 'I'm glad I stayed aboard this ship because, even though we were only 300 yards away, I nearly gagged at the stench emanating from the *Enterprise*. I think I preferred being seasick!' exclaimed Col.

'I know what you mean,' said Rob, 'it's certainly an acquired smell, one you have to get used to. They're forever boiling whale blubber and rendering it down to produce the oil before barrelling. It's not a pleasant task, blood and guts everywhere.'

'Stop there,' said Col, 'I'm off to windward to get a breath of fresh air. You've only been aboard the *Enterprise* for a couple of hours and you reek of it. Talk to me tomorrow,' he laughed.

'Make full sail,' ordered Fitzjames in the distance. 'Steer Nor' West by North helmsman.'

Soon the vessels were picking up speed in the light South Westerly heading for Lancaster Sound.

CHAPTER FIFTEEN

A Plan of Action

Sir John squinted through his spectacles at the Admiralty orders. The hierarchy's expectations of a successful outcome of the expedition were abundantly apparent. Failure was not an option!

In addition to the main aim of locating a route through to the Pacific were listed several tasks or experiments to conduct of a scientific nature and at key locations. He grunted as if to confirm his own understanding of what was required, before turning in his chair, raising his eyes above the spectacle rims and addressing Crozier.

The ships were 'hove to' in Wellington Channel, some five days after the meeting with the *Enterprise* and *Prince of Wales*. Commander Crozier had joined him for some strategic planning and would stay aboard for a day before returning to the *Terror*.

'Francis, glad you could join me. I'm looking forward to our discussions, as the past weeks of keeping things to myself have become a trifle tiresome. We will, of course, be joining Fitzjames and the other offers in the wardroom for dinner, but we have a lot to consider before then. I've arranged for a bunk to be made up for you tonight and you can rejoin the *Terror* tomorrow morning.

Crozier, an experienced explorer himself was not only Sir John's second in command of the expedition, but also a lifelong friend. Their paths had crossed on several occasions, not only in an official capacity, which was to be expected, but also socially. They had many mutual acquaintances and friends and, therefore, felt relaxed in each other's company.

'We're to explore the possibility, that the area north of Cornwallis, known as Penny Strait, may provide the opening to the Pacific, but if nothing is found, we'll round the island and return via the west coast of Cornwallis, turning back to Beechey Island before wintering there. We'll need some time to establish a base ashore, to supplement our meagre stock of meat by hunting. I'd prefer to keep the majority of the coal in reserve, by the way, as we'll need all the power for the engine if we're to force our way through the pack ice. No doubt we'll encounter a few 'leads'[16] to help us on our way. Unfortunately, that means restricting the heating somewhat.'

'Crozier nodded in agreement, but added, 'A pity we didn't consider taking on a few more tons of coal. The twelve tons hardly seems adequate when you consider that the heating and the engines require an enormous amount of fuel!'

'Yes indeed Francis. Of course, hindsight is wonderful and may help us with for future voyages, but it doesn't exactly help us now. No matter, I believe the tree-line to the south of the arctic circle will be within our reach next summer. A few tons of timber may just be the answer to our problem. We should make our base camp on Devon to afford the best protection from the prevailing winds. It will be bitter enough when the temperature drops, but the arctic winds threaten to make it considerably worse. We may even see the

---

16 'Leads' – breaks in pack ice through which navigable passage is possible.

temperature fall to minus 40 or 50 degrees Fahrenheit,' he paused, 'Remind me to speak to the engineers, Col and James Thompson on your vessel. We must emphasise the importance of maintaining an ambient temperature, whilst preserving as much fuel as possible.'

'Yes, of course, John,' replied Francis, for once dropping the 'sir', while they were in the privacy of Franklin's quarters. 'I'll have a private word in Thompson's ear prior to bringing them together for a final winter briefing.'

They were silent for a few moments, each considering other aspects of the voyage, thus far, until Francis broached a familiar subject. 'I don't anticipate that the presence of ice in this channel has escaped your notice. We've sighted a few 'bergs'[17] and many 'bergy-bits' and there's certainly a lot of 'growlers' around. So far they haven't caused problems because we took the precaution of iron plating the bow at the refit, but it has to be said that the 'growlers' are difficult to spot if the seas are anything above slight.

'Yes, we have hit several and it has rattled the china somewhat,' chuckled Sir John, 'but our speed will have negated the likelihood of any damage. Carrying less canvas enables us to proceed with relative safety, but do impress the importance of vigilance to the able seaman on 'lookout' duties.'

'That's duly noted, John, but I have already doubled up on the lookouts since we entered the channel.'

'Shouldn't have doubted you, Francis; in some respects you have more experience than me in these regions,' complimented Sir John with a genuine smile. 'Anyway what concerns me most is the allocation of rations. We cannot

---

17 Bergs/bergy-bits/growlers – Forms of ice of varying size

rely on our fresh and salted stores alone and we must conserve our quantity of canned goods supplied by Goldner, if the expedition is to last in excess of three years. If we can supplement our stocks with game meat ashore, it will be to our advantage. We should arrange a regular hunting party and ascertain if this really is possible or, indeed, practicable. We should also be aware of what is 'on offer' from 'mother nature' herself. The arctic summer usually provides an abundance of plants when the temperature rises dramatically. We might be able to use some 'greenery', don't want any scurvy aboard!'

'We certainly do not', emphasised Francis, echoing Sir John's sentiments. 'We've gone a long way in resolving that particular problem since the days of Captain William Bligh and the 'Bounty' expedition to Tahiti. By the way, how are your fishing skills, John?' questioned Francis, cocking an amused eyebrow and knowing full well that Sir John would never, ever look at a fish, unless it was served on a plate, without its head...he never did like the eyes staring back at him!

'I'll leave that to you Crozier, my esteemed friend', once more reverting to his surname. 'You're the experienced one, remember?' he laughed...

'Actually, that is something else we should explore,' interjected Francis. If we can supplement our supplies with fish, full of protein I believe, then that's bound to benefit the ships' complement. I recall on a previous expedition, observing an Inuit[18] cutting a hole in the ice...must have been two feet thick! He proceeded to bait a line with a small fish, then sat for an hour or more, before whipping out a seal! Unceremoniously clubbed it to death before hauling it

---

18 Inuit – Eskimo (Esquimaux)

on to the ice. Only problem was, that within, let me think, possibly only ten minutes, the scent of blood enticed a Polar Bear to the kill; a massive and brutal beast and certainly to be feared. I wasn't surprised that the Inuit deemed it prudent to make a fast exit and leave the bear to it! Our party was only a couple of hundred yards away and didn't even see it approaching. Luckily for us, the bear was intent on stealing the Inuit's catch and didn't want us for breakfast!'

'They're a magnificent animal nonetheless, but certainly one to avoid, especially the females when they're intent on feeding their cubs, around March, April I think.' advised John.

'Point taken,' acknowledged Francis. 'When we conduct our allotted tasks and experiments, we need to be vigilant and extremely alert to that particular danger. We don't want a marine or one of our 'succulent' lieutenants on a Polar Bear's menu,' he joked.

John considered a repost on the lines of 'poor taste' but then considered it inappropriate. 'Hmm, perhaps black humour isn't really warranted when we've both seen remnants of seals on the shoreline, obviously bear kills. They leave little for other scavengers such as wolves, arctic foxes and seabirds, of course, but the fact remains they're cunning and dangerous and can move fast on ice or in the water.'

'Which brings us to the tasks and experiments them-selves,' said John matter of factly. 'We've three to conduct. The first will be ongoing and requires us to log the magnetic variation around the North magnetic pole. We surmise that the earth's field may change, giving rise to the suggestion that the magnetic pole itself may change its position over many decades. By monitoring the variation[19] in several

---

19 Variation – Name given to the variation in degrees + or – between True and Magnetic North.

locations, we should be able to determine the difference between true and magnetic north and thus be able to compensate our compass courses and headings. It will be interesting to discover if magnetic north does in fact subscribe an oval or circle around true north. Seems the Earth may have a slight magnetic 'wobble',' eh Francis?! 'The second concerns us with the gathering of meteorological data,' continued Sir John. 'This will be ongoing and I've designated Lieutenant George Hodgson to co-ordinate and correlate the findings on board the *Terror*, supervised by yourself. We'll be monitoring wind direction and speed, sea and ice conditions, currents, temperature, daylight hours etc. This should be undertaken in parallel with the taking of soundings in the narrower channels and the mapping of coastlines so far unexplored. I've no doubt the hydrographer aboard will have his hands full with that one. Our third task will be to monitor and observe the flora and fauna during the summer months when the Arctic comes to life. The nearest trees, for instance, are around eight hundred miles south in mainland Canada, but summer brings out many varieties of wild flowers such as arctic poppies, which flourish in sheltered spots. We've already observed sedges, saxifrages, heathers and prostrate willows in some areas. As for the animals, there are arctic hares, caribou, which we've seen on Ellesmere and a variety of birds, including Terns, Rock Ptarmigans and Snow Buntings.'

'I rather fancy some jugged Hare,' laughed Francis. 'I wonder if it tastes the same in these parts.'

'Can't imagine it would,' returned John. 'Their diet would be different in England's green and pleasant land, but maybe not so much in the Highlands of Scotland. I'm beginning to feel hungry, now that you've mentioned jugged hare! Still it's not long before we're due to dine with the officers. Might I suggest a brandy before we conclude our meeting?'

'Thank you, I will,' responded Francis.

Their toast was for a successful expedition.

CHAPTER SIXTEEN

'A Beeching New Year'

A successful transit around Cornwallis, which included systematic charting of the coastline, impressed Franklin and Crozier. They had not succeeded in finding the elusive waterway to the Pacific, but they had circumnavigated the island. The ships crews had behaved impeccably from the onset and proved their worth with only one minor mishap. John Diggle, the cook on the *Terror*, sliced the end of his finger whilst overenthusiastically carving up an arctic hare, shot by Marine, Henry Wilkes.

The shore party, which landed on the island as part of the hydrographic survey, took the opportunity for a spot of recreation. They had not, of course, been privy to Franklin and Crozier's conversation some weeks earlier, but fresh meat was always considered a bonus 'jugged' or not. The end result was that John Peddie, Surgeon, got to practise his needlework, in which he always took a distinct pride. He then gave the cook two days off in which to recover. He didn't want the 'end' dropping off into one of the indescribable '*Terror* broths', for which Diggle was dubiously famous.

Rob Golding, the ship's boy took over temporarily...some aboard breathed a distinct sigh of relief for even this brief respite from Diggle's galley offerings.

❧

Col, aboard the *Erebus* and James Thompson, engineer on the *Terror* were now fully familiarised with the workings of the engines and conversant with all the associated pipe-work, whether for heating, fresh water or the 'heads'[20]. The heads utilised a header tank filled frequently, using a rotational pump. Four men cranked the horizontal bar in a circular motion, which in turn operated the pump. A couple of hundred turns filled the tank and kept the able seamen fit. David Bryant, the Royal Marine Sergeant, having observed this practice over a number of weeks, came to the conclusion that a competition should be organised, open to the marines and seamen of both vessels. Whatever team completed the task of filling the header tank quickest had the bragging rights.

The competition, now in its seventh week, was proving to be a great pastime with only seconds between all four teams. Tug-o'-war was added to the entertainment as the rivalry became more competitive as the spirit of camaraderie blossomed. However, the more established off watch pastimes, were enjoyed by the majority.

Friends amongst crew members were now firmly established and groups played cards, Nine Men Morris, Chess, Draughts, Dominoes and other games. Others carved scrimshaw, repaired clothes, sewed canvas with palm and sail-twine in the true tradition of mariners' off-watch time.

Rob's 'whale tooth' was coming on a treat. He was becoming quite adept with his small toolkit of 'hot needle', file and penknife. His 'square rigger' on one side looked impressive, even if he did say so himself, but he did need help with the chart of their proposed exploration area, he

---

20 'Heads' – Toilets

intended to etch into the reverse of the tooth. For this he consulted Lieutenant Graham Gore, navigator and hydrographer, who was only too happy to assist in his endeavour.

॰ঌয়৵঴

Christmas was fast approaching, the first of the expedition to be spent near Beechey Island in Resolute Bay. The winter nights were long and very cold; colder than expected, according to Franklin and his experience of the region. All that could be done had been accomplished. They were virtually battened down, only venturing out for brief periods of exercise and essential duties as temperatures allowed.

The men's clothing and uniforms, whilst not especially commensurate for the voyage, were adequate, but many of the crew were thankful for the extra woollens and other garments given to them by family, prior to leaving London.

The heating system, such as it was, was also adequate, if temperamental. However, Col and James were keeping a watchful eye on the coal supply, which had been supplemented by the gathering of driftwood by the crew on the shoreline, but it amounted to very little in real terms.

Their fresh supplies of meat and vegetables were also dwindling and it would soon be time to break into Goldner's cans, some eight thousand of varying size. Three days before Christmas, Davy and the cook took the opportunity of inspecting the store area in which they were contained. Dick Wall fished into his apron pocket as they approached. He removed a large iron key, inserted it into the lock and opened the gate. Cans were stacked uniformly, in such a fashion so there could be no possibility of movement should the ship roll. 'Locking stows' were second nature to all aboard and prevented mishaps. Items could fall, such as barrels and easily break a seaman's arm or leg, or worse.

'Okay Davy, let's see if these cans bear any resemblance to Goldner's manifest. He turned up pretty late by my reckoning and looked a bit shifty. Wouldn't be the first chandler or supplier to try it on.'

'Which ones are we checking, Dick?' asked Davy, addressing him by his Christian name. Davy was a lot younger than Dick, but realised that Dick at forty-five years, was no fool. They had a good working relationship and Davy appreciated Dick's affection for his two cats, Mitzi and Fritz, now past their kitten stage and into occasional rat catching.

'See that batch on the starboard side,' indicated Dick. 'We'll have a look at those. I've not had much to do with cans prior to this voyage but they're supposedly the future in the Navy, not to mention a market ashore...Hmm, I'm not taken with the lead soldering on this can, looks more like the back leg of a donkey! I'll send this one over to Diggle on the *Terror* to put in one of his broths. It won't bother him that he can't read the label!'

'Shall I take another for us to try?' queried Davy.

'Aye lad...why not?' responded Dick. 'In the meantime, tally up the larger cans, we'll probably be using them first.'

Christmas Day passed without incident, notwithstanding the fact that Franklin and Crozier agreed to allow a ration of 'grog'[21] to be issued to the crews. This produced a few sea shanties and reels, but no extreme behaviour and no drunken revelry. Everyone realised it was important to

---

21 'Grog' – Rum diluted with water.

remain alert in such a demanding environment. Those officers and men who remained on duty took their responsibilities to heart, whilst the majority enjoyed the festivities, meagre as they were, in time-honoured fashion. Some received gifts from wives and girlfriends, hidden aboard by shipmates until Christmas Day itself. Tom and Davy were among the fortunate few.

'I've been hiding this woollen scarf from Marie in my kitbag for months, see, there's a note attached,' explained Davy.

'Let me have it then,' urged Tom. He proceeded to wrap it enthusiastically around his neck before bowing and exclaiming, ''Ow do I look?'

'Magnificent,' grinned Davy. 'A right toff.'

Tom grunted, not quite sure if it was a compliment or an insult as he read the note. *'Something to keep you warm when I'm not there. Think of me always,' Love Marie xx'*

Tom was not one to give way to emotion, but a slight tear appeared to form at the corner of his right eye, the only acknowledgement of his love. He brushed it away quickly and held out a clenched fist to Davy. 'Here you are then, here's yours!'

Davy ducked away, thinking he was about to receive a cuff, as he had indeed witnessed the telltale tear; however, he was mistaken.

Tom pressed him. ''Ere, take it'.

'Take what?' questioned Davy.

'This,' he said indicating to Davy that he should open his hand. With that, he dropped an inch square green velvet pouch into Davy's palm.

Davy looked at it incredulously. 'Is this it?' he asked.

'Yep, that's it,' affirmed Tom. 'Well open it then!' he instructed.

Davy peeled open the small flap and dropped the content into his hand. Inside was a small silver button bearing an exquisite portrait of Catherine. A neatly folded miniature message in keeping with the gift lay beside it. He turned his back on Tom to read the words, not wanting to show his emotion. Actually, he needn't have bothered because Tom already knew the sentiments it conveyed. After all, it had been in his keeping since May.

Davy read it slowly...*'Sew it on the inside of your tunic, so that I'll always be with you. I love you, Catherine xx' PS Please come back safely.'* It was both simple and heartfelt, a genuine message of love from one individual to another, who both knew where their destinies lay from the very first meeting.

Tom coughed awkwardly in the palpable silence that enveloped them as Davy gazed at Catherine's portrait. 'Ne'er mind lad, it won't be long before you're looking at the real thing.' Tom commiserated, before leaving him alone with his thoughts...

'Thanks Uncle Tom,' he whispered, acknowledging the bosun's obvious concern for his nephew.

'Try this,' suggested Diggle to John Torrington. 'Heat it up on the boiler in the engine room when you're on duty...here's a pan.'

'Thanks, I will,' responded John.

Diggle continued. 'We're not supposed to be having these until the New Year proper, but I'm interested to find out what the contents taste like. 'It'll look suspect if I'm using them in the galley before I'm supposed to, so you can be my 'guinea pig'...just keep it to yourself. It's one of the small cans, so you'll be all right. Chuck the can overboard afterward.'

'Right you are,' grinned John.

John Torrington turned twenty on the outward bound voyage and was looking forward to celebrating the New Year in two days time. He'd volunteered for the Navy just seven days prior to the commencement of the expedition as a leading stoker aboard the *Terror*. Originally from Manchester, he'd gained some experience with steam boilers at a foundry, which gave him an incentive to try his luck in the newly appointed engine room, aboard one of Franklin's vessels. He was even more pleased to have been paid fifteen pounds and twelve shillings; a princely sum by any standard, which constituted double pay for three months in advance no less! He'd promptly sent twelve pounds of this sum to his mother as a heartfelt thank you for her encouragement, love and help in his adolescent years.

The boiler room aboard the *Terror* offered an extra degree of warmth to those working there. Clothing was constantly being dried on the pipes, next to the boiler itself; consequently, the stokers received a steady stream of visitors wanting a favour. But now it was quiet and John took the opportunity to open the can with a chisel before inserting it into the burning coals, using the back of his shovel. It wasn't long before the liquid, annotated beef broth, was bubbling. He was just about to locate his spoon when his name was called.

'Are you there John?' It was too late to conceal the can as two men from the *Erebus* confronted him, a marine and an able seaman. 'Wot yer got there then?' questioned Bill Braine.

John Hartnell, accompanying the marine sneered accusingly. 'That's shocked yer! Caught in the act eh? Tell yer what, let's 'ave some and we'll say nowt.'

Torrington was alarmed, but immediately decided to offer his two visitors a portion of broth. He pulled out three tin mugs and poured three generous glutinous shares. 'Ere you are then, sit down and keep quiet. What are ya 'ere for anyway...not spying on me?'

'Nah', replied Bill. 'Col the engineer sent me over with Hartnell here to collect a heavy wheel spanner. He's 'aving trouble with a valve, needs freeing up...says you've got one?'

'So I have,' replied John. 'I'll get it once we've supped our broth. Just remember to keep your mouths shut!' he reminded them quite prophetically.

They ate and chattered until the marine and able seaman left with the wheel spanner, returning to the *Erebus*. Torrington disposed of the empty can with ill concealed relief.

New Year's Eve dawned and Franklin and Crozier, who'd formed quite a bond, were approaching 1846 with fortitude and optimism. The voyage so far was proceeding according to plan.

Meanwhile in the boiler room, John Torrington was experiencing double vision. Worse still, he felt extremely weak. He decided to sit awhile and drink some water, but even that didn't help as he had difficulty swallowing. He closed his eyes and edged closer to the boiler for warmth. Beads of sweat appeared on his forehead, but he felt decidedly cold. He needed the 'Heads'. Stumbling out of the boiler room, he headed to the lower deck facility...but did not make it, throwing up before he got there. He managed to drag himself the rest of the way before quickly dropping his trousers...just in time, he thought, as a vile smell invaded his nostrils. 'Was that me?' he muttered to himself, before passing out completely...

John was vaguely aware of the administration of Alexander McDonald, assistant surgeon, for some hours before he eventually passed away. It was early in the morning, New Year's Day 1846.

Alexander was shocked. He did not know what could have caused Torrington to die so horrifically and dramatically in such a short space of time from the onset of his illness. Alarmingly, two other men aboard the *Erebus*, William Braine and John Hartnell were also suffering the same symptoms, but at present were holding their own. Stephen Stanley and Harry Goodsir, surgeon and assistant surgeon were monitoring them, but could not determine the cause of their illness either.

❧

John Torrington was laid to rest three feet down in the gravelly permafrost on a desolate spit of land on Beechey Island. The burial party found it impossible to dig deeper, even with pickaxes. His grave was marked with a simple wooden headboard. A service conducted by Franklin himself was attended by the majority of both ships crews, but their mood was sombre, which reflected private thoughts of a none too auspicious start to the year.

❧

Three days later both John Hartnell and William Braine died without gaining consciousness. This didn't help the surgeons in determining the reason behind their deaths.

'Torrington's death occurred within twenty four hours and Hartnell and Braine, within three days,' commented

Stephen Stanley. 'Whatever it was, it was exceptionally virulent and fatal. Have any others been reported as having the same symptoms?'

'No, Sir,' responded Harry Goodsir.

'Well at least we can be thankful for that eh?'

Harry acknowledged Stanley's observation before introducing another issue. 'I believe Hartnell's brother, he joined with him, wishes to see you, before you prepare John for burial…he has a request apparently.'

'Yes, of course, Harry. Send him in,' confirmed Stanley.

Tom Hartnell, the brother of John stood in the doorway and doffed his cap. 'Permission to enter, Sir,' requested Tom.

'Please come in, Hartnell, how can I help you?'

'Can't help *me* really,' suggested the distressed brother, 'but me mam would be really upset if I didn't give John a good send off. She really wanted us boys to be smartly dressed whenever the money allowed. Well, I've brought along this fine cotton shirt…I know it's got my initials on… TH…' His voice broke and he gulped, before continuing, 'John always admired it…and I'd want him to 'ave it…so would mam!'

'I quite understand. I'll ensure he's presentable for your mam and yourself. I'm sure he will have appreciated your final gift,' said Stanley in commiseration.

'Thank you, Sir, you're a gentleman,' responded Tom as he left with tears in his eyes.

John Hartnell and William Braine were buried a day later, alongside John Torrington, just as the weather conditions on Beechey Island improved. They were given the same respect afforded to their shipmate. Franklin again gave the eulogy, although visibly upset at the latest deaths.

'Let's hope that's the last we'll have to suffer on this expedition,' remarked Crozier to his friend and Commander.

Franklin refrained from replying. His thoughts were elsewhere as he remembered his wife, Jane's words: *'The expedition is madness...you're too old.'*

Later, as he sat down in his cabin to compose three more letters of condolence to the crewmen's relatives, his pen hand started shaking. *Must remind Fitzjames to make an entry in the Logbook concerning their deaths,* he reflected.

❧

'What did you do with that can we took from the store, Davy?' enquired Dick, the cook.

'Oh, sorry, forgot to mention that I'd opened it just before New Year and heated it in the galley. Unfortunately, I knocked it over and only managed to save a small portion, which I gave to the cats. Mitzi growled at it and Fritz sniffed before walking off. I've not seen them do that before, so I smelt the stuff myself. It wasn't pleasant I can tell you, so I threw it away.'

'Fair enough,' commented Dick. 'Can't be too careful. There's been a lot of 'Tommy Rot'[22] in London Town recently, so who knows what's been put in those cans. Remind me to check before we use any more.

'Done,' agreed Davy.

---

22 'Tommy Rot' – Less than perfect meat, passed its optimum time for eating and sold by unscrupulous butchers/pedlars to unsuspecting and or poor customers.

CHAPTER SEVENTEEN

'Spring/Summer 1846'

'Enter', instructed Sir John in a friendly tone, as he was in good spirits at last. Three months had elapsed since the expedition suffered its first casualties, apart from James Stanley in London at the onset of the expedition. He was thankful that he was able to inform the relatives directly of James' demise and offer his condolences. However, he did wonder how many months would elapse before his three other letters, informing the relatives of Torrington, Hartnell and Braine's deaths, would arrive on their doorstep. Col stood on the threshold of Sir John's dayroom. 'Come in, come in and do sit down,' enthused Sir John.

'Thank you, Sir,' responded Col.

'Tea?' enquired Sir John.

'I don't mind if I do. It's been a long time since I've had the pleasure of drinking from such a fine service as yours. Thank you again.'

The two men had formed a good working relationship since Col's appointment in London. It was now time to plan the expedition's next passage for which Sir John would need Col's expertise in manoeuvring the vessels through the many leads in the pack ice around the islands. Col and James on the *Terror* had already worked wonders in conserving as much fuel as possible needed for the passage between Somerset Island and Prince of Wales Land. However, their goal, this time incorporated transits of several straits: Barrow, Peel, Franklin and Victoria. They would be difficult and probably not without incident, but if everyone worked effectively as a team, they had reason for optimism.

'I've requested that Captain Crozier, Lieutenant Little and James Thompson join us from the *Terror*. Fitzjames, my second in command aboard this vessel will also attend,' advised Sir John. 'Feel free to discuss any concerns that you may have at this juncture or they may be forever 'frozen' in time,' he laughed.

'You may be assured that I will,' confirmed Col as Sir John welcomed his other officers into the dayroom. All were well aware of each other's importance in bringing the expedition to a successful outcome, so introductions were merely perfunctory.

Francis Crozier started the ball rolling. 'We don't anticipate any serious problems negotiating the pack ice, which should be breaking up considerably now that the sun is over the yardarm. There'll be plenty of 'leads' to be followed in the southerly direction we wish to follow. If Col and James can maintain the engine speed at around four knots in 'brash' or pack ice, the reinforced bows of both vessels should break up any stubborn obstruction impeding our progress.'

'It will be important to maintain momentum in those circumstances,' interjected Fitzjames. 'If one vessel follows closely in the wake of the other, there will be minimal likelihood of the ice closing in again before the second is through.'

'I concur,' commented Col as James nodded in total agreement with his fellow engineer. 'We'll save more fuel if we move as one, whenever possible. What should be avoided, if at all possible, is an engine movement astern.'

'Quite right,' added James. 'If the ice closes in, around the stern of the vessels, we risk damaging a propeller. Far better to maintain forward propulsion as Captain Crozier suggests.'

'Hopefully, the summer months will provide sufficient clear water for us to navigate safely, without recourse to the engines,' remarked Lieutenant Little. 'However, I appreciate the need for caution, should we encounter inclement conditions.'

'Thank you for your observation, Lieutenant Little,' said Sir John, 'but I should stress that our chances of locating the North West Passage may entirely depend on the efficiency of the engines of both the *Terror* and *Erebus*.' These sentiments were unanimously confirmed by positive rumblings from everyone present. 'Efficient navigation will also play an important part in determining a way through,' continued Sir John. 'You will, of course, be aware from our previous discussions that 'lines of soundings'[23] are important as are bearings of coastal features. Hydrography of all the coastal areas is of vital importance. Some features will be familiar from previous expeditions, but we need to reaffirm and monitor progress as concisely as we are able.

The meeting continued for a further two hours before closing. Agreement was reached on many important issues. Tomorrow they would depart Beechey Island, but not without memories of crew members lost to them in unfortunate circumstances.

---

23 Soundings – depths taken at regular intervals with 'line and lead' a simple device for measuring depth.

Davy positioned himself on the foc'sle head, bracing his legs for the occasional impact of a small 'bergy-bit'. He took in the panoramic vista, overawed at its stunning magnificence contained in the mountainous sheer cliffs of rock and blue ice.

'Quite a sight, eh Davy?' whispered Rob in his left ear, who'd crept up behind him unnoticed.

'Words can't describe what I'm feeling right now!' enthused Davy. 'How can an area like this be so beautiful and yet so dangerous!' It was obvious that Davy had learnt a lot in his first year aboard.

'Makes it worthwhile doesn't it? No wonder your Uncle Tom signed on again...most people will never be privileged to see such sights...make the most of this because it won't be long before you're back in a thick London fog!' He laughed at his own erudite remark, but wasn't convinced he wanted to swap the clean crystal air of the Arctic for London right at that moment. 'Better get on with taking some soundings with the 'hand leadline[24]' for Fitzjames, otherwise he might think I'm 'swinging the lead' and just chatting to you up here on the foc'sle.' Rob laughed again at his own humour. It wasn't a bad job taking soundings compared to other more arduous tasks, hence the phrase which came to mean 'avoiding other duties'. 'Watch out! Here comes 'Cookie', closely followed by Mitzi and Fritz. I'll bet one wants you to do some work by the meaningful look on his face and the cats obviously need feeding.'

'No time for sunning yourself up here,' remarked Dick good-humouredly. 'We've a meal to prepare.'

---

24 Hand leadline – a line marked up to twenty fathoms for use in shallow water – one fathom equals six feet.

Reluctantly Davy left with Dick, leaving Rob 'swinging the lead' and calling out the marks. Rob was fully conversant with the procedure, always making sure that the number of fathoms were the last part of the call. He was aware that the recording officer generally hears the number of fathoms called, even if the wind or other factors prevent the first two or three words being heard.

Rob called out his first mark. 'A quarter less eight,' which the officer understood to be forty-six and a half feet.

'Check the bottom, Rob,' instructed Lieutenant James Fairholme.

Rob turned over the lead and inspected the hole in the bottom, 'Mud,' affirmed Rob.

'Let's have another!'

Rob heaved the lead on the weather side once again and reported. 'By the deep six!'

Fairholme determined that the channel was becoming shallower as subsequent soundings indicated a steady decline in available depth, with a consequence that the *Erebus* altered course to mid-channel as a safety measure.

'Well done, Fairholme!' congratulated Fitzjames. 'We were closing in too fast on that promontory and it was prudent to be cautious!'

'Thank you, Sir,' responded Fairholme.

'Sir John's concerned that the 'Fast ice'[25] is pretty stable in this region, which doesn't bode well, as we're coming into summer. We should really expect more 'brash' and 'rotten' ice as the temperature rises.'

'I've noticed it myself, Sir,' affirmed Fairholme. 'From my limited experience it could mean a series of cold summers

---

25 'Fast ice' – sea ice which remains fast in the position of growth throughout the winter and remains even during the ensuing summer.

and possibly extreme winters. Any idea what Commander Franklin and Captain Crozier are thinking?

'I'm sure they're aware of the possibility Lieutenant. We'll know what's in their minds in due course.'

❧

'Signal Crozier on the *Terror* and send this message,' instructed Sir John.

'Yes, Sir,' Fitzjames answered, at once beckoning a signaller to the task: *'Proceed to the Bay south of Cape Rendel on the Boothia Peninsula. Follow Erebus, but keep three hundred yards astern on her port quarter in case we run aground – Opportunity to replenish supplies, water and conduct experiments for Admiralty.'*

An acknowledgement from Crozier was promptly received with a rider – 'I'll welcome stretching my land legs.' He was aware that the bay had been sighted previously, on another expedition in 1819, but was never explored because it was difficult to discern where the pack ice ended and the land began. He was looking forward to rectifying this oversight.

Two days later on 7th June they anchored in the bay and cleared away two boats from each vessel crewed by several able seamen and marines, under the command of Fairholme and Irving.

CHAPTER EIGHTEEN

'An Encounter'

Crozier braced his legs and supported his elbows on the bulwark[26]. This practised posture enabled him to use his telescope to best advantage whilst scanning the shoreline from north to south.

'What do you see?' queried Sir John.

'Very interesting! Not at all what I expected,' replied Crozier

'Well, what *do* you see, Francis? Don't keep me in the dark,' said Sir John impatiently.

Crozier smiled, but kept the telescope fixed to his right eye, before responding. He collected his thoughts...'To the north east and south east of the bay are two inlets which look extensive...could reach inland for a few miles. The bay itself is a natural anchorage with gently sloping cliffs, culminating in many shale and rocky beaches. Not much ice here, most of what's left is 'brash' or 'rotten', but the best news is that there's an abundance of wildlife. I can see several groups of seals, arctic terns and other seabirds.

'That's good news for the shore parties!' remarked Sir John. 'I'll leave their instructions in your hands while I concentrate on mapping the area. Charts for this 'neck of the woods' are sketchy to say the least, so I'll liaise with our

---

26 Bulwark – ship's side, about 4' high above deck level.

respective hydrographic officers on the task. Perhaps we should name the bay and inlets while we're about it. What do you say, Francis? Torrington Bay and Hartnell and Braine Inlets will be more than appropriate and it will please the crews. I'll annotate the ship's log to that effect along with our observations, if you've no objections?'

'No, not the slightest as I agree with your sentiments,' confirmed Crozier. 'It was a shock to lose three men in quick succession and unexpectedly. I'll organise the shore party's departure. They're already standing by expectantly! Here take the eyeglass[27] and have a look for yourself, there's reason to be optimistic now.'

༺༻

Tom and Rob were selected for the shore party, with a complement of fourteen all told, including the two officers, Fairholme and Irvine. They would split into two parties to hunt game and find fresh water; one party to proceed along the northern shore and one to the south.

Tom and Rob were assigned to the northerly contingent under Fairholme along with Able Seamen John Morfin and Henry Lloyd, plus Marines, Sergeant David Bryant and Corporal Alexander Pearson. The latter two carried the firearms and ammunition. Both were experienced in hunting, having previously undertaken similar excursions. Sergeant Bryant was pleased to have been placed in the same group as Tom and Rob, as they had become great friends 'off watch'. Their 'card game' was a regular pastime and small amounts of money changed hands frequently without anyone gaining an advantage overall. Consequently,

---

27 Eyeglass – Telescope

there was insufficient cause for any animosity or friction. Dave Bryant, short of money on one occasion, promised to instruct Tom in the use of one long barrelled musket, should he lose the following hand, which he subsequently lost! According to Dave, Tom was apparently a 'lucky sod' but he still needed to pay the debt at some point.

The shore parties landed without difficulty or mishap. They were soon picking their way through the boulders and scree on the shore when Dave Bryant caught up with Tom. 'Might be able to repay our small wager, if Fairholme agrees. He's a good sort for an officer and won't mind you using the musket if you're given proper instruction.'

'Sounds good to me, Dave,' enthused Tom producing a broad grin. 'Didn't fancy tackling one of them huge bearded seals with my deck knife...as sharp as it is.'

'Just point it away from me when you pull the trigger!' countered Dave. 'In fact, all six of us plan to stand behind you...just in case.'

'Cheeky bugger, it can't be that difficult can it?' laughed Tom.

'Not if you've been taught by an expert I suppose,' grinned Dave, continuing the 'needling' just a little longer than necessary.

'What's this?' laughed Fairholme. 'Planning a shooting party on the grouse moors are we?' He was obviously joining in the fun, having heard the previous exchanges. 'Actually, I'm fine with your 'tuition' Sergeant Bryant. You never know, we may need the bosun here if your trigger finger develops frostbite and falls off!' Fairholme laughed once again before staggering off over the rough terrain with his telescope at the ready.

'There you go then,' encouraged Dave, glancing in Tom's direction. 'We're on for a shoot!'

''Ere ya are then. Now you're one of us marines, you can carry the musket, it's heavy!' Fairholme himself carried a side arm in a leather holster, which was a new edition to the expedition's armoury. His 'naval colt' based on the American 'Captain's colt' was being produced in England at the Pimlico factory. Although weighty, it packed a punch at close range, but its accuracy was partially dependant on the man pulling the trigger, so definitely something to be desired. Consequently, it was no coincidence that the lieutenant could be heard practising on the poop deck from time to time, much to the annoyance of off duty seamen in need of sleep. However, he had persevered, if not exactly becoming a crack shot in the process.

Minutes passed before Fairholme's party rounded a small promontory when he motioned them to hunker down behind several black rocks. Before them lay an expanse of shale beach, about a mile and a half from one end to the other. In the central area a group of large bearded seals were lazing in the sun, almost three hundred yards away and unaware of the men's presence. It would obviously be unwise to approach directly, so they took the precaution of skirting around the base of the cliff face, which afforded them some element of surprise.

'Here Tom,' whispered Dave Bryant, pass that musket rifle and we'll load up, it's quite simple once you know how.'

'I'm watching,' indicated Tom. 'Now don't go too fast or an ordinary bloke like me won't 'cotton on''. He winked at Davy and Rob, sharing his humour conspiratorially.

They laughed quietly but were intrigued at how quickly and efficiently Bryant loaded the firearm.

'Okay, brace yourself behind this low rock and support the barrel on the lichen, growing at the top so it won't slip. Make sure the stock is firmly into your shoulder and sight the two metal strips in line with the target…Target a seal by the way, not Lieutenant Fairholme!'

Just at that moment, the Lieutenant spoke a word of urgent warning. 'Wait! Looks like the 'Esquimaux[28] ' have the same plan as ourselves. There's two Inuits with harpoons, downwind of the seals stalking them…hold on there's something else!'

Fairholme rapidly unsheathed his telescope from its leather case and focused on an area just behind the hunters. He'd noticed a flash of white in the sunlight and was now astonished at the size and sight of an enormous predatory bear hunting the hunters. The two men were in imminent and grave danger.

Tom was the first to react and although he had never fired a musket before, swivelled it in the direction of the bear, which was now only twenty yards away from the hunters on a loping charge. He took aim as best he could.

'Squeeze the trigger now,' Dave shouted frantically, in the knowledge that he hadn't any chance of retrieving the firearm from Tom before the bear attacked the Esquimaux.

Tom fired; the recoil knocked him backwards on to the shale, so he didn't see the unfolding drama. His hurried shot had somehow hit its mark. The bear collapsed in a tumbling fall, only five yards away from the astonished hunters who were lucky in that they survived the surprise attack intact. The seals, amidst all the commotion took flight and headed for the sea, bellowing their anguished concerns.

---

28 Esquimaux – French name for Eskimo or Inuit

'Good shot,' exclaimed Fairholme, congratulating Tom...'but I don't remember giving you the order to fire!' he joked.

Tom raised his eyebrows while the rest of the party stood up and cheered.

The two stunned Inuits remained where they were, waiting silently for the *Erebus's* contingent to approach.

Fairholme unbuckled his holster containing the colt pistol, but did not take out the weapon, having determined that the Inuit were probably friendly, considering the circumstances of their somewhat abrupt encounter. He noted also that the swarthy skinned hunters were displaying lopsided grins from under sealskin fur hoods and that their harpoons lay harmlessly on the shale beach. 'Shoulder your muskets,' he whispered to the marines, as silently as possible, so as not to alarm the Inuits. He needn't have worried; the two men were obviously in awe of the white man's long distance firepower and held out their 'empty' hands in friendship and gratitude.

The elder Inuit approached Fairholme chuckling and although diminutive in stature compared to Fairholme, hugged the Lieutenant in a massive chest high greeting of thanks.

The surprised officer was more than a little taken aback, but even more so when the Inuit pulled him by his neck to within inches of his face and rubbed noses with him. Fairholme had heard of this practice amongst the natives from officers who'd encountered Inuits during the 'Back' expedition, but he'd not witnessed it first hand...until now! He couldn't help noticing a faint smell of 'seal' during the brief nose session, but disregarded it for the sake of diplomacy.

'Come Kabloonans[29],' beckoned the younger Inuit, displaying probably the only word of English he possessed, 'Umiaq[30]'.

Tom and Rob acknowledged his cryptic pronouncement by looking at each other questioningly before following the man to some large rocks a matter of yards away. He indicated that they were to take what they required from their kill of seals, recently slaughtered on the beach, which lay alongside their Kayaks[31]. It was obvious from his hand motions and smile of gratitude that this was his way of thanking the *Erebus's* crew for saving their lives.

He tapped his chest; 'Kayat!' then repeated it, 'Kayat!' then pointed at Tom and Rob in turn. Tom cottoned on quickly and pointed at Rob. 'Rob,' indicated Tom, then fingered his own chest, 'Tom'.

'Aah,' returned the hunter, 'Rob, Tom,' then smiled again in a time honoured universal acceptance of friendship.

'Over here,' shouted Tom to the other marines and seamen. Their colleagues meandered over, realising that the 'gift' of meat would mean an early return to the ships, without expending too much time or energy.

Meanwhile, Fairholme was examining the massive white bear with the help of 'Taka'. The elder Inuit had also introduced himself and was now exposing the bear's very white and large incisors for the lieutenant to admire.

'Hell, they look sharp,' he exclaimed to no one in particular. 'Wouldn't fancy meeting a live one, he'd have me for breakfast!'

---

29 Kabloonans – white men
30 Umiaq – boat
31 Kayak – canoes/small boats

Taka heard the words and by their intonation, guessed their meaning. He nodded in understanding and jumped back in mock alarm after touching them, to jokingly shock the lieutenant.

A crimson stain was spreading over the bear's white fur, just below the entry wound in his brain. *It was definitely a lucky shot*, thought Fairholme, but didn't dwell on the consequence of Tom missing the target, although this brief acknowledgement left him momentarily queasy. The size of the beast's claws and gargantuan bulk was the stuff of nightmares, worse than a night out in London's *East End* he thought. Still laughing to himself, he began watching Taka intently. The Inuit was expertly removing the fur from the carcass of the bear with what looked like an extremely sharp and efficient flint 'knife'. His movements were well practised and it was soon being watched by the shore party. All were intrigued and mesmerised at the spectacle.

Kayat lent his expertise to the task of butchering the beast, as did Tom, to the immediate surprise of both the Esquimaux hunters. The mammoth fur was put aside for the Inuit to keep for themselves, as their need for adequate clothing from the chilling winter months was paramount. All the meat was offered to the crew of the *Erebus*. Taka indicated that the 'taste' would be good, if strong. He did this by placing a morsel in his mouth and then flexing his biceps at the shore party whose jaws were dropping at the prospect of having to emulate the Inuit chewing on raw meat. Luckily, Taka did not expect them to copy his demonstration.

Lastly, in acknowledgement of Tom's lucky shot and help with the butchering, Taka presented him with a bear's claw strung on a piece of hide cord. Tom beamed, blissfully unaware of what Taka actually said to him in Inuktitut,[32]

---

32 Inuktitut – Inuit language

although he understood the gist of it. 'Thanks my little friend!' exclaimed Tom towering above the Inuit.

'Thanks' repeated Taka successfully imitating Tom's London accent.

Soon afterward the Inuits were gone, waved off by the sailors who had helped stow the Kayaks with the bear's fur, bundled efficiently into a manageable load, shortly before loading their own boats with meat for the return trip to the *Erebus*.

'Exciting day, eh,' said Rob, grabbing Tom's arm conspiratorially. 'That pair of Esquimaux certainly took to you and seemed extremely grateful. It's not every day that you save someone's life!'

'I suppose not,' said Tom whose reply, understated as it was, reflected his reluctance to accept an accolade of any kind. His unassuming personality was a trait that Rob admired in Tom from when they'd first met, with a consequence that they'd become firm friends.

'Let's have a look at that trinket?' teased Rob, pointing to the bear's claw around Tom's neck. 'Better watch out or you'll cut your own throat...then what would I tell Marie back in London?'

'Better give it to you then!' guffawed Tom. Giving as good as he got.

'No thanks,' grinned Rob in mock horror. 'That thing looks lethal.'

The return trip to the Erebus was uneventful and the parties were welcomed back enthusiastically.

'Let's search out Davy and Col and tell them about our adventure!' prompted Tom.

'With or without boasting?' countered Rob.

Laughing riotously and slapping each other on the back they left the deck to Diggle the cook who thought Christmas had come early with all the meat on offer.

CHAPTER NINETEEN

Summer 1846

During the summer months, several excursions were undertaken to ensure adequate supplies for the expected tough winter of 46/47. Crewmen took turns in 'stretching their legs' ashore and welcomed the distraction from the life aboard the two ships.

Inuits were sighted on numerous occasions, but the exciting close encounter experienced by Fairholme's party at the beginning of summer was not repeated. The nearest anyone came to an actual meeting came when Col, mesmerised by the rugged scenery, caught a glimpse of Inuits in two kayaks tracking several seals in what they now knew as Hartnell Inlet. They'd exchanged a friendly wave but they were soon out of sight, engrossed on their mission. Col was aware that, despite the sun's warmth, a distinct chill was beginning to creep remorselessly into early evening, now that July was coming to an end. His tunic seemed barely adequate – thank goodness a warm engine room beckoned for the winter, an abstract thought in the midst of such splendour, before he was jolted out of his reverie by the bosun. Tom startled him, having crept up silently, before growling in his ear in a gross imitation of a bear.

Col shot forward in alarm and a second or two passed before realisation dawned. 'Bloody Fool!...you didn't 'alf give me a fright Tom.'

'Couldn't resist it Col, you 'ad your head in the clouds and were obviously daydreaming...admiring the scenery again?'

Col answered belligerently, 'Well, what if I was, there's an ethereal beauty in this part of the world which I can't quite get to grips with, 'it's mesmerising!'

'Whoa there,' said Tom, 'you'll 'ave to explain that to me in plain English. You've lost me with that one!'

'Sorry Tom,' apologised Col. 'Got that one from my mother, she paints you see and most of her paintings have this surreal quality about them'

'There you go again,' protested Tom. 'Just tell me in simple terms, befitting an ex butcher and new found friend, what you're actually talking about?'

'Aah, all right, like in a dream, a wonderful vision,' explained Col.

'That'ull 'ave to do then,' guffawed Tom in token exasperation. 'I'm just glad that one of us knows what we're talking about!'

They both laughed, sharing the joke before Col continued. 'Chilly now isn't it?'

'Colder than I've experienced before,' mused Tom. 'Could be in for an early cold spell. Anyway, it's time to return to the ships, we've enough 'game' for the winter now, so my guess is there won't be any more shore visits, unless Franklin's planning an experiment or observation of some 'planet' on behalf of the 'Lordships' or those fellows at the Royal Observatory at Greenwich.

Tom was not mistaken in his premise and in early August he was conscripted with Col and Rob plus two officers and two marines to ascertain the potential for mineral wealth on the Boothia Peninsula, initially along the coastal perimeter and then inland. Copper and iron were essentially their prime motivation, but tin and other minerals were also targeted. Col, having some experience of metallurgy and smelting would accompany the party to enhance the limited knowledge of the officers. He was overly pleased to do so as he was already gaining an affinity with the rugged terrain and wanted to explore to improve his knowledge of the region.

Lieutenant Graham Gore leading the shore party planned to stay on the coast for five days. They would sleep in tents and collect rock specimens in an area of interest encompassing twenty square miles.

Franklin's briefing still rang in Lieutenant Gore's ears as they reached the shoreline –

'Be sure to keep a good lookout at night. Post sentries accordingly and maintain a fire to ward off bears and wolves. They're less likely to approach. My experience near the Thiew-ee-choh-desseth, that's the Great Fish River, proved invaluable, consequently you should heed my advice!'

Col also received a briefing from Franklin, more a potted history, prior to leaving the *Erebus*, which he mulled over in like manner –

'Samuel Hearne, a European explorer, back in the 1770's encountered 'Yellowknife' Indians during his search for the legendary copper deposits in the region. They helped him transit the Arctic tundra from Hudson Bay to the Arctic Ocean in exchange for tools and other items. They were still the largest and most powerful tribe until the Dogrib almost wiped them out in the 1830's. Some have inter-married and formed new communities based on mining and trading furs,

but others retain their old disputes and hatreds. Rumour has it that gold has also been found which brings me to my point...There's certainly iron and copper in this region which suggests opportunities, but gold brings another dimension to the arena, although our primary concern, of course, is locating the North West Passage. Anyway, enjoy your time ashore and bring back some rock samples before winter sets in!'

Col fully intended to keep his eyes open armed with his newly acquired knowledge. These 'Copper' or 'Yellowknife' Indians interested him greatly. Franklin revealed that their traditional lands were some hundreds of miles away from the ships' present location, but he was sufficiently intrigued to learn more. He reminded himself to gain another audience with Franklin when they returned. Sir John was always pleased to see him, exchanging knowledge and anecdotes, albeit from different backgrounds and upbringing.

A base camp was established in a sheltered location and their tents erected in close formation around a central fire point.

'I reckon we've enough driftwood to last out our stay at this location,' commented Rob to no one in particular.

'The prevailing currents seem to have deposited a good amount in this cove and over many years by the look of it,' responded Lieutenant Gore. 'We'll not have to worry on that score at least, so we'll be able to maintain a fire for cooking and protection, night and day, while we explore the terrain.

'I'll be glad of that,' chipped in one of the marines, who'd been with Tom's party, when Tom killed the bear with a lucky shot. 'I'll be keeping a watchful eye and my powder dry never the less! That beast gives me the jitters whenever I think of it.'

He still looked worried so Tom made an attempt to cheer him somewhat. 'Want me to teach you how to shoot?' This raised a laugh from the rest of the group who knew Tom's claim to fame rested on his 'one and only' shot to date.

The marine looked at Tom askance, until he realised the implication of the joke, then joined in and laughed with them.

❧

Three days passed quickly and many rock samples were collected. Rob was extremely excited over one find, having listened to Lieutenant Gore and Col one evening discussing the possibility of finding gold. He'd rushed over to Col and exclaimed deliriously, 'Look at this, I'm rich!' as he handed over a small chunk of rock which glistened gloriously in the fading rays of the sun.

Col, seemingly amused, commented, 'Hope you're not going to try and use that as a 'stake' in our game of cards?'

'Why not?' asked Rob. 'It must be worth a fair bit?'

'Fraid not,' advised Col. 'It's only 'Fools' gold.'

'Calling me a fool are you Col? I thought we were shipmates.'

'We are,' laughed Col, 'but I'd not be your mate if I let you believe it's the real stuff; it's only 'iron pyrites' and a lot bigger than any gold nuggets you're likely to find, unless you're prospecting near the San Fernando Mission in South California...that's on the other side of this continent.'

'Who told you about that?' queried Rob.

'Oh, Franklin,' replied Col. 'He's a 'mine' of information, by the way, but you've as much chance of going there as I have meeting a woman in this cove!'

His words were quite prophetic in that they became aware of the presence of six Inuits standing silently in the stillness of the evening some yards away. Not one of the sailors had noticed their silent approach, but as all were smiling profusely, they were not alarmed.

'Tom! Rob! Greeted Taka and Kayat as they approached the ship's crew. Tom was delighted...he still retained the bear's claw around his neck, which Taka noticed and obviously appreciated, seeing as it had been his gift.

Lieutenant Gore, Col and the others were introduced with the customary hand signs, closely reminiscent of the first meeting. Kayat introduced his family, which included his wife, two daughters and a son.

'Perhaps you will get to California after all, Rob,' prompted Col, 'as it is, we've just met three women, not one!'

'Don't get any ideas,' whispered Lieutenant Gore, 'I'd prefer to keep the natives friendly...not that the women look much different to the men in all that sealskin and fur hooded attire.

'I see what you mean,' countered a thoughtful Col, squinting slightly in an effort to discern the women's features from beneath their hoods.

'Come over,' gestured Rob to their visitors and eat some food. He placed his hand to his mouth in an eating pantomime to convey his intentions, which they easily understood and soon all were enjoying the tasty stew conjured up by one sailor. He'd actually made a better job of cooking than 'Diggle' on the *Terror* or Wall on the *Erebus*.

Communication didn't prove too difficult in the circumstances until Taka became fascinated by a pocket watch on a chain, after Col took the item from his tunic to check the time. He let Taka examine it and soon the intrigued Inuit was making motions to barter for the timepiece. He instructed the young boy to bring some items from their sleds some distance away and it was only then did the sailors notice the sounds coming from the huskies, who'd obviously been resting quietly after an undoubtedly arduous day pulling the sleds.

Col, on observing the dogs, filled a bowl with the remains of the stew and some smaller left over chunks of meat and went over to inspect the beasts. He was fond of all animals and had already formed a relationship with Davy's cats Mitzi and Fritz who had their own special warm place in the engine room. What amazed him immediately was their bulk; massive heads and jaws and a stocky frame. He soon had their full attention when distributing the food among them. The lead dog, with exceedingly intelligent eyes, took to him immediately which put him in a good mood and receptive to Taka's encouraging offer of 'barter'.

Taka laid out an Inuit outfit on the ground beside the campfire, amidst several inquisitive onlookers. It consisted of a fur-lined jacket with integral fur hood, trousers, fur lined boots and gloves to complement the jacket. All were immaculately stitched and waxed to prevent the ingress of cold winds or water and obviously lovingly created by women with many decades of experience. Taka's wife demonstrated her skills to the sailors by showing them, before stitching the clothing together, how she chewed along the skin to soften the material. Then, by using a sharp ivory needle, the skins were transformed into efficient clothing.

'I reckon you'll need two pocket watches for that lot of bespoke tailoring,' joked Rob.

'If I had one myself I'd not hesitate,' added Tom. 'You never know when you might need an outfit like that.'

Col didn't hesitate for long; he beamed at Taka, indicating a deal should be struck. He wasn't sure he'd even wear the garments, but at the back of his mind he recalled the moment when he questioned the quality of his naval issue uniform tunic. 'Is it really fit for purpose in these climes?' he murmured questioningly to himself.

'What's that Col?' asked Rob.

'Oh nothing,' responded Col. 'Just thinking out loud.'

'First sign of madness,' cajoled Tom. 'You've spent too much time with all those pipes and gauges on the *Erebus*!'

❦

All the sailors learnt something that night from the Inuits who lived, hunted and survived in what was undoubtedly a very hostile environment. By dawn they had left, their dogs hauling the laden sleds into the distance with Taka and Kayat waving a beaming goodbye. Their impressive departure conveyed a definitive statement of their society and their place in this wilderness.

That very night back on board the *Erebus*, Col laid out the Esquimaux outfit on the naval issue blanket, which covered his bunk. He stroked the fur hood abstractedly whilst examining the exquisite stitching as only an engineer could, revelling in the precision of each stitch and shape of the garment. A distinct chill enveloped him at that instant, could it be the harbinger of a bad winter or was it his imagination playing tricks on him? Whatever the cause, an odd feeling of dread sent a shiver along his spine...Tom would have described it as 'someone walking over his grave!! He tried to dismiss it, but failed miserably, lying awake for several hours before falling into a fitful sleep just before dawn.

CHAPTER TWENTY

Dark Leaden Nights
February 1847

'Thanks, that's a good job you've made of that oven door Col,' congratulated Richard Wall, the cook on the *Erebus*. 'Reckon that will last the rest of this voyage. Maybe a bowl of hot broth will be welcome, as I'd not be able to fix the door myself.'

'Don't mind if I do, it's colder than I imagined for February, even for the Arctic,' responded Col with enthusiasm.

'It's good broth, by the way, made from only the best meat brought back by the hunting parties last year. Franklin's instructed me to mix a few of Goldner's tinned provisions in with the basic ingredients, but ever since Diggle gave me the 'thumbs down' following Torrington's death last year, I've been a bit cautious. Of course, I've been inspecting the cans and the contents before using them, but I reckon the lead soldering leaves a lot to be desired. Your oven door's a masterpiece of engineering compared to the tins!' He gave a hollow laugh which didn't go unnoticed by Col. 'Apparently, some of the crew have been complaining of headaches and mild fever and one or two look a bit grey around the gills, but maybe that's because we're cooped up in this damp, dark hull with little opportunity for any exercise topside.'

'Harry, the assistant surgeon, who I was talking with last night reckons that his boss, Stephen Stanley, is at a loss at the pallor of some of the crew. He's been talking to Peddie and McDonald on the *Terror* and they're none the wiser. Apparently McDonald himself is feeling lethargic and out of sorts, so if he, as assistant surgeon, can't determine what's wrong with himself, we're in trouble. I think I'll stick with the stuff we brought back from Boothia, rather than chance Goldner's cache of cans,' confirmed Col.

'Davy Young, his uncle Tom and Rob the carpenter are of the same opinion,' said Richard. 'Call me Dick by the way... They're usually around the galley at mealtimes to watch the two cats, Mitzi and Fritz...if our furry friends turn their noses up at the offerings, them three either go without or pester me for something else. Whose to say if they're on to something or not?'

'I see what you're saying!' answered Col. 'But I know what I'll be doing in the future...I've always had a soft spot for those crazy cats...maybe not so crazy eh?'

Dick laughed at his comment. 'One thing I do know is that they're a pretty lively duo, always running around my feet when I'm busy, so there can't be too much wrong with them.

There's some crates of cans marked with yellow paint: *'Especially for the officers'*, according to Diggle on the *Terror*. Apparently Goldner made a point of presenting Commander Fitzjames with some extra special cans for the officers. Must be really good stuff in them and not for the likes of us ordinary folk. I'm supposed to be including those cans in their meals over the coming months. Fitzjames instructed me to start on them to improve the humour in the wardroom. Apparently, even the officers are feeling the effects of this bloody cold winter. Lieutenant Gore is already wishing he could begin the next experiment ashore, but if the freezing weather keeps the ships locked in the ice, he's not likely to start out until May. He reckons there'll be a party of two officers and six men. Davy's going along to cook and Tom and Rob have also volunteered...must be mad! I don't fancy trekking some distance and then setting up tent in this wilderness. Prefers me 'ome comforts, even if it's in this hulk, do I!'

It was Col's turn to laugh this time, but he couldn't help wondering how his mates would fare once they embarked on this latest venture. He knew he wouldn't be allowed to join the group this time, as they would venture further afield and he would be needed aboard to maintain the heating and engine in working condition. He made a mental note to mention to Franklin that they would need to turn the propeller at the first opportunity this summer when the ice melted and leads appeared.

He could not have known that the *Erebus* and *Terror* were in the midst of the severest prolonged period of cold experienced in the arctic for many years.

CHAPTER TWENTY-ONE

Planning an Expedition
April/May 1847

Tom poked his head around the galley entrance and called, 'Davy! We're wanted by Lieutenant Gore and the mate, Charles Des Voeux, to discuss our expedition in May. He reckons we'll be leaving in about three weeks time, so he needs to finalise the arrangements and ensure we're well prepared.'

'All right Tom, should I let Rob know?' suggested Davy.

'Yes you can, but less of the cheek, it's bosun, or Uncle Tom in private; you're still my sister's 'boy',' he laughed, although he knew in his heart that Davy had matured considerably in the many months since their departure from London, nearly two years ago. It had passed by deceptively quickly and seemed far shorter than their many experiences indicated.

When one is busy, one can achieve many things, but now time was slowing, being stuck in the ice, caged up in a darkened hull, wasn't the best environment for maintaining morale. Some of the crew and marines were complaining about the cold and the food. The frequent laughter from earlier in the passage was slowly dissipating, along with the camaraderie. Where once everyone joined in the games and shanties, many were now keeping to themselves, especially those who had developed sore throats and aching limbs.

Rob almost completed his scrimshaw in early January, but needed a finishing touch. It wasn't until just before Lieutenant Graham Gore's party was due to leave on 24th May that he knew what this must be. He etched in the ship's position in their present location. Charles Des Voeux had said they'd not be going anywhere for a while due to the ice, so they'd be sure to find them in the same spot on their return – 5 leagues Nor', Nor' West of King William Island.

Col peered over Rob's shoulder inquisitively, as Rob completed his last etched letter with a flourish. 'What's a league[33]?' enquired Col.

Rob laughed at his friend's lack of knowledge then added. 'Almost forgot Col. You're obviously a great engineer, but still a landlubber at heart. Never heard of a league eh?' I'm sure they use the term in deepest Manchester, but you must have buried your head in them technical books for too long... Listen and learn,' he joked. 'A league's equivalent to three miles, so by my reckoning, our shore party excursion to King William Island is about fifteen miles. Tom hopes we'll make it in a day, but even if we don't, the ice is thick enough between here and the island to support the whole ship's complement. Of course there's only eight in our party so not much chance of a ducking, although I'd much prefer sheltering on the island...far safer! I don't like the sounds the ice makes when it grinds and shatters, especially at night, it sends shivers up me spine.'

'I know what you mean,' commiserated Col. 'I've lain awake on numerous occasions listening to its malevolence, which reminds me of some mythical beast I heard of as a kid, crunching up bones in a dark cavern!'

---

33 League = 3 miles

'Bloody 'ell Col, you've fair put the wind up me,' admitted Rob. 'The sooner we're on land; I'll feel a lot better. Thank goodness we leave in two days. That reminds me, I'm due to join Tom, Davy, the three marines and the two officers for a briefing with Franklin and Fitzjames later today, something to do with magnetism and observations of the Northern Lights. They called the 'lights' by another name, but I can't pronounce it. Maybe I'll learn their proper name on the trek inland.'

'I bet you will,' laughed Col. 'Want me to look after the scrimshaw while you're gone? I'm fascinated by it and might be able to pick up a few tips, should I try some etching myself.'

'Yeh, sure, but don't go practising on the gaps on that one, it's finished, find yourself another whale tooth,' warned Rob convincingly.

CHAPTER TWENTY-TWO

A Malevolent Presence
24th/25th May 1847

The crews of the *Erebus* and *Terror* watched on silently as the shore party, led by Lieutenant Graham Gore, and Mate, Charles des Voeux disembarked. The ropes of the jumping ladder glistened in the pale light as the wood battens and rungs clunked on the hull under the men's weight as they climbed down the ladder to the ice.

A few less than spontaneous words of encouragement emanated from those remaining on board, cajoled to some extent by the Sergeant of Marines, always an optimistic and happy character. Two of his men were leaving with the party, along with many words of advice from himself.

Joe Healey and Will Read were in some respects ill equipped mentally for their support role, but acknowledged the sergeant's 'Good Luck', with a smile and a wave. The other marine, Henry Wilkes, Harry to his mates, was seconded from the *Terror* and became the last man of the party of eight. Davy, Tom and Rob gathered around the efficient lightweight sled, expertly created and constructed in the last few weeks by Rob and which he'd subsequently tested on the terrain. It contained all the supplies required for the expedition; food, tents, blankets, oil for cooking, arms and ammunition and several technical apparatus stowed in small wood boxes, along with other essential items, including warm clothing.

Each man was provided with a leather harness, which buckled at the front, chest high. At the back was an attached iron 'O' ring, two inches in diameter, centred between the shoulder blades for extra purchase in hauling the sled. A sisal rope was attached to the 'O' ring with a bowline knot which in turn was attached to the sled with a simple clove hitch. Six men, including the officers were expected to pull the sled at any one time, with two men resting whilst walking alongside. Three lengths of rope would be in use, ensuring that each pair hauling the sled would not impede another pair while walking, two abreast.

Gore and Des Voeux planned to monitor the sled for any problems, which might manifest themselves when negotiating the undulating and fractured terrain for the first two leagues, whilst the marines and the crew concentrated on the physical task.

'I feel like a trussed up chicken in this rig,' quipped Harry, the marine from the *Terror*. 'It's worse than kitting out in my dress uniform back at the barracks.

Davy, who paired up with Harry because of their equivalent height and build, responded in like manner. 'If you were a chicken on the *Erebus*, you'd be on the menu, so think yourself lucky!'

'Point taken,' laughed Harry, but I didn't think you ate as well over there as we do on the *Terror*!' This caused him to guffaw more loudly at his witty attempt to tease the young sailor, but Davy only chuckled himself in response.

Davy knew well enough that the remaining food, which included Goldner's cans, was not of the highest quality. He'd managed to bring along some 'good stuff' which Richard Wall, the cook and his Uncle Tom had stashed on the sled, without too much attention. This included a bottle of port which Franklin had given to Col for his birthday during one of their lengthy conversations and which Col had given to Tom later, stating his need was greater than his own!

꿍

The party made good progress over the ice and it soon became obvious that they would make landfall the same day. The sled and the harness arrangement was working well and the men weren't overly fatigued, as they changed positions frequently.

Lieutenant Gore, was ecstatic on reaching the coast near Victory Point earlier than expected, and gave instructions to Davy to start on the stew, which he'd already partially prepared aboard the *Erebus*, while the others were engaged in setting up camp. Once the camp was established and everyone replete with Davy's stew, the three marines posted a lookout. Each were to keep watch for a period of four hours, to guard against natural predators, mainly foxes, wolves and bears. Some of the crew had already experienced close contact with arctic wildlife and weren't that comfortable with the thought of another encounter!

'Keep yer powder dry, Will,' prompted Joe Healey, 'and don't drop off like you usually do aboard ship,' he said jokingly, although he was actually quite serious about Will's predilection for snoozing on watch. So far he hadn't been knobbled, but there was always the first time and he didn't want that to be now, as the consequences of that were too frightening to contemplate.

Two tents housed the eight men; the officers and two marines shared one, while Rob, Davy, Tom and Harry shared the other. A fire they'd started for the stew had provided a modicum of mental and physical warmth, but was now extinguished. Its dying embers, now long gone, were fragmented into charred remnants of charcoal.

Joe was on duty, having relieved a drowsy Will for the next watch, two until six. He considered Will's parting shot, which mimicked Will's own warning to him. 'Now don't drop off like you usually do!' He'd laughed heartily, before responding with a 'Cheeky sod!' and 'You could have at least kept the fire going!'

Joe, too was drowsy, partly because of the cold and partly because he'd had difficulty sleeping in the strange environs of a tent.

It wasn't long before he dozed off. The sounds of the others slumbering had tipped him over the edge. His rifle slid to a position near his feet, although he remained in a sitting posture, supported by a flat rock to his back.

He dreamed of home, of his wife and children. He could smell the fresh bread baking in the oven and a smile flickered at the corners of his mouth when a strange sensation overwhelmed him. He was being lifted vertically and his head ached abominably, as if an iron band encased it. Another smell invaded his senses in the brief moment before he left this world, as the fetid breath of a mammoth polar bear entered his nostrils. His skull was crushed in an instant as the bear's 'gin trap' jaws silently tore his head from his body. This male bear was not alone, his rival and a much stronger, older bear was ripping apart the officers tent with vast swings of his giant claws. Those inside never stood a chance. The beast towered over them, biting and tearing into their flesh with impunity, until all were massacred in a matter of seconds.

The first bear, encouraged and enraged by the taste of Joe's blood, tore at the second tent. Harry screamed 'God have mercy on us.'

'Never mind him, ready that musket!' shouted Tom as he grabbed the marine's bayonet and stabbed at the bear's hind leg, wounding it convincingly, but this only angered the beast as it bludgeoned both Davy and Rob into a bloodied motionless state. Tom was petrified; he'd just witnessed the nightmare of both his nephew and best friend being cast aside like two rag dolls, but still had the presence of mind to shout to Harry. 'Shoot the other bugger, now!!'

Harry didn't hesitate, he let off a round into the skull of the bear that had done for Will and the officers, just as the bear charged. It was a killing shot, but the bear's momentum knocked Harry into a sharp rock snapping his spine like a twig. As Harry's eyes glazed over, Tom alone faced their wounded arctic predator. Snorting with pain from Tom's bayonet wound, the beast eyed him malevolently. Tom knew he didn't stand a chance but steeled himself to go down fighting. He just had enough time to remove his deck knife from its sheath and change weapon hands. With the bayonet now in his left hand and the knife in his right, he experienced a nightmare sensation that no man should ever face. The bear, now oblivious to his wound...charged! Tom had just one infinitesimal moment to reflect on the fact that someone had told him that polar bears hunt alone! 'Oh God!' Tom muttered, forgetting himself momentarily, as he was not a religious man, 'Marie will never forgive me for getting killed.'

CHAPTER TWENTY-THREE

Searching
Early June 1847

'The shore party are long overdue.' Genuine concern tinged Francis Crozier's voice as he crossed his legs in the upright chair adjacent Franklin's cabin desk.

'Yes, Francis, something must have happened to them I think. Lt Gore may have extended their observations by a couple of days, but it's been almost a week now. I'd like you to organise a search party. I would have sent Bosun Terry, but, unfortunately, he was one of the party. I hope we haven't lost any of them, but especially him...such a strong character and very dependable.'

'I second your thoughts Sir John; I'll get on to it straight away. I'll send four men from the *Terror*, Lieutenant Little plus a sailor and two marines.

'Search the area in the immediate vicinity of Victory Point and then if nothing's found, extend the search inland to the south east where they were to conduct observations into magnetic variation.'

'Certainly, Sir John. I think that's the way to proceed. It's more than likely that they would have run into difficulties further inland, but you can never tell. Lieutenant Gore was confident of setting up base camp at Victory Point on the first or second day, but the Arctic can be a strange forbidding place at times. I hope nothing serious has occurred.'

Crozier left the cabin deep in thought, but intent on

locating the eight men as soon as possible. He knew that their supplies were by now exhausted, even allowing for the contingency provision, which included some canned food.

∞⧉∞

The search party made good time in reaching the destination but they were totally unprepared mentally or physically for what they were about to encounter as they approached Lieutenant Gore's camp at Victory Point.

Lieutenant Little stared in disbelief at the horrific scene, which greeted his small 'rescue' party. The scattered remnants of tents, provisions, equipment, clothing, two broken muskets and ammunition, lay in a state of utter confusion, but what horrified him most were the three corpses, mangled beyond belief and almost unrecognisable, lying in copious amounts of congealed blood, now frozen in obscene testament of the vicious attack. One of the marines was so appalled that he fled the immediate scene to throw up behind a rock, but only encountered Harry, staring into eternity, half covered by a huge white bear. He still had the presence of mind to loose off his weapon into the bear's back before he realised, it too, was dead. Gibbering incoherently, Marine Hammond stumbled back to Lieutenant Little and tried to convey his anguish through tear stained eyes.

Lieutenant Little, although visibly shocked, surprised himself. 'Get a grip Hammond, what did you fire at?'

'Sorry Sir,' Hammond managed to mumble, 'a dead bear, was all!'

'You mean you killed it?' queried Little.

'No, Sir...already dead. Harry...sorry, Wilkes, looks like he knobbled it before copping it 'imself, Sir. It crushed 'im or summat!'

'Anyone else there? Any survivors?' asked Lieutenant Little.

'No Sir, none, just the bear and Wilkes...'is spine's gone, Sir!'

Lieutenant Little turned and once more surveyed the carnage. He could identify the victims...just, as Lieutenant Gore, De Voeux and Marine Reed. Healey's body was to be seen decapitated some yards away, but Little was puzzled, Hammond had already identified Wilkes as the fifth victim, but what had become of Bosun Terry, Carpenter Ellis and Young the ship's boy?

He could not contemplate that just the one bear, huge as it was, had created so much havoc. It was obvious that the campsite had had some later visitors, wolves or perhaps another bear had scavenged the bodies and maybe carried off the other men.

He widened his search, but at the end of two hours, decided it was fruitless. His only recourse seemed to be to give the men a decent funeral under a rocky tumulus to prevent further mutilation and return with the grave news. He considered taking the dead bear as evidence, but came to the conclusion that this was an impossible task. His men had had enough difficulty hauling the bear off Harry. A return trip lugging a bear would be nigh on impossible.

His parting thought was that Harry's killing shot, right between the eyes, did the marine proud. He would ask Franklin if he could write to the man's family himself to express his admiration for the man's obvious valour in such a traumatic situation.

❦

Franklin's mood was sombre. The news Little brought was not what he expected. The loss of one or two men would have been bad enough, but all eight was a real catastrophe. He would address the crews tomorrow, but he knew in his heart that it was probably unnecessary in that they already knew the gory details via the search party. At least he could try and offer some comfort on the loss of their valued shipmates and friends.

Col sat alone in his cabin and contemplated the horrific demise of his three good friends, until jostled out of his grief by the purring of two others.

'What's to become of us now?' he asked aloud of his two furry companions, Mitzi and Fritz who seemed to sense his misfortune...and theirs.

CHAPTER TWENTY-FOUR

June 1847

Sir John Franklin, alone at the stern rail of the Erebus, looked to the west. *Where,* he thought, *in this vast wilderness of ice is the gateway to the Pacific. I've committed the men under my command to this search; they may have done so willingly in the first instance and out of respect for myself and other officers and their country, but how far does their loyalty go, I certainly don't deserve it...we've lost too many good men already and they must feel demoralised being stuck in this forbidding ice, going nowhere for many, many months. How can I boost morale and keep up their spirits in such a desolate place, which is so spectacular yet so daunting?*

Significantly, a line from a long forgotten poem alighted on the periphery of his consciousness:

> *'Day after day, day after day,*
> *We stuck, nor breath nor motion;*
> *As idle as a painted ship*
> *Upon a painted ocean'*[34]

He laughed, almost hysterically, unconsciously glancing around to ascertain if anyone had observed him, thinking

---

34 Lines from English poet, Samuel Taylor Coleridge, 1772–1834 – 'The Rime of the Ancient Mariner', which alludes to the 'Doldrums' –

that he may have turned the corner into madness. In any event, he was most certainly, if not literally, in the 'doldrums'[35]. He was shocked to see someone standing in the shadow of one of the ship's cutters, but instantly relieved when Col stepped out, a man who he truly respected and with whom he'd had many interesting but occasionally controversial conversations. *Not that that mattered, a good debate never harmed anyone. After all, debate and resolution were the spice of life.*

Sir John beckoned Col to join him; he'd spent too long musing on the events of the last few days. It was time to be positive and would draw on his experience from the past. 'Col, my engineer friend, I'll tell you a story about a man whose ambition was second to none, whose determination to succeed probably outweighed his capacity to achieve all the goals he set himself!' Sir John spoke quietly, while Col listened in the eerie light thrown by the solitary oil lamp. It was cold even by summer standards and the breath of both men condensed rapidly in the night air. Sir John paused—

'Go on, I'm listening,' encouraged Col.

'Do you know I was at Trafalgar?' asked Sir John, not expecting an answer. 'I was about the same age as Davy Young, but I'm still here...and he's not, such is the fragility of life,' he said, pausing again. 'That was a battle Royal' and I'm proud to have sailed in the fleet with Nelson, though I doubt whether he noticed me...but that's not important. He gave me inspiration and that's why I've undertaken four journeys to the Arctic and charted over three thousand miles of the coastline of North Canada.' He coughed apologetically before clapping his hands together as he remembered one

---

35 'Doldrums' – An area of little or no wind between the equator and 10º North approximately, both in the Atlantic and Pacific.

vaguely amusing anecdote. 'I'm aware we have an inordinate amount of canned food on this expedition, but I remember in 1821 on my second arctic 'forage' that we were forced to eat many of the leather parts of our uniforms, belts, boots and such like...we tried stewing them, but they were still tough!' he laughed.

'Not quite at that point yet, Sir John, are we?' laughed Col with him.

'Anyway, we survived and I met my second wife, Jane... we haven't any children of our own you know, but I love her dearly. I nearly refused this appointment as Commander, although I wanted one last stab at the 'passage'. She warned me...no advised me...that I wasn't as young as I used to be and that this journey would be an enormous undertaking. It was with some trepidation and indeed, sorrow, that I insisted, but I've retained her misgivings in my soul...perhaps I should have listened to her. She was happiest when I was Governor of Tasmania, but, unfortunately, I always had itchy feet and wished to retain my sea legs. There's a certain excitement that envelopes you when you leave port...it's an adventure and a privilege. Anyway, I've probably bored you enough for tonight, but I've been thinking while I've been talking and now I've an idea to boost morale, because what we do in life echoes in eternity. Goodnight Col.'

'Goodnight Sir.'

Sir John immediately set about organising a special celebration with the help of Francis Crozier the following day. Both crews were to be given extra rations and a spit roast planned on the ice between the two vessels where the ice was judged to be thickest. A hog or even a suckling pig wasn't, of course, available, much to Sir John's chagrin, but Diggle assured him that a tasty substitute in the form of a side of oxen could be found. It was also agreed to broach the cans in the yellow crates for the good of morale. Although Diggle and Richard Wall questioned this particular decision by raising their eyebrows at one another at the planning meeting, they kept their mouths shut. This did not prevent them examining the cans for any imperfections later, convincing themselves that the contents would be all right and safe to eat.

Sir John was mindful that it would have been Davy Young's birthday on 9th June, so he intended the party to be a tribute to him and the other seven. A remembrance service and a celebration of life...he hoped the ships' crews would appreciate the gesture and remember their shipmates accordingly.

He also hoped, somewhat despairingly, that there wouldn't be any more such occurrences resulting in the deaths of more crewmembers in the future and would strive to avoid any more mishaps by careful planning. Feeling more positive and with renewed vigour, he took up his pen to write a letter to Jane. He placed a sheet of ice while vellum on his blotter and considered his opening paragraph, although the opening greeting would always be 'My Darling Jane.' No sooner had he written this, than he coughed alarmingly. Recovering his equilibrium he observed his paper and blotter...no longer white, but flecked with red!... Shocking as this was, Sir John regained his composure before sending for the surgeon, Stephen Stanley.

'What can I do for you Sir?' enquired Stanley. Sir John pointed at the parchment and blotter on his desk in a parody of the grim reaper extending a bony finger at the condemned, as they approached Charon[36] the Ferryman, for the crossing over the River Styx.

'I require an honest appraisal from you, Stanley and a prognosis. It's not the first such occurrence and I've been suffering from a persistent cough for a couple of weeks. I'm no fool, so please be direct.'

Stanley stroked his chin whilst considering Sir John's predicament. He admired their commander as a leader and as a man and would not, therefore, give him anything but a truthful answer. 'In all honesty Sir, I don't doubt that it could be a bad case of bronchitis, but judging from the amount of blood, the worse case scenario may be consumption. A few of the men are showing similar symptoms, but it's hard to tell at present. I'm treating them with variants of cough linctus, but so far I've not administered any Laudanum for those awful pains associated with a sore larynx and inflamed bronchial membranes in the lungs.

'Better give me some of that stuff too. If I'm to address the men at the spit roast, I'll need something to ease my throat...it won't do to cough up blood on my audience...bad form indeed,' he laughed, but this brought on another coughing fit. 'Better stop laughing, eh Stanley?'

Stanley frowned his concern, but insisted, 'No, don't stop laughing, but I will give you something. I'll be back shortly.'

'Thank you, Stanley...I appreciate your candid diagnosis... I'm obliged.' Franklin watched as the surgeon left his cabin. He did feel decidedly unwell and fatigued, but would keep up a resolute façade as long as he was able.

---

36 In Greek mythology, Charon or Kharon is the ferryman of Hades who carries souls of the newly deceased across the rivers Styx and Acheron that divided the world of the living from the world of the dead. A coin to pay Charon for passage, usually an obolus or danake, was sometimes placed in or on the mouth of a dead person.

CHAPTER TWENTY-FIVE

Tragedy

The 'celebrations' were held on the ice on the 9th June. In reality, everyone knew that it was a 'wake' for those lost on the recent expedition. Those closest to Rob, Davy and Tom were not able to fully embrace the intended morale boost hoped for by Franklin. They tried their best, especially Col, but their attempts to smile seemed as bleak as the vastness of the ice, which encompassed the ships.

The officers exuded similar bravado but the sadness in their eyes at the loss of Graham Gore and Charles Des Voeux emphasised the meaningful camaraderie that had grown between them during the voyage. The marines, huddled together in a small group, conveyed to anyone watching, a similar sadness at the loss of Wilkes, Healey and Reed. They chewed despondently on the 'oxen' roast and toasted their departed comrades in grog.

'God rest their souls,' rasped Sergeant Dave Bryant, still suffering from a bad sore throat, as he raised a tankard, clunking it dramatically into those wielded by his diminishing band of marines.

'Aye we'll drink to that!' seconded Sergeant Solomon Tozer. 'God rest 'em! At least they're not having to chew on this burnt offering. Diggle's surpassed himself with this piece of charcoal.

'It was supposed to be 'oxen' wasn't it?' chipped in Will Pilkington, which raised muted laughter and instigated a discussion on Diggle's other culinary delights.

The sombre mood had not gone unnoticed by Franklin and Crozier. Franklin's speech raised dutiful cheers and a few 'God bless 'em's' during his praise of the eight who perished, but he knew he'd lost the initiative to inspire the men which had been his intention. He hoped that this was not the turning point on which the expedition would founder, but the invisible signs were irrefutably there nonetheless. He excused himself early to Crozier and escaped to the solitary confines of his cabin, feeling tired and dispirited.

A pallid watery sun greeted the crews on the morning of the 10th June, which only proved to emphasize their isolation.

In addition to Franklin, six seamen were also causing concern. All six were taken to the sick bay with fever and sickness and all were vomiting black watery bile, which alarmed both Stanley and Goodsir his assistant surgeon. So much so that Peddie and McDonald their colleagues on the *Terror* were consulted to discuss their present dilemma.

'What do you make of the symptoms displayed by the seamen?' enquired Peddie of the small group of surgeons congregated in a tiny annex adjacent the sick bay quarters.

'Could be a number of things,' mused a worried McDonald, who was also suffering from some of the symptoms himself. 'I've not come across the black bile, other than in cases of Typhoid and that's only second hand information given to me by a surgeon who worked in India. I consider it unlikely as the conditions aren't right, more likely to be food poisoning from yesterday. Game from ashore maybe?'

'Similar to Torrington's symptoms,' suggested Stanley. 'In which case, we need to be worried as he died unpleasantly, as I recall.'

McDonald paled at Stanley's remark, but steadied himself, keeping his composure.

'None of the six are improving unfortunately and four are markedly worse,' added Goodsir.

'That also applies to Sir John,' said Stanley. 'But that particular information stays only between us four surgeons... agreed?'

They nodded silently.

'He's not displaying all of the symptoms of the others, but one or two are similar. I am concerned, as his fever is not abating. In fact, I'm very disturbed.'

'Not good then,' stated Peddie matter of factly, before continuing, 'Well all we can do is attend to their needs as best we can. I'll be administering Laudanum for the pain they are obviously experiencing in their more conscious moments, but the shaking and fever concerns me. I suggest we burn any cloths or clothing, which are contaminated by the sickness just in case. All of us should ensure we keep ourselves clean and as a further precaution, wear a gauze mask when attending the men.'

With that, the surgeons left to administer to their sick colleagues.

Franklyn awoke abruptly in the early hours of 11th June in a cold sweat. His head ached abominably and blood lay on his pillow. In addition, his breathing seemed erratic and his ability to think seemed beyond him, as did his ability to stand. He fell forward, hitting his head on the corner of the oak desk before he collapsed in a heap of aching limbs and overwhelming tiredness.

He closed his eyes, as a resigned smile lightened the grey pallor in his cheeks. 'I'm not dead yet,' he thought, 'but at the present moment I've nothing to show for my life except myself, here, right now. I'm poorer in the true sense of the word and yet my life is more precious and richer in the uncertainty of my present predicament.'

At that moment, Surgeon Stanley, on station outside Franklin's cabin burst in. He'd heard Franklin fall; concern showed on his face as he lifted Sir John back on to his bunk. Nasty wound on your forehead, Sir John, we'll have that fixed in a jiffy. Just relax while I summon my assistant.'

Franklin muttered a faint acknowledgment in return. 'Thank you, Stephen,' addressing the surgeon in this instance by his Christian name. 'Although I fear that before you tend to my head wound, I'll not be around to witness your practical skills!'

Stanley stopped in mid stride on his way out of the cabin door...he was distinctly alarmed at his commander's statement, so matter of fact and seemingly resigned to his fate.

'Call Crozier immediately!' shouted Stanley to the acting orderly stationed in the alleyway beyond Franklin's cabin door.

Stanley lifted Franklin's head and supported it in the crook of his arm whilst proffering the commander a sip of water, which he received gratefully and with exceptional calm.

'I'll not see another dawn, Stephen.' Sir John whispered. 'There's a letter to my wife, Jane, in the desk drawer...make sure she receives it please and if you ever manage to see her in person, tell her I love her and say sorry for my determination to take on this formidable expedition, which I know was against her wishes.'

Sir John fell silent as Stanley watched his commander intently. He observed the grey pallor and the gaunt cheeks of this once great man. The eyes still sparkled in appreciation of Stanley's presence, but in an instant, that too was extinguished as they too glazed over and Sir John Franklin died, his head falling on to Stanley's chest in a final farewell.

Stanley closed Sir John's eyelids with his finger and thumb, just as Crozier burst in, anguish and concern showing on his face.

'I'm afraid you're too late, Captain, he's gone.'

Crozier stared in disbelief at his friend and commander's lifeless body cradled in the crook of Stanley's arm, before taking Sir John's hand between his own two hands. 'I'm so sorry, John,' he managed to enunciate, although choked with distress. 'Whatever will I be able to say to Jane?'

A tear appeared at the corner of his eye, which indicated to Stanley the loyalty and friendship, which Crozier had for Sir John. A few moments passed before Crozier collected himself. 'I'll make arrangements for Sir John's funeral and inform the crews,' once more assuming his role of Captain, now Commander of the expedition. 'Please give him the dignity you would a man of his stature whilst preparing his body for burial at sea. Thank you, Stanley, I know you will do the best you can.'

A few moments elapsed before Crozier released Sir John's hand from his own, begrudgingly leaving the cabin to begin his sorrowful tasks.

Stanley watching as he departed, heard him whisper under his breath...'My God, what's to become of us now?'

Sir John Franklin was not alone in his passing, four more sailors also died within hours of each other. The cause of death was undetermined, but suspected to be some form of poisoning, possibly botulism.

Entries were dutifully recorded in the ships logs dated 11th June 1847 by Crozier, whose suspicions were growing as to the real reasons behind the recent deaths.

Absently, without thinking, he wrote a name on the blotter beside the log book – 'Goldner!'

Two days later, assistant surgeon, Alexander McDonald and the remaining two sick sailors joined the list of dead.

That same day, Crozier presided over the funeral of Sir John Franklin. Every crew member attended, including those suffering from similar symptoms. The shock of losing their leader was almost beyond belief and showed clearly on their faces as they contemplated their own fate, which was now in Crozier's hands.

CHAPTER TWENTY-SIX

Aboard Erebus and Terror – A Dire Decision
April 3rd 1848

Francis Crozier fidgeted uneasily as he contemplated the unenviable but necessary decision to abandon both vessels to the elements and make for the nearest settlements some six hundred miles to the south.

He'd sat in Franklin's chair, at Franklin's desk for more than two hours, hoping for inspirational thoughts, which may prevent or even delay this seemingly inevitable decision, but if nothing else, he was pragmatic. He knew in his own mind that if the ship's complement were to survive, then he should make the drastic decision sooner, rather than later.

He mulled over the facts, all of which indicated to him that this course of action was the best in the circumstances.

He was jolted out of his thought process by a loud knock on the cabin door, which indicated the arrival of Col and James Thompson, the engineers from the *Erebus* and *Terror* respectively. He'd requested their presence to discuss the rapidly diminishing fuel supplies, but had been momentarily surprised at their early arrival, although it transpired that they weren't early at all. Two hours had passed since he'd asked Edmund Hoar, his steward to instruct the engineers that he wished to see them at 'eight bells'[37]. They were, in

---

37 'Eight bells', end of watch – in this case, noon/midday

fact, extremely prompt, which pleased him greatly, although it did indicate that his ruminating of the task ahead had engrossed his consciousness completely.

Crozier eased himself out of his (and Franklin's) chair. He stood erect and adjusted his uniform, fastening the top button of his tunic. He needed to convey to the two engineers that he was in control of the situation and that a realistic, if optimistic approach was warranted to ensure a successful exodus from the vessels.

'Enter!' Crozier's voice boomed out from the cabin office, surprising both himself and the engineers with its voracity.

'You wished to see us, Sir,' stated Col on behalf of himself and his colleague.

'Yes indeed,' responded Crozier. 'Please be seated; I wish to speak to you both to ascertain your considered opinions before we are joined by Fitzjames, who's now acting Captain aboard the *Terror* and Lieutenant Little.

'You will be aware that we're in a tight spot right now gentlemen. Our present predicament is untenable in the long term. In actual fact, our short-term survival prospects aren't much better. I'm sure you will agree with my brief synopsis, suffice it to say we're well and truly stuck in the ice!' Crozier hesitated before continuing, but as Col and James seemed to affirm their agreement of his brief statement by nods and muffled 'hmms', he launched into his plan.

'We've enough fuel left to sustain our situation for another three weeks or so according to your calculations, which you provided yesterday. I can't say I'm surprised, although I hoped we had sufficient to last until summer when the ice might diminish sufficiently to enable us to proceed into open water.'

'We could try to break free now, Sir,' suggested James. 'I've noticed some slight movement around the stern of the

Terror; we might be able to manoeuvre ahead, then astern. If we can break up some ice around us and gain some forward momentum, we could force our way back to a navigable channel.'

'Thank you, Thompson, I have, in actual fact, given some thought to that particular argument but it gives me some optimism now that you've reciprocated my thoughts. Of course, we'll use more fuel in the process, which will reduce our reserve if we fail. However, I believe we should make an attempt to free ourselves. Let's trial it on the *Terror* first. If we can free her, then it will be possible to break up the ice around *Erebus*. Luckily, both ships' propellers were in place before the ice set in and the blades should be below the ice. As a precaution, have the Bosun, John Lane, bore a hole in the ice near the stem with the auger and use that periscope tube device to check the free movement of the blades before we proceed.'

'I'll inform him of your wishes on my return to the *Terror*, Sir,' confirmed Thompson, just as the arrival of Fitzjames and Little was announced by Edmund Hoar.

'Come in, please join us,' gestured Crozier. 'I wish to appraise you of our present situation. I've outlined a plan of action to the engineers, which involves attempting to break free of the ice. However, should we fail, I'm afraid we do not have the luxury of remaining with the vessels.'

This last statement was not unexpected by any of the four seated in the new Commander's office, but their faces still betrayed their innermost feelings. Fitzjames looked shocked, whilst the others portrayed different stages of incredulity. The last thing any sailor ever wanted was to abandon ship, whatever the reason or cause.

Crozier still maintained a resolute composure, but Little detected a slight reservation in his eyes, which he found disturbing.

'We've, or rather I've, been in a similar situation before,' stated Crozier. 'A trek to survive in fact; but if we pull together, we'll win through. Consequently, we'll need to formulate a contingency plan. I've already considered the implications, but I need your input to ensure the best possible strategy, which will involve building sledges to haul our food and other supplies over six hundred miles of ice and rugged terrain.'

Col gasped, he'd not realised the extent of the problem until now and so spoke quickly. 'Just how will that be possible?' I'm no expert, but from what I've observed, this region is formidable.'

'Formidable, yes, but not impossible,' responded Crozier. 'It means that every man will have to work in a team; I propose two in actual fact. My intuition tells me that the best format will be to maintain the crews as they are, one from the *Terror* and one from the *Erebus* and not to integrate them. In that way, the officers will have a better understanding of the men's strengths and, unfortunately, their weaknesses, which they must allow for at the onset. It will be necessary to instil confidence in all of them and to justify the decision to abandon the vessels. Consequently, I intend to inform everyone tomorrow of my decision. Please arrange for both crews to assemble at noon so that I may address them,' he instructed, with a nod of affirmation to Fitzjames and Little.

'The building of the sledges, should they indeed be necessary, will begin immediately after our attempts to break free of the ice, should that of course fail. I do not wish to give the men false hope, but we must try; one hurdle at a time eh? This begins in earnest tomorrow when Thompson here fires up his 'Copperknob' auxiliary engine...Good luck to you, Sir!'

'Thank you, Commander, I'll do my best,' responded a flushed Thompson, who felt he'd been given the responsibility of saving the expedition in its entirety at that particular instant, but wasn't even sure if he could deliver a head of steam, let alone a positive result.

'And you Cautious Col,' Crozier joked pointedly, admitting in essence to the engineer that he had some prior knowledge of the man's first interview with Franklin back in London, 'should assist!...Check the pressure on the boiler instruments or whatever you engineers do in that complex world of pipes and pistons!' He laughed heartily and so did the others in an attempt to lighten the gravity of their situation.

'Better fire up the *Erebus's* auxiliary engine too, Col. If the *Terror* breaks free then we don't want the ice closing in again before we're under way. You'll have to 'hot foot' across the ice of course, but if you leave *Erebus's* engine idling under the supervision of John Cowie, the lead stoker...I believe he's a capable soul...then we may have a chance.'

'I think I'll manage, Sir, as long as I don't fall on the ice. Perhaps I'll throw 'caution to the wind' this time and sprint the two hundred yards between the vessels.' He laughed, acknowledging Crozier's reference to his nickname, although he did wonder what else Franklin had told Crozier of his interview with the great man.

After the engineers departed, Fitzjames, Little and himself finalised an action plan with respect to the building and supply of the sledges. Crozier suggested that a small boat from each vessel be taken along, as a contingency to ferry men across open water, possibly in relays, should the occasion demand. However, he did consider that this was unlikely, as most open water was frozen over in the harsh winters already experienced by the expedition. They would, of course, double as shelters with the addition of suitable canvas windbreakers in time of need.

One other thought occurred to him at the briefing...if they did encounter open water, either a river or an area of sea with brash ice, say...then how would they float the sledges? He put the argument to Fitzjames and Little. 'Any ideas gentlemen on how to provide buoyancy for the sledges?'

Little, slightly bemused at this latest problem replied first. 'If we take along some empty casks together with those we are storing our food in, then we could lash them to the sides of the sledges. As we use the food, we retain more casks for buoyancy. In addition, we should experiment with tarred and greased canvas. Our sail-makers are adept with a needle and palm and a portable bellows will inflate the canvas bags we fabricate. The only problem I foresee applies in both scenarios; the weight of the items! We're dragging the sledges remember, consequently, our first consideration will be food and clothing, then weapons and ammunition, as we won't know what we're likely to encounter—'

'Actually, you do know,' interjected Fitzjames. 'I'm fairly certain, after your search party experience, to ascertain the whereabouts of Gore's men, that a gigantic white bear is foremost in your thoughts!'

'Point taken!' replied Little. 'I never want to encounter such a beast again. I still have nightmares when I remember that frozen tableau—'

'All right, gentlemen,' interrupted Crozier. 'If you formulate anymore interesting ideas, please let me know. The weight of the sledges and their flotation could be a problem. However, I'm sure you'll find and propose solutions. I'll speak to you both before I address the crew tomorrow.'

Little and Fitzjames took that as their cue to depart and left Crozier to his deliberations.

'What do you make of all that?' enquired Fitzjames of Little in the alleyway adjacent Crozier's office.

'I'm not sure,' replied Little, 'but it's desperate, if we have to abandon.'

Fitzjames nodded, not even attempting to hide the concern, which showed in his eyes and in his glum expression.

CHAPTER TWENTY-SEVEN

Expectation
April 4th 1848

Captain Fitzjames, recently seconded to the *Terror* and Engineer James Thompson, welcomed Col aboard the ship.

'Everything ready?' questioned Col.

'As ready as it ever will be, this bright Tuesday morning,' answered James. 'What about the *Erebus*?' he asked, nodding in the direction of Col's ship some two hundred yards away.

'Well, we've checked that the rudder and propeller are in position away from obstructions. As far as we can tell, they're clear of the ice too, but it's far from obvious; the periscope device gives an indication up to a point, but it's dark under the ice, even on a bright day such as this one!' expanded Col.

'We think we're clear too, anyway, we'll soon find out. Will Crozier be giving the signal to start the engine soon,' queried Thompson.

'I expect so, he's raising a flag astern and we're to acknowledge by doing the same. If we run into trouble, we're to lower the flag.'

'Let's keep it flying then,' said Captain Fitzjames optimistically. 'We are bound to get some movement ahead and astern with these reinforced hulls.'

'When you do,' remarked Col optimistically, 'I'll return to the *Erebus*. If the *Terror* can open up a lead, we'll double up on your efforts and maybe we'll free the ships from this icebound situation.'

'Crozier's hoisting the flag now!' observed Fitzjames, ' better go below and 'fire her up' Thompson.

'Aye, aye, Sir, I'm on my way. There'll be lots of vibration as I increase the revolutions, so be prepared.'

'Duly noted, Thompson, thank you!'

As Thompson disappeared below, Fitzjames fixed Col's gaze and asked him a direct question. 'What are our chances Col?'

Col held his gaze, but pressed his lips together before responding, which gave him time to think. 'Well, providing we maintain steam pressure and there aren't any obstructions below the ice, we may succeed in breaking free, by first going ahead and then astern. There will be a delay between engine movements, as we don't want to shatter or twist the propeller shaft...not designed for rapid changes in direction you see! Anyway, I'm hopeful we'll break free, but how far and for how long, I'm not sure. From what I've seen, the ice has a habit of closing in rapidly and that's not a good sign.'

A rumble from below precluded any further conversation. Any misgivings either of them had were lost in the vibratory noise emanating from the engine room.

'Here we go then!' shouted Fitzjames, above the clanking and hissing of steam from the boiler. Let's go on deck astern and observe our attempts at freeing ourselves from this infuriating ice.'

They were not alone; most of the crew who were not engaged in other duties were aligned shoulder to shoulder along the bulwarks on both the port and starboard sides of the vessel.

Crozier's signal flag hung limply from the stern mast of the *Erebus*, which rather forlornly heralded the commencement of the operation. However, expectations were high and improved tremendously following an ahead movement of the engine.

'The ice is cracking at the bow, Sir,' exclaimed one seaman, leaning over the bowsprit, whilst hanging precariously on to a stay to obtain a better view.

Then the engine stopped abruptly! Fitzjames cast a look of consternation and concern in Col's direction, but Col smiled encouragingly. 'Thompson will be stopping before putting her astern,' explained Col. 'There will be several of these engine movements before any progress is made.'

Fitzjames began counting. On the sixth movement ahead a discernable gap in the ice had opened at the bow. Significantly, several square yards had opened up at the stern, although large chunks of ice still peppered the surface.

The marines began cheering, which incited the seamen to join in. Their enthusiasm swiftly infected those aboard the *Erebus* who reciprocated by joining in and shouting encouragement.

'Come on *Terror*,' bellowed Edward Couch, the mate on the *Erebus*, renowned for his deep bass voice, which could cajole even the laziest of seaman to extra efforts.

At that very moment of excitement, enthusiasm and optimism, the whole ship lurched three feet in an upward direction at the stern and the bow dipped alarmingly. The menacing sounds of metal grinding on ice, coupled with a whiplash crack, stunned the crews into silence. Fitzjames gripped the stern rail to prevent himself falling as the ship settled. Col was already rushing to the engine room to aid Thompson, but in his heart, he already guessed what might have happened.

Thompson's anguished face betrayed his thoughts as he met up with Col. Icy cold water was creeping into the stern bilges at a fast rate. 'Reckon we've lost a blade on a big chunk of ice, which in turn has probably damaged the stern tube. At any rate, the *stuffing box*[38] must also be damaged as water's coming in fairly rapidly.'

'We'll have to man the pumps immediately! I'll get on to it right now,' stated Col, 'then we'll appraise the situation again and inform Crozier and Fitzjames.'

Col needn't have worried on that point as Crozier had already boarded the *Terror*. He'd heard the horrendous 'crack' from the deck of the *Erebus* and immediately proceeded across the ice to the crippled *Terror*, not waiting for any lowering of a flag as previously arranged. 'Damn it, Fitzjames! What happened?'

'We've lost a blade according to a stoker, but I'm still awaiting information from Thompson himself, as to the extent of the damage. We seem to be settling by the stern... it looks bad I'm afraid,' commented an obviously concerned Fitzjames.

'That's probably an understatement, Fitzjames,' agreed Crozier, 'but if the pumps can't evacuate the bilges faster than the incoming water; we may have to abandon. Better prepare your men for that eventuality. We may need to transfer stores and equipment to the *Erebus*. Go now! I'll liaise with Col and Thompson!'

'Aye, aye, Sir,' said Fitzjames and left abruptly to complete the unenviable tasks ahead.

Just at that moment, Col appeared beside Crozier. 'Bad news, Sir,' gasped an out of breath Col. 'Water is coming in rapidly. The pumps are only just holding their own, but for how much longer, I'm not sure. It's coming in around the

---

38 Stuffing box – device through which the stern tube containing the propeller shaft is fitted through the aft bulkhead and then the stern post to prevent ingress of water.

stern tube; the stem post is obviously damaged and that caused the stuffing box to fail at the aft bulkhead. I'm pretty sure we did in fact lose a blade on a chunk of ice; hence the horrendous crack everyone heard. Sorry Sir, but it's as bad as it can be.'

'Thank you Col for your candid opinion,' replied an outwardly calm Crozier. 'I'm sure Thompson and yourself will do your utmost, but we will abandon if necessary! Please keep me informed.'

'Of course Commander,' responded Col as he rapidly left Crozier's presence on a task that was becoming increasingly impossible.

No sooner had Col spoken than a tremendous explosion rocked the *Terror*. The whole ship shrieked her defiance as she ground against the ice, which held her in its insidious embrace.

'The boiler's gone!' gasped Col. 'The icy water must have breached it!'

Crozier was stunned and became momentarily silent as the ship settled. Several of the crew on deck, thrown around like skittles, clambered to their feet, shock and horror portrayed on each and every face. They turned their eyes upward in expectation to where the officers' were gathered, but there were none willing to convey any optimism.

'Check for casualties,' Crozier instructed mechanically and only partially recovered from the blast himself. 'It's too much to assume there aren't any, judging by the violence of that explosion!' He was only just aware that several 'Aye, aye Sirs' punctured the turmoil in his mind.

John Peddie, surgeon, accompanied by mates Fred Hornby and Robert Thomas organised a small contingent of men to investigate the blast. There was a strong smell of blood mingled with smoke and iron that greeted the searchers as they entered the engine room. The hull was seemingly intact, but the scene that greeted them was gory beyond belief. One sailor threw up, then raced back to the deck...it was all he could stand. The rest gritted their teeth before commencing a fatalistically gruesome task...to identify the bodies. No one in the engine room could possibly have survived the carnage.

They were wrong, almost...James Thompson, *Terror's* engineer, with severe chest injuries lived for two hours before he too, died. Col was beside him at the time, promising to convey a message to his wife and mother, although he did wonder if that would ever be possible. A dire situation had suddenly become worse...much worse.

Several hours later, the *Terror's* main deck was submerged in icy cold water. Crozier considered that the only thing keeping her afloat now was the ice itself, which had closed in around the vessel once again. His feet were firmly positioned on the *Erebus's* deck, so his weren't wet, unlike the unfortunate few who were clearing away the last of the salvageable equipment aboard *Terror*.

His thoughts turned back the clock and stripped away the years, as he reminisced on his meeting with Ross and Franklin prior to the commencement of the voyage. They'd discussed the sternpost being shattered and displaced out of true. *Could this and the subsequent repairs have contributed to their present situation,* he wondered absently?

The sternpost was supposedly strong, being strengthened by iron bands, but they had been cut in two to accommodate the propeller shaft.

When they'd tried to force their way out of the ice, could this have been a contributory factor? The blade may still have broken off on the ice, but the subsequent flooding of the vessel would only have occurred through a weakness... or maybe in this case, through several weaknesses! But the explosion wasn't expected. 'No matter!' he exclaimed out loud, the *Terror's* doomed now!

'Beg pardon, Sir?' uttered Fitzjames questioningly.

'Oh, nothing,' lied Crozier. 'You've excelled yourself today and so have the men in such dire circumstances. Convey my thanks will you and start building those sledges at first light tomorrow, after we attend to the dead.'

'Yes, Sir!' affirmed Fitzjames, although anxiety betrayed his resolve. He left Crozier's presence in an emotional vacuum, wondering just how he would cope with several more funerals.

❧

The following morning, the *Terror* was, remarkably, still stuck fast in the ice, although scant attention was given it. All the crew were engaged and preoccupied in arranging funerals and making ready to abandon their second ship... the *Erebus.*

Crozier made what was to be the penultimate entry into the logbook: *'Several dead due to a boiler explosion on the Terror. Remaining crew preparing to abandon Erebus.'* He then listed the dead, painstakingly writing the names in neat copperplate handwriting, before lapsing into melancholy reflection.

He recalled that after they'd repatriated the five sick and injured seamen on the *Rattler*, a total complement of one hundred and twenty nine men remained. Since then, twenty-four had died, nine officers and fifteen men, including his friend and Commander, Sir John Franklin.

CHAPTER TWENTY-EIGHT

Concern
April 22nd 1848 – London

Lady Jane Franklin rang the call bell, handily placed on a small Jacobean table next to her chaise longue. Her recently appointed maid, Catherine, attended to her call almost instantaneously, as she wanted to begin and maintain an aura of efficient awareness throughout her employment.

She was already highly regarded by Lady Jane, who considered Catherine was a cut above the other servants and obviously highly intelligent, if not well educated. She made a note to resolve that particular shortfall as she was sure her new maid was ambitious and more than wiling to learn. What convinced her, in this particular regard, was the amount of classic reading material Catherine had brought with her on entering her employment and which now stood on a functional wooden bookshelf in her compact upstairs attic room at Lady Jane's London residence.

'Aah Catherine, prompt as usual,' Lady Jane smiled her encouragement. 'Please be good enough to inform Jenkins that I will require his services in two hours time. I intend visiting Admiral Millership at Greenwich this morning to press for a search expedition to the Arctic. It will be nearly three years since my husband sailed on the *Erebus* with the *Terror* to search for the North West Passage and that's a long time to wait without news. The last information we have is that the expedition was in contact on the 26th July 1845. Captain Dannet on the *Prince of Wales*, a whaling ship, kindly agreed to deliver letters from the crew, which I and others received that September...' Jane hesitated momentarily and turned her head away from Catherine as tears began to well up in her eyes. She dabbed the tears away with an exquisite silk handkerchief, before continuing, 'Please excuse my emotional state Catherine. After three years of separation, my mind's in turmoil. No wonder Sir James Ross declined the offer to lead the expedition; he obviously wasn't convinced of its viability, before it was offered to my husband. John couldn't resist the opportunity you see...one last adventure and one last chance to seal his ultimate place in history...vanity perhaps?'

'There's no reason to be embarrassed ma'am, your concerns are completely understandable.'

'Thank you Catherine,' acknowledged Lady Jane. 'Your intuition belies your age.'

It was Catherine's turn to hesitate now as she remained motionless, whilst gazing intently at her employer. Should she confess her real reason for seeking employment in Lady Jane's house or remain silent for a while longer. A few seconds elapsed before she decided to reveal all, in the hope that Lady Jane would identify with her own desperation. She had had little success in ascertaining information as to the whereabouts of the expedition herself. Those people she had managed to reach at the Admiralty had not been forthcoming, possibly because they actually knew nothing themselves. So in exasperation she'd decided to enlist the assistance of someone who might. She realised that her subterfuge might be her undoing, but calculated that the risk may be worth her 'change of career' from singer to maid. Fortunately, Lady Jane had taken her to her heart from the onset of her employment and had shared a degree of intimacy in their recollections, albeit their ages were far apart.

It was at that moment that Lady Jane interrupted her thoughts. 'What is it Catherine? You seem distressed and preoccupied yourself.'

'Forgive me ma'am, but I have something to confess. I hope you will be able to see beyond my deception and realise my anguish, for I too have emotional ties to the expedition.'

Lady Jane raised her eyebrows at this unexpected outburst, but smiled her encouragement. If Catherine was also distressed, she would try hard to understand. 'Perhaps you should start at the beginning,' prompted Lady Jane, 'then perhaps I will understand and be able to help...please take a seat beside me, I've a feeling this could take some time. My visit to the Admiralty will have to wait a while longer I think. Jenkins lunch won't be interrupted today,' she laughed.

Catherine sat and wiped away a tear of her own with a corner of her crisp linen apron. She hesitated, collecting her thoughts, then launched into her story. 'Well ma'am, I too have someone special on the *Erebus*. From the moment I met him, I knew that our destinies were entwined. My friend at *The Jolly Sailor*,' she paused, 'Oh that's public house in Whitechapel ma'am. I dare say you won't be acquainted with an establishment of that ilk, but it was home to me for a while. I used to sing there, actually, I still do when I've time off from my duties here, infrequent though that might be.'

'Please continue,' prompted Jane.

'Well, one night, shortly before the *Erebus* and *Terror* sailed, Marie, that's my friend, introduced me to Davy...our eyes met and I felt I could see into his soul. It was obviously reciprocated and we spent an idyllic two weeks or so together, when our respective duties allowed. Marie is walking out with his Uncle Tom. They've known each other a long time and will marry on his return...if they return! Catherine stumbled at this point in her story, but collected herself. 'He's bosun on the *Erebus* by the way, so you can see why I wanted the position in your house. Marie suggested I apply after she watched me sing one evening. Do you know that there's a tribute to you in song which is now popular?'

'Not exactly, but I'd love to hear it, will you sing it for me?'

'Of course,' replied Catherine as she stood to compose herself. 'It's called...I hope you won't be offended...'Lady Franklin's Lament[39].'

'Oh dear, I hope it's not an omen,' responded Lady Jane, 'but please continue.'

Catherine began, slowly picking up momentum as only she could. The accolade bestowed upon her by her admirers 'The sweetest voice in Whitechapel' was a just acknowledgement of her talent, soon to be greatly appreciated by Lady Jane.

When she'd finished, Lady Jane remained silent for several seconds before commenting, 'What a wonderful singing voice you have Catherine. Thank you so much, I'd not heard it before, although Jenkins advised me of the ballad's existence I suppose I didn't want to acknowledge the depths of its meaning, because I've not given up hope that both crews are alive and well.'

'That is my hope too ma'am!' reciprocated Catherine. 'Are you annoyed that I wanted this position in your household out of what you will undoubtedly regard as

---

39 'Lady Franklin's Lament' circa 1850 (although for the purpose of this story 1848). Also Bob Dylan's 'Dream' circa 1980.

selfish motives? I'll understand if you see fit to dismiss me, as I've not been entirely truthful, but I have enjoyed working in such a grand household. The bonus, of course, was that I might learn more about the *Erebus* through yourself because I am aware of you pressing the Admiralty to do more in the way of search parties.'

'Exactly,' confirmed Lady Jane. 'Anyway, I'll hear no more of your dismissal from my service. We're in the same boat, so to speak, but as a precaution, we'll keep your 'dual' personality to ourselves for the moment, as I do have other staff to consider. I don't want to be seen as having favourites, which I'm sure you'll agree is not good for morale.' She coughed surreptitiously and conspiratorially at the moral judgement directed at herself, then laughed, which alleviated all tension between them. 'Anyway, better call Jenkins now and then come back and tell me more about young Davy!' winked Lady Jane.

Catherine smiled, she thought it quite funny in that 'young Davy' was actually his name in reverse and explained to Lady Jane accordingly.

Lady Jane saw the humour too, before shooing away her maid. 'Away with you then *young* Catherine, be good enough to advise Jenkins of my trip to the Admiralty. 'Oh, by the way,' Lady Franklin probed quizzically, as Catherine opened the heavily panelled door, 'Will you marry him on his return?'

Catherine turned, blushed imperceptibly, but indicated that she would with a discreet nod of her head.

'Thought so!' teased Lady Jane with a knowing wink at her maid.

∽∾∾

An hour passed before Jenkins appeared at Lady Jane's study door. 'Your carriage awaits at the main entrance m'lady. Oh and Catherine wished me to give you this.' He handed over a single sheet of parchment with neat legible writing containing five verses entitled 'Lady Franklin's Lament!' She said that she hoped it wouldn't upset you,' confirmed her coachman.

'Thank you Jenkins, I'll be down shortly.' Lady Franklin read the verse so recently and feelingly sung to her by Catherine. She contemplated the penultimate line, *'Ten thousand pounds I would freely give.'* She knew in her heart that Sir John's life was more important than any amount of money and would gladly give all her wealth to have him back.

She sobbed silently for five minutes before gathering herself to join Jenkins for her trip to the Admiralty, resolute and determined after Catherine's unexpected revelation.

Before leaving, she again read the lines on the single sheet of parchment:

'Lady Franklin's Lament'

We were homeward bound one night on the deep
Swinging in my hammock I fell asleep
I dreamed a dream and I thought it true
Concerning Franklin and his gallant crew

With a hundred seamen he sailed away
To the frozen ocean in the month of May
To seek a passage around the Pole
Where we poor sailors do sometimes go

Through cruel hardships they vainly strove
Their ships on mountains of ice were drove
Only the Eskimo with his skin canoe
Was the only one that ever came through

In Baffin's Bay where the whale fish blow
The fate of Franklin no man may know
The fate of Franklin no tongue can tell
Lord Franklin alone with his sailors do dwell

And now my burden it gives me pain
For my long-lost Franklin I would cross the main
Ten thousand pounds I would freely give
To know on earth, that my Franklin do live

Then she folded it in two and placed it in her purse, armed with renewed determination.

CHAPTER TWENTY-NINE

Ghost Ships
April 22nd 1848

Crozier surveyed the scene before him with a practised eye that denoted his familiarity with a position of command. He considered that the preparations for abandonment had gone well and that an air of trepidatious expectation emanated from the reluctant gathering of the combined crews before him.

A contingent of men still lined the deck of the *Erebus* but most of the crew were waiting patiently on the ice for Crozier to give the order to abandon. The men were eerily silent, which conveyed a mixture of apprehension and fear of the unknown to the officers. Until this point, they had little time to think of the consequences...they had been too busy preparing sledges, equipment and stores for the trek south.

Tom Blanky, Ice Master, from the *Terror* turned purposefully, but stared vacantly at the *Terror's* forlorn hull. It seemed to him that this once proud ship's spirit had diminished since the boiler explosion several days ago. Although the ice still held her fast, it was obvious that she was sinking slowly and listing to starboard.

'I'll give her a week before the ice claims her!' muttered Giles McBean, *Terror's* second master. He'd observed Blanky's solemnity and made an attempt to engage him in conversation, but the response he received was not encouraging.

Blanky, suffering as he was from a persistent sore throat, croaked back, 'Aye, you're not wrong there! I've seen 'bad ice' before, but this season's took a turn for the worse. If it can crush a ship's reinforced hull, makes you wonder what it can do to skin and bone?'

McBean cast an apprehensive glance at Blanky, he wasn't an expert himself, but as Ice Master, Blanky would know what he was talking about, which sent a shiver down his spine.

'Trying to put the frighteners on me are you Blanky? If so, you're doing a good job. I'm not looking forward to this hike one bit...a ship offers protection, unlike what's out there!'

'Sorry McBean,' apologised Blanky, 'but we're in for a rough time. I was talking to Lieutenant Hodgson and he reckons we'd be better off staying together, instead of splitting into two crews, heading in different directions, albeit southward. Apparently, Crozier considered leaving several men aboard *Erebus* in case anyone's looking for us, but thought better of it. Reckons our best chance is to leave in two parties. You're with Fitzjames, same as me and most of the *Terror* crew. He's a good officer and made of stern stuff, but one or two are already questioning his ability on land and ice, it's not the same as seafaring!'

'Let's hope he's up to it then,' remarked McBean optimistically. 'Otherwise we'll not make Fort York in Hudson Bay!'

'Where's Crozier's party heading for?' asked Blanky.

'They're hoping to make Fort Resolution, after they transit the ice, by following the Great Fish River. It's longer than our route but possibly less arduous, according to the rumours, but there isn't an easy option.

Their conversation was interrupted by Crozier himself. His voice boomed out in solemn reverence of their present predicament, as he addressed the two parties, 'Men, you are well aware of our impending departure. My decision to abandon has not been taken lightly, but I consider it to be in our best interests. Indeed, our survival depends on it,' he paused to let the implications reach home, noting it was having the desired effect. 'We have prepared well! The crew of the *Terror* under the command of Captain Fitzjames, will head for Fort York. I will command the crew of the *Erebus* and head for Fort Resolution. Both destinations are some hundreds of miles away to the south over difficult terrain. All of you will need strength and determination to succeed in reaching our goals. I'm sure I can rely on everyone to support each other on this undertaking, which will be daunting and not without considerable hardship. However, I need to tell you this in the belief that you will overcome all difficulties.

'Provisions for this trek have been divided equally between the parties. The canned goods you will take with you are estimated to last longer than the projected time needed to reach the forts. Hot food may be a problem, but Diggle and Wall have been briefed as how best to achieve a decent allocation for everyone.'

At this point in Crozier's address, a murmur of laughter emanated from within the gathered crews. One wag shouted, 'Wot, like dining at Mivart's[40] in Mayfair?'

Crozier welcomed the light relief and laughed with the men before continuing, 'Exactly,' confirmed Crozier, 'but don't expect three courses at every meal!'

The crews cheered. Realising that his briefing was coming to an end, Crozier took his cue, 'Lastly, I wish you to remember Nelson at the battle of Trafalgar, a defining moment in our

---

40 'Mivart's Hotel', founded in 1812, was the pre-cursor to Claridge's in Mayfair

history. Before the battle commenced, he inspired the crews of his fleet, by raising a flag hoist...

'England expects every man will do his duty,' quoted Crozier.

Silently the crews digested the message.

'Good luck and God speed gentlemen,' shouted Crozier.

This time the crews acknowledged his heartfelt message, cheering and clapping loudly.

Several minutes later, the two parties assembled prior to setting off in their separate directions. Shouts of 'good luck' interspersed with other more ribald comments, shot from one group to the other, until the order was given to proceed.

It wasn't long before they were out of sight of one another on a path to their separate destinies, leaving the ghostly apparition of the *Erebus* and *Terror* in their wakes.

Crozier cast one backward glance at the tops of the masts, still visible from his vantage point atop an ice hummock. He reflected that *Erebus*, now twenty two years old and *Terror*, nearly thirty five years, had 'lived' eventful lives, but knew they were doomed and lost forever. Their story, however, would still be told in the 'logs' held by himself for the *Erebus* and by Fitzjames, now leading the *Terror's* party...God willing!

Cautiously, Crozier checked that his leather bound logbook, contained in an oilskin cover, was secure on the sledge. Relieved it was still where he'd stowed it earlier, he made a mental note to log all events on a daily basis, until they reached Fort Resolution.

CHAPTER THIRTY

The Hand of Fate
26th/27th May 1847

Taka and Kayat were once again hunting seal near Victory Point, but known to them by another name entirely, 'Natsiq Nuvuk'[41]. They rounded the promontory where Gore's camp was sited. Their dogs began barking vociferously and were straining at their hide leashes as the stench of fresh blood filled their nostrils. The men hauled them back, as a truly terrible sight came in to view.

Taka motioned Kayat to remain with the dogs as he readied a harpoon and gingerly approached the scene of devastation. It was immediately obvious that there were four mangled bodies near the remnants of a tent and another close by, which seemed intact, save that it was almost entirely covered by a massive bear, three times the size of the man himself. Both were seemingly beyond redemption, but as a precaution, Taka tentatively prodded the bear in the middle of its back with his harpoon, before swiftly retreating. There was no response, much to Taka's relief; the bear was as dead as the unfortunate sailor. The only other time he'd got close to such a large bear was when Tom saved both his and Kayat's life with a lucky shot and he

41 Seal Headland

was in no mood to take chances with this most recent of encounters.

He surveyed the scene: His intense gaze took in the gruesome horror of a vicious bear attack. Fearing there may be another, he swung around abruptly to address an imaginary second predator, possibly stalking him! He calmed himself sufficiently to drop the fur-lined hood of his sealskin suit and listened intently. The dogs were no longer barking, Kayat had obviously calmed them and they were now under control. He stood silently for a long period and was just about to move when he sensed a low moan, almost a whimper coming from behind a large rock some fifty yards away. He approached the rock slowly and cautiously, harpoon again at the ready. Ten yards from the rock he stopped and listened, detecting a barely audible anguished intake of air. Whatever was behind the rock appeared to be in dire trouble. Fortunately, Taka identified the sounds as human and, spurred on, covered the remaining distance quickly. What confronted him shocked him to the core. Taka was used to the sight of blood; a true hunter's right of passage was to kill to live, but the three men before him were in a real bad way. Two were bloody and unconscious. The third, with a gaping wound right across his chest where a bear must have slashed him with its massive claw, held a musket in readiness for whatever emerged from behind the rock.

Rob's piercing eyes met Taka's in a shocked embrace, before realisation dawned on Rob's face. The corners of his mouth turned up in a feint smile and he lowered his musket as he recognised the Inuit, before passing out completely.

Taka stared in disbelief at the wounds of the three men, barely recognisable as his friends from the ship. Their clothes were torn and tattered from the bear attack and blood oozed from wounds on all three men. It was obvious that the men's lives hung by a tenuous thread. The attack could only have occurred within several hours of this chance meeting, but they were in grave danger of dying unless their wounds were tended immediately.

Taka shouted for Kayat to join him with the dogs and the two sleds and soon they were administering to the sailors' injuries.

Kayat instantly recognised Tom and Davy wedged behind Rob who was protecting both men's unconscious bodies. He surmised that Rob must have dragged them here, away from the killing area before stationing himself in front, brandishing his musket. *A very brave man indeed,* Kayat thought, as he wouldn't have known if another bear was prowling around while he was accomplishing his painful task.

Rob drifted in and out of consciousness, but was aware of the presence of the Inuit. At last he could relax and allowed himself to be manhandled onto a sled, along with Davy, who was unaware of anything.

Taka covered them with furs and strapped them down on one sled, then assisted Kayat in hauling Tom on to the other. *A big man beyond doubt,* thought Taka and definitely in need of a whole sled to himself.

Before setting off, he retrieved Rob's musket and ammunition, then set a fast pace ahead of Kayat's sled to the settlement several miles to the north where his wife and family awaited the return of the hunters. They would know what to do. Wounds would be effectively cleansed, stitched and dressed, but what concerned him was the damage to their heads...he'd known deaths occur after long periods of unconsciousness in his own tribe. All they could do would be to watch and wait and hope.

Taka believed this was his chance to truly repay the *Kabloonans* for saving his and Kayat's lives earlier that year, so he determined to make a supreme effort to achieve that goal. He also knew that if they'd attempted to return the men to the ships, they would be dead before they arrived, so realised a return to his small settlement was undeniably the best option. Plenty of time to contact the ships, providing the weather holds up, he mused, but this year's winter signs were already forbidding. Subconsciously, he had doubts in his ability to contact the ships, despite his best intentions. It could be months before that would even be possible. If his 'guests' survived, they would have to learn the way of the Esquimaux! He chuckled, breaking into laughter, despite the gravity of the situation.

Taka turned to observe Kayat following his own sled. The route they were taking was over difficult terrain, but they were moving at a productive pace. His wife would be surprised at his 'catch' on this occasion, but they'd been together for some time now and nothing seemed to surprise her when it came to his expeditions and forays, but surprised she was! True to form, however, she immediately took over, organising the men's initial aid and their road to recovery. Whilst the Inuit women tended to the three injured seamen, Taka and Kayat resolved to recover the bear, killed by Tom, before the weather closed in. They could not waste the opportunity, so took one sled with extra huskies. They agreed it would be impossible to bring both bears back for the fur and meat, but one was possible. However, in the true tradition of the Inuit, they would leave the slaughtered men where they lay...and allow the elements of wind, ice and time to dispose of their mortal remains.

They returned in a little more than two days with Tom's bear lashed to their sled, staring into eternity.

✑

A pale glow emanated from the Kudlik,[42] sited in a recess above Tom's head in the igloo.[43] He groaned, the pains in his arms, legs and body ached abominably. He eased his eyes open to observe a diffused aura of light from behind a head of dark hair, the face indistinguishable. 'Am I dead?' he asked aloud of no one in particular. 'Are you St Peter perhaps?'

'No, you're not dead and I'm not St Peter,' answered Rob with a cautious laugh, relieved to hear Tom speak after several days of fever and discomfort. 'Glad to have you back in the land of the living.'

Tom squinted some more and took in the glistening sides and rounded orbit of the igloo. 'Where the bloody 'ell am I then, if I'm not in the afterlife?'

'Well it's a long story, but you're certainly one lucky bugger. You're in an igloo, along with myself and Davy.'

'What's an igloo?' queried Tom.

'Never mind that,' countered Rob. 'Just listen and learn, but don't attempt to sit up just yet, you've a lot of wounds that need time to heal, you've also suffered a broken leg by the way.'

'Ouch,' grimaced Tom, attempting to raise his left leg, which was encased in a heavy splint, fabricated from animal bone. 'It's coming back to me, that was a bloody big bear that attacked us...who invited him for tea, I'll have his guts for garters![44] Wasn't you was it Rob?' he queried, instantly regaining his humour, 'or young Davy perhaps?'

---

42 Kudlik – oil lamp with significant symbolic meaning of Inuit culture, family and community.

43 Igloo – Esquimaux Ice Home

44 'Have his guts for garters' – Meaning you are in deep trouble. Comes from the serial killers of the early 1800s who would use the guts from their victims to make garters that were sold on market stalls.

Rob's face dropped into a frown at the mention of Davy, who still lay in a feverish state on the other side of the igloo. 'He's not too good,' responded Rob. 'Suffered a broken leg and arm and other slashes across his back where the bear caught him. He's a fighter, but you're the first to recover. I was luckier, in that I only got done for a slash across my chest and an attempted bite on my shoulder. Managed to stick him with a bayonet, so he released his bite before much harm was done to me, although he did for Davy.'

'Ah yes, I'm beginning to remember. Wilkes put one in the first bear,' stated Tom sombrely. 'Just before copping it himself, then the second brute had a go at me. Reckon I took out my deck knife to the fellah, along with another bayonet, but I didn't fancy my chances. I'm big, but he was enormous,' he said jokingly. 'Then everything went blank.'

'You were lucky,' agreed Tom. 'I was watching in horror as he went for you. I was amazed you stood your ground. The bear charged, but stumbled and you thrust the bayonet up through his throat to his skull. Must have died instantly, but not before he careered into you, knocking you unconscious and breaking your leg. You were still clutching your deck knife by the way...it's beside you. You now hold the dubious accolade of having dispatched two bears in one season!'

A blast of cold air interrupted their conversation before Taka, Kayat and Taka's wife entered, beaming smiles at the unfortunate sailors. Taka's wife immediately 'set to' in administering to Davy's needs. He was the one causing most concern to the Inuits. She raised Davy's head carefully and whispered soothingly in his ear. Neither Tom nor Rob understood what she said, but knew instantly that she had the young lad's welfare as her first priority. She raised her eyebrows and looked at the two men, acknowledging their mutual understanding of Davy's predicament. Davy's eyes flickered open, in vague awareness, but initially failed to recognise anyone within the confines of Taka's abode.

A small vessel containing a mixture of herbs and Inuit traditional medicine was pressed to his lips. Although his senses were dulled, he knew he must drink the pungent fluid, which was not unpleasant, but a trifle strange. His eyes met those of Taka's wife and for a brief instant he believed he was at home with his mother, Eve, nursing him back to health as a youngster, but then the pains in his leg jolted him out of his trance like state. He was instantly wide-awake, staring at the dark skinned homely lady dressed in sealskin attire, who was staring back at him with compassion and concern.

Davy focused on Rob and Tom. 'Where am I?' asked Davy.

'You're safe and being well cared for,' replied his relieved Uncle Tom. 'Can you remember what happened?'

Davy hesitated, his face portraying abject fear as he recalled the dramatic events of that fateful night. 'Yes I can,' he managed, 'but I don't want to remember.'

'Aye lad,' agreed Tom. 'I'll not blame you for that. It was a truly awful experience, one that I'm not anxious to repeat. We've survived, but the others, save Rob, you and me, didn't make it.'

David nodded in acceptance of the fact as he remembered more of the traumatic incident in detail.

Taka's wife felt him tremble, so hugged him closer, gesturing to the men with one hand, that that was enough. She whispered something in Inuit to Davy, which indicated to Tom and Rob that she meant for the boy to sleep now. Davy didn't need encouragement and instantly returned to a deep sleep borne out of exhaustion and the effects of his wounds. He had been unconscious for nearly three days, which had raised deep concerns in Taka's immediate family, although they now knew that the critical period was over.

Tom was overjoyed to see Taka and Kayat again and attempted to raise himself sufficiently to embrace them, but they were having none of it and implored him to remain firmly on the hide bed by a series of hand gestures and smiles. He was also feeling exceptionally hungry. Although Rob had eaten prior to Tom's recovery, Taka anticipated the need and soon produced bowls of steaming broth for them.

'I've been given this stuff before,' explained Rob pulling a face.

'What's in it then?' queried Tom.

'Better not to ask,' responded Rob. 'It tastes better than it looks and it surpasses some of Diggle's brews. He supplemented *his* soup with several of Goldner's cans, if you recall. God knows where the meat came from for those, not from a slaughterhouse that's for sure. Still, try Taka's broth, you'll not be disappointed and you'll feel much better.'

After they'd eaten, Taka and Kayat squatted on their haunches and attempted conversation with the two men. In a mixture of hand signals and Inuktitut, interspersed with a few words of English, Taka explained how they'd come across the sailors' ravaged party, how they'd crudely tended their needs and why they'd returned to the Inuit camp, rather than the ships' location.

It was surprisingly warm in the igloo, so Kayat encouraged them to admire his and Taka's wife's needlework, after he indicated that they divest themselves of their 'new' sealskin tunics.

'Oh my God!' exclaimed Rob. It was the first time he'd examined the wound across his chest. It was heavily poulticed with a criss-cross stitching of seal tendon, stretched to an exceptional thinness for easy working. He noticed absently that the same pattern of stitching had been incorporated into his sealskin tunic...a fact that he thought faintly humorous, although he was aghast when Kayat showed him the sharp carved ivory 'needle' they'd used on them all.

His outburst caused the onlookers to collapse in a heap of hysterical laughter, including Taka's wife, who they now knew as Tapeesa[45], having been introduced formally after Davy awakened earlier.

'I suppose you think that's funny,' remarked a rather disconsolate Rob. 'You'll not be so cocky when you see your own, which looks more like one of Col's railway lines he was telling us about on the ship. You've another one on your backside by the way...perhaps Taka's got a mirror...if you're unlucky! Otherwise take my word for it, it's not a pretty sight!'

Tom's response was his usual, 'Bloody 'ell,' or rather a sheepish version of his well-known phrase, of which he was modestly, but justifiably proud.

'You've several more by the way, but not so life threatening,' continued Rob, beginning to enjoy Tom's discomfort and pressing home his advantage. 'I'd keep that one on your backside under wraps if I was you!' was his last gambit. He was well aware that Tom would have had the last laugh, but for his broken leg. Had they been on the ship, he would have chased him halfway up the mizzenmast!

Tapeesa was again busying herself over Davy. He'd opened his eyes once again and with Rob and Tom's encouragement, made him eat some of the broth.

---

45 Inuit female name – translates as Arctic flower.

'It'ull give you strength,' suggested his Uncle.

Davy did actually feel much better afterwards and was even able to converse for a while, until his eyelids closed again in sleep. Tapeesa studied him closely before bestowing an Inuit name on the boy. She caressed his cheek and uttered the word 'Uki'[46] before kissing him on the forehead. Had they known what it actually meant, they would have been impressed.

Several weeks elapsed. With their health improving, Kayat determined that he would try and learn some English while the sailors' attempted to learn some Inuktitut. Taka and Tapeesa joined in with enthusiasm. They started with simple words making obvious comparisons, which proved successful in building up a minor vocabulary. Not quite as dramatic as Dr Johnson's dictionary of the previous century in England, but an enjoyable interlude while the sailors' convalesced. The first word learned was 'Aput' meaning 'snow' and the second 'Aputi' meaning 'snow on the ground'. Everyone agreed that it was an excellent starting point, before they moved on to more exacting and complicated words, such as 'Aqakuktuq', which meant 'catches a fish'

Davy, always intrigued by the Inuit, learnt many things about their culture and traditions. Some things shocked him; marriages could be arranged at birth to ensure survival of the family, because men and women needed to be together to survive. Actual marriages were simple and apparently sometimes occurred only after the birth of a first child. Families exchanged gifts, as witnessed by the three

---

46 Inuit male name – translates as 'Survivor'

sailors on one occasion, although the actual ceremony almost went unnoticed.

Strangely, men and women knew their place in society, having what seemed equal amounts of prestige, influence and power, although men were considered as heads of their family, a far cry from Davy's relationship with Catherine and Tom's with Marie.

He observed the Inuit sharing food between families and communities, men would hunt and fish, women would collect berries, birds eggs and prepare basic medicines from natural sources.

The most bizarre practice, one not followed by Tom in his butchering days was the realisation that all kills needed to be butchered immediately, otherwise the carcass would freeze with no hope of dissecting it later. Women were responsible for most of the butchering, skinning and cooking of animals caught by the men. They sometimes accompanied the men on the actual hunt, unless engaged with childbirth or the tutoring of girls. Males usually instructed the young boys in the hunting techniques required to survive.

Davy picked up a trick or two himself when on one brief trip he was inducted in the art of fishing through the ice, although Tom and Rob never witnessed such an occurrence.

Kayat intimated that in a very bad winter many years ago, when food was extremely scarce, the families in the community had, through necessity, resorted to infanticide. Infants were killed to preserve the majority's survival. Taka described this gruesome practice perfectly and without hesitation by drawing his knife deftly within a hair's breadth across his own throat: It left nothing to the imagination and even Tom felt extremely queasy after the demonstration, whilst Davy went outside to throw up. All three were reminded in this instance of how fortunate they'd been to be unconditionally looked after by the family of Inuit who had asked for nothing in return. Their new sealskin suits, expertly sewn together, were testament to the Inuit's generosity. Tom and Rob were at a loss as to how they were ever going to repay them, although they hoped to be given an opportunity.

⚜

The days spent with the Esquimaux were long and sometimes arduous, as they were unable to exit the encampment for even small periods, often less than one hour in duration, but they learnt well whilst they all recovered their strength. Their time aboard the *Erebus* seemed to pale into insignificance; although Tom and Rob were concerned that word of their survival should reach Franklin by some means. Unfortunately, the winter of '47/'48 did not offer even the slightest chance of renewed contact.

Days became weeks and weeks became months until Tom, using his 'homemade' calendar calculated the date. The conditions outside were dramatically clear that day, 22 April 1848. They could not have known, but it coincided with the exact day the *Erebus* and *Terror's* remaining crews abandoned their vessels, which were stranded beyond redemption in a vice like icy grip, with a distinct probability of breaking up and disappearing forever.

CHAPTER THIRTY-ONE

Fitzjames
Winter 1848/'49

Log Entry *Terror* February 1849

'Beginning to despair of ever leaving this God forsaken land of ice and forbidding terrain.

Since abandoning vessels, several months have passed. Out of a total complement of fifty-three souls, fifteen remain. We have lost our way on several occasions and encountered many obstacles since depositing the brief but concise documentation in the cairn at Victory Point...'

Fitzjames stopped writing to massage the remaining three fingers of his right hand. Many of his men had suffered from frostbite and he was no exception. Huddled in the small canvas tent with his one surviving officer, John Irving, he determined to record their plight for posterity. Those at home needed to know their story, if none from the *Terror* survived. He shivered at that prospect but courageously heated up the inkpot once more over the flickering oil lamp to continue writing. It wasn't the first time that the ink had frozen, but he considered that it might be the last.

John Irving watched Fitzjames going through the motions

of completing the log entry. 'What's the point, Sir? Who's going to find it, let alone read it?' asked Irving pointedly.

Fitzjames raised his eyes almost apologetically at Irving's incisive comment. 'There is a point, John; our families and loved ones deserve to know what happened to us. If I can't tell them in person, then this will be the next best thing, assuming, of course, that we don't make it and our prospects aren't looking good!'

Irving dejectedly acknowledged Fitzjames and nodded his affirmation. 'The men are exhausted and so are we. Our food is almost gone and we're still hundreds of miles away from York by my reckoning. Those cans we've lugged around with us have contributed to our downfall. Damn that Goldner, whoever he is! I'd like to get my hands on him now and show him how thirty reasonably fit men can die like flies within three days of each other. What on earth did he put in those cans anyway?' voiced an angry Irving.

'If it's any consolation to you John, I'd personally place a noose around his neck...given the opportunity...unlikely as that may be in our present circumstance. We relied on those cans to see us through, instead they did for us! Without much back up in the way of game meat, we've not much else to rely on. Which brings me to my next point...I've been listening to the strongest men's barely concealed murmurings and guarded comments. I'm not naïve in any sense but I am acutely aware of ancient traditions concerning survival. Let me put it this way; I believe the weakest will be invited to draw the short straw in their incoherent capacity to determine right from wrong. They'll believe, by making the ultimate sacrifice, that they're helping their shipmates to survive!'

Shocked and disbelieving, Irving stared at Fitzjames, mesmerised at his Captain's matter of fact résumé of their present predicament.

Fitzjames continued, 'We've sufficient ammunition to hunt game, but we're not fit enough or motivated enough to even consider looking for any, let alone finding any. So what's left to us? We've some meagre scraps of gristle and bone from an oxen carcass, which may provide a weak soup, but when that's gone, we'll die, or...' Fitzjames eyes fixed Irving with an intensity, as disturbing as the unspoken revelation itself, whilst Irving retreated into his innermost soul, completely horrified at the prospect.

Fitzjames coughed, which broke the spellbound Irving out of his nightmare. 'Here', offered Fitzjames, 'take my colt pistol; you will undoubtedly need its reassurance in the next few hours and possibly days. It's not much good to me as I can hardly use my finger to pull the trigger. I can just about manage to write an entry into the logbook, but even that is painful.'

'Thank you, Captain, I'll do my best to prevent the last vestige of our small civilised society disappearing.'

'You do that, John and don't be afraid to use the colt if you have to...there's the holster and spare ammunition over near the oil lamp,' he indicated with his three fingers to a pile of equipment. 'If I were you, I'd practise loading the weapon in case you need to fire multiple shots. Much better than a rifle or a musket when you're up against several men.' Fitzjames smiled benevolently at the junior officer that left him in little doubt as to the importance of being prepared.

Irving weighed the pistol in his hand, alarmed at the prospect that he may actually have to use it. Absently, he half remembered the maniacal glint in the eyes of 'wild man, Eric' when they'd encountered the whaling ship *Prince of Wales*, some three and a half years' previously, although it seemed like yesterday. They'd been happy and optimistic then and would not have dwelled on the circumstances of Eric's time in an open boat. How many 'Erics'' were there in the remaining *Terror's* crew? he wondered acutely, haunted now by the evil vision contained in the eyes of the *Prince of Wales'* crew member. 'I'd better check on the crew, Captain,' suggested Irving, relieved that he'd found an excuse to divorce himself from the confines of the tent, to achieve something practical.

'A good idea, John...try and ascertain what their thoughts are and assess their state of mind, without alarming them too much,' requested Fitzjames.

'Aye aye, Sir, I'll try my best.'

When Irving exited, Fitzjames busied himself replacing the logbook in its hide folder, then painstakingly into a waterproof oilskin. He was not prepared to take a chance on the pages spoiling after all his hard work recording their epic journey in the attempt to reach Fort York.

Secure in the knowledge that the log was safe and secure, Fitzjames sighed and made himself as comfortable as possible within the cramped confines of the canvas tent. He dozed fitfully, hardly awake at times, but still aware of his surroundings...when suddenly and abruptly he became alerted by a heated argument and commotion emanating from the direction of the crew's encampment. His imagination ran rife when he heard angry shouts and then sounds of a scuffle and lastly five shots in rapid succession, then a lull. It was momentarily quiet until a deep voice boomed out 'Bastard Officer', which left him in no doubt as to the inevitability and outcome of the altercation.

Within seconds he became conscious of many agitated voices outside his tent. He struggled to his feet, but was only briefly aware of his own impending doom as the tent collapsed, its pole crashing against his forehead as he lost consciousness. Fitzjames had written his last log entry.

The crew secured but a brief respite from their fate, following their drastic action, although not all were willing participants.

The cooking pots bubbled and boiled obscenely for several more days, until the fuel ran out. Even the hardiest were revulsed and disgusted at themselves and retched at the prospect of chewing on human flesh. In desperation they attempted one last push south, but only succeeded in trudging another seven miles, scattering equipment and artefacts along their route, no longer relevant to their existence. One by one, all of the remaining crew succumbed to the freezing temperatures and extreme conditions. Soulless and conscience weary they'd staggered to their sad and tragic end.

CHAPTER THIRTY-TWO

Crozier
Winter 1848/'49

Log Entry *Erebus* February 1849

'Our journey is taking its toll. There have been many
days when we've been unable to move out of our
tents. The winter of forty-eight/forty-nine has not
been kind to us, several men, thirteen in total, out of
our original complement of fifty-two have died,
through extreme cold, frostbite, illness and starvation.
We were unable to utilise the canned provisions. Most
of the contents were found to be contaminated and
five men that risked eating from them, early on in our
trek, died in what I can only describe as 'gruesome
consequence.'

Their deaths prompted me to issue an order that
the remaining cans be abandoned, notwithstanding
the fact that they constituted four fifths of our
available sustenance. I hoped that by careful
management of our dry and salt meat stores that we
could survive until game and other sources of food
became available. Unfortunately, the extreme winter
has almost halted our progress en-route to Fort
Resolution, so we have not escaped the Arctic Tundra
nor the confines of the Adelaide Peninsula.

It is two days since we encountered a group of Inuit.
We took the opportunity to barter for a seal, which

shared between thirty-nine souls will only provide brief respite from our hunger. What concerns me most is the incidence of scurvy, now quite pronounced in all of us, including myself. The absence of any fruit or vegetables makes concentration difficult, as does our ability to chew anything. Our teeth are loosening from the gums and are becoming painful. All of our complement have lost considerable weight, which makes hauling the sledges and boat more difficult, so much so that I've taken the difficult decision to send an advance party on ahead. They will be able to move at a faster pace to seek assistance from whatever source is available, possibly a settlement where fur trappers co-exist with the indigenous population of Yellowknives and Dogrib Indians. Franklin encountered such people before when following watercourses and river systems as far as the Great Slave Lake; consequently, an opportunity exists to make contact. I have delegated three men to undertake this important mission: James Reid, Ice Master, Sergeant David Bryant, Royal Marines and Col Fryer our engineer. They will leave tomorrow, 28th February, after our briefing this evening...'

❧

'Close the tent flap behind you gentlemen,' instructed Crozier, 'it will be much cosier,' he laughed, knowing full well that it made little difference to the temperature, albeit the chill wind was prevented from entering.

The four men crouched around a low makeshift table, on which lay an unusually concise map of the region south of the Arctic Circle.

'One of Franklin's?' suggested Col.

'Well yes it is,' replied Crozier.

'I've poured over this one before, during one of my visits to the Commander's quarters,' admitted Col. He was proud of this particular one, which gives an insight into his attention for detail. His anecdotes enhanced the map somewhat, which convinced me that, in some of the areas, I was actually there.'

'That will stand you in good stead then,' confirmed Crozier. 'The knowledge you gleaned from Franklin, coupled with Reid's experience will undoubtedly compliment each other for this hazardous mission. Sergeant Bryant's skills should provide support in catching game, which you'll need to survive, as you'll be travelling fast and light. Your goal is the treeline initially and from there, contact with any settlement that could mount a rescue mission. I don't expect such a rescue to be accomplished without reimbursement to those concerned, so I am trusting you with this money belt, containing enough gold sovereigns to buy sufficient food and supplies along with the men to deliver it.

'We will, of course, continue to press southward along the track you've taken, but I doubt we'll be able to trek a vast distance. Ultimately, we'll be relying on you three.'

'That's a very sobering thought,' commented Sergeant Bryant, 'quite a responsibility, I just hope these other two are up for it Sir,' he guffawed, gesturing with his thumb in their direction.

'I'm sure they will be,' smiled Crozier. 'I've organised a lightweight sledge to be constructed, which two of the men have painstakingly assembled for you. It's a miniature version of the one Rob Ellis fabricated for Lieutenant Graham Gore on his ill fated expedition...No doubt you remember the circumstances well gentlemen, so be aware of the possibility of encountering the brother or sister of that particular family of bear.'

At the mention of the incident the men's eyes locked in fear, in the realisation that they must be alert from the onset if another tragedy was not to be repeated. The larger contingent of nearly forty men was enough to keep predators at bay, but three men alone was an entirely different proposition.

'Anyway,' continued Crozier, 'the sledge will be easier to haul in this terrain. One man on his own can easily manoeuvre the device with its lightweight load.'

At this point, Col interrupted Crozier's flow, 'Beg pardon Sir, but I have a request providing Bryant and Reid don't raise an objection.'

'Please enlighten us Col,' suggested Crozier.

'Well it's fairly straightforward really. I wish to take the copper plaque from the engine room of the *Erebus*. It weighs very little and it will denote where we've come from, should we not make it.'

Bryant and Reid shifted uneasily at this comment, but agreed to the proposal.

'Oh and one last request,' continued Col, 'I must insist on taking Mitzi and Fritz along as well, as they've been good friends to me since Davy, Tom and Rob's demise. They've also prevented me from eating the spoiled food from the cans, which makes me believe they bring good luck. I know they are nearly as skinny as we are, but that's not prevented some of the crew from casting covetous glances in their direction. Many consider that they'd make a fine stew and maybe two fur hats!' although to me that's a somewhat macabre joke. Nevertheless, I'll not leave them!'

Reid smiled in response, 'Good luck you say, then aye why not?'

Bryant also reciprocated by raising his hands in the air, palm upward, indicating that an objection would be useless, as Col seemed determined anyway.

'I think you have your answer,' continued Crozier, 'I hope your feline friends really do bring you luck. Incidentally, you've led me on to another point. I assume you're intending to wear that fur lined Inuit suit you exchanged that timepiece of yours for a while back?'

'Yes, indeed Commander, I'm certain that it will provide me with good protection against the elements.'

'Excellent,' encouraged Crozier, 'I've kitted out Bryant and Reid with our own version, which the sail makers have had a hand in. I doubt that the stitching is as fine as the Inuits', but they've made true facsimiles from oxen skins and also the Arctic fox we've killed for food. Their fur should keep you warm, eh gentlemen?'

'We hope so,' replied Bryant on behalf of them both. 'The sail makers have been burning the midnight oil with sail twine and beeswax to fabricate them. We are in their debt; I only hope we prove our worth and return as planned.'

'Yes, of course. Well, finally, I suggest you all get as much rest as possible before you leave early tomorrow. There will be a hot meal before you depart. All that remains is to wish you good luck and God speed.'

'Thank you Sir,' came the response in unison.

Their departure early the next morning was burdened with desultory looks and fixed bleary-eyed stares, but not much enthusiasm. The optimism generated by Crozier was not reciprocated down the ranks, as they didn't consider that the advance party would be successful. Some would have preferred to have eaten the cats as a means of prolonging life, in the hope that some game would cross the crew's path in the near future. In the event, Mitzi and Fritz were cushioned in a fur lined canvas and oilskin container, securely lashed to the lightweight sledge, probably wondering just how many of their nine lives remained.

Col was comfortable in the knowledge that at least the three of them were engaging in a positive undertaking. His suit was warm and for the first time in a year he felt exuberantly optimistic.

By noon, four hours later, they had marched six miles, more than the main group had managed in six weeks.

CHAPTER THIRTY-THREE

River Camp – March 1849

Col Fryer, James Reid and David Bryant roused themselves from oft interrupted slumber as the dawn of another day beckoned. Weary limbs and tired minds were optimistically cast aside by all three crewmembers who had become firm friends, supporting each other through many adverse situations. When one was downhearted, the other two cajoled and inspired until courage and optimism returned and vice-versa.

Six weeks had passed since Crozier's hand had shaken theirs in a passionate grip of understanding and hope. Now they were in sight of an important staging point along their planned route...the Back River, south of Franklin Lake.

They'd successfully negotiated the Adelaide Peninsula, catching small rodents along the way to revive body and spirit. Bryant even bagged an Arctic Hare on one occasion with a long shot he was still boasting about two weeks later, much to the annoyance of Col and James. What pleased them most was the fact that they'd passed the line of latitude designated as the Arctic Circle itself and were now well into the tree-line where conditions for survival were ever present. What they hadn't encountered were signs of habitation; no matter, the temperature was increasing, as were opportunities to supplement their meagre food supply. Frostbite was no longer a feared foe; their clothing had done its job admirably. Even Mitzi and Fritz were enjoying their freedom and catching small prey as 'gifts' for the sailors, although they never strayed far from Col's side, purring frequently as they settled beside him each evening, after camp was established.

If anything, Col was more aware of the dangers now, than ever before, so ensured they kept a watch throughout the night for bears and other predators and maybe 'humans'.

A few days ago, Reid regaled him with a tale of fearsome Indians in the Canadian outback who weren't averse to murdering settlers for their valuables. He'd been minded to keep a sharper watch ever since and frequently fingered the sovereign money belt, also his deck knife, for reassurance. What was it Reid said he'd read? 'Last of the Mohicans'[47] by a James Fenimore Cooper. He wondered if any Mohicans lived in this neck of the woods, which were more intimidating at night. The only consolation was that he was sure Crozier hadn't mentioned 'Mohicans' in his briefing. All he'd really advised was, 'Make sure you've something to barter and the means to defend yourselves. If *they* think they can take your valuables anyway by taking your lives first, *they* will!' Crozier didn't emphasise the point but all three were left in little doubt as to the importance of such a warning.

---

47 The Last of the Mohicans: A Narrative of 1757 (1826) is a historical novel by James Fenimore Cooper. It is the second book of the Leatherstocking Tales pentalogy and the best known to contemporary audiences. The Pathfinder, published 14 years later in 1840, is its sequel. The Last of the Mohicans is set in 1757, during the French and Indian War (the Seven Years' War), when France and Great Britain battled for control of North America. During this war, both the French and the British used Native American allies, but the French were particularly dependent, as they were outnumbered in the Northeast frontier areas by the more numerous British colonists.

Their campfire burned invitingly and another hare they'd caught earlier in a loop snare was cooking magnificently on a makeshift spit above the fiery embers of small dried out logs. The plentiful supply of wood meant that a hot meal awaited them after each day's march in the general direction of Fort Resolution.

The three waited patiently in mouth-watering anticipation of their small feast, a far cry from the deprivations of the last few months. The cats, sitting side by side on their haunches watched intently; the men weren't the only ones salivating on this occasion...only a matter of time before they'd all be licking their lips, fingers...and paws when they tasted succulent pieces of hare cooked in its own juices.

Eventually replete and completely satisfied with the day's march and catch, the three men discussed their next move. Franklin's map, retrieved from its hide and oilskin container was spread out on the ground, weighted down with small smooth stones gathered from a tributary of the Back River, located several yards away down a gentle slope.

'We should plan to follow the Back River as far as Baillie, recommended by Franklin's party on a previous expedition. We're more likely to encounter a settlement near a river than in the denser part of the woods,' suggested James Reid.

'Agreed,' responded his two companions without the slightest hesitation, although Dave Bryant quipped, 'But just why we should be taking advice from an 'Ice Master' in a forest is beyond me!'

Col laughed loudly at this exchange of good humour, before reinforcing the real reason behind their trek. 'Let's not forget that even if we find a group of people willing to help us, it's still going to be another six or maybe seven weeks before we make contact with Crozier again, after backtracking to his expected position. That's three months since we parted company.

'We'd better find someone sooner rather than later in that case,' urged James with genuine concern.

At that moment, the cats stood upright as one, tails twitching and hissed. Their gaze fixed on a dense patch of forest immediately behind Bryant, who swivelled rapidly to ascertain the cause of their agitation.

Bryant grabbed his already loaded musket and crouched, pointing it in the direction indicated by Mitzi and Fritz.

Reid, immediately behind Bryant probed cautiously in his kit for his colt revolver, one of three from the *Erebus* armoury. Seconds passed; Col tensed as Reid checked the chambers of the colt before cocking the weapon ready to fire. Col's own hand rested on a small hand axe, which gave him some assurance...but not much.

They waited, their breath shallow and their hearts pounding.

'What do you reckon?' Reid whispered in Bryant's ear.

'Can't see a bloody thing in all that greenery and evening mist,' came the response.

'Keep watching then,' Col beseeched. 'If it's a grizzly, shoot it before it gets anywhere near us!'

'What if it's human?' asked Bryant. 'It could be just as dangerous.'

'Shoot it before it gets anywhere near us!' whispered Col grinning, despite his concern.

'You're a laugh a minute,' whispered Bryant in return. 'Remind me not to go camping with you in future.'

He'd hardly finished his comment before a buck deer broke cover from the undergrowth directly in their gaze, thirty yards away, before disappearing again in the mist.

Reid let out a sigh of relief as the tension of the moment dissipated. Bryant regained his full height after crouching at the ready for what seemed like a lifetime, but what was actually only minutes; Reid did likewise.

Col, however, remained motionless. He was observing the cats still staring intently at the position where the buck deer broke cover. 'Don't relax yet,' warned Col, but it was too late. Bryant let out a choked gurgling sound as an arrow pierced his windpipe, the arrowhead reappearing at the back of his neck. He fell to his knees, releasing the musket instantaneously, before collapsing head first into their campfire.

Reid's anguished scream was cut short as a second arrow entered his chest and cut through his heart. He was dead before he rolled to the ground. Col reacted in the only way possible, he ran, zigzagging toward the river as a third arrow nicked his ear, drawing blood, although he was hardly conscious of it. His predominant thought was to run for his life and not look back.

He reached the fast flowing river, breathless and afraid. To have survived this far against the odds, was an arrow to be his fate? 'Think man, he shouted at himself, although no sound came from his lips. 'Look ahead, what do you see?' he forced himself to stop briefly and survey his surroundings. Beyond a fallen tree and a rocky outcrop, a small but virulent waterfall fed the river course. He would head there. He clambered over slippery rocks in his desperation to escape his unknown foe, only once turning frantically to ascertain if he was being followed.

On reaching the waterfall, he could just make out an overhang, underneath which, he may be able to hide. In an instant, he decided he could, the water would shield him from view. At the overhang, he hunkered down, out of sight, beaten and alone. 'Time to take stock of the situation Col,' he encouraged himself. Unbelievably, he still held the small axe...! *Just how did I manage that* he thought? But he had, although not much else escaped with him, apart from his

Inuit suit and a knife, which hung from his belt in a hide sheath.

'Calm yourself Col, it will soon be nightfall and keep a sharp eye out in the meantime!' he reminded himself...He was only just aware of five Indians searching the opposite riverbank before a belated weariness overtook him as he sat with his back against a dry rock wall under the overhang.

He drifted into an uneasy slumber, but awakened suddenly and dramatically to the sounds of fighting and blood curdling aggression. He feared his hiding place had been discovered and frantically scanned the immediate area around the overhang. Cautiously, he peered out. What he saw both astonished and mesmerised him. He was unable to move as he witnessed the unfolding drama before him.

His five assailants were themselves becoming victims of a massacre. They were surrounded by at least twenty Indians who had obviously ambushed the small band. A hail of arrows preceded a full on attack with clubs and hatchets. Screams and groans filled the air, adding emphasis to the bloody scene. The killing of the five took little more than a minute, but to the engineer, it seemed much longer. Col's overworked brain was near to bursting from his head and his nerves jangled alarmingly, but he remained motionless. He watched intently while the bodies were stripped before the raiding party departed, their copper sheaths containing fearsome knives glinting in the failing rays of the sun.

Col exhaled, in welcome relief that his ordeal appeared to be over. Sleep beckoned and for the second time in less than an hour, his eyelids closed, despite his anxiety.

Daylight streamed through the falling water and woke him with a start. He looked around apprehensively before realising where he was...his limbs ached abominably from his exertions and he knew he had to move, but not before ascertaining if it was safe to do so!

He left the safety of the overhang and proceeded cautiously in the general direction of the camp. He had never in his life felt so alone, so took the precaution of skirting the camp, three hundred yards to the north, where he had the advantage of some high ground. He watched and waited, surveying the macabre scene, which overwhelmed his senses. Bile rose in his throat and his knuckles showed white from his grip on the axe handle. He fingered the dried crusty blood on his left ear to remind him of his mortality and the need to be wary. A motionless two hours passed before he picked up the courage to investigate.

Just as he considered it was safe, he felt the hairs on the back of his neck raise in the certainty that he was being watched. He turned around quickly, frantically scanning the dense undergrowth for movement; there was none, but two pairs of eyes stared back at him, reflected in the pale sunlight. Ears straining, with his whole being on alert, he detected the familiar sounds of two cats purring simultaneously, wherein he relaxed noticeably.

'Mitzi, Fritz! He called, barely audibly, for he was still cautious. They came running over to his position, where he couldn't determine which of them was more pleased at their reunion, the cats or himself. Col smiled, despite his predicament; he was no longer alone. He didn't hesitate any longer, with the cats scampering after him, he descended to the camp.

The bodies of his two friends lay naked amidst the debris of the camp. Their clothing and other items, including the pistol, musket and ammunition had been taken. Only Franklin's map remained, obviously discarded by their assailants and caught on a thicket, as being of little value. Col retrieved the item and secured it in his tunic before turning to his other task...burying his friends, Reid and Bryant.

He decided to bury them under a small tumulus of stones, gathered from beside the river, which took him the best part of the remaining day. Although weary, he was proud of his achievement and hoped that they would have done the same for him had their roles been reversed. Mitzi and Fritz watched patiently throughout his endeavours, as though they too wished to pay their respects.

Col returned to their campfire of the previous evening... was it less than twenty-four hours ago...it seemed like days!

The fire still smouldered, exuding feint whiffs of smoke. Luckily for himself and the cats a small portion of the hare remained, enough to appease an immediate hunger, but not to sustain them for very long. He would need to find food tomorrow, but for now they would move on before nightfall to find a place of safety, away from the killing ground.

Col found a piece of canvas from their tent, discarded by the Indians and fabricated a crude harness for the cats to 'ride' on his back, should he encounter any difficult terrain, although he thought wryly, they'd be more sure footed than himself. Still, he'd feel comfortable with them watching his back. With that thought in mind, he retrieved his axe and trudged off into the evening.

Col travelled only another hundred yards beside the river, when he was vaguely aware of a presence behind him. An almost silent footfall preceded a sharp thud at the side of his head from a war club, before he lost consciousness completely.

PART TWO
'TRANSITION'

A Fond Farewell
September 1848

Davy, Tom and Rob realised that they must make contact once more with the Expedition. They knew in their hearts that despite the circumstances and the dire consequence of them being thought of as deserters or worse, as mutineers, they must report their story to the Commanding Officer, Franklin.

Theirs' had been a painful recovery and the time taken to recover after such excruciating injuries were not in any way excessive, but their consciences troubled them greatly.

Some sixteen months after their encounter with the bear, the three sailors were fully fit and recovered from their wounds. Suitably attired as honorary Inuits, they bid farewell to the settlement that, unbelievably had been their adopted home for well over a year.

There were tears from Tapeesa, but also smiles from the many men and women gathered to see them off. They would travel light and use a lightweight sled, pulled by two huskies given to them by the community. Davy had a fondness for both animals, which bore significant parallels with his feline friends Mitzi and Fritz aboard the *Erebus*.

Taka and Kayat were to accompany them as far as Victory Point, which meaningfully completed the 'circle of life' for the Inuits. Victory Point was where they'd found the sailors and Victory Point would be where they said their goodbyes.

The huskies were harnessed to the sledge, seemingly acknowledging the fact that this would be their last time in the encampment. They were unusually quiet but their piercingly blue intelligent eyes conveyed to Davy, Tom and Rob that they were prepared.

'Better give Tapeesa a hug and a kiss young Davy,' suggested Rob. 'She will miss you greatly, treated you like her own son, she did!'

'I will,' whispered Davy. 'I'll always remember her and intend recounting every detail to my own mam, Eve, should we make it back home.'

'You bet we will!' encouraged his Uncle Tom, 'but first we have to make contact with the *Erebus* and *Terror*, although I'm not sure how we'll be received.

'We'll cross that bridge when we come to it,' insisted Rob. 'I wonder if Diggle's improved his cooking; if he hasn't I'm coming back here!'

Tom and Davy broke out laughing and so did Taka and Kayat who understood their meaning perfectly, after many months in their company. If anybody wasn't impressed with the Inuit evening meal, Taka would solemnly declare, 'Diggle! Ugh!' which never failed to raise raucous laughter.

The party were waved off by the Inuit community, which was not so much an occasion as an acceptance. What it actually achieved was to acknowledge a friendship that would remain in their respective hearts forever.

'Goodbye my little Uki,' shouted Tapeesa tearfully.

❧

Two days later they reached Victory Point with trepidation and fear. Rob seemed particularly disturbed. His action alone had probably saved Davy and Tom's lives, but in his mind's eye, he retained a surreal, but vivid recollection of the scene as he clutched his musket in readiness, whilst shielding his shipmates. It would stay with him forever. However, little remained to indicate any carnage had happened; save for a cairn of stones, the area was strangely barren of debris.

'They must have come looking for our party, after we failed to return,' stated Rob.

'Can't have been pleasant,' remarked Tom.

'Aye that's for sure, I reckon they buried what was left of Gore, Des Voeux and the others under that Cairn...could have been us, save for Taka and Kayat...that's fate that is... makes you wonder what life's all about,' suggested Rob.

'Quite profound,' agreed Tom.

'What's that mean?' queried Rob.

'Oh, sorry,' replied Tom. 'That's what comes from talking with Col. He was always coming up with strange words...it means you are thinking deeply, or summat.'

'Right you are then, I see what you mean. I wonder how he's getting along?' asked Rob.

'We'll soon find out,' Davy butted in. 'I hope he's been looking after Mitzi and Fritz while we've been gone...with some help from Diggle of course.'

Taka and Kayat smiled somewhat resignedly, some distance away, realising that the time for their farewell was approaching. 'Hope to see you again,' pronounced Taka in near perfect English.

'And you my friend,' replied Tom in Inuktitut.

A flurry of hugs prevented more conversation, although, essentially, any spoken word would have denigrated their heartfelt emotion.

The three turned to leave, waving as they did so, but eventually when they looked back, minutes later, Taka and Kayat were only small specks on the horizon.

Tom, Rob and Davy made good progress and after one night on the ice, sighted the *Erebus* and *Terror* in the distance.

'Bit of an odd angle on the *Terror*,' observed Tom. 'Listing to port and down by the stern.'

'Strange,' commented Davy. 'I can't make out any activity on deck from this distance, but we'll soon be there. They must have a problem...perhaps the ice is crushing her and she's letting in water.'

'Maybe lad,' said Tom. 'Let's find out.'

They approached to within a hundred yards of both vessels, which were strangely eerily silent.

'Ahoy there,' bellowed Tom, but a response was not forthcoming. Tom shouted again...nothing. The three cast quizzical glances at one another, which conveyed a feeling of mutual dread. Surely, they hadn't been abandoned?

Realisation dawned as suddenly as the question entered their consciousness. The unthinkable was true...they stared at the ghost ships in disbelief for several seconds, before Tom choked out his own personal fear, 'They have abandoned, but we must go aboard the *Erebus* and find out what happened.'

Davy and Tom followed with heavy hearts. It was obvious to Tom that nobody remained aboard the *Erebus* and he suspected that none remained on the *Terror* either. She was listing at such a crazy angle that it precluded the prospect of habitation.

'I'm off to Franklin's cabin,' confirmed Tom, making his way up a companionway until he reached the alleyway leading to the Commander's quarters. The atmosphere aboard was dark, dank and uninviting. 'What on earth could have happened?' muttered Tom under his breath.

The cabin door was ajar. Tom entered, followed by Davy and Rob. Nothing seemed out of place, but their attention was drawn to a single sheet of paper on the oak desk, fixed by a paperweight.

Tom picked up the sheet but suggested Davy read the content, as he passed it over to him.

'It's signed Crozier,' said Davy mystified.

'That's odd,' said Rob. 'You'd have expected to find something from Crozier on the *Terror*, not the *Erebus* and no mention of Franklin himself, that's really puzzling.'

'Odd and very strange indeed,' agreed a concerned Tom. 'Anyway Davy, what's it say?'

Davy held it up to the porthole to shed light on the document. 'It states that the crews of *Erebus* and *Terror* abandoned the vessels on 22 April...that's months ago... They split into two parties, one under Fitzjames and one under himself. Fitzjames is attempting to reach Fort York, via Victory Point, with fifty-three men and Crozier, Fort Resolution via the Adelaide Peninsula, with fifty-two men.'

'I wonder what happened to Franklin and the rest? That's only one hundred and five men in total,' queried Rob. 'There were at least another twenty men when *we* left.'

'I daren't think, although it could have had something to do with the *Terror* by the look of her,' responded Tom. 'Anyway, they've left and from what we've seen on our way up here, they didn't leave in a hurry, so we must assume they were well prepared.'

'What are we going to do Uncle Tom?' asked Davy.

'Well, we've two choices, follow Fitzjames or follow Crozier. We've learnt from our Inuit friends that some trade exists with Fort York in Hudson Bay, but I've no idea where Fort Resolution is located, unfortunately, so Hudson Bay it is! Check and see if there are any charts remaining in the chart drawers, Davy, which maybe of assistance. One thing is for certain, we can't stay here and certainly not if Crozier considered it mandatory to leave...he's no fool.'

'All right Uncle Tom. I'll see what I can find.'

A few minutes elapsed before Davy returned clutching two sketchy charts of the Hudson Bay area. 'I've found these Uncle Tom, but I am of the opinion that they took the best ones with them. These two will be of some use when we reach the bay itself, but the hinterland doesn't look promising. There are one or two rivers marked, but not much else.'

'What's 'hinterland'?' questioned Rob.

'Well, according to Lieutenant Gore...God rest his soul; it's an inland area away from the coast. I remember him saying that not much is known about the area, unlike the Back and Great Fish River to the south west, explored by Franklin,' explained Davy.

'Perhaps we should follow Crozier's route after all,' suggested Tom.

'Let's not be hasty on that score Tom,' cut in Rob. 'We at least have a partial chart and Fort York offers the prospect of finding a ship to return to England in the summer, or early autumn, when the bay is mostly free of ice.'

'He's got a point, Uncle Tom,' agreed Davy.

'You two are not as green as you're cabbage looking!' laughed Tom. 'I'll bow to the consensus of opinion and stick with the original idea. Fort York it is then! I think we should search the ships for anything we need before we leave. I noticed that the small skiff[48] is still aboard. We could take

---

48 Skiff – small boat.

that along. With the addition of some runners, which Tom can make fairly quickly, we can attach the boat behind the sledge. Those huskies are fairly powerful, so won't notice the extra load once it's moving. You never know when we'll encounter open water or a river, so it could be an advantage to us. Right then, we'll spend the night aboard and start out first light tomorrow. We'll head for Victory Point, retracing our steps, then travel south-east. We may find evidence of the route Fitzjames has taken, so keep your eyes peeled.'

'Aye aye Bosun,' quipped Davy.

'Aye aye Bosun,' mimicked Rob, before stating, 'I'd better make those runners and fix them on the skiff, or I'll have no peace this afternoon.'

'Better feed the huskies, Davy,' advised Tom. 'They'll need rest and a good feed before we start off. However, before you do that, fire up the galley stove; I looked in on Diggle's 'pantry' before we got to Franklin's cabin and there are still some logs we can use, but use the meat we brought with us. Leave Goldner's cans, if there's any to be found, where they be!' emphasised Tom.

'Will do,' answered Davy.

Shortly afterward, the galley stack began emitting huge volumes of black smoke as Davy's stove roared into life, providing warmth and, subsequently, a hot meal for the three men.

'Good job,' remarked Tom when he observed Rob's handiwork with the runners...anyone would think you'd been a carpenter in another life!'

'Hah, hah, now who was my apprentice when we fitted the stage at *The Jolly Sailor* in Whitechapel...could that have been you by any chance Tom?'

'Point taken Rob, but we must be on our way. Davy's harnessed the dogs and loaded a few items on the sledge. I emphasised that we needed to travel light...just like the Inuits. He got the message loud and clear...must have learnt something this past year, or so, eh?'

The three gazed once more on the *Erebus* and *Terror*. *What was to become of the once proud ships?* thought Davy.

They turned as one, but not before Rob observed Davy's inner turmoil. 'I bet you're wondering about the ships' fate aren't you Davy?'

'Is it that obvious?' Davy countered.

'Fraid so,' continued Rob, 'but you're not alone on that one, I'm also fearful. I reckon the *Terror's* already a 'goner'; it won't be long before she sinks. The *Erebus* will last longer and probably drift south-westward with the pack ice and prevailing current. Eventually, the ice will crush her too; an inglorious end to our once proud ships, but we can't dwell on it as we've much to do to survive. 'Chin up' lad,' Rob encouraged.

'Let's find Victory Point gentlemen,' spoke a determined Tom. 'The first way point of many, I'll be bound.'

The huskies heaved on the sledge, picking up a reasonable pace, in spite of the extra load.

'Mush Taktuq, Mush Tikanni,' ordered Davy. The huskies picked up the pace, enjoying their run.

Tom reflected on the fact that Taka had named the huskies well; Taktuq meant 'Fog' in Inuit because even in a 'white out' the husky always found a safe way home. Tikanni was fearsome and a protector. His name meant 'Wolf'.

CHAPTER TWO

Revelations

Davy, Tom and Rob reached Victory Point for the second time in three days. They rested near the cairn, believing the stones represented a tribute to their own fallen shipmates, but nothing more.

Tom pushed back the fur hood of his Inuit suit and stood head bowed. He began reciting the Twenty Third Psalm, recalled from the dark recesses of what seemed like another life entirely. Davy and Rob watched silently, uncertain of their need to join in; the recollection of the deaths of Gore, Des Voeux and the others too raw and painful to want to remember.

Tom replaced his hood and turned to face them. 'Let's move on, Sou' Sou' East through the valley. I reckon that's the route Fitzjames would take.' He undid a bone toggle on his suit to access a hide pocket, especially sewn into the garment by Tapeesa at his request. He withdrew an article from within, drawing comfort from the bevelled edge and smooth surface. The inscription never failed to inspire him. It shouted the simple message loud and clear: *'To Tom, may you always find your way back to me, love forever, Marie.'* He unscrewed the bevelled cap to reveal the compass and checked the direction against the rudimentary chart, which Davy had retrieved from the oilskin holder.

'Let's hope that thing's accurate, we don't want to be wandering round in circles,' jibed Rob.

'Should be, if it was good enough for a Dutch sea Captain and most of them are experienced navigators, it's good enough for me.'

'Me too,' chipped in Davy.

'I'll bow to your better judgement…and Marie's in that case. She'll not want you to get lost, you made her a promise remember.'

'Aye, that I did and I intend to keep it too,' confirmed Tom.

'Good for you, Uncle Tom,' said a supportive Davy.

'Well, if we've finished our enjoyable conversation, I suggest we move on, before we're too old to move. Sou' Sou' East it is then.'

The three returned to the sledge and skiff in good heart.

'Mush Tikanni, Mush Taktuq,' ordered Davy once more.

⟨❧⟩

The three men made steady progress during the next two weeks, covering an estimated one hundred and eighty miles, ably assisted by the huskies, who more than proved their worth.

Tom was sure they were following in the footsteps of Fitzjames, which on the thirteenth day was confirmed by the sighting of an abandoned sledge and many of Goldner's cans.

'My, my,' exclaimed Rob, when they stood over the sledge. That's one mammoth construction. 'I reckon it would take about twenty men to pull that one and, as far as we're aware, *they* haven't any huskies.'

'Do you think that's why they've abandoned it?' asked Davy.

'I expect so, too heavy by far…they'd be exhausted lugging that monster around,' explained Tom.

'What about the cans?...Either they took too many from the ships, which weren't needed, or they found the physical task of transporting them too wearying,' hazarded Rob.

'Why don't we take a few along to supplement our own meagre stores? We're still reliant on catching small game and the huskies need feeding,' continued Rob.

Davy, alarmed, spoke immediately to dissuade them, 'I would advise against taking any, however tempting. There's something sinister about them. I'd sooner we take our chances on finding game.'

Davy went on to explain the events that led him to believe that the lead soldering was suspect and the contents may be spoiled. He mentioned Mitzi and Fritz's reaction to 'Diggle's can' and the rumours surrounding other cans consumed by members of the crew, including Torrington. 'I also overheard Franklin and Crozier discussing and expressing reservations about their quality with Surgeon Stanley one morning,' confirmed Davy.

'Eavesdropping young Davy?' prompted Rob.

'Not exactly, I was delivering a pot of tea to the officers. They stopped when I knocked, but not before I'd heard some of their concerns.'

'Just as well you did...leave them be then...we'll not risk it,' affirmed Tom.

❧

That very afternoon, they encountered a party of six male Inuits travelling north. The leader hailed them from a distance, which Tom acknowledged in Inuktitut, which may have explained their total surprise when they eventually closed with each other. They stopped abruptly in their tracks as the huskies bellowed and barked.

Their leader hesitated before giving an appropriate greeting. Tom's party looked like Inuits, spoke in Inuktitut, admittedly just a few words so far, had a sledge and dogs *but* were towing a small boat on runners? He was extremely perplexed, but as the three men offered no visible threat, he relaxed.

'Which tribe are you?' the leader asked.

Tom, as spokesman responded in his 'best Inuktitut', as he, Davy and Rob lowered their hoods.

The Inuits were astounded; they'd just encountered 'Kabloonans', looking and speaking like their own kind.

Tom laughed, as did the leader, which broke the stalemate and it wasn't long before all were conversing in Inuktitut and swapping stories. This included the strange tale of the three men's year with another Inuit community.

Their leader, named Anik, did not know Taka personally, but had heard of him through others. What he told them, however, was alarming and filled them with dread.

'*Several weeks ago, we encountered many dead Kabloonans in tents, on the ground and near an upturned boat. There were cooking pots in the encampment with,*' Anik gulped and paled visibly before continuing, '*with pieces of human remains, tulimak*[49] *floating in an evil, foul smelling and stagnant congealed brew. We also came upon several others some miles distant, not together, but all dead, seemingly ravaged by 'scurvy' and very skinny. Their clothing inadequate and ragged, not suited for here,*' he gesticulated, sweeping his arm around in a wide circle. '*They appeared to have been escaping the camp and died where they fell hours or days later.*'

---

49 Tulimak – ribs

Davy, Tom and Rob's grim faces portrayed their revulsion. Anik's description of his encounter was perhaps too vivid, but they thanked him for his account and for the implied knowledge of the Fitzjames's crew.

'One last question,' pressed Tom. Anik nodded acceptance. 'Were any alive?'

Anik turned to the others in his group. *'Did you see anyone alive?'* he asked.

They all shook their heads in solemn recognition of the fact that, in their opinion, none had survived.

Anik turned back to Tom and sadly shook his head too, although Tom already knew the answer.

What Anik said next stunned him to the core. *'I counted forty, maybe forty-two dead, but how many ended their lives in the cooking pot, I cannot say.'*

At that very instant, Davy determined that whatever happened, he would make it back to England, firstly for Catherine and, secondly, to make 'someone's' acquaintance. He then ran to a small hummock, away from the group and was violently sick.

'Better see how he is, Tom,' suggested Rob. 'I propose that we skirt around Fitzjames's encampment in the circumstances. The elements will do a decent job of hiding the evidence. I couldn't stomach it.'

'Neither could I,' sympathised Tom. 'We'll go the Inuit way and leave everything to nature.'

Before Anik's party left them alone once more, Anik brought over a hide bound book covered over with oilskin. *'Kabloonans' script,'* said Anik circling his hand over the documents and indicating that they had little use for such articles in Inuit society.

'Thank you, Anik.' Tom accepted the package, realising its importance immediately.

'*We go now,*' informed Anik. '*Fort York many days to the south. We wish you luck.*'

Tom, Davy and Rob waved them off. All three wondered just how important was this chance encounter. They would leave the place where they met the Inuits the following day, but first, Tom would read the logbook.

Tom settled down in their tent and took out the document. He read the last entry first...tears streamed down the big man's face, before he reached the last sentence, as he vividly remembered the vibrant smile of Lieutenant Fitzjames.

Several days passed in which the three made excellent progress, covering nearly ten miles a day, due in no small part to the stamina of the huskies. Once again they came across an occasional item obviously discarded by Fitzjames's party, which indicated that the route they were taking paralleled his route. They served as a constant reminder of the harrowing tale relayed by the Inuits. However, their account was not put into any meaningful context until they rounded the last promontory on the south coast of King William Island. A grotesque frozen tableau, surreal in its simplicity and framed as if in a painting, challenged their sanity.

All three stopped in their tracks, as did the huskies; even they remained silent, transfixed on their haunches.

Tom lowered his hood and scratched his head before speaking. 'Would you look at that?'

'I'm looking,' replied Rob, 'but my brain's having difficulty taking it in.'

Davy surveyed the scene. An abandoned clincher[50] built boat attached to a large unwieldy sledge. In the boat sat two

---

50 Clincher built – horizontal overlapping planking on the boat's hull.

frozen sailors, hunched under the gunwale[51], staring fixatedly into a far distant eternity. Beside each were muskets and watches laid flat, but frozen to the thwart[52].

Tom approached the boat and peered inside. At the sailor's feet lay a variety of surprising items. Tom was perplexed, it was as if these silent sentinels were standing guard over many useless items; several towels, books, sponges and most surprising of all, silk handkerchiefs.

Rob eased himself over the gunwale before levering the muskets off the thwarts, using his deck knife. They parted company with the ice holding them with a loud crack. 'They're both loaded, must have been expecting trouble,' remarked Rob absently, before placing the weapons in an upright position to the side of each man. 'We won't be needing these ourselves, so we may as well leave them with our shipmates,' he added sombrely, but respectfully.

'Did they die of the cold?' asked Davy.

'I don't know young Davy,' replied Tom, 'but that large empty can may have had something to do with it, if it wasn't the cold. Anyway, we're leaving now! This place gives me the creeps.'

---

51 Gunwale – top section of boat side.
52 Thwart – wood plank seating which spans width of boat, usually several on an individual boat.

CHAPTER THREE

A Chance Meeting
Admiralty Buildings, London 1849

Lady Jane Franklin alighted from her coach, ably assisted by Jenkins and gazed at the impressive façade of the Admiralty headquarters. It was not the first time that she had undertaken the task of lobbying support for a search party to be sent to the Arctic to determine the whereabouts of the expedition. It was, however, the first time that John Ross, Sir James Clark Ross's uncle would be joining her, in an effort to sway the authorities thinking and to perhaps loosen the purse strings for such a venture.

The Admiralty were not, in fact, actually averse to authorising an expedition, but were minded in essence to do nothing, bearing in mind that the original undertaking was scheduled for a period of three to five years. It was conceivable from their perspective that the expedition may be experiencing difficulties and may be icebound somewhere, but was probably not in danger. Since there hadn't been any information regarding their whereabouts, which in itself was not surprising, given the nature and climate of the Arctic, *'no news was good news'*. This consensus of opinion amongst the hierarchy had not been tested, until Lady Jane began her own minor crusade to change their view and approach to the situation.

Rear Admiral John Ross, no stranger to Arctic exploration himself, greeted her in the expansive lobby, adjacent to the main entrance. He smiled encouragingly and whispered in her ear that several interested parties in senior positions, including business icons with a financial interest in locating the passage were attending. He also mentioned that several relations of the officers were beginning to ask questions.

'Where are the ships?' That's what they're asking, I've no doubt,' confirmed Lady Jane, 'which they have every right to do.'

'Quite,' replied Ross. 'I know one or two personally and they are extremely concerned, especially because no one has reported encountering the expedition. That to me seems exceedingly strange.'

They proceeded to an upper floor where the meeting was to take place. As they approached the double oak doors of the conference room, Lady Jane noticed two men in deep conversation, obviously agitated.

'Who are they...do you know?' enquired Lady Jane of Sir James.

'Ah yes, indeed I do, much to my chagrin,' confirmed John Ross. 'That's Stephan Goldner and an Admiralty supply agent. He provided the canned food for Sir John's expedition!'

Ross moved to open the door for Lady Jane, just as Goldner and his associate brushed past them in their haste to obtain advantageous seating. Goldner appeared not to notice, or acknowledge their presence in any way.

'What a rude man,' exclaimed Lady Jane pointedly, ensuring that he heard her, even if he had, apparently, ignored them completely.

'Believe me, he has a reputation to match his rudeness, but the Admiralty continue to use him as a supplier nevertheless,' explained Ross.

'Why is he here?' queried Lady Jane.

'I expect he'll want to supply any search expeditions, so he'll have a vested interest in this meeting, which in itself is probably a good sign that he's been invited.'

'I suppose so,' agreed Lady Jane, 'but that won't prevent me disliking him.'

'I suggest we present the case for a search and ignore his presence. He's not likely to influence their decision anyway and it's them we have to convince.'

'I agree.' Lady Jane calmed herself to address her immediate concerns, but at the back of her mind, she wondered if that would be the last she heard or saw of Stephan Goldner.

⁂

Two hours later, Lady Jane and her escort John Ross emerged from the meeting room having successfully convinced the Arctic Council representatives at the Admiralty to agree in principle to a preliminary expedition to search for Franklin's ships. The search would be partly funded by Lady Jane herself. Goldner would supply the canned provisions, although a ship and date were yet to be decided upon.

The Admiralty gave an undertaking to Lady Jane that she would be kept informed in confidence of progress in this regard.

⁂

Catherine was overjoyed at Lady Jane's news and was pleased that she had sent for her immediately on her return from the Admiralty.

'Don't get your hopes up too much Catherine, advised Lady Jane. 'I've been in this position before and it doesn't do to be too optimistic, although on this occasion, I do feel some enthusiasm that action will be taken.'

'Thank you so much,' enthused Catherine. 'Will I be able to tell Marie as well, or do I have to keep it a secret?'

'I don't see why not,' agreed Lady Jane. 'However, do emphasise that until any expedition becomes known publicly, I expect the information to be held in confidence.'

'Of course,' affirmed Catherine respectfully. 'Marie's not one to gossip; she won't say anything to anyone and neither will I.'

'Well that's settled then... we'll find them soon,' Lady Jane promised, less optimistically than she sounded.

Several days later, Lady Jane received a communiqué from, none other than, Sir James Clark Ross, with good news. It stated that his uncle, John Ross, now a sprightly seventy three year old had convinced the Admiralty that a search expedition was warranted. Indeed, he had intimated to his nephew, prior to the Franklin expedition's departure, that if such an undertaking was warranted to 'rescue' the expedition, then he was prepared to lead it.

In consequence, two sea borne rescue missions and one land expedition were to be authorised in the spring, which acknowledged John Ross's insistence that action was urgently required when they met with the Admiralty and the Arctic Council.

CHAPTER FOUR

Yellowknives

Col was aware that his head ached abominably, moments before daring to open his eyes. He peered through half-closed lids to take in his immediate surroundings. *Where am I?* his brain asked, while his heart, gripped with fear of the unknown, increased its rhythmic pulse. He turned his head to the left and tried to rise from his prone position, but was unable to do so. His wrists and ankles were tied to the low level rustic bed on which he lay.

Alert at last, he opened his eyes fully and surveyed his surroundings, some sort of circular peaked tent, with an opening at the top. Someone was watching him from the hide flap, which served as the entrance, but it was dark outside so he was unable to make out any features of the person watching him, only a silhouette.

A feminine voice called out, 'Akaitcho!' followed by something unintelligible to Col, although he assumed it was a call for assistance. He was correct in his assumption. Several footsteps indicated the fact that one or more persons were interested in his recovery...*Oh yes, that's why my head aches...someone hit me with something heavy!* He would have felt his head, but the tied wrists precluded even this simple task.

Two men entered. The woman, who'd called the men, lit a simple stone oil lamp. Col could now make out their features clearly and was impressed with their dress and presence, despite his predicament.

He was even more impressed, but totally shocked when the first man introduced himself in excellent English.

'My name is Akaitcho[53], chief of the *T'atsaot'ine,* who you may know as Yellowknives or Copper Indians, or perhaps not. No matter, it is of little importance. This is my son, Akilinik, who may have hit you too hard down by the river, which is our territory.'

At this point Col observed Akilinik smiling in the background. He obviously thought he *hadn't* hit him too hard.

Akaitcho continued, 'This is my daughter, Tala[54], who also speaks your language. She has been attending to you since we brought you here, but be careful, her name translates as 'She Wolf''.'

Col nodded his appreciation, albeit with some trepidation, but was rewarded with a genuine smile from the attractive young woman.

'She already has a name for you, Englishman. Do you wish me to tell you or shall we call you by your real name?'

Col was intrigued, but still bound by his wrists and ankles, which Akaitcho noticed.

'Ah you wish to be released; we are sorry, but it was a precaution, in case you awakened and felt the need to escape before we could talk to you. Tala, please release...?' he looked at Col questionably and expectantly.

'Col,' said Col, relaxing perceptively.

'Please release Col,' Akaitcho continued.

Tala approached him and gentle hands untied his wrists and then his ankles. Her face came close to his as she

53 Akaitcho meaning 'like a wolf with big paws'
54 Tala meaning 'She wolf'

accomplished the task and her eyes sparkled as she smiled again.

Col immediately realised why she was named Tala. Her irises were quite remarkable, comparable to an intense blue ice crystal of a she wolf's eyes. Col rubbed his wrists and sat up.

In anticipation of Col's next question Akaitcho stated, 'We mean you no harm and would like to ask you a few questions, but first, do you wish to know what Tala has named you?'

Col laughed despite himself and the strange situation he'd inherited. 'Why not?' he agreed.

Tala brought over a wicker basket and placed it on the bed beside him. '*Two Cats*,' she said in clear concise English. 'That is your *T'atsaot'ine* name and these belong to you.' She opened the lid and Mitzi and Fritz stared at him before tentatively leaving the basket to sit beside him.

Col, caught up in the emotion of seeing his furry friends again began to remember the circumstances of his being there in the first place. 'Bryant and Reid?' he uttered abruptly.

'Dead, but you were aware of that already,' answered Akaitcho. 'We followed you to your camp the following day, after we killed your attackers. They were *Dog Rib* and, lucky for you, our traditional enemies.' Akaitcho made this remark matter-of-factly and without emotion. 'It would have been only a matter of time before they found and killed you too.'

Col shivered at the prospect; but realised that trust had now been established between himself and the Yellowknives.

'Oh, we have everything that they looted from you...it is here in this tent,' he indicated, pointing to a pile of possessions near the entrance. 'We are sorry we could not save your companions...we will talk more in the morning, but now, rest.'

Col nodded, assimilating the poignancy of Akaitcho's remark, before responding, 'We will, but just one question before you leave, it's important to me.'

'Yes,' countered Akaitcho.

'How did you learn to speak English?'

'My grandfather knew Samuel Hearne,' came the cryptic response and then he was gone, leaving Col less informed than before.

Who the hell was Samuel Hearne? thought Col, but decided patience was the best policy in the circumstances, as Tala brought him a bowl of 'interesting' broth.

'Eat,' she instructed, 'and then sleep.'

Before she left, she offered the cats some strips of smoked meat, which they ate quickly. They too were hungry.

Col awoke the next morning as the sun streamed into the tepee[55] from the entrance flap. He cagily moved his legs to the ground and felt the rough texture of the dirt beneath his feet. He still ached all over, but was relieved to find that his hands and feet remained free. He rubbed his eyes and focused on the doorway. Tala stood at the entrance with a wooden bowl containing water and a soft cloth.

'Awake at last *Two Cats'* she jested. 'You've been asleep all night and most of this morning. Your 'friends' have been hunting since the early hours.'

Col was amused and smiled at the reference, but responded good humouredly, 'That's because they haven't been hit over the head with a war club.'

---

55 Tepee – tent

'Yes, he may have hit you too hard, but he will be chief when my father dies,' she hesitated, 'although that may be many moons away, he has to prove himself now.'

Col mulled this one over in his mind, but decided to move on to something else, something that slipped his mind in the confusion of yesterday, but was now of paramount importance. Crozier's party! 'I must speak to your father, it's a matter of urgency.'

'Yes of course,' answered Tala, 'but first wash and dress, then I will take you to him. I will leave you alone while you attend to these matters.'

'Thank you,' he replied, thinking that she was leaving him to preserve his modesty while he dressed. Had he known, he would have been somewhat embarrassed. Tala had already bathed his naked unconscious body and attended to his cuts and abrasions shortly after the Yellowknife warriors had brought him into camp.

She smiled mischievously as she left.

⟨⟡⟩

Tala returned later. 'Akaitcho is ready to speak to you. I will escort you to his tepee. He wishes you to bring your possessions with you; I will help.'

They proceeded to the meeting with Akaitcho. His son and two other warriors, obviously elders, sat with them.

'Sit.' It was neither an instruction nor a command, merely a request, which put Col at ease. He sat.

'You have urgent business according to my daughter,' stated Akaitcho. 'Just what is this business?'

'It is a very long story, but I believe time is running out for many of my shipmates. Without help, I fear they may die.' Col leant forward to add emphasis to his concerns and launched into a brief but concise rendition of the circumstances of his being there, explaining the expedition's purpose and the role of the *Erebus* and *Terror*.

Akaitcho and the two elders, watched closely by Col and Akilinik, seemed deep in thought. At first the three conversed in their own language before Akaitcho swivelled on his haunches to face Col and address him, speaking compassionately, 'The horizons of our territory are wide and extensive, from the *Tinde'e*[56] to the *Thlew-ee-chow-desserth*[57] and from the *Akilinik*, or Thelon River, as far east to the place you call Hudson Bay. My son is named after that river.' He glanced at his son then continued, 'We have great authority in this region and our communication between tribes is legendary, so what I'm about to tell you will undoubtedly come as a shock. We believe that all the men from your ship are dead.'

Col stared at Akaitcho in disbelief. 'How could you know that?' he asked incredulously.

'It's true, I'm sorry Col. Our scouts and runners as far away as the area you know as the Adelaide Peninsula report many deaths. Not all in one place, but spread over a wide area. It appears that some succeeded in almost reaching the Great Fish River, before succumbing to the cold or the ravages of some kind of illness, lying dead where they fell. Our nation is used to death and hardship but to hear what befell some of your countrymen is truly terrifying. Although this information has been passed down to us through several mouths, it is still hideous and incredible. There is much more and most of it you will not wish to hear. It will not be

---

56 Tinde'e – Great Slave Lake
57 Thlew-ee-chow-desserth – Great Fish River

pleasant. We should talk more tomorrow...today is a day of sadness and you may wish to be on your own.'

Col returned to the original tent in a trance like state. His colleagues were dead, despite his efforts, if Akaitcho was to be believed of course, but deep down he knew it to be true. He collapsed on the rustic bed and curled up into a ball in the realisation that he and he alone was probably the only survivor of Crozier's group.

Unnoticed, Mitzi and Fritz curled up beside him as if they were aware of his pain and unhappiness.

CHAPTER FIVE

A Decision

A solemn and subdued Col awoke the following day, having slept fitfully for fifteen hours.

Chief Akaitcho had promised to speak with him again today, so all he had to do was find the Yellowknife leader. Fortunately, Tala entered the tent at that moment bearing a hot drink for him, which he took gratefully for he was extremely thirsty. He gulped the liquid in quick mouthfuls, finding it pleasant and refreshing.

'It's made from mixed berries and herbs, Col. Not only will it refresh you, but it will help with your aching limbs.'

'Thank you Tala,' responded Col, adding, 'Do you know where your father is at the moment because I have much to discuss with him? I have a proposition. I need a guide and possibly an escort. I intend searching back along the route Bryant, Reid and myself took. I cannot believe everyone died; there must be someone alive.

'He's bathing at the river, but he'll be back soon. I know he wishes to speak with you again. You can wait for him in his tent,' informed Tala.

They made the short walk along a narrow path to the chief's tent, where Tala left him alone. His possessions still lay in the same position from the previous day, so he took the opportunity to examine what remained of his worldly goods. He was astounded to find the money-belt containing the gold sovereigns that Crozier had trusted him with, still in Akaitcho's tent. This spoke volumes as to Chief Akaitcho's character and control of his tribe. Col's understanding of human nature seemed at odds with that of the Yellowknives.

If a money-belt containing such a vast amount gold coins had been left unattended anywhere in Britain it would have 'walked' in the blink of an eye. He was impressed.

He'd just retrieved the copper plaque from the meagre pile and was examining it when Akaitcho entered. 'Ah, *Two Cats*', he greeted Col with a smile. 'I see you've found what you thought you'd lost? Such fine engraving, obviously from your ship,' stated Akaitcho before continuing matter of factly along the same lines, 'Also, your gold coins are 'ex-quis-ite'.' Akaitcho pronounced the word in three distinct syllables, which emphasised his knowledge of English.

'Your Chief is a woman?' added Akaitcho, which indicated to Col that he had indeed examined the money-belt.

'That's Queen Victoria,' explained Col, 'our Monarch.' He took out one coin from the belt and handed it to the chief. 'The coins were minted in 1845 and they show our young queen facing west.'

'Minted?' queried Akaitcho.

'Pressed or stamped out,' indicated Col, imitating a 'press' as best he could. 'On the reverse is a shield which contains two sets of the three lions of England and other heraldic symbols. The writing is Latin, 'Britanniarum', 'Regina Fid Def'. I'm no scholar, but roughly translated it means 'Queen of Britain'. You can keep this one.'

Col offered Akaitcho the coin, which he examined again minutely, before transferring it to a tiny leather drawstring pouch, which hung around his neck, then nodded his appreciation in mutual understanding of the gesture. 'Now the Chief of Britain and the Chief of the Yellowknives travel as one!' emphasised Akaitcho sagely.

'Queen,' prompted Col.

'Ah, yes, Queen,' Akaitcho corrected himself, before launching into a potted history of his own historic tribe, which included another reference to Samuel Hearne.

'We have encountered many explorers since my grandfather met with Sam Hearne, nearly eighty years ago. Some have sought to exploit us, where others have traded and worked alongside us in mutual benefit, including John Franklin, which may surprise you.'

Col was visibly shocked, Franklin had never mentioned Akaitcho in their conversations aboard ship, but it was apparent that Akaitcho knew Franklin personally. 'Why didn't you mention that you knew Franklin when we spoke yesterday?' asked Col with some concern.

'Because I was never entirely sure of his motivation, but above all else, he seemed to be obsessed with locating his *North West Passage*. I wasn't surprised to learn of his death in 1847 from your own lips, but I was sorry about the deaths of so many of the crewmen aboard the two ships.

'You ask how I knew Franklin, well we were recruited by the North West Company to act as guides and hunters for the Royal Navy. We agreed our services at Fort Resolution in exchange for cloth, ammunition, tobacco and iron products, also the cancellation of our past debts to that company. During 1820 and 1821 we guided the party as far as the Arctic Ocean, initially along the Coppermine River. We left them there, agreeing to leave food and other supplies for their return, along the chosen route and at Fort Enterprise. Although I believed Franklin's expedition to be folly, we assisted as much as we were able, losing several of our own tribe, when they fell through ice on a frozen lake. I doubted we'd ever see Franklin alive again, but may be his obstinacy drove him on. Luckily, we encountered him again, preventing him starving to death along with his party, partly due to a George Back[58] who convinced us to return to Fort Enterprise. Despite Franklin's failure to supply the goods and ammunition agreed with our terms, we assisted, which saved his life. A pity he lost it twenty-six years later, searching for his elusive passage.

'I mentioned yesterday that Yellowknife lands are vast, extending north and north east of the Great Slave Lake, the Tinde'e is our language. There are many rivers and bays in our land, the Coppermine, Thelon and one you may know as the 'Back' River or Thlewechodyeth, which translated means 'Great Fish'. Our existence relies on our empathy with our rivers. The one's I mention are few, although others, too numerous to name individually, contain the life-blood of our ancestors within their waters. They are like the veins on our hands.' Akaitcho held his hand up in front of Col's face for effect...'guiding and shaping our lives. We travel great distances, from the Great Lake to Hudson Bay and the Arctic Ocean. Our knowledge is vast and trade is extensive. Inuits trade fur for our tools, which prompts me to ask you a question...Just how did you obtain such a fine Inuit suit?' Akaitcho's question remained unanswered as he immediately launched deeper into his dialogue, giving Col insufficient time to even open his mouth, let alone offer an explanation.

'Hearne recognised that an association with our tribes was paramount. We helped him find viable routes from the Arctic tundra to Hudson Bay, opening trade links with settlers

---

58 Back Expedition – Principal participants, George Back, Explorer, John Franklin, Leader of the Expedition, Midshipman Naturalist Robert Hood, Doctor John Richardson, Ordinary seaman John Hepburn.

and other tribes as far apart as Granville[59] and the Fraser River, on the West coast and Quebec and the St Lawrence to the East. The names given to us around this time, *Copper Indians* or *Redknives* explains our affinity with the metal. It is undoubtedly the bedrock on which our civilisation has succeeded in recent times, but it is not our only resource; there is much hidden in our hills!'

Col listened intently, not wanting to disturb Chief Akaitcho's rhythm.

'Your sovereigns, I believe are much sought after as a currency between peoples of the world. We too value gold in its purest form, its allure and lustre is quite remarkable. Unfortunately, many would kill to own but a small nugget, such is the greed of the prospector who feed on the rumours that the yellow metal can be found in abundance in Yellowknife territory.

'We have to protect our lands from those who wish to exploit us, although I already fear it is too late. Our way of life is already changing and Akilinik, my son, fears it most because it will be his generation that must fight for survival. That may be why he hit you a little too hard, but try not to hold that against him,' he laughed. 'He realised, after we examined your belongings that you had brought gold and, therefore, were not one of the new breed of prospector... and perhaps my daughter also persuaded him that you weren't a threat to our way of life!'

'Oh,' muttered Col, for that was all he could think of to say as he felt the bump behind his ear, colouring slightly as he did so.

---

59 Granville – now Vancouver

Akaitcho watched Col intently for a few seconds before speaking again, 'You have a request I believe?'

'Yes, I need your assistance. I have to retrace my steps and return to the area where I left Commander Crozier. It's not that I disbelieve the account provided by your scouts, but if there's a remote possibility that some men are alive... even one man, then I must return. If there aren't any survivors, then I should attempt to contact the crewmembers of the *Terror*. They undertook a different route, under the command of Captain Fitzjames, heading for Fort York. I hope they have been successful.'

'We do not have any information concerning the men from the *Terror*,' interjected Akaitcho, 'but your knowledge of their route indicates they're far to the east of our territory. They may have succeeded in finding a way through, although in some respects, the terrain is more treacherous than the one your Commander, Crozier undertook.'

'Perhaps I could intercept them, but that would be extremely difficult, as I haven't any knowledge of the area,' said Col glumly.

Akaitcho frowned, but formulated a suggestion in his mind which he proceeded to outline to Col, 'Difficult, but not impossible. You say you departed the ships on 22nd April; well, that's over three moons ago, fourteen weeks in your time. By my estimation of their progress, I would have expected them to have reached a northerly point on the coast of Hudson Bay...Wait—' instructed Akaitcho, as he rummaged through the contents of a leather bound roll of what looked like parchment, but was, in fact, fine animal skins. Akaitcho was a map-maker it seemed. He spread several of these in front of Col, who was delighted at their clarity and apparent accuracy. All overlapped, which made identification of the whole area easy to interpret.

'Almost as good as the charts aboard the *Erebus*,' Col muttered 'almost' to himself.

Akaitcho frowned in exasperation as he had heard the comment. 'Better!' he insisted, although he'd never set eyes on any hydrographers' chart in his lifetime. Ignoring the muttered insult, Akaitcho prodded his own map, which depicted an inlet to the north of Hudson Bay. 'Here's where I'd search! It's probable that they'd head there before proceeding south. The Inuits call it Tikiranjuaq. Hearne named it Whale Cove. If you don't find them, I'd advise that you head southward toward Fort York, if that is your wish. To help you in this endeavour, I am prepared to offer you the assistance of four of my followers to guide and escort you, but it will not be for you alone. Theirs is also a trading mission for our tribe, which is important.'

'What do you want from me in return?' Col asked pointedly.

Akaitcho pursed his lips as if deep in thought, as though he'd never considered such a question. 'Well, the plaque impresses me...it will be a reminder of our meeting should you leave it in our safekeeping.'

'Of course Chief Akaitcho,' agreed Col.

'Oh yes,' continued Akaitcho 'and perhaps we could agree on you leaving several copies of your Queen, so that I may appreciate and study the *heraldic* symbols you introduced into our conversation.'

'Agreed,' confirmed Col, realising that Akaitcho was indeed as shrewd as he looked, 'but just how many had you in mind?'

The Chief engaged his most disarming smile once again before replying, 'For saving your life...nothing; for the four guides to escort you, possibly as far as Fort York...ten sovereigns, but only five for myself,' he indicated by raising his right hand, palm toward Col. 'That will leave you with many more to negotiate, should the need arise. There are many perils in the wilderness, but the majority of those walk on two legs...I will not deprive you of that capability.'

Col felt his indebtedness to Akaitcho was increasing by the minute, but was anxious to leave, as time seemed of the essence. If his preparations to find possible survivors were completed quickly, he could be on his way.

Akaitcho noticed his impatience and accepted it as a consequence of the responsibility placed upon him by his Commander Crozier. However, he hadn't any intention of allowing Col to leave without an additional favour. 'I almost forgot,' added Akaitcho, 'It is obvious to me that you will need an interpreter, one that can converse in the many tongues of the tribes that inhabit our lands...one that can also speak your native tongue, English.'

Col looked questioningly at the chief; could he mean his son, Akilinik?

Akaitcho, as if reading Col's mind, pre-empted the unspoken question, 'No, not my son, but my daughter, Tala. She is very intelligent and extremely capable. She will need little protection I can assure you, but she is very precious to me...please remember that!' He stopped for effect before continuing, 'Oh, you may wish to know that it was her idea to accompany you and once my daughter decides on anything, there is little, I, as her father, can do to dissuade her. You are a lucky man in that you will have the pleasure of her company for a few months.'

'Thank you Chief Akaitcho,' was all Col managed to say in response, having been totally taken by surprise at the turn of events.

'One last request, *Two Cats*,' Akaitcho chuckled, 'Mitzi and Fritz go with you! Goodbye and good luck.' The

Chief turned and left the tent, leaving Col to begin his preparations.

❧

A day later, the group left the settlement watched by Akaitcho and Akilinik and many of their tribe. Tala waved, but showed little visible emotion at their departure.

CHAPTER SIX

Terrible Consequences

*'...Then only the cook and me was left
and the delicate question, 'Which
Of us two goes to the kettle?' arose
And we argued it out as sich...'*

Two weeks into the journey, Col was still struggling to keep up with the pace of the four Yellowknives accompanying him. Tala was sympathetic, but her own lithe, tuned body, accustomed as it was to the hardships of these northern territories, put him to shame none-the-less.

It had taken Bryant, Reid and himself nearly six weeks to travel the same distance, so in one respect his fitness and wellbeing must have improved. 'Pat yourself on the back Col,' he spoke out loud.

'Is it madness to speak to yourself?' enquired Tala. 'Or perhaps you prefer your own voice to mine?' Her remarkable eyes flashed mischievously, already aware of the effect she was having on him.

'No, no of course not,' came his embarrassed reply. 'I love our conversations and I'm really pleased that you convinced your father that you should act as interpreter. I would have been very lonely without you to talk to, with all due respect to your tribesmen. I only know one or two words of your language and similarly they only know a few words of English.'

Tala raised one eyebrow before teasing him again, having succeeded on several occasions since leaving her father's camp. 'So, you love our conversations and you would feel very lonely without me. I like that *Two Cats*...I wouldn't want you to be lonely.'

Col realised that Tala was having an *uncomfortable* effect on him. His world so far largely consisted of cogs, flywheels and boilers. Not surprisingly the attentions of a woman had so far eluded him. His thoughts were interrupted when one of the Indians pointed to a range of hills, twenty or more miles distant. He conversed with Tala at length before she advised Col of the content. 'He says that beyond the hills, you will find what you are looking for...but it will not be pleasant. A scout from a friendly tribe, who Makwa met two days ago when skirting their village, confirms the information brought by runners to our settlement before we left. I'm sorry *Two Cats* but we must prepare ourselves.'

'So be it then,' admitted Col resignedly, 'but I must go there myself and see the scene with my own eyes, as terrible as it may be.'

༺✿༻

Two days later, chief scout Makwa discovered the first signs of Crozier's men's struggle to survive; two tin cans, which had obviously been crudely opened by a bayonet or something similar. Sharp irregular edges seemed to indicate that a desperate man or men had hacked at them haphazardly to retrieve the contents.

Col realised that it was distinctly colder here; patches of snow and ice peppered the landscape, which indicated an early autumn and a return to the rugged mountainous terrain beyond the Arctic Circle. He shivered uncontrollably, until Tala placed her hand on his arm. 'Come, we must follow

Makwa's lead,' urged Tala, 'See he is beckoning us over toward that hillock.'

Makwa stood atop the hillock, head bowed, waiting for the others to join him. He eyed the ravaged body of the dead sailor speculatively. The clothing was tattered and shredded, only partially covering an already decimated skeleton that was more skin and bone than the flesh of man.

It was obvious that several wild animals had chewed their way through the carcass some time ago. A leg bone was to be seen, several yards away from the main remains, which indicated some animal had dragged it there to enjoy a slightly more peaceful meal, while others stayed at the main banquet.

He wasn't repulsed by the sight, but realised that the Englishman's perspective would be different, so shouted to Tala, before they could reach his position.

'Makwa's found someone...' she advised. 'He says it will be the first of many. Are you still willing to find out what happened?'

"I must,' came the reply as he trudged over to the hillock before steeling himself for the inevitable shock...the recognition and identification of one of his own.

'Daniel Arthur,' whispered Col, recognising the frayed insignia of the quartermaster on the remnant of clothing. 'I'm so sorry, Dan, you were a good man...I'll remember our conversations aboard the *Erebus*. Rest in Peace.' Col mouthed a short prayer before addressing Makwa, 'Let's move on,' he said determinedly.

They travelled several more miles that day, sighting more bodies and possessions with increasing regularity, but it wasn't until the following day that they reached what Col instantly knew was Crozier's final destination.

The camp, or what was left of it was in disarray. It was obvious from the cooking pots and utensils, that some attempt was made to feed the last of the survivors, but what with, was unclear, until an ashen faced Tala pointed to a human thigh bone within an overturned pot. Col, appalled, turned away, not wanting to acknowledge the unthinkable. Even Makwa was subdued and removed himself from the scene to investigate the perimeter. His three followers did the same, casting worried glances at each other as they left the killing ground.

Col faced the mountains and took a deep breath before noticing a collapsed tent on the periphery of the camp, which he recognised as Crozier's. He approached with trepidation and some fear of what he might find, but dragged open the canvas flap at the entrance with resigned determination. Crozier was not inside. Col was both disappointed and relieved as he surveyed the jumble of possessions. In the centre stood a crate with distinctive yellow markings, containing a few of Goldner's cans, atop which, sat an oilskin package, instantly recognisable.

'Crozier's log,' he explained to Tala. 'Hopefully a record of what has happened here since I left. We must take it with us, but I'm not sure I'll want to read it. As for the rest, I've seen enough to believe what your scouts reported at your village. We'd best leave everything here for the elements to take their toll. By next spring there'll be little left anyway and I've neither the will nor the strength to bury so many poor men. I believe it's the Inuit way of life and death.'

Tala understood his anguish and felt his sorrow before compassionately leading him away from the confines of Crozier's tent. It was truly a time of despair, but also one of hope in that the *Terror's* party succeeded where Crozier's failed.

'We need to try and find Fitzjames's party before winter sets in,' insisted Col.

'Yes, Two Cats, it will be difficult,' replied Tala, 'but we will try. Makwa should lead the way eastward.'

Despite a final search, Col did not locate Crozier, only 'Diggle' the cook was recognisable amongst the bodies; was he one of the last he thought, as he remembered the man himself and the difficult and emotive job he'd undertaken. He'd tried his best to please everyone, despite the ongoing joking and ridicule, which accompanied that particular position aboard ship.

CHAPTER SEVEN

Searching – 1849/1850

'Ice, ice and more ice!' muttered a tetchy John Ross. His promise to Franklin and, more recently, Lady Jane Franklin to find the *Erebus* and *Terror* had not been fruitful so far.

The entrance to the Peel Channel was severely hampered by the presence of thick ice and had been for several years since Franklin apparently entered the Channel in 1846.

Ross rubbed his left thigh, which was 'playing up' again. 'Damn these temperatures, they'll be the death of me,' he declared vehemently to an officer on the bridge of the largest of the two vessels, he'd both financed and led to the Arctic. 'Absolutely no sign of him, but I'll not risk taking these ships any further. If Sir John couldn't fight his way out, we can't fight our way in. Knowing him, he's probably found the North West Passage and is sunning himself in the Pacific somewhere, with no way of informing us,' he laughed, although neither he nor the officer were convinced of that hypothesis. 'Do you know there are fifteen vessels searching for the expedition this year alone?' asked Ross of the officer.

'No Sir, I didn't, in fact I assumed we were the only ones.'

'Well we aren't; even the Americans have two ships in the area. Lady Jane, the wife of Sir John has financed another herself. She'll not give up on him. Met her at the Admiralty a while ago, gave her my support you know, but I doubt she really needed it. I've never met a more determined woman in my life. Anyway, I've kept my promise to a dear friend, but I must confess this search is like a 'needle in a haystack' and this seventy three year old's eyesight isn't used to finding needles. Without access to the 'Peel', we're scuppered!'

'Beg pardon, Sir,' queried the officer.

'By way of explanation Mr Allen,' responded Ross. 'This ice has been in the Peel for years. You can see by the build up of hummocks and the way it glistens. If he's in there, he's stuck...well and truly and so will we be if we remain here! We'd better head for Beechey Island and see what we can find there. The admiralty has already sent Austin to search that area on the *Resolute*. In addition, I believe Will Penny may also have started searching to the west and north of Devon Island on the *Sophia,* in conjunction with *H.M.S. Lady Franklin*, so we may eventually cross paths and possibly exchange information, meagre though that may be. Anyway, break out the charts Mr Allen and let's plot a course for Beechey Island.'

'Right away, Sir,' responded Allen, busying himself at the slim chart drawers, before producing two, well surveyed charts of an area. They encompassed the Wellington Channel, between Cornwallis Island and Devon Island and the Barrow Strait, north of Somerset Island.

'That's more like it,' boomed Ross. 'Plot a course via Resolute Island in case Franklin's sightseeing up there and then on to Beechey Island,' ordered Ross.

'Aye, aye, Sir,' responded Allen.

'Better plot a course for home too, along Lancaster Sound to Baffin Bay. We'll not be achieving anything more this season by staying more than a few days at Beechey. The ice is closing in already and I'd much prefer to be heading for Cape Farewell in clear water.'

'I'll have them ready for your approval very shortly, Sir,' confirmed Allen.

'Thank you, Allen, now for some hot tea, I think we deserve it,' suggested Ross.

~◈~

Beechey Island provided at least some information relating to the expedition, which Ross viewed positively. It was slightly unsettling to realize that three men from the expedition had died and were buried on the island. Headstones denoted the names and the dates in 1846 of their demise.

It was obvious to Ross that Franklin had wintered there due to the evidence of fire marks on the ground and the preponderance of large empty cans discarded in a heap of rusting metal.

What he hoped to find was a message from Franklin himself, but the area was devoid of any stone cairns. As Ross knew, it was the custom of the time and expeditions in general to deposit messages in bottles or similar containers and to secrete them inside a cairn. He therefore assumed that Franklin was confident at this particular juncture, despite losing an 'acceptable' number of men and, therefore, proceeded to the Peel Channel as planned, without reporting anything amiss.

Satisfied with his summation, Ross departed Beechey for England in the summer of 1850. His intention, on the passage home, was to write a report for the Admiralty and Lady Jane Franklin. He determined that he would deliver his findings personally to Lady Jane at her residence in Spilsby, Lincolnshire, in the belief that she would be pleased to receive him with first hand knowledge, albeit with not as much as she had hoped.

CHAPTER EIGHT

Winter/Spring – 1849/1850

Despite the efficiency of the Yellowknife trackers, Makwa could not find any trace of Fitzjames and the crew of the *Terror*. Reluctantly, Col and Tala took the decision to head southeast and gain the tree-line before the harshness of an Arctic winter effected their own abilities. Their plan now would be to reach Fort York in the spring, but in the meantime, Makwa was keen to resume what, in his eyes, was the prime objective...securing enough beaver pelts to make their journey worthwhile.

'Makwa and my tribesmen are experienced hunters,' explained Tala, 'and know this area extremely well. They are aware of the beavers' way of life, gleaned from many years of observation. When and where they build their dams, when they have their young and their daily habits and rituals. Just one beaver pelt can make 'good trade,' affirmed Tala with enthusiasm.

'I can see why,' replied Col, fingering his now familiar sealskin Inuit suit, which he had little intention of discarding now, or in the future.

'We will barter and trade at Fort York,' advised Tala. 'I have been there once before, but Makwa and the others have been there many times, so are wise to the ways of the white man,' she laughed at this point, wanting to see his reaction, but all he did was smile, as he too knew how devious 'men from across the water', could be. There was more than an element of truth in her observation. Indeed, he trusted Chief Akaitcho and his tribesmen, a great deal more than his own countrymen, in some ways, as he recalled the 'sovereign money-belt' and the honesty of the Yellowknives back at the camp.

Spring came earlier than usual in 1850. The Yellowknives, ably assisted by Col and Tala were tremendously successful in accumulating many beaver pelts on their final push to the Hudson Bay coastline, made easier by the mild conditions and navigable rivers and lakes. The purchase of two canoes from a tribe of Chipewyan Indians made their journey almost enjoyable. Tala explained that on their return to the area, they would again barter with the Chipewyan, returning the canoes for other goods to take back to Chief Akaitcho. This shared approach benefitted the different tribes. Makwa confirmed through sign and a mixture of his own language, tinged with English, that the practice had served them well for many generations. Their own copper products were much sought after by other tribes, although Col considered that their 'smelting' process could be improved, so made a mental note to mention it to Tala. He was sure that his suggestion would be well received, although he could not play an active role in the process itself. His main objective was to secure a passage back to England from Fort York for himself and the two cats. Sadly, he was now totally convinced that they were the only survivors of the Franklin expedition; consequently, he felt it incumbent on himself to retell their story. Strangely, as if in confirmation of his unspoken decision, both Mitzi and Fritz became instantly alert, watching him intently from their vantage point, atop a beaver pelt.

'If only you two could talk,' he said aloud, but the only response he received was a continuation of their enigmatic stares.

'Did you say something?' questioned Tala.

'Oh no, nothing really,' replied Col. 'Just talking to the cats, but I'm not expecting a response.'

Tala frowned, then smiled understandingly. She appreciated that this man, who she was becoming increasingly attracted to, had many facets to his character. She more than hoped he felt the same way, as she calculated just how long it would take them to reach Fort York. *Was that enough time?* she thought, as she turned away from the campfire to gaze at the stars in the night sky.

'Nothing is impossible.' Tala spoke precisely so that Col heard her clearly. Now it was his turn to be perplexed.

'What was that?' he asked.

'Nothing is impossible,' she repeated.

This time, he just said, 'Oh.' Which left him wondering if she really thought that the cats would talk some day or was she thinking something else entirely?

Just then Makwa entered camp with something of interest to report. He spoke rapidly to Tala who translated swiftly. 'Makwa says that by tomorrow we will reach Hudson Bay, about eight hours distant. He's detected smoke blowing inland from the coast, so it's likely there's a camp of sorts, which means we should be wary until we know who they are. They could be fur traders or Indians, but it's better if we approach cautiously.'

'I'll bear that in mind. I'm just glad that I'm with you and Makwa's brave men. I doubt if I'd have made it this far without you; this country is so vast and beautiful, but so daunting and dangerous.'

'I would never live anywhere else,' Tala emphasised pointedly. 'This lake, 'Kaminak', is one of the many beautiful lakes between here and my father's lands. In the Fall, the colours of the dying leaves are particularly brilliant, which makes me feel excitingly alive. I believe Samuel Hearne used the word 'paradox' to describe the effect of how one species dying, could make him so ecstatic about being alive. I love it here.'

'I can see why,' Col conceded. Anyway, I'll be on my guard, as you advise, when we approach the coast tomorrow.'

CHAPTER NINE

Dawson Inlet – March 1850

Makwa approached the shoreline slowly and cautiously, where smoke was rising vertically just beyond a tree-lined headland, two hundred yards away from his present position. He motioned to the others that they should keep silent and remain where they were until he considered it was safe to proceed. Tala acknowledged him with a wave and a nod, then relayed his intentions to the others. Col, acutely aware of potential danger, after his experience with the Dogrib Indians, was more than a little relieved to remain stationary and allow Makwa to reconnoitre. However, he was amused when he observed Mitzi and Fritz stalking Makwa, before rapidly overtaking him and taking off in the direction of the headland.

'Would you look at that,' whispered Col. 'I think they associate food with the smell of smoke.'

'Let's hope they don't alert whoever is beyond those trees to our presence,' warned Tala, as the cats disappeared out of sight.

Makwa gave them a quick glance, consternation showing clearly in his features before silently pursuing his furry friends for whom he'd a growing affection. Their antics never failed to amuse him around their own campfires, but possibly less so now, in view of the circumstances, which required silent observation in the first instance.

On reaching the trees, Makwa crouched. His practised eyes took in the pebble beach and the gently lapping water. Several yards away, three men who Makwa assumed to be Inuits from their sealskin attire were huddled around a small fire, roasting fish on a makeshift spit.

A large canoe lay nearby which made him suspicious as to their real identity, as he was aware that Inuits' preferred mode of water transport was a Kayak.

He stroked his chin in thought, deciding to observe a while longer, before returning to Tala, Col and his tribesmen. He was just about to leave when he saw Mitzi leap on to a smooth rock, not five yards away from the men. Fritz remained hidden beneath the rock. She then sat on her haunches, curled her tail around her paws and gazed intently at the trio.

One of the men adjusted his posture to turn the fish on the spit, at the same time noticing the cat sitting on the rock. 'Bloody 'ell,' said the man, 'I've not seen one of them since the Erebus.'

The others' turned to look in the cat's direction. 'Good job it's not a Grizzly, otherwise he'd have had us for breakfast along with the fish,' suggested one. 'I never noticed it creeping up on us, we must be more careful; not that it looks dangerous of course, but that Mohican when we traded the dogs in exchange for the canoe, did warn us about wildcats.'

'That's not a wildcat,' offered another, they're much bigger.'

'Looks well fed to me,' commented the first man, just as the cat leapt from the rock. In an instant the feline reached their campfire, before sitting again, eyeing the fish and licking its lips.

Open mouthed and clearly astonished, the men stared incredulously at the cat.

'Mitzi?' queried one.

'Nah, don't be daft,' said another unconvincingly.

'Well if it's not, it's one damn good lookalike,' observed the third.

'Where'd you come from?' asked two of them in unison. As if on cue, Fritz decided to make an appearance, encouraged by Mitzi's boldness.

'Well, would you believe it, I'm either dead or seeing things,' stated the biggest man.

'You're neither, that's Fritz alright and if they're alive, there are survivors from the ships and not far away.'

They looked around but failed to see a well hidden Makwa, observing them from a distance. He'd detected the English language and their reaction to the cats, but still couldn't connect the clues of their identity.

He decided to report back with his strange encounter and within minutes was relaying it to Tala, whilst casting a concerned glance at Col.

'What's Makwa saying,' asked Col.

Tala smiled before replying, 'Briefly...there are three men...speaking your tongue...who seem to have greeted your cats with some heartfelt affection.'

Col's eyes opened wide in astonishment. 'Could there possibly be others alive and well?' he conjectured. He'd almost given up hope, thinking he was the only survivor... but was it possible?

He didn't waste any time in negotiating the route recently taken by Makwa and as he rounded the promontory, came face to face with three men garbed in Inuit style dress, similar to himself, not ten yards away. All four stopped in their tracks, staring unbelievingly at each other.

'Col, you bloody brilliant engineer,' shouted Tom. 'How the bloody 'ell—'.

He stopped as Col shouted back at them, 'Tom, Rob, Davy...you're alive...thank God, but how? We thought you all perished two years back.'

'It's a long story,' explained Rob as they closed together, hugging each other in amazement and heartfelt relief.

Just then, Davy noticed Tala and the Indians, becoming instantly alarmed.

Col recognised the fear in Davy's eyes, but explained rapidly, 'Don't worry, they're with me...my escort to Fort York in fact and my friends.'

'Well, any friend of yours is a friend of mine,' confirmed Rob, noticing at the same time that Tala was a very attractive woman with astonishing and unusual blue eyes for an Indian.

Col introduced Makwa, Tala and the three tribesmen, 'They're Yellowknives,' he explained 'and you're not the only ones with a story.'

'Have any more of the crew survived?' asked Davy, not really wanting an answer.

Col responded solemnly averting his eyes, 'No, I don't think so, although I've no real way of confirming it.'

The gravity of the statement, left all silent for several seconds before Tom chirped in, 'Well, let's hear your story Col. We've plenty of fish for all, including Mitzi and Fritz, if they haven't already eaten them while we've been chatting,' he laughed heartily which reminded Col of this remarkably optimistic man from the Erebus. He felt happy to be back in his company and that of Davy and Rob, too.

While Col, Davy, Rob and Tom exchanged stories around the campfire, Makwa took the opportunity to retrieve the canoes and beaver pelts for their onward journey to Fort

York. Tala remained with the remnant of Franklin's crew, eager to listen to their individual experiences.

Col was the first to offer up his story, beginning with the realisation aboard the vessels that they believed all Lieutenant Graham Gore's party had perished in the ferocious bear attack at Victory Point. 'We were horrified. The search party found a dead bear amidst the bloody carnage of several mutilated bodies. We surmised that another bear must have been involved and had carried you three away somewhere to be eaten!'

'Quite a sobering thought,' interjected Tom. 'We were certain that would be our final resting place, although Rob did us proud; Davy and I were totally out of it and badly injured. Rob, too, had lost a lot of blood, but did enough to protect us, until Taka and Kayat turned up unexpectedly, but fortuitously. So began our year long convalescence at the Inuit camp.'

It was Col's turn to interrupt this time. 'We even had a memorial service for you, you buggers! Had you sent one of those new fangled telegraph messages, everyone's talking about at home, we could have saved ourselves the glowing eulogy we bestowed on you three,' emphasised Col sarcastically.

'Was it that good?' chipped in Rob. 'We never knew you cared. Just what did you say anyway, apart from how handsome and talented we were…still are!'

'Hmm,' laughed Col, 'let's just be thankful that our friends the Inuits found you before another bear. 'I like your sealskin suits, by the way, they match mine, although I'll bet you never traded a treasured timepiece for them.'

'Made to measure by experienced Inuit tailors, but completely free,' offered Davy. 'Without them, we'd have perished in the extreme winter of '49' when really desperate and short of food. That was in a place which we've since learned was named Tikiranjuaq from a Mohican Indian. We traded our two huskies for his canoe, about two weeks ago. We've hugged the coastline since, making camp at night and travelling by day.

'Tikiranjuaq was our low point,' explained Rob. 'If it wasn't for Tom, Davy and I would have been 'goners'. I remember chewing on a piece of meat from an Arctic Fox thigh bone…must have been dead for ages…frozen solid, but Tom chivvied pieces off before cajoling us into another supreme effort.'

'The huskies really saved us,' added Davy. 'Their energy kept us alive and mobile; it was a great pity to see them go, but the canoe trade offered us a better chance of reaching Fort York along this coast.'

'You did well,' Tala congratulated Davy. 'If you had decided to travel overland with the huskies, you would have encountered many long inlets and near impenetrable forests, making your journey much, much longer.'

Davy was as surprised as indeed Tom and Rob were at Tala's logic, not because of her opinion, but in the way she spoke to them in clear and precise English.

Her eyes flashed disarmingly and she smiled as all three raised their eyebrows in unison.

'Ah, she's special,' Col pointed out rather unnecessarily.

'And attractive too,' Rob murmured under his breath, wondering just how far Col had succumbed to the Indian maiden's charms.

'It's good to know that we've made some good decisions,' replied Tom, looking at Tala in admiration, 'but our great fortune was being saved by the Inuits.' His lengthy story followed, while Col listened intently. Tala was attentive and intrigued, which helped Tom finish his monologue.

Now it was Col's turn and their turn to be astonished at the sequence of events, which preceded and superseded the abandonment of the Erebus and Terror and the death of so many in harrowing detail. Davy found it almost unbelievable, especially the demise of Franklin himself.

They considered Col's trek with Bryant and Reid to be an extremely brave and arduous task to undertake, virtually into the unknown. Crozier must have realised that the main group's chances were slim, but felt the risk was warranted.

'Poor old Bryant and Reid,' sympathised Rob when Col reached the part in his story of the Dogrib attack.

'I was lucky to survive that night,' stated Col, 'and so were the cats, although they've an acute instinct for survival. It was then that I encountered the Yellowknives,' continued Col.

'And I gave you your new name,' interrupted Tala.

'Oh, you have a new name?' commented an amused Davy, 'and what might that be?'

Col coloured slightly and hesitated, 'You'll never guess,' he said, but before he had chance to inform them, Tala answered in her own language, which sounded impressive and left them in awe.

'Oh, in your language it means...' her eyes twinkled mischievously as she enunciated the words very meticulously, 'Two Cats'.'

Tom's laugh, which boomed out across the inlet and was probably heard in Fort York, started everyone laughing, including Col.

'Could have been worse,' stated Col, 'could have been 'Man who hides under waterfall!'...The Yellowknives do have names to suit circumstances, or an event of some kind. Anyway, I'm really quite proud of it; sorry Davy, I know they're your cats really but I did look after them when we'd thought you'd gone.'

'That's all right,' replied Davy, 'you seem to have done a good enough job anyway.'

At this point, Col's demeanour changed, a period of thoughtfulness bordering on melancholy prevailed as he remembered the more recent past. He began recounting how his group of Indians came upon the pitiful remains of Crozier's men, one or two at first and then the rest at the final camp. Col choked away his obvious distress to complete his story. 'They'd given up on Crozier's leadership and themselves. They'd gone feral; reverting to cannibalism to survive...the scene at the camp will live with me for the rest of my days. Tala's men were appalled and couldn't look me in the face until the following day.' Col paused to regain his composure, while his three friends watched feeling his pain. He cleared his throat with a cough then continued...'We couldn't bury any of the poor sods, the ground was too hard anyway, so we left them where they lay...the elements will do the job for us no doubt. I did manage to retrieve the log of the Erebus from Crozier's tent. I've put the record of my trek with Bryant and Reid in the same oilskin package to keep everything together. I've not added anything since they were killed, because I considered it prudent not to, mainly to protect my Yellowknife friends from any blame...you know how stories can be misrepresented; people might think they may be responsible for the deaths as a viable alternative to cannibalism amongst the crews.'

'You're a wise man, 'Mr Engineer',' stated Tom, 'but we're not out of the woods ourselves either, because effectively we're deserters. Rob, Davy and I discussed it a few days ago and it could be a problem if and when we get back to civilisation. We don't want to be held responsible for anything that we haven't done if there's an inquiry, especially with regard to the cannibalism,' stated Tom.

'So we've decided to change all our names before we reach Fort York...just in case and blend in as fur traders. Let's face it, we look the part,' Davy laughed as he displayed his Inuit suit to best advantage.

'That's right,' emphasised Tom, 'especially as we learned from Anik's party, another group of Inuits, that Fitzjames and the Terror's crew appear to have suffered the same fate. Their description of the death of so many men shook us to the core. We were left in no doubt as to the authenticity of their story. The ultimate proof was contained in Crozier's log, which Anik found there and gave to us. I've read it and can't imagine what the folks at home will make of it...if we hand it over.'

'Best if we don't,' suggested Rob. 'Their families don't deserve to be inflicted with the truth, better that they retain the good and happy memories, rather than the alternative.'

Col nodded his head in agreement before adding, 'we did try and find Fitzjames's party ourselves but it was a near impossible task. We headed south for the winter instead. Right now, after hearing your account, I'm glad we did. Finding Fitzjames's as well as Crozier's men would have done for me. My despair at encountering the Erebus crew was bad enough, but the misfortune of the Terror's crew in similar circumstance would have been too much for any man.'

'God rest 'em,' offered Tom, then all fell silent, unable to continue their conversation.

'Best put all the logbooks together, until we decide what's to become of them,' suggested Davy.

'Aye lad, we'll do that,' agreed Tom. 'Make sure they're well bound in the oilskins and wrap them again in one of Col's beaver pelts for safekeeping, if Makwa agrees.'

Begrudgingly, Makwa did agree, although he did think that would be the last he saw of one of his precious beaver pelts.

Tala, seeing his reluctance, chastised him in her own language, but his good humour returned when Col offered two gold sovereigns for his loss.

'So,' continued Tom, 'if we all agree, we've to decide on our aliases. I'm not one for taking chances if the Admiralty are looking for scapegoats.'

'Agreed,' said Rob and Davy in unison.

'Me too,' affirmed Col.

'Well 'Two Cats,' you've got yours,' laughed Davy, 'but I'm for something sensible. I reckon Stephen will be fine and I'll keep the surname.'

'Sounds good. Does that mean I've another nephew?' queried Tom, not expecting an answer. 'Anyway, I'm keeping my Christian name, otherwise I'll get confused.'

'Same with me,' said Rob, 'but I'll adopt 'Carpenter' as a good fit for a surname.'

'Right you are then, Mr Carpenter, now what do you think to 'Harding' for mine? That'ull please Marie at least, should she ever recognise me as the same person.'

'A good choice,' Uncle Tom, enthused Davy, which only left Col grumbling and undecided. 'I'll leave mine until later,' Col insisted.

'We should leave at first light tomorrow,' stated Makwa in his best English, interspersed with sign language.

'Agreed,' said Tom, impressed with Makwa's language skills.

'We need rest now,' suggested Tala. 'It's been an eventful day and the cats are already asleep, which indicates to me that we should be too! Tomorrow will be a long day, but if we make good progress, we'll be in Fort York in seven more.'

'God willing,' said Davy.

CHAPTER TEN

Fort York, Hudson Bay – April 1850

Davy, Tom and Rob's lives were transformed from the first moment they'd set eyes on Col's party of Yellowknives. They seemed imbued with a real sense of renewed hope and approached it with vigour and resolve. So much so, that they made excellent progress along the coast, following a route frequently employed by the Yellowknives themselves.

Makwa gave them guidance on how to conserve energy when paddling their canoe. Until recently, their brave attempts at controlling the vessel in difficult offshore and inland currents had met with limited success, which gave rise to much mirth and laugher amongst the Indians. Eventually, they could stand it no longer and volunteered to instruct the 'white men' by taking it in turns to exchange places, one at a time, in the Mohican canoe. The instruction was initially slow and painful, but a week into the journey to York, all three managed a passable 'image' of Yellowknife expertise.

'Easy,' said Rob, congratulating himself on a difficult manoeuvre around a large round rock.

'Easy,' mimicked one of the Indians, raising his eyebrows in anticipation of the imminent collision with a second boulder, hidden behind the one Rob had just negotiated.

Rob just managed to shout, 'spoke too soon,' before their canoe overturned and his comrades received a ducking, which included Mitzi and Fritz.

Fortunately, they were only a few yards away from a riverbank and the bedraggled cats were first to reach safety, although clearly annoyed.

Col was in stitches and couldn't stop laughing. That instigated more infectious laughter as the Yellowknives joined in, but not before they assisted in dragging the canoe to the bank.

It was obvious that they should make camp at that spot for the night, their clothes needed drying and a campfire needed to be lit. Tala took the opportunity of their embarrassment to brief the sailors on what to expect at and around Fort York.

After they'd eaten and their clothes were dry, all nine gathered around the fire to discuss their intentions and formulate a plan.

'We don't want to create suspicions regarding ourselves as strange travelling companions,' advised Tala, 'so Makwa should go on ahead to open negotiations with the 'Cree' and 'Assiniboine' Indians, who inhabit the areas around Fort York. We cannot trade directly with the Hudson Bay Company and must use the services of these tribes as a go between. We have to respect their role, as these are their lands on which they trap, hunt and fish for the benefit of the population of the Fort.

'We trade with them, they obtain the goods we want for our tribes and they make a living for themselves. We have benefitted from this exchange for many moons, almost since my grandfather met Samuel Hearne and it works well.

Tala continued, 'The fur trade here is well established and no one will be suspicious of your presence once our bartering is complete. I believe you will be able to blend in, using your aliases and arrange your passage home on one of the many ships which call in the summer months.'

Makwa intervened at that point. He was obviously giving advice through Tala regarding the geography of the Fort and factory facility. She nodded appropriately and rarely interrupted Makwa during his advice, save to ask a question. Makwa's satisfied smile indicated that he'd said his 'piece' and waited for Tala to translate.

'Makwa wishes you to know that the buildings of the Fort—' she paused, drawing a plan in the dirt with a stick, 'are laid out in an 'H' formation, with the depot building...he says 'Great House', which the Cree call 'Kichewaskahikun' in the centre of the 'H'. The sides house fur stores, provision shops, trading rooms, officers' and servants' quarters of the Trading Company. There is also an armoury; all are contained by a wooden palisade. The main gate is directly in line with the entrance to the depot.

'Outside the palisade, further from the river, *Hayes*, he believes it's named, are manufacturing shops and other dwellings on boardwalks, like a village you told me about *Two Cats*. They have a Blacksmith, a bakehouse and traders dwellings. There is also a graveyard and the beginnings of a church and school. Barrels are made at a Cooperage, I think that is the word and a house that sells drink, which makes men swear and stagger!'

Tom pursed his lips to hide his smile, but refrained from any comment, as it obviously was not to Tala's liking. Rob, too, noticed, but he'd quickly turned away, hiding his face from view.

Tom felt obliged to offer an explanation with respect to the taverns of London, as clearly, Tala's understanding of the 'evil' drink, was limited. 'We have such places where we live, in the big city. In fact, my Marie runs one.'

Tala was impressed. 'Is she a chief?' she asked.

'Not exactly Tala,' replied Tom, 'but she certainly knows when to 'throw out' the men who swear and stagger.' He laughed somewhat unconvincingly, as he was not sure how Tala might react. The image of a lady manhandling drunkards might be difficult to comprehend. However, Tala clenched her fists, raised her arms and uttered, 'Strong Woman,' which apparently indicated her approval.

The following day, Makwa wasted little time in conducting his business with the Cree tribe he respected. Previous negotiations in other years formulated a lasting bond of trust and friendship. Both tribes had gained and prospered from the relationship.

Unbeknown to Makwa or his followers, a French fur trader who was also conducting a transaction with the Cree, observed Makwa proudly displaying his two gold sovereigns to his Cree friends. Leduc, never one to ignore any unscrupulous avenue of making money, overheard their conversation with reference to a *'Whiteman's'* money belt, with whom they were travelling. Pierre Leduc's curiosity was instantly alerted to the prospect of relieving this particular *Whiteman* of his money belt, although he was averse to tackling the inordinately powerful Makwa to relieve him of his two sovereigns. He determined that he would follow Makwa when he left the Cree settlement.

Leduc was patient, waiting until Makwa left alone, later that evening. Fortunately for Leduc, Makwa's three fellow Yellowknives opted to stay with the Cree until the following day.

Tracking an Indian was difficult at the best of times, but Leduc succeeded in keeping a safe distance, until Makwa arrived at Tala's camp. Leduc was surprised at first to be confronted with a group of Inuits and a Yellowknife girl, but soon realised they were in fact 'White men' and 'English'. He frowned in consternation; which one was in possession of the money belt?

'Patience, patience,' Leduc reminded himself. However, he couldn't believe his luck when he observed the Yellowknife girl helping one of the men divest himself of his tunic in the subdued light of the campfire.

'You need some balm on that abrasion, Col,' explained Tala, as she examined his shoulder. 'It's not good to capsize a canoe and not expect an injury.'

Col grinned sheepishly, but allowed Tala to administer some balm to the wound, which gave Leduc enough time, quite fortuitously, to sight Col's money belt.

'Well now,' said Leduc to himself, 'that's saved me some time.' With that he departed the scene. He would need help to relieve Col of the hoped for gold sovereign cache.

Leduc and two other frontier men, Armand Picard and Louis Riel sat conspiratorially, but unnoticed by the many traders of the well-frequented tavern, outside the palisade. Their position in a corner booth, hunched over a rough-hewn trestle table attracted little attention. The light from the flickering candle hid their features, but reflected on the bottle of fine cognac and their three glasses.

'There'll be plenty of this stuff once we get our hands on those sovereigns,' encouraged Leduc.

'Is that so,' hedged Armand. 'And just what do we have to do to secure them?'

'Pretty obvious, I'd say,' Louis butted in.

'Yes, all right,' continued Armand, slightly irritated, 'but just how are we going to go about it?'

'I'll explain, so listen carefully,' said Pierre, 'we can't afford any mistakes.'

⊰※⊱

Tom, Davy and Rob left camp that evening to reconnoitre and assess the prospect of securing a passage on one of the ships berthed at Fort York. Makwa's intention was to return to the Cree camp to collect the goods bartered for the furs and join his fellow tribesmen for another night of exchanging stories and companionship, which left Tala and Col alone.

'There's an opportunity for them to get to know each other,' joked Tom knowingly. 'Have you seen the way they gaze into one another's eyes?'

'I don't believe there's much doubt as to their feelings,' commented Rob. 'Much the same as your besotted, if drunken approaches to Marie at *The Jolly Sailor*. God only knows what she saw in you that night Tom, but she must have seen something, otherwise she wouldn't have agreed to marry you!' Rob laughed to emphasise his good-humoured remarks, although Tom knew his friend too well to take offence.

'All right, I admit I was slightly merry. Anyway, that's beside the point, are we looking for three berths aboard or four? Our engineer friend may not be joining us I fear.'

⊰※⊱

The three Frenchmen approached the camp with caution, after observing the departure of Tom, Davy, Rob and Makwa.

'We make this quick,' emphasised Pierre. 'Take out the Englishman with a blow to the back of his head, relieve him of his money belt and maybe have some fun with the squaw.'

Riel and Picard's eyes glinted salaciously at the added bonus; they weren't adverse to the suggestion and actively welcomed the prospect; women were in short supply at the Fort.

'We'll be on our way back before she realises what's happened to her,' sneered Pierre.

'That's not going to happen,' said Riel pointedly. 'There'll not be a witness.' He drew out his knife and felt the edge of the blade with his thumb to emphasise the point. 'We're agreed then?'

The others nodded, accepting the implied solution with barely a thought as to the consequences.

'Right then, let's go,' ordered Pierre and all three proceeded to the edge of the camp, where they halted momentarily to ascertain the position of their victims.

Col and Tala were facing away from them, warming their hands in front of the fire.

Quickly and stealthily, the three Frenchmen crept up behind them. The element of surprise was complete. Realisation dawned too late as Col was hit a glancing blow to the side of his head, which rendered him immediately unconscious.

Tala turned and encountered a grinning Louis Riel, bearing down on her at pace. She tumbled to the ground as Picard stifled her scream midway through, but not before her half cry echoed around the surrounding valley.

'Did you hear that Davy?' asked Tom with concern.

'Sounded like a scream, but incomplete,' replied Davy.

'Could have been an owl,' suggested Rob.

'Nah, I've not heard an owl hoot like that, don't be daft.'

'Well, let's just listen awhile,' persisted Tom.

The three, some four hundred yards from camp, crouched down and listened, but heard nothing. Meanwhile at the camp, Picard and Riel wasted no time ripping away Tala's clothing, exposing her bare thighs and femininity, whilst holding her down and preventing her from screaming again. Louis cuffed her around the head, warning her to keep completely silent, but she still struggled to prevent what she knew they wanted. They had little intention of being thwarted from their lust.

'Hey you two, I've not retrieved the money belt yet,' admonished Pierre. 'Help me first.'

'Not a chance,' answered Riel, 'we're busy.'

In that instant, Mitzi and Fritz joined the fray, claws flexed, hissing, growling and spitting, as only cats can do when they're fighting, usually each other. Mitzi leapt at Riel, slashing his face and eye, whilst Fritz attacked the back of Picard's head, causing him to scream in agony, as claws and teeth raked his neck. The astonished and bloodied men released Tala in their frantic haste to rid themselves of their furry nightmare. Picard managed to dislodge Fritz and dashed him on to a rock, breaking the cat's hind leg, but Mitzi hung on to Riel. His screams could be heard miles away. Consequently, Tom, Davy and Rob were left in no doubt that trouble brewed back at camp. They rushed back and were soon face to face with the attackers. Riel, who was totally incapacitated, his face slashed to ribbons by Mitzi and now blinded in one eye, with blood obscuring the other eye's vision, crawled, moaning and uncomprehendingly toward the campfire. Mitzi had finally left him alone, but still hissed menacingly.

It was now the three Englishmen's turn to confront Picard and Leduc, who had successfully relieved Col of the money belt. Leduc held the money belt in his left hand and the wooden cosh, with which he'd hit Col, in his right.

'If you want this back, you'll have to take it,' warned Pierre, indicating his prize.

Tom glanced at Rob, then Davy before raising himself to his full height and producing his deck knife. Rob paralleled Tom's movements and took out his own knife, whilst Davy skirted to his right, picking up a Yellowknife axe on the way, to prevent the Frenchmen escaping.

What happened next both appalled and fascinated the three sailors, as a Yellowknife execution followed swiftly before their eyes.

Tala crept up on Picard, slashing his ankle tendons with a crisp movement of her own sharp blade, wherein he collapsed in anguished pain before a returning Makwa, who'd also heard the scream, despatched him with an arrow to his throat. Leduc, his next victim, had only a split second to react before Makwa's second arrow pierced his eye, continuing through to his brain. He was dead before he hit the ground.

Makwa signalled to Tala. The mesmerised Englishmen were only spectators to what followed. A mercenary Tala took her cue. She walked slowly toward the campfire and took Riel by the hair, jolting his head back before cutting his jugular in one swift movement of her knife. His life ebbed away, but terrifyingly he witnessed, with his one remaining eye, the squaw removing his trousers to cut away his genitals, before throwing them on the fire.

Tala, seemingly unmoved by any of the events, headed toward where Fritz lay injured. She picked him up lovingly, shushing him with tenderness and concern, in sharp contrast to her recent actions. She laid him on a multi-coloured blanket, then proceeded to fashion a splint for his broken leg, before binding it securely with leather thongs, whilst Mitzi looked on with strange understanding.

Makwa was the first to speak in broken English, 'I return quickly, bad sounds, much to do.'

Tom nodded, making a mental note not to cross any Yellowknives in the future.

'Help Makwa dispose of bodies in river,' the Indian continued, referring to himself unnecessarily.

Davy, Rob and Tom were more than willing and did his bidding. They'd consider the consequences of their actions later.

A short while after the exertion of ridding the camp of the bodies, Col regained consciousness. 'What happened? Oh my head aches,' muttered Col.

'Where do we begin,' said Davy, still trying to make sense of all that he'd witnessed.

At that moment, Tala came over, 'Fritz is sleeping,' she explained. 'I will tell Col, it is better that I tell him 'everything'.

'You're a very brave woman,' said Tom matter of factly.

'I know,' replied Tala without modesty. It is our way and a new day is fast approaching...we do not have time for regrets or bad memories in this life.'

Davy, listening intently, was not so sure, as a man named Goldner fleetingly impacted on his own memory.

CHAPTER ELEVEN

A Hasty Goodbye

An uneasy silence prevailed as none in the Yellowknife camp felt capable of meaningful conversation. Daylight brought the events of the night into stark reality.

Tala, still tending to the injured Fritz, seemed strangely defiant in spite of her ordeal. Save for the evidence of Fritz's broken leg and Col's sore head, an observer would not know anything unusual had occurred. Col, appraised in detail of the Frenchmen's attack by Tala, could only admire her fortitude and determination.

Tala was the first to speak. 'We cannot stay here; it will only be a matter of time before the bodies are found. It will be obvious to some that the wounds on the traders were caused by arrows.'

'Makwa,' she instructed, 'you must go to the Cree camp and obtain our traded goods and return with our men. Then we must say goodbye to you, Davy, Tom, Rob and...' she hesitated, 'you too Col, before returning to our homelands. I think you will be safe my English friends, if you proceed with your plan to obtain passage on one of the ships.'

'There is someone who may be able to help you at the school. I met her last time we traded here, helping her to revive a child who had fallen into the river and was not breathing. She's also French, but speaks good English, better than me,' Tala said modestly. 'Her name is Marie Cayer.'

'I reckon I'll remember that,' said Tom, 'same as my Marie back in London.'

Tala continued, 'She knows many people, so you will be in good hands. Mention my name and that of Makwa who revived the child, but last night's events must remain unspoken, as should your association with the expedition.'

While this conversation was taking place, Col was looking on in anguish. His obvious distress did not go unnoticed by Davy. 'Anything wrong with Tala's advice?' enquired Davy.

'No, nothing at all,' Col lied, but an unconvinced Davy persisted.

'You're not a very good liar, what's really troubling you?'

'If I say, your Uncle Tom and Rob will give me a lot of stick. It's just that I can't believe Tala is abandoning us now, after all we've been through this past year.'

'Abandoning you, I think you mean Col,' probed Davy.

'Yes, all right, me then, or is it that those Frenchies had a serious effect on her and she's washing her hands of all us foreigners?'

'Could be, or it might not be that at all,' continued Davy. 'Why don't you ask her?'

However, Col, deep in thought, was not given the opportunity, as Tala turned to face him and address him personally. Their eyes met, as the others watched. Col was surprised, her smile radiated a warmth that he'd not experienced before and her eyes conveyed a mystique that he found himself powerless to resist. At that moment he truly believed that eyes were the windows of the soul and that he could see into her innermost being.

What she whispered was certain to change his life forever. She gestured with open hands, palms upward, to where Mitzi and Fritz sat on the blanket. 'Two cats, leave...*Two Cats*, stay.' Her meaning was abundantly clear and Col's hesitation lasted but one fleeting moment.

'Time to throw caution to the wind, Col,' suggested Tom with amusement.

'Aye lad, you'll not do any better,' Rob contributed, 'guess we'll only be booking a passage for three.'

Col acknowledged his friends and vigorously shook their hands as Tala placed her arm around his waist. Confirmation of their future together was understood. Even Makwa looked on encouragingly, as already he too had great respect for *Two Cats*.

'Now all you have to do is tell Akaitcho,' advised Makwa in their own language.

'Oh my father knew before we left,' replied Tala, which Makwa found hilarious.

He laughed outrageously and so did the others, even if they were unaware of what they were actually laughing about.

⸙

By mid-afternoon, their campsite was cleared and little remained of their occupation. Tala, Col and the Yellowknives faced Rob, Tom and Davy for the last time, as Tala gave one last piece of advice to Davy. 'Remember to check Fritz's splint regularly, he should heal very quickly as it is a clean break, but prevent him from chasing anything. Keep him tethered and feed him well. If it wasn't for Mitzi and Fritz attacking the French invaders and alerting everyone, Col and I would be dead,' she shuddered momentarily, before crossing the small distance between them to kiss each on the cheek in turn.

'Maybe our paths will cross again. You will be welcome in the lands of Tala and *Two Cats*,' she promised. 'But now we must leave.'

Col once again shook everyone's hand and hugged each of his shipmates in turn. He personally doubted that they'd set eyes on each other again, but he would remember them and their friendship for the rest of his days.

෴

Soon Davy, Rob and Tom were alone once more as the retreating Yellowknives disappeared beyond a hill.

'Incidentally, Col gave us this,' indicated Davy, brandishing the money-belt. 'Reckons we might need it on the way home, or to convince a captain to take us aboard. I'll keep it safe, along with my tunic from the ship in this oilskin, it's too obvious as a money-belt.' They too, turned to leave on the route to Fort York.

෴

Rob shouted to the others, 'There's the school Tala mentioned.'

They approached cautiously, not wanting to alarm the young woman who seemed to be having difficulty repairing a gate at the centre of a picket fence, which marked the entrance pathway to the school. The school itself was obviously incomplete. Rough hewn timbers, some in position, some lying on the ground indicated that the project was well underway. All four walls were in position, but the roof was only partially completed.

'Marie Cayer?' enquired Rob, while Davy and Tom looked on; Davy, holding Fritz in a makeshift hide and wicker basket, with Mitzi peering inquisitively from between his legs.

The woman turned to address them, smiling in amusement at their appearance; dressed as Inuits, but obviously English, with two cats in attendance, one in a basket and one eyeing her speculatively, as if food might be in the offing. 'Whom, might I ask, wishes to know?' she hedged.

'Oh, I'm Rob *Carpenter*,' replied Rob, using his alias, 'and this is Tom *Harding* and *Stephen* Young, he's the young man holding Fritz the cat.'

'And the other one?' the woman prompted.

'Oh, sorry, I see what you mean,' apologised Rob. 'That's Mitzi, our other cat.'

'Isn't she gorgeous,' enthused the woman, not expecting an answer. 'Well, I am Marie Cayer, so, just how can I help you? But first, please tell me how you know my name?'

Rob, warming to the woman, who seemed to be around his age and attractive in a traditional way, began a lengthy explanation, beginning with their mutual acquaintance, Tala.

'Better come inside and continue your story, it's warm, if a little cramped under the temporary canvas roof. I can offer you a hot drink.'

'Thank you, that's very kind,' replied Rob on behalf of them all.

They sat on a crude bench, little more than a plank of wood, whilst Rob told their abbreviated story, of living with the Inuits and existing as fur traders, eventually coming into contact with the Yellowknives and Tala. Whether Marie believed them or not was open to interpretation; nothing untoward showed in her demeanour, as she seemed intrigued and interested in their story.

Marie listened intently for more than an hour, until Rob finished the tale. Although *Stephen* and Tom's embellishments were frequent and excitable, the interruptions only served to enhance their story.

Marie was impressed, especially with the fact that they were able to converse in Inuit, but essentially, she still wished to know why they'd come to her for assistance.

Rob sensed that she would ask again, so pre-empted her question. 'Why are we here? Well, Tala advised that you are well acquainted with the hierarchy within the Hudson Bay Company and for that matter, some of the captains', officers' and crews' from the many vessels visiting York. We're intent on obtaining a passage on one of them. Perhaps you may be able to assist?'

'Well, yes, I do know that the *Prince Rupert* is due in about five weeks time. We're expecting some equipment and books to be on board for the school. I hope we'll be able to finish the roof by then, otherwise the books will be in a sorry state if we're still dependent on the canvas. Once the damp gets to them they're practically useless.'

Tom chipped in, 'Well, you look as though you're nearly there with respect to your slate roof.

'Not exactly,' explained Marie, 'we've all the Welsh slate we need, but our carpenter suffered a fall two weeks ago; he was supervising the men on constructing the roof timbers. Anyway, all work's stopped, as it has to be right with the pitch, because of the snowfall here in York. I don't suppose your name lends itself to a past occupation before you became an Inuit does it Rob?' she said jokingly.

Tom looked at Rob questioningly and *Stephen* hid his face, pretending to attend to Fritz, although he couldn't help muttering, *'it might.'*

'Sorry *Stephen*,' apologised Marie, 'I didn't quite hear you.'

Rob pulled a face in *Stephen's* direction, but smiled at Marie a second later. 'What he's trying to say, is that you've hit the nail on the head, so to speak. That's exactly what I'm famous for,' Rob said, proudly and immodestly, 'and maybe I can help, at least until your carpenter recovers, assuming that occurs before the *Prince Rupert* sails for England.'

'That would be wonderful and very generous of you to offer your time and skills for the school,' enthused Marie, 'although I'm unable to offer you much in return, save for accommodation and food...for all of you of course,' she added. 'I've no doubt that I'll be able to help when I speak to David...oh, he's the Captain of the *Rupert*, who has helped with funding for the school, cajoling others for donations. He's been with the ship for a while now and knows many people and potential benefactors both here and in England. We have a good relationship, so I'm sure he'll assist with a berth on the ship.'

'That sounds promising,' said Tom speculatively. 'I believe I've heard of the *Prince Rupert*, a four masted barque named after a cousin of Charles II.'

'How do you know that?' enquired Marie.

'Saw her once in London. Her bosun knew all about the ship's history and was only too keen to share his knowledge over a drink,' explained Tom.

'I take it you're familiar with the ways of the sea then, Mr Harding?' stated Marie.

'In my early days, yes,' replied Tom. 'I have some experience of ships and seafaring.'

'Good, that will help me when I speak to Captain Herd.' Marie seemed pleased that she'd have something to offer when the time came.

Before Marie continued, they were interrupted by another visitor, obviously familiar with the school, who flamboyantly sat down next to Marie, before casting a quizzical eye on the three men. 'Whom might these fine fellows be? You must introduce me at once,' insisted the young woman.

'Of course, Valerie, they're my guests who will be helping with the building works until they secure a passage home to England. Tom, Rob and *Stephen*, meet Valerie Davies, she helps with the teaching here and also assists her father at the church where he preaches. They're also in the midst of completing that building. It's a wonder she finds time to teach as well as supervise the construction. Valerie is very practical and determined,' complimented Marie.

Valerie smiled in appreciation, before adding, 'I do have some failings gentlemen, but my friend and I need all the help we can muster, so welcome.'

Valerie, younger than Marie, but about the same age as *Stephen* impressed the men with her forthright personality, taking to her immediately, especially *Stephen*. It was the first time since meeting Catherine in *The Jolly Sailor* that he'd noticed another female, apart from Tapeesa, who'd mothered him unconditionally. His inner embarrassment was compounded when she looked him straight in the eyes, smiled disarmingly and then asked directly, 'Just why are you dressed as an Inuit, *Stephen*?' ignoring Tom and Rob completely.

Stephen, unprepared as he was for any question from this young woman, coloured noticeably before stammering a response. 'Tapeesa made it for me.'

'Is she your girlfriend?' teased Valerie, causing Rob and Tom to guffaw loudly.

'No, no,' he managed, 'she looked after me when I was sick...she's old,' he spluttered.

Tom turned to Rob and whispered, 'methinks he protests too much.'

The remark didn't go unnoticed by Marie, but she came to *Stephen's* assistance by retelling an abbreviated version of their story, which seemed to satisfy Valerie...for the moment.

'Anyway,' said Valerie, 'I'm sure we'll be seeing a lot of each other if you're assisting Marie for a few weeks.'

'We'll look forward to that,' offered Tom.

'Oh, nearly forgot,' beamed Valerie, 'I brought you this from father, Marie; he's been baking again, how he finds time I don't know.'

'Madeira cake?' guessed Marie.

'Of course,' replied Valerie. 'Perhaps *Stephen*, Tom and Rob might like a piece?'

Tom looked at his nephew and *Stephen* reciprocated, both chuckled, although *Stephen* was still flustered by her presence; his bewildered countenance providing a great source of amusement for Rob and, indeed, Marie.

Valerie was just about to take her leave when her father appeared in the doorway, slightly out of breath. 'Oh hello everyone, didn't know you had company Marie, sorry for the interruption.'

Marie hurriedly introduced her new acquaintances as Patrick seemed agitated and wished to impart some information.

'They've found three bodies on the riverbank downstream, French fur traders, but they're in a pretty sorry state. They are bringing them back to the church for burial, after the authorities are satisfied there's been no foul play; mind, just how they are going to achieve that I'm not sure. However, I'm certain they are the same three who accosted Valerie and Marie, making lewd suggestions after the evening church service last Sunday, when the congregation had all but left. It was a good job I appeared when I did, as they seemed intent on mischief.'

'I believe they wanted much more than mischief, father,' emphasised Valerie. 'Marie and I were frightened...they exuded evil, so I for one won't be troubled by their deaths. They probably deserved it.'

'Valerie, that's very unchristian of you. Do you always have to be so forthright?' asked Patrick.

'Well it's served me well in the past and I like speaking my mind,' replied Valerie. 'At least they won't be bothering Marie and I again. Their presence last Sunday made us both feel extremely uncomfortable.'

'That's as may be, Valerie, but they're dead now and it's my duty to provide a Christian burial.'

Valerie raised her eyebrows at her father's statement, but refrained from comment. She'd made her point on behalf of Marie and herself.

While this conversation was taking place, the three men exchanged worried glances, which didn't go unnoticed by Marie.

'Well, that's the news anyway,' said Patrick. 'I'm very pleased to meet you all by the way,' he continued, before retreating as swiftly as he'd entered.

'He's always busy,' explained Valerie.

The following morning, Marie showed Rob around the school and explained her ideas and requirements for the roof structure.

'I'd like to thank you again for 'volunteering' to help,' emphasising the actual word and placing her hand on his forearm at the same instant.

Rob was pleased and ecstatic at her closeness. It seemed a long time since an attractive woman had made such a simple overture to him. She smiled encouragingly, letting her hand dally a mite longer than was absolutely necessary.

'You're most welcome, Marie, I'm actually grateful to be doing something I really enjoy,' Rob explained, enlarging on the work he'd done for Tom's Marie, those many years ago in London. 'Tom and *Stephen* intend to 'pitch in' as well, so with a bit of luck, we'll be finishing your roof and maybe a few other things by the time the ship sails.'

'Oh good, but it's a pity you're not staying longer, as I've desks and benches that need a skilled carpenter's attention,' qualified Marie with another disarming smile.

Rob felt himself waver, almost promising to stay longer and maybe securing a passage on another ship later, although he knew at the back of his mind that that might not be possible, if the ice blocked the channels in the *Bay*.

The next four weeks passed rapidly, with everyone working hard to achieve what was closest to Marie's heart...a roof for the school.

Fortunately for Rob and his colleagues, the three Frenchmen were dispatched underground by the Sexton and Patrick without anyone discovering what actually happened to them. The deaths of three 'ne'er do wells' in a society where arguments were common and deaths frequent was hardly worth much of a mention after the event.

Only Valerie remained inquisitive...three men arrive and three men die...surely, she thought, it must be coincidental? Her misgivings, however, were put to one side in the hustle and bustle of building works, until one evening, when visiting Marie. She'd noticed the oilskin packages amidst the men's belongings, which they'd moved to facilitate the fabrication of some benches.

'What are those Marie?' she asked.

'Well, Rob says they contain some artefacts from the Yellowknives, which they're taking back as curios. He says there's a market for them amongst the rich folk in London,' explained Marie.

'Oh really, do you think they'd mind if we took a look?' hedged Valerie.

'I'm not sure, but I don't suppose they'd mind,' she replied, handing the smallest to Valerie.

Valerie opened it carefully, so that she could re-seal the package, without anyone realising it had been opened. Marie looked on nervously, but was pleased when Valerie only discovered an item of clothing – a sailor's tunic. A disappointed, 'hmm' emanated from Valerie's lips, but she persisted, examining the outer pockets until she came across an inch square green velvet pouch.

'What's that?' enquired Marie.

'Something and nothing,' replied Valerie. 'It's a velvet pouch with a very small message inside.'

'What's it say?' encouraged Marie, forgetting her earlier reticence.

'It's only just legible, but I can make it out: *Sew it on the inside of your tunic, so that I'll always be with you. I love you, Catherine xx. PS Come back safely.*'

Intrigued, but equally disappointed, Valerie examined the tunic more closely. 'Does this package belong to *Stephen* by any chance?' enquired Valerie of Marie.

'I believe it does,' she replied.

Valerie nodded in acceptance and at the same time located a silver button on the inside of the tunic. She gazed at the miniature portrait of another attractive young woman, contained within the parameters of the button itself. 'How exquisite,' she murmured, then, 'Lucky you'. Why is it, Marie, that when I set my eyes on an apparently eligible bachelor, they're already taken?'

'I thought you'd set your sights on *Stephen* from the start,' commiserated Marie, 'but it looks like you are right. That's a beautiful miniature portrait.'

'Oh well…' she began to say, before Marie interrupted—

'Quick, replace the tunic, I hear them coming back.'

Valerie had just enough time to accomplish the task before the door opened and the three men entered.

'You look guilty of something,' joked *Stephen*, unaware of just how near he'd come to witnessing their inquisitiveness.

Marie and Valerie exchanged glances.

'If only you knew,' teased Valerie, without giving anything away. 'Actually, I've some good news, the *Prince Rupert* has docked this afternoon. Marie says she'll introduce you to Captain Herd tomorrow. He'll be at the Hudson Bay offices, while the ship unloads her cargo.'

'That's good timing,' smiled Tom, 'we've finished the roof already and Rob's started on some benches; he's really enjoying himself.'

Rob, catching Marie's obviously sad demeanour, winked encouragingly, which immediately revived her more natural optimism.

Valerie also noted the exchange, realising that she was not the only one harbouring affectionate thoughts.

'Well,' she said to herself, 'they haven't embarked on the good ship *Rupert*, yet.'

CHAPTER TWELVE

Meetings and Consequences
May/June 1850

The *Prince Rupert*, a majestic four masted, three hundred foot barque, lay alongside the substantial wooden jetty, adjacent the Hudson Bay offices, its decks a hive of activity. The hatch boards and tarpaulins, which previously covered the cargo holds, were stacked neatly to one side, to enable the cargo to be offloaded by local gangs of stevedores. The gangs contained a mixture of nationalities, including indigenous Indians. Her own crew supervised the discharge under the practised eye of the *Rupert's* mate, Eugene Conlon, an irascible, non-compromising mariner, whose weather beaten features spoke volumes and true testament to his seafaring capabilities. His only failing was a drop or two of gin in his off duty moments, which undoubtedly cost him promotion to Captain on more than one occasion. However, his expertise and knowledge of stability, navigation and sailing ships in general left others in awe, which afforded him great respect overall.

Captain David Herd, the Master of the vessel also held the ageing seafarer in great esteem and trusted him completely, when absent himself, whilst engaged in negotiations ashore with officials from the 'Honourable' Company.

Captain Herd was a frequent visitor to the Fort and, consequently, well known to most of the hierarchy at the offices and even the lowly clerks whose duties involved recording, in meticulous detail many official documents and ships' manifests. Cargoes were complex issues and profit and loss were dependent on the accuracy of such an 'apparently' mundane occupation. However, David Herd acknowledged the clerks' importance and often directed a cheery word in their direction, which gave rise to a welcome and mutual respect.

'Good morning David! How the devil are you?' The enthusiastic greeting metered out by none other than the General Manager of the Hudson Bay Company at Fort York, gave an insight into their relationship, nurtured over several years of admiration and understanding.

'Good morning, Sir Geoffrey, none the worse for wear as it happens, in answer to your question. Our passage this time was thankfully uneventful and we made good progress, actually saving a day to boot.'

'Excellent, glad to hear it, I know what the North Atlantic can throw at our ships' on occasion. If you're not battling fierce storms and heavy seas, you're always on the lookout for those large chunks of ice.' Sir Geoffrey Short laughed at his own joke, but did not underestimate the power of the sea or the perils of encountering an iceberg. Fortunately, David Herd knew his Hudson Bay friend's personality and character, so treated the remark as it was meant to be taken, which was noticeably light hearted and without offence. 'But first things first, may I offer you some refreshment?'

'Thank you, I will,' replied David. 'Tea would be most welcome.'

'Of course,' responded Sir Geoffrey, 'and perhaps after our official duties, you'll join me for lunch. I've invited a mutual acquaintance of ours to join us, Marie Cayer, from the school. Apparently, she has a request to ask of you. My wife always enjoys her company, so a convivial lunch with female companionship sounds good to me. What do you say?'

'I'd love to,' enthused David. 'Marie's an intriguing lady and an interesting conversationalist. Your own wife, Ann, can inject some thought provoking ideas too, so I'll look forward to an entertaining lunch.'

'Good, that's settled then, I'll send a message to Ann, to arrange the meal,' confirmed Sir Geoffrey.

Soon afterward, both men were engaged on the more mundane issues surrounding the *Prince Rupert's* visit.

'I've been invited to lunch with Sir Geoffrey and his wife Ann,' advised Marie. 'Captain Herd will be there too. Ann informs me that I'll be able to broach the subject of securing a berth for the three of you aboard the *Prince Rupert*, during the lunch. David's quite approachable and I'm sure I'll have little difficulty in convincing him to take on some extra crew, intent on working their passage to England. He's quite fond of me you see.'

Rob frowned at Marie's last remark, which didn't go unnoticed by Tom and *Stephen*, or, for that matter, Marie herself, although she feigned ignorance of his troubled expression. *Maybe Valerie has a point* thought Marie delightedly.

'Thank you Marie, but a brief introduction is all that we require. I'm sure that we'll be able to explain our situation to him personally. So, if you're able to arrange a meeting with him later today or tomorrow, if he's not too busy himself. I'm sure we'll be fine,' explained Tom. 'We have some experience of seafaring you see, before we broadened our horizons with the Inuits and Yellowknives in these lands. Admittedly, it does seem a long time ago, but you never forget the joy and freedom of the oceans.'

'I'll do my best then gentlemen, although David is always obliging when it comes to helping me with equipment and books for the school.' This time she turned deliberately and smiled disarmingly in Rob's direction. Rob was almost lost for words as their eyes met, but still managed a feeble, 'Thank you' too, clearing his throat rather unnecessarily, as he broke eye contact.

'Oh, by the way,' said Marie, as if suddenly remembering something she'd forgotten, but actually hadn't at all, 'Valerie mentioned that she'd acquired some second hand clothing at the church, suitable for budding seafarers, as opposed to adopted Inuits. She suggested that you might like to sort through them, *Stephen*, while Rob and Tom finish off their jobs at the school. Her father considered the clothing would be more appropriate if you were all to meet with Captain Herd.'

'That's a good idea Marie; I'll walk over at midday and see Valerie. We do need new clothes, although our sealskin tunics have served us well, they're slightly cumbersome for what we have in mind.'

'That's settled then, I'll send word to Valerie to expect you,' confirmed Marie.

❧

Stephen approached the church gate, which in some ways reminded him of the entrance pathway to the church where his mother Eve took him on a Sunday as a small child. Valerie beckoned to him from a side door, leading to the vestry, where he assumed the clothing was stored, in preparation for his visit. He stopped in his tracks a few steps before the entrance. He couldn't fail to notice that Valerie was attired in a most stunning green velvet dress with lace cuffs and collar. She'd obviously paid significant attention to her jet black hair, which hung in attractive ringlets to her shoulders, while her eyes smiled seductively in welcome.

Stephen, taken aback at first, felt himself drawn to this woman, her sensuous lips were slightly parted, revealing perfect white teeth. She drew her tongue across them slowly, before speaking, although *Stephen* knew beyond doubt that she had already said everything without uttering a word.

'Are you coming in *Stephen*? You seem transfixed to the spot...is there a problem?'

'No...no not at all...yes of course...are the clothes inside?' he asked somewhat inanely.

'There's plenty of choice and I'm sure most will fit you and Rob. Unfortunately, Tom's such a big man, so there's only a few items his size, I think. Why don't you try some on while you're here? Father won't be back for a couple of hours. He's collecting some items brought over on the *Prince Rupert*, so you won't be disturbed in the vestry,' confirmed Valerie.

Just why Valerie wished to emphasise the whereabouts of her father left *Stephen* with a few misgivings, but he went ahead with her suggestion anyway. He believed that, as they were in an annex to a place of worship, her suggestive teasing would remain just that...teasing.

Reluctantly, while she remained the other side of the vestry door, he disrobed, before selecting an excellent blue cotton shirt and dark navy trousers, along with a double-breasted naval style jacket and black boots. He placed one boot's sole to the sole of his foot to check the size and seemed pleased with the result; still room for a thick woollen sock. He was just about to select a cotton neckerchief, when Valerie entered.

'Oh dear, sorry *Stephen,*' apologised Valerie, 'but I thought you'd be kitted out by now.' However, she refrained from averting her eyes, taking in his naked body avidly. Instead of retreating, she closed the door purposefully behind her and approached to within touching distance of him.

'My, my, you're a handsome man, Stephen,' complimented Valerie, 'with a fine physique. A shame about the scars,' she continued, daring to run her finger along Tapeesa's fine needlework stitching, which had by now healed magnificently, adding an air of masculinity to his bearing.

Stephen stared at her incredulously, dumfounded at her forwardness, he hardly dare breathe, let alone move any muscle in his body.

'Do you find me attractive?' asked Valerie, looking him steadfastly in the eyes.

'Yes,' *Stephen* stammered, wondering if he'd actually said it himself, or could it have been another person hiding in his head?

'Do you want to make love to me…now, *Stephen*?' suggested Valerie seductively, as she moved to kiss him firmly on the lips without soliciting a reply.

Stephen was incapable of resisting her any longer and responded eagerly, returning her kiss passionately, whilst holding her against his naked body. Feeling incredibly guilty, but monumentally aroused, he began raising her velvet dress to a position above her thighs. She was delighted with his response and shifted her position to allow him to caress her virginity.

'I'm not wearing anything under my dress,' she murmured encouragingly.

Before he could continue, a male voice, whom he recognised, boomed out. 'Are you there Valerie? I need some help with the items I brought from the *Rupert*.'

'Oh hell,' expostulated Valerie irreverently, 'just when I was beginning to enjoy you. Quick *Stephen*, put the shirt and trousers on and pretend you're trying on the boots.' She hurried out, carefully smoothing down her dress on the way. 'Coming father!'

Only seconds had passed since her father made his presence felt, but it seemed his whole life passed before him in those moments. He realised he'd had a lucky escape, but continued with the deception, rather than upset Patrick. He donned the outfit he'd selected earlier, chose more clothing for Tom and Rob and carried them out to the churchyard.

'Oh, hello, *Stephen*,' greeted Patrick. 'I see you've acquired a set of clothes; you look almost human again. Oh sorry, I don't mean to be disrespectful to the Inuits.'

'No offence taken, Sir,' replied *Stephen* blushing, although not from the comment, but still in anguish from the consequences that might have befallen Valerie and himself moments before, had it not been for Patrick's unwitting warning shout.

Stephen hurriedly offered an excuse to leave, but thanked Patrick for the clothing. He glanced at Valerie, but refrained from making eye contact again. Fate had intervened, hastening his departure. The relief showed plainly on his face as he exited the church gate en-route to rejoining his colleagues working at the schoolhouse.

CHAPTER THIRTEEN

Homeward Bound
July 1850

'I've spoken to Captain Herd over a very enjoyable lunch with Sir Geoffrey and his wife Ann,' informed Marie. 'He's willing to spare you some time this afternoon aboard the *Rupert* and suggested four o'clock. You're to make yourselves known to the first mate; his name's Eugene Conlon. Apparently, he'll give you the 'once over' and, according to David, he'll have a shrewd idea if you're 'swinging the lead' with minimal seafaring experience. He added, that if you have any misgivings in that direction, then you shouldn't bother attending.'

'Sounds fair enough to me,' admitted Tom. 'What say you two sea-salts?' he jovially enquired of Rob and *Stephen*.

'You don't have to worry on our account, Davy and I have years of experience between us,' replied Rob, before adding, 'Admittedly most of them are mine.' He started laughing until he noticed Marie's quizzical expression, which stopped his joviality abruptly.

'You mean *Stephen*, don't you Rob?' asked Marie, raising an eyebrow.

Up to that point Rob, Tom and Davy himself had kept up the pretence of shielding their real identities, using pseudonyms. Unfortunately for them, Marie was notoriously sharp and quick witted and noticed Rob's *faux pas* immediately.

'Well, Mr Rob Carpenter, am I to assume *Stephen* allowed Patrick to re-baptise him at the church earlier or does *Stephen* just prefer to be called Davy now?' she probed.

The three men fell silent momentarily and glanced at one another with ill-disguised alarm.

'Curiouser and curiouser,' Marie speculated, placing her hand on Rob's arm affectionately. 'Perhaps we should sit down for the explanation. By the look on your faces, I'm certain it's probably a lengthy tale.'

'Can we trust you Marie?' asked Rob earnestly.

'Well, Rob, if that is actually your real name.'

'Oh it is, it is,' confirmed Rob.

'Then I should tell you that I have wondered about you all, although it's obvious you are good men at heart...but you do have secrets!'

'If only you knew,' whispered Tom under his breath, which Marie still heard clearly.

'Actually, that's the second time I've heard that expression in as many days. The first time was when *Stephen*, or is it Davy? said, Valerie and I looked guilty of something, when you returned earlier than expected. She used the phrase, 'if only you knew'. Well, what she was alluding to was the fact that, 'we' were guilty of prying. We opened the oilskin package belonging to *Stephen* and found the miniature of a girl.'

'Catherine,' confirmed Davy.

'That's when we heard you returning, so we quickly packed it away again. We've not repeated our inquisitiveness, although Valerie determined that you were still worth pursuing, despite the portrait. She does like you very much,' explained Marie.

'So I found out at the church,' humphed Davy exasperatedly. 'It's a wonder I escaped with any clothes at all,' he complained.

His Uncle Tom raised an eyebrow at his nephew's statement, but refrained from comment. He bit his lip instead to prevent himself from laughing out loud.

However, Rob did laugh, despite the circumstances, which seemed to embarrass Davy more than his experience with Valerie herself.

'Perhaps we should offer Marie an explanation,' suggested Tom. 'She has helped us tremendously and I'm sure she'll respect our motives.'

'Perhaps I've as much to lose as you,' stated Marie, winking at Rob. 'Valerie isn't the only one interested in you men-folk' she insisted, without any hesitation or coyness.

Rob wasn't alarmed or unhappy at Marie's overtures; in fact he was secretly pleased. In the passing weeks, since Col's departure, his feelings for the schoolteacher had grown. He felt at ease in her company and shared moments of mutual understanding, interspersed with good conversation. He also found her physically attractive, but up to this point dared not tell her, because if he reciprocated, he'd effectively be abandoning Davy and Tom in the process.

Tom watched Marie and Rob intently. He was already ahead of the game, seeing in Rob, his lifelong friend, what Rob was failing to see clearly himself. He resolved to give his friend a nudge!

'I reckon that, after the explanations are over, Davy and I will be the only ones requesting a berth on the *Rupert*,' suggested Tom.

Rob looked at Marie, who smiled at him encouragingly before he cleared his throat to speak again. 'Aye, reckon you're right Bosun, it won't be the first time you've saved my life!'

'Two berths it is then. Come on Davy, let's see Mr Conlon and leave Rob with the explanations.'

Davy and Rob approached the *Rupert* kitted out in their second hand or possibly third hand clothing.

'Where can I find the mate?' enquired Tom of an obviously harassed third mate, currently engaged on ensuring a wooden crate remained secured in a cargo net.

'Bloody fool,' muttered the third mate. 'Not you...'im with is 'ead in the clouds, 'e'd 'ave 'alf the cargo in bits, spread all over the jetty if left to 'is own devices. Wot you want 'im fer anyway?'

'A berth aboard,' answered Tom.

'Well, good luck, 'ope yer better un this fellah...yer both luk the part...Conlon's topside near the mainmast.'

'Thanks for the compliment and the information,' acknowledged Tom as they made their way to the gangplank, before boarding the vessel.

'Eugene Conlon?' said Tom pointedly; ignoring the fact that it was totally obvious that this rugged seafarer before him was none other than the mate himself.

'Who wants to know?' replied Conlon gruffly.

'Tom *Harding* and *Stephen* Young,' responded Davy, using their agreed aliases.

'Ah yes, Captain Herd advised me earlier that you'd be coming aboard.' He eyed up Tom in an instant. 'Don't I know you Mr Harding?' he enquired. 'You're a big man to forget easily and I've a good memory.'

'Not that I recall,' replied Tom. 'Perhaps we've seen each other around the London docks on occasion, before *Stephen* and I left England to try our luck on this side of the Atlantic.'

'That's probably the case then, as I've met a few men in my time over the years. The good ones you remember,' said Con disarmingly.

His next act seemed comical to Davy as he grabbed two short lengths of sisal and threw them at him and Tom. 'You, he said,' indicating Tom. 'Tie me a 'Running Bowline' and put me an eye splice in the tail end and you, young man, put a 'Killick Hitch' around that spar, then tell me what it was also used for...if you can?' Conlon raised an eyebrow in expectation. 'You've a minute,' he instructed, seemingly amused.

The pair wasted little time and both completed their tasks, but only just.

'Not bad at all,' admitted the mate, you've both got seafarers hands, so I reckon you'll be a good bet on deck and up aloft. Know your sails do you?'

Tom and Davy proceeded to 'reel off' the sail and rigging configurations on the *Rupert* to Conlon's satisfaction, before he smiled. 'Oh, one last thing young *Stephen,* you nearly got away with explaining what use the 'Killick' had in the past, but perhaps not so much nowadays...Do you know?'

'Well, yes I do...I've read David Steel's *Elements and Practice of Rigging and Seamanship*. It stated that a 'Killick' referred to a small anchor and that the knot used to secure such an anchor, took on that name itself,' explained *Stephen*.

'An academic as well as a seaman, you'll be wanting my job next,' he laughed, before continuing, 'Be good enough to bring your kit aboard in two day's time...we sail in four.'

'One last request, Mr Conlon if you please?' added Davy.

'What's that young man?' Conlon asked.

'We've two cats to bring along.'

'Fond of them are you?' asked Conlon with a smile.

'They've been with us a long time,' explained Davy.

'Aye, why not lad, they can catch the rats. There's a few down the bilges.'

'Thank you, Mr Conlon,' said Davy.

'Don't thank me just yet...you'll earn your keep and theirs,' Conlon jested as they left.

Marie regarded the pair in a different light on their return. Rob had explained in detail their harrowing tale, which left nothing unsaid and Marie, in awe of their experiences. Instead of commenting on the decision to keep their identities secret, she adopted a different approach. 'Well Mr *Harding* and young *Stephen,* you seem pleased with yourselves. I take it David agreed to sign you on?'

'Actually, no he didn't,' replied Tom. 'That's because we reported to the mate on your instigation. We never laid eyes on Herd, but Mr Conlon wasn't a pushover, he certainly knew what he was about. We felt we'd been through the wringer in five minutes flat. Suffice to say he's no fool when it comes to engaging crew. Anyway, we sign on in two days and sail in four, so we're very near to saying our goodbyes,' explained Tom.

'You'll be sadly missed,' stated Marie.

'Aye and by me too,' conceded Rob, who'd overheard Marie's last statement, as he'd entered the room. We've been through a lot in the last five years, but maybe we're better men because of it...at least I'd like to think we are... and we're still alive, unlike those other poor sods on the expedition.'

'That's a fact, Rob,' agreed Davy, 'and that's why Uncle Tom and me and, dare I say on behalf of Col too, we're leaving the remainder of the Gold Sovereigns with you and Marie, as a donation to the school. Col would be in agreement with such a gesture, so consider it a lasting legacy and a tribute to the men of the *Erebus* and *Terror*.'

'I'll make sure we used them wisely,' promised Marie.

'We know you will. I've no doubt about that,' confirmed Davy.

Marie asked many questions of the men in their remaining hours at Fort York, but soon it was time for them to leave.

Valerie failed to put in an appearance at the school before their departure, whether by design or through embarrassment associated with their 'encounter' at the church. However, Rob was convinced Marie had warned Valerie to keep her distance, after she knew the full story about Catherine and her relationship with Davy back in England. Whatever the reason, there wasn't to be a repeat seduction in the vestry.

On the morning of the *Prince Rupert's* departure, Rob and Marie walked hand in hand behind Davy and Tom, until they reached the wooden jetty. All that needed to be said had been spoken the previous evening, but there seemed to be poignancy about their impending goodbye, which would remain with them forever.

Tom and Davy stopped short of the gangplank, before turning to face the couple. Davy refrained from saying anything as he kissed Marie on the cheek in farewell, before grasping Rob's hand in a challenging handshake, which proved to Rob that Davy already missed him greatly. No sooner had this occurred than Tom embraced him in a tremendous hug, worthy of his stature. He held him longer than normal decency dictated, but on this occasion, he didn't care…releasing him eventually.

'I'll miss you *Mr Carpenter*, my lifelong friend. I hope we'll meet again someday, but in the meantime, enjoy your life with Marie.'

'You too, you big bugger,' laughed Rob, making one last joke, as Tom realised the implication of his own statement.

'Marie Harding will be waiting for you at *The Jolly Sailor*... I'm certain of it.' said Rob passionately.

'I hope so; otherwise all this will have been for nothing! Ready to go aboard Davy?' asked Tom.

'That's not his name,' Marie reminded.

'Sorry,' continued Tom. '*Stephen*, ready to go aboard?'

'Aye, I'm ready.'

'Haven't you forgotten something?' queried Rob matter of factly, as he handed over the wicker basket, which not only contained Mitzi and Fritz, but also the ships' logs concealed within their calico mattress.

'Bloody 'ell,' muttered Tom. 'My mind's in a turmoil, I'll forget my own name soon!'

Laughing, they climbed the gangplank, turning to wave one last time, which seemed strangely reminiscent of the past, when they waved from the deck of the *Erebus* in London.

It wasn't long before the crew gathered on the foc'sle and afterdeck to reclaim the mooring ropes as the men ashore released them from the bollards.

The *Prince Rupert* moved off the berth in slow motion, before turning into the vast expanse of Hudson Bay and onwards to the Atlantic.

What lies in store for Davy and Tom now? thought Rob absently. His future was settled, but he knew they were on a mission.

CHAPTER FOURTEEN

The Crossing
July/August 1850

Under the guidance of Eugene Conlon, the *Prince Rupert* made steady progress to the mouth of Hudson Bay, passing Ivujivik and the Digges Islands to starboard, before sighting Nottingham Island in the far distance to port. Captain Herd made only brief appearances to check courses. However, his randomness in this regard served to keep everyone alert and on their toes to ensure effective navigation in the Hudson Strait. Even a simple error in these latitudes could prove disastrous.

Eugene Conlon watched Tom intently, as the former *Erebus* Bosun expertly kept the vessel on course, with little deviation and only slight adjustments of the ship's wheel. He recognised in *Tom Harding* the mark of a true seaman, who within a few days had a true 'feel' for the *Rupert*, when steering the vessel in different sea conditions.

'You handle this barque well,' complimented the mate. 'Sailed on others have you?' he enquired.

'One or two,' answered Tom, non-committedly, before adding, 'I've crossed the Atlantic before on the Boston, New York run and once stopped off at St John's in Newfoundland.' Tom paused, then changed the subject, 'After we round Resolution Island, will Captain Herd be heading for Cape Farewell or does he intend plotting a more southerly course?'

'He'll probably go south initially,' hedged Conlon. 'He's not one for taking risks. Royal Navy man were you?' he persevered…'I mean before you strayed on to the other side of the Atlantic in search for…gold and other riches perhaps?'

Tom laughed, despite his apprehensiveness at Eugene Conlon's persistent questioning. 'Not exactly,' he replied. 'I was a butcher for a while, before joining the Royal Navy.'

That part was true, thought Tom to himself, so he didn't feel uncomfortable in its telling, but immediately Conlon added, 'and then?'

Tom was silent for a few seconds before he continued, 'And then I decided to broaden my horizons and ply my skills aboard a merchantman,' continued Tom rather lamely.

'Interesting,' countered Conlon. 'I take it you only made a few voyages before exchanging your sea legs for those of a landlubber on the continent we've just left. Whatever inspired you to do that when you've obviously so much natural ability aboard ship?'

The compliment was not lost on Tom, but he remained impassive with his response. 'I like change, Mr Conlon,' he replied. 'I've experienced life with the Inuits and *Yellowknife* Indians and learned a little about the fur trade…but no gold or vast riches I'm afraid, in answer to your question. Anyway, I'm richer for the stories I can tell to my children and grandchildren.'

'You'll have to tell me about them sometime,' encouraged the mate. 'However, that will have to wait, we're due to change course shortly and Herd will be on deck to observe, I'll be bound. He's a stickler for accurate navigation and he doesn't like to be left out of the 'loop'.'

As if on cue, David Herd appeared on deck clutching his telescope. He proceeded to snap the sections into place before making a slight adjustment to focus the instrument.

He smiled, instantly recognising the familiar feint markings on the final cylinder near the eyepiece, scratched in by himself many years before. Eugene Conlon and Tom looked on with amused interest, although they were careful to keep their expressions neutral.

Herd scanned the horizon several times, until seemingly satisfied, reducing the telescope to its diminutive state once more. He moved to the compass, bracing himself, legs apart, against the rolling of the ship. With deft movements of his practised hands, borne out of many years seafaring, he manoeuvred the azimuth ring above the compass and took several bearings to give him a 'fix' on their position. Ignoring the two men completely, he proceeded to the chart table where he accurately transferred the three figure bearings, held accurately in his brain to the current chart. Next, he checked his pocket watch against the chronometer, secured in its gimbal box mountings and was pleased that his timepiece reflected that of the chronometer. Finally, he registered the time of the fix in pencil, alongside their position on the chart, before returning to the men.

'Steer East, South East helmsman,' he ordered.

'Aye, aye, Sir, steer East, South East,' Tom repeated, as he began to bring the ship around to its new heading. A minute passed before Tom spoke again, 'East, South East, steady as she goes, Sir.'

'Thank you Helmsman,' said Herd, accepting the affirmation of his order. 'Let me know immediately if you suspect the presence of any ice, Mr Conlon, if you please.'

'Yes, Sir,' responded Conlon, as Herd left the deck. 'Now where were we?' asked Conlon of Tom.

'I'm off watch shortly, so my stories will have to wait Mister Mate,' he replied.

His announcement, however, didn't phase Conlon in the

least, as he shrugged non-committedly, before forming an incisive response. 'Aye, that we will Mr *Harding*...that we will!' emphasising the *Harding*, which pointedly made it sound more like a question, than an actual name.

❦

Five days later, the *Rupert*, now well into the Atlantic and past Cape Farewell, was encountering a problem.

The 'glass' is dropping Eugene, rapidly too. I suspect we're in for a bit of a 'blow', stated Captain Herd.

Conlon raised his eyebrows at Herd's familiarity, whilst on deck, which indicated concern. The barometer's fall had not escaped Conlon's notice, of course, but the Captain's use of his Christian name, only used in the confines of their cabins before now, indicated unease and a sense of foreboding. The wind was indeed freshening and coming from the South West. Conlon stroked his chin in thought. Experience told him that this could be the tail end of a hurricane, mixing with a low weather system, originating in North America. 'Better we reduce canvas now, Sir,' suggested Conlon.

'Indeed, another hour and it will be too late,' agreed Herd. 'Send the watch aloft and reduce sail, but retain sufficient to maintain steerage. If the situation worsens, we may have to run with a bare minimum of canvas or rely on our sea anchor, but for now, we'll continue to beat into the wind and steer a course away from the storm centre.'

'Understood Captain,' confirmed Conlon. 'I'll keep everyone on standby, just in case.'

'Thank you Eugene. I'm going on deck to check on the cargo holds, but I'll need assistance. Instruct the new men, *Harding* and Young to accompany me. You seem to hold them in good regard and I've also noticed their proficiency.'

'Yes, Sir, they will be with you shortly.'

Tom and *Stephen*, summoned by the third mate on Conlon's orders, reported to Herd in oilskin and sou'westers. The weather was already cutting up rough, acknowledged by Herd himself, who was similarly attired.

'Ah, *Harding* and Young, glad you could join me,' growled a stern looking Herd. 'Grab those mallets and check holds one and two. Ensure the wedges are holding the tarpaulins in place over the hatchboards and also that the fore and aft iron bands are secured. If this storm is as bad as I think it will be, judging by the rapid fall in pressure, we don't want the added implication of an ingress of sea water entering the holds. If the tarpaulins give way, the hatchboards are next in line. Once they're gone, our stability's gone too and I don't want to think of the consequences of that happening. Make sure you do a good job,' Herd emphasised, holding eye contact with both men, in an intense instant of understanding.

Tom was in no doubt as to the importance of the task, wedges and tarpaulins had a habit of coming loose, even if checked regularly. His nod to Herd, accompanied by a quick, 'Aye, aye, Sir,' signalled both his and his nephew's compliance. Both scurried away, while Herd attended to number three hold. He was never one to avoid getting his hands dirty and prided himself on never asking any man to do something he couldn't accomplish himself.

Tom and *Stephen*, sweating profusely because of their exertions, but also because of the moderately warm air blown rapidly north eastwards along the eastern seaboard of America in their direction, proved beyond doubt that Herd's theory was correct. The long swell, increasing in height and wind speed picking up rapidly, was a sure indication that a low pressure system storm, borne out of a hurricane in the lower latitudes, five to fifteen degrees north of the equator, prevailed.

Half an hour later, their task completed, the three breathless men gathered near the stern, bracing themselves against the pitching of the vessel.

'Well done lads,' Herd rasped hoarsely as a 'green 'un' cascaded over the bow. Tom anticipated the flow and dived behind the stern mast as a powerful stream of water ran along the whole length of the vessel, either side of the hatch coamings. Captain Herd and *Stephen*, less anticipatory than Tom, were swept off their feet in the surge and tumbled somewhat ungraciously, fetching up in the stern sheets bulwark next to a freeing port.[60]

Herd and *Stephen* laughed at their inglorious moment as they regained their feet and composure. Nether were hurt, save for minor bruises, but it did prompt Herd to instruct the two seamen to rig a grassline[61], running the whole length of the vessel on both sides.

'Something to hang on to, to prevent a recurrence,' stated Herd ruefully before rejoining Conlon and the current helmsman; the former preparing to reduce sail to a minimum, enough to maintain steerage and prevent the ship 'broaching to'[62].

'We're close hauled, six points off the wind at present Captain,' stated Conlon. 'Upper and lower topsails are down and we've reduced canvas on the foremast, mainmast, mizzen and spanker. The foresails are down, save for the aft staysail, but I've a feeling we'll be shedding more canvas very soon, whilst beating into the wind.'

---

60 Freeing Port – Gap, low down in the bulwark, to allow water to escape.

61 Grassline – Coir rope line

62 Broach to – vessel becoming beam on (sideways) to sea and capsizing.

'Aye, we will, Mister Mate,' agreed Herd. 'If this storm is too fierce and we can't follow the wind round, we'll be forced to run with it with minimal canvas, until it overtakes us or abates. Fortunately, we've plenty of sea room, no nasty rocks around. Most appealing, don't you think Eugene?'

Conlon knew his Captain was referring to his own two unique experiences aboard vessels, which had founded. The last, aboard the London Barque, *Arietta*; Swansea bound with Cuban copper ore. She struck the 'Mixen' shoal at midnight near the Mumbles in heavy seas, becoming a total loss. Thirteen souls survived, including Conlon, by rowing to the Neath tug *Dragonfly*, eventually making Swansea harbour.

Luckily, he'd survived the turmoil, preferring the open sea, nowadays. Making a landfall in bad weather still left him queasy to the pit of his stomach. Nevertheless, he responded positively, 'Of course, Captain,' managing a grin in the process.

'Have all watches on standby, we may have to reduce canvas in a hurry,' continued Herd. 'Who's our best helmsman?'

'That'ull be *Harding*, Sir,' replied the mate.

'Right, have him take the wheel in half an hour.'

With that, Conlon scurried away to inform the watches and Tom *Harding*. *Quite a reputation you have already Tom*, thought Eugene as he left his Captain pondering a best course of action.

'Glad you could join us,' shouted a genuinely concerned Herd as Conlon returned with Tom *Harding* to relieve the present helmsman, already tired from the massive exertion of maintaining course ten to fifteen degrees off the wind, which was blowing hard. In addition, the swell was heaping up, increasing in height and already a massive thirty feet high.

'Eugene, I'm going below for a few minutes, I've something to attend to urgently,' stated Herd.

'Aye, aye Sir,' answered Conlon unwaveringly, without for one moment considering what could be so urgent.

'Perhaps he's putting a message in a bottle for his wife,' suggested Tom irreverently when Herd was out of earshot.

'Unlikely Mr Harding, unlikely!' replied Conlon, 'but we'd better concentrate on the task in hand, because if he is, he'll need a leeside to heave it over and if we've capsized due to 'our' incompetence...he'll be somewhat annoyed.'

Tom laughed at Eugene's understated jocularity, but instantaneously gripped the wheel as he watched the bows lift and begin to climb the next long swell, before reaching the crest. Then the barque plunged alarmingly into the chasm on the other side. No sooner had the bows and deck cleared themselves of hundreds of gallons of seawater, which cascaded in fountains from the freeing ports, than the next climb began. The *Rupert* shuddered as she climbed the following crest, regaining equilibrium in the process.

'Lucky we didn't sail two days earlier,' observed Conlon, raising his voice once more to be heard, 'otherwise, we'd already be in the storm centre. Even the *Rupert*, as strong as she is, would have been hard pushed to survive. As it is, we've a fighting chance on the edge of it, as long as the helmsman's up to it!'

Tom grinned, despite his exertions and the fact that he hadn't any intention of joining the many seafarers who'd been on ships that had founded and ended up in 'Davy Jones's Locker'. He and his nephew had come this far through many a daunting experience, so this storm, as powerful as it may be, would not defeat him.

'Bugger the storm,' swore Tom vehemently, 'it'll not get the better of this ship.'

'That's the spirit,' cajoled Conlon as he took courage

himself from Tom's remark, just as *Stephen* heaved himself on to the deck beside them using the 'grassline'.

'Captain's compliments,' Mr Conlon, shouted *Stephen*, 'he'll be with you shortly. All hands are on standby. Says I should assist with the steering. He reckons that two hands are better than one.'

'Aye, he's right there,' responded Conlon, as Tom raised his eyebrows, although secretively relieved. His arms already ached despite his own undoubted strength. Sharing the duty with his nephew, where he could also keep an eye on him, increased his own confidence, despite the dire circumstances.

The strain on the rigging was audible above the storm's ferocity. The remaining canvas snapped and twisted as spars groaned under the physical demands of the incessant gale. Herd, now on deck observed them all with practised eye. His experience and seamanship dictated his actions with a consequence that he changed helmsmen frequently to rest tired limbs and the intense effort required in steering the vessel. He conceded that Tom was indeed the best helmsman, as Conlon advised, but he knew the storm, which would last for hours through the night and into the dawn, would not respect tiredness. Rest was important.

Several hours passed in which the *Rupert* hauled itself relentlessly over the increasingly massive swells, now fifty feet high, spindrift punctuating their contours in directional wind lines, until she encountered one exceptional, seemingly near vertical swell. Audible gasps escaped from the lips of those sailors struggling to reef a sail on the mizzen mast, which reached the ears of those at the ship's wheel, including Tom and *Stephen*, just relieved of steering duties.

The *Rupert* climbed the huge column of water, teetering for an age at the summit, before plunging into the abyss on the falling side of the crest. The violent slide caused the helmsmen to lose their footings, sending the wheel spinning. The *Rupert* veered off the wind to starboard, just as a violent gust caught the mizzen, whipping the canvas away from the astonished sailors' hands in their attempt to reef the sail. The strain on the mast stay became too great and with a tremendous snap, it parted, catapulting two unfortunate men over the side into an unforgiving and relentless sea.

The mast, no longer supported, dangled crazily before crashing sternward in a tangled jumble of rigging blocks and rope, which whiplashed into Eugene Conlon and the helmsmen, but missed Herd, Tom and *Stephen*.

Conlon cried out as his leg, hit by a spar, snapped in the instant a wave took him over the leeside. By sheer luck, he grabbed at a line, which arrested his fall, but now he dangled helplessly upside down, painfully gasping for breath, suspended in the water by a rogue rope to his good leg.

In that brief moment, *Stephen* and Tom, galvanised into action at the distressing scene, made simultaneous decisions: Stephen grabbed the wheel, while Tom sprinted to the leeside, avoiding most of the debris from the felled mast. While *Stephen* steadied the vessel, bringing the bow back into the wind, Herd's bellowed instructions to the remaining crew succeeded in resurrecting a spread of canvas. Fatalistically, Tom swung himself over the side, dragging a wood and metal snatch block with him. Issuing a stern order of his own to two mesmerised seaman, the ex Erebus bosun injected an urgency into their fuddled brains. 'Throw down a bight of rope and attach one end to that stanchion,' instructed Tom.

Their reaction was relatively quick, as Tom proceeded to engage Conlon's sturdy belt with the hook of the snatch block, whilst bracing himself rigidly, arm around a broken spar, jammed firmly in a freeing port.

With both hands free, Tom released the hinged clamp, inserted the bight over the sheave, then rapidly closed it again. 'Heave aweigh,' ordered Tom and the seamen hauled on the rope. Conlon shrieked in pain, but was soon clear of the water. As Eugene drew level with Tom, he conveyed his appreciation, through gritted teeth, despite being half drowned and in obvious agony. A relieved Tom stared back, but couldn't resist a jibe. 'Dunking for apples were we Mister Conlon?' which raised a semblance of a smile on Eugene's face. 'Let's get you aboard and find a splint for that leg,' he suggested.

'Aye, you do that,' Conlon managed before passing out through exhaustion and excruciating pain.

Two hours later, with the winds abating and the huge swells diminishing, Conlon awoke in his own cabin. His bunk was small, so the splint encasing his broken leg seemed to occupy most of it. He was in pain, but his battered body was still able to acknowledge the change in the ship's motion. *We're through the worst*, he thought. *Thank God for that!* He was just about to reach for his bottle of gin, when interrupted by the third mate.

'Good, you're awake, Herd wants to know how you're feeling?'

'Bloody awful,' replied Conlon, 'but still alive, thanks to *Harding* and the other two.'

'We thought you'd bought it when the stay snapped and the mast came down. We lost Jones and Wright overboard... they'd no chance in that sea,' confirmed the third mate. 'Herd's already organising repairs; my guess is we'll soon be back on course now that the storm has passed. Oh, by the way, *Harding's* waiting outside to see you, shall I send him in?'

Conlon frowned before agreeing and as the third mate departed, reluctantly relocated the bottle of gin in his locker adjacent his bunk. A knock on the cabin door indicated *Harding's* presence.

'Enter,' instructed Conlon.

Tom's bulk filled the doorframe as he entered and the small cabin did little to accommodate the large man's bulk.

'Cosy isn't it?' joked Conlon.

'Not big enough for me, if we'd lost you overboard, if that's what you mean,' answered Tom. 'Not that I'd want to take your place, I've not got the experience.'

'I doubt that Mr *Harding*, but I do want to thank you for saving my life, perhaps I can repay you in some way?'

'No thanks needed Mr Conlon. I'm glad you survived, me and *Stephen* both.'

'Ah yes, I believe he took over the helm, while you practised your rope work,' smiled Conlon.

'Yes, he did a good job, stayed at the wheel until the storm abated,' proffered Tom.

'You're close aren't you?' queried Conlon. 'Anything more than that?' he continued.

'Actually, he's my nephew, my sister's son,' Tom replied.

'Well you taught him well Mr *Harding*, or should I say, Mr Terry?'

Tom stared at Eugene Conlon in disbelief and some anguish, before responding, 'How long have you known?'

'From the moment you stepped aboard at Fort York. You're a hard man to mistake once known. Saw you in London once; my second mate knew who you were, said you were an accomplished seaman. I obviously didn't think any more of it until you walked aboard that day, but don't worry, your secret's safe with me. However, I expect we'll have plenty to talk about during the rest of the passage home. Do you know that speculation's rife with respect to the fate of the *Erebus* and *Terror* in London town by the way?' enquired Conlon.

'No, I didn't, but it's not what you think.'

'Undoubtedly, but I'm intrigued, especially so because one Tom Terry sailed as bosun aboard the *Erebus* in '45',' expanded Conlon. 'What happened in the intervening five years, I wonder?'

'It's a long story and not without consequence,' stated Tom.

'Come and see me tomorrow, but, as I said before, your secret's safe,' assured Conlon.

Tom nodded as he left, now less concerned than he was initially. *Could he really trust Eugene Conlon*, he reflected.

꙳

At the same time as Tom was in conversation with Eugene Colon, *Stephen* was being congratulated by Herd in the captain's cabin. 'Well done lad,' expressed Herd jovially. 'I do believe that if it wasn't for your quick action in taking the wheel, the *Rupert* would have 'broached to'. I'll be recommending a reward once we reach London. The 'Company' owe you their thanks, as will the underwriter's at Lloyds, who have a 'sixty-fourth'[63] share in this enterprise.'

'Thank you, Sir,' expressed a surprised *Stephen*, who seemed at a loss for words, especially with the Captain's following comment:

'Everyone aboard owes you their lives and that is not a

---

63 Lloyds underwrite insurance for ships, taking 1/64th share of the risk. Some may take more, but the basic idea is to share the load, i.e. If a ship founders, the cost will not be as great for any one person or company involved.

mere statement of fact, but I genuinely feel, is heartfelt by all the men. In fact, sir, you're a hero! Let me shake your hand. No doubt many will do the same before we reach London in a few days' time.'

'Anyone would have done the same, Sir,' said *Stephen* lamely.

'Wrong, Mr Young...most would freeze. You've got quick reactions,' confirmed Herd. 'Actually, you remind me of a young man we repatriated to England, not long ago. Worked for the Hudson Bay Company in Fort York for a while, but destined for better things...like you. We had many interesting conversations. He's publishing a book, possibly based on the experiences of others, as well as his own, titled *The Young Fur Traders*. Could have learned something from you, if you had been around in '46. Apparently, there is another he is working on...*Coral Island*...*R. M. Ballantyne* by name. I dare say, that with a few more voyages under your belt, you'll also have a tale to tell, eh Young?'

'Maybe, Sir,' replied *Stephen*, raising his eyebrows, but secretly thinking he'd already enough experiences to write several.

'Anyway Young, well done. Oh one more thing, please ask Mr *Harding* to come and see me too. I believe congratulations are in order with respect to his actions in saving Mr Conlon. He's a valuable asset to the 'Company'. I'm glad *Harding* was able to save him.'

'I'll inform him,' *Stephen* acknowledged, as he left the Captain's cabin.

'Conlon knows,' whispered Tom to his nephew.

'How?' replied *Stephen*, alarmed at his own brief question.

'Apparently, you can't fool an old seadog, whose eyeballed you before at London Docks! He's known since we came aboard, but kept it to himself. Says, now that he's time on his hands, wants to hear the whole story. Says he'll keep quiet because I saved his skin.'

'Can we trust him?' asked *Stephen*.

'I think so, but he is partial to a drop of gin when he might spill the beans,' responded Tom.

'Well, I hope not, but even if he mentions our story when drunk, I doubt whether anyone would believe him. Anyway, it's too farfetched and it's second hand. Most, on hearing his ramblings, would put it down to the meanderings of the mind of an old seaman who likes tall stories.'

'Maybe, but we've only another five or six days before docking in London to convince him that silence is the only option. With respect to him, I don't envisage him talking. He already knows a part of our story and he's heard of Goldner… there's no respect there. On one of his voyages, most of the crew were violently ill, due to the contents and condition of the cans shipped aboard from Goldner's factory.'

'Have you mentioned anything about our resolve or intentions once we return to England?' queried *Stephen*.

'I though it best not to,' answered Tom. 'Especially as we've not any clear ideas ourselves.'

'Agreed,' said *Stephen* with conviction.

CHAPTER FIFTEEN

Arrival

Despite the storm damage and the makeshift mizzen, the *Rupert* continued to make steady progress and passed Dover on the South coast of England in the early dawn seven days later.

'That sou'westerly's pushed us along nicely,' commented Tom to the amazingly sprightly Conlon, now on deck despite his broken leg.

Conlon, wedged into a corner adjacent the wheel, was still obviously in pain. His good leg supported his wiry frame, while his heavily splintered leg rested on a firkin[64] specifically placed and fixed to support it.

'Indeed,' agreed Conlon. 'We'll be in London tomorrow and I'll be off to my sister's for a spot of convalescing. I reckon I'll be right in about six weeks, thanks to you. I'll not ask what you've planned or where you're going, but my advice to yourself and young Davy, sorry, *Stephen*, is to depart quickly once you've signed off with Herd. He's not got an inkling with regard to your past exploits but he did try to cajole me into persuading you to return to the *Rupert*, along with *Stephen*.'

'We'll leave quickly and quietly; thanks for the advice,' said Tom.

---

64 Firkin – quarter barrel

'I'm glad you confided in me,' continued Conlon solemnly, 'and I'm truly amazed and overwhelmed by your story, but not a word will pass my lips, of that I can assure you. I hope we'll meet again, but if we don't, good luck friend.'

The following morning, the *Rupert* passed Gravesend, then Grays, without incident. Their passage from North Foreland to the Thames Estuary, whilst slow due to light winds, was uneventful. Proceeding carefully, they passed Greenhithe on the port side. *Stephen*, as helmsman on duty, glanced apprehensively and with some anguish at the quayside, where he'd last seen Catherine, some five years previously. *Did she think he was dead, would she still be waiting for him, or worse, had she found someone else?* His confused brain refused to comprehend the numerous possibilities flooding his mind, which momentarily caused him to lose concentration.

'Steady helmsman,' ordered Herd, which jolted *Stephen* into a hasty correction of course.

'Aye, aye Sir,' shouted *Stephen* in response to the command, shaking his head as he did so to clear his vision of so many memories.

Herd frowned, *unlike Young* to lose attention, he thought. 'No harm done,' he whispered to himself. 'Prepare to make fast the steam tug,'[65] instructed Herd. Instantly, several seamen, supervised by the third mate, engaged themselves in hauling a heavy hawser aboard, followed by a second, shortly afterward, as the *Rupert* neared Woolwich. With the

---

65 Steam vessels were occasionally used as tugs in sheltered anchorages, or wide rivers, such as the Thames.

tug secured, the ship made excellent progress, reaching their destination at St. Katherine's dock around midday, which unbeknown to *Stephen* coincided with Catherine's arrival at Spilsby.

The hustle and bustle of a ship commencing discharge began immediately after the last rope engaged with the bollards on the quayside. Dock workers streamed aboard, while the crew removed the tarpaulins and shifting boards to gain access to the holds. The ship's agents and chandlers[66] jostled together in their determination to arrange and conclude their business with the Captain, as soon as decency allowed. Herd looked on with amused stoicism...nothing he hadn't seen before of course, but he was used to it and took comfort in the fact that another successful voyage had been completed, if not without incident. This evening he would be reunited with his own wife and family. A decent interlude this time, before his next voyage...three whole weeks! He determined to enjoy every moment.

Down below, Tom and his nephew were preparing to leave, whilst Mitzi and Fritz sat expressionless, but patiently, atop a wicker basket.

'Not long now, Uncle Tom and we'll be on our way. I've stowed the oilskin packages containing the logbooks at the bottom of both our kitbags. I've kept Rob's scrimshaw wrapped in my tunic. I'll not leave my *Inuit* suit, even if it's a bit bulky.'

'Neither will I,' Tom responded, 'but we best not be wearing them when we turn up at your mam's. She'll be shocked to see us standing there, 'large as life', without scaring her half to death!'

---

66 Chandlers – A ship chandler (or ship's chandler) is a retail dealer who specialises in supplies or equipment for ships, known as ship's stores.

'I've really missed her, Uncle Tom.'

'Aye, I know lad, she'll be glad you're safe and well,' promised his intuitive Uncle, before following it up with, 'That's providing she even knows who you are, after five years,' he laughed, punching his nephew on the shoulder to emphasise the joke. 'Anyway, Eve will look after us for a couple of days, enough for us to find our bearings and decide what to do. We've some big decisions to make,' he emphasised, stuffing his deck knife and Marie's compass into his own kitbag. 'All set, *Stephen* or Davy, whatever it is going to be, now we're off ashore again. Let's go and see Herd and Conlon before we depart. Better secure Mitzi and Fritz in the basket, they've come too far to be left behind now.'

Davy smiled as he placed Mitzi then Fritz, his leg now completely healed, into the basket. Their eyes seemed to convey an unanswerable question, as he closed the catch on the small wicker door at the side of the basket. *What kind of adventure are you planning for us now Davy?*

Herd was sorry they'd not agreed to sign on again, but wished them well. Conlon was well aware, of course, but kept an impassive outlook on their departure, save for a whispered remark as they approached the gangplank.

'I know cats have nine lives, but I reckon you two have several more. It was a privilege to meet you and to be trusted with the tales of your exploits. I hope I don't hear about you in the newspapers!' The macabre joke was not lost on the pair, but they knew it was well meaning as Conlon tapped the side of his nose, which implied his own silence. 'So gentlemen,' he continued, 'Good luck and goodbye...and thank you for saving my life.'

Tom nodded his own appreciation. 'Don't take that splint off too soon Eugene...your leg might drop off!' came his parting shot.

Conlon's raucous laughter rang in their ears as they walked on to the quay. One final wave in the *Rupert's* direction and they were gone; Woking Common some forty miles distant and Eve's small dwelling awaited their arrival.

'What say we try that new steam train, eh Davy?' suggested Tom.

'Sounds good to me,' said Davy with enthusiasm.

Davy and Tom stepped down from the third class carriage on a small rural platform in the heart of the English countryside, a far cry from the wilds of the Arctic. The journey from the impressive Waterloo Bridge station had begun three hours previously, with several stops along the way.

'We can walk from here to the cottage,' announced Davy. 'It should only take us half an hour.'

'Let's move on then,' suggested Tom, shouldering his kitbag. This remark jolted them out of their reverie, reminding them of their daunting trek southward, away from King William Island.

Tom shrugged off the painful memories and instantly replaced them with a visual memory of his sister, Eve, Davy's mother. Her parlour beckoned them...the smell of cheese with homemade bread, tea and Madeira cake, already overwhelmingly invading his senses.

Davy approached the gate at the centre of the picket fence. Happiness and anxiety fused together and his heart beat faster. He opened the gate and trod purposefully along the path to the quaint stable door, which was slightly ajar. He pushed the top half open and caught a glimpse of a figure disappearing into the scullery.

He tapped on the door. 'Mam, he called softly,' but received nothing in response. 'Mam,' he called again. This time, an audible gasp emanated from inside, followed by a swift shuffling of slippered feet. A second passed before Eve Young appeared, framed in the scullery doorway, wiping her hands on her pinafore. Her happy eyes brimmed with tears as she held out her shaking hands to her long lost son.

'Oh dear...oh Lor',' she managed. 'Is it really you Davy... and Tom too?'

'Yes, mam, it really is Uncle Tom and me,' he stammered back.

'My 'giddy aunt',' she muttered.

Eve rushed to greet him and embraced Davy in welcoming arms, while Tom, filled with emotion himself, looked on. 'They said you were all dead,' she cried, clutching him closer still.

'I told you I'd bring him back safe,' affirmed her brother and I don't break my promises.'

Eve smiled gratefully at her brother then beckoned him over and all three embraced in a huge hug that conveyed more than any words; indeed, words would have been inappropriate.

Recovering her composure, Eve motioned them to the small sitting room, where sunshine danced through the windowpanes. 'Come, sit down,' she instructed. 'I'll make some tea. You can tell me what's happened...all five years of it,' she complained happily, 'but you'd better introduce me to your two furry friends first, they obviously want to be in my garden and not cooped up in that open weave basket any longer than necessary.'

'Oh, that's Mitzi and Fritz, who, if they could talk, would also have a tale to tell,' explained Davy.

'Really,' exclaimed Eve as she released them from the basket, before watching them explore her garden. 'There, they're much happier now.'

༻❦༺

The sun had long since gone down before Tom and Davy finished re-telling their story. Eve lit candles and prepared a light supper for the pair, before she attempted a comment or response.

A palpable silence prevailed, as she looked from one man, her brother, to the other, her son, now a grown man himself. *Do I recognise my little boy,* she thought. *Is he present in this man's sturdy frame...of course he is,* she admonished herself, *that twinkle in his eyes could never be extinguished, despite all the hardships.*

She took a deep breath to speak, 'Those poor, poor men,' she managed. 'I'm so blessed and lucky to have you both back safe and well.'

'That may be,' Tom warned, 'but for all intents and purposes, we are 'dead' and must remain so, especially as we have things to do.'

'And what might they be, may I ask?' enquired Eve, raising an eyebrow.

'Better you don't know,' hedged Tom—

'But,' interrupted Eve—

'No buts, I'm afraid, sis,' insisted Tom. 'We've some unfinished business, that's all.'

'Sorry, mam, it's for the best. You've not seen us and for now we're using our aliases, Tom *Harding* and *Stephen* Young.

'Oh,' was all she could say in response, until Davy went on to explain all the implications of why such subterfuge was necessary. Eventually, she understood and promised her unconditional co-operation.

'We have to leave the day after tomorrow,' announced Davy.

'So soon, oh dear,' said Eve sadly.

'But we'll be back, I promise. I've missed you mam. We have to find two ladies,' stated Davy with a smile.

'I see…would that happen to be Catherine by any chance, in your case?' enquired Eve, knowledgeably.

'How would you know that?' Davy asked incredulously.

'Ah well, a mother knows these things. Actually, she's been to see me several times and helped me in the garden. I like her and I might even know where she is now,' she smiled, as she imparted the information.

'Well, where is she? Don't tease me mother,' he admonished cheerily.

'She's in Spilsby with Lady Jane Franklin,' replied his mother.

Now it was Davy's turn to be surprised and he looked at his Uncle with some alarm.

'Don't worry,' she said, touching his arm to calm, him. 'Catherine works for Lady Jane now and is accompanying her to Lincolnshire for a visit. Marie's well aware of the situation,' she emphasised pointedly, looking in Tom's direction. Now it was Tom's turn to be shocked and it left him speechless.

'They're both single, by the way; never given up hope that their men on the Erebus survived and would return. Some women didn't, of course, but those two are loyal beyond reproach. Marie's at *The Jolly Sailor* still, but she's thinking of moving on to Colchester Tom…in case you're wondering? She's left a note for you…over there on the mantelpiece…in anticipation, or hope that you returned here first.'

Tom blushed as Eve smiled again. She was enjoying their discomfiture.

'Where the hell's Spilsby, or Lincolnshire, for that matter,' asked an anxious and exasperated Davy.

'Language, dear,' admonished Eve.

'Sorry, mam,' expressed her chastised son, realising that no matter what he'd been through or achieved, she was still looking after his wellbeing.

'Well, I'm not sure, myself, somewhere near the East coast I think, but my best advice is to ask Marie when you see her. Try not to surprise her, by the way, she'll be shocked to see you both I'm sure. Better if she's on her own too, if you're pretending to be someone else,' Eve warned. 'There's many a prying eye in *The Jolly Sailor*, by all accounts.'

'Thanks, mam, we'll do that, but now we'd better sleep, we've some long days ahead of us,' warned Davy.

As Tom and Davy trudged wearily up the narrow staircase, where they would share a small room prepared by Eve herself earlier, she relaxed in a worn but comfortable rocking chair. A feint smile graced her lips, as her eyes closed and she fell into a contented sleep, after the many anguished and unhappy years of wondering what had happened to her son and brother.

PART THREE
ENGLAND

CHAPTER ONE

August 1850

'Good morning Lady Jane, I've brought some refreshment with the letters received this morning.'

'Thank you, Catherine, I'm sure they will contain nothing more than the usual bills and invoices, but I'm still optimistic that I will be the recipient of some good news; although the pessimist in me thinks they will probably contain reminders from the bank, warning that funds are running low. I've little doubt that my 'friends' in that establishment consider my expenditure, financing search missions, excessive and unwarranted. I dare say that if it wasn't for my constant lobbying in certain circles for funds and the good will of John Ross, I'd already be on the verge of bankruptcy.'

'Is it really as bad as that?' asked Catherine anxiously.

'Well, I've known better fiscal times in the past, but I'm still confident that by prudent management of all my assets, some cajoling amongst many of Sir John's friends and some industrial benefactors, we'll manage. It seems Sir John has attained legendary status with the public at large, becoming a national hero in the process. It's unlikely the admiralty will give up on the expedition at this juncture, as they've still a vested interest in finding the North West Passage. I suspect that some search parties are not actually looking for Sir John anymore, but more likely continuing an alternative objective, that is, the Passage; if they chance across the expedition, that will be a bonus in their eyes. Were you aware that fifteen ships entered the Arctic last year alone, ostensibly searching for the expedition, including two American?' stated Lady Jane.

'No ma'am, I wasn't. That's an incredible number for a person like me to imagine,' answered Catherine. 'Oh, that reminds me,' she continued, 'there's one envelope with John Ross's seal—'

Lady Jane stopped her in mid-sentence, as she grabbed the bundle of letters, exclaiming, 'Which one, which one?' as excitedly as a child with a new toy.

Lady Jane hurriedly discarded the obvious bills, before locating John Ross's envelope. She slit the white vellum with an ivory handled paper knife and extracted the single sheet in an anxious state of expectation and possible fear. She began to read:

> 'My dear Lady Jane,
> I trust you are well and in good spirits, despite the circumstances of our mutual heartache. Sir John is, of course, never far from our hearts and minds, but it is with regret that I must report my mission to locate the expedition has gone unrewarded...'

Jane's demeanour changed immediately. She crumpled the letter in her hand, in similar fashion to that of her husband when he'd received news of the accident involving the ship's boy on the Erebus in 1845, prior to them sailing. Stifling her tears and disappointment, she bit her lower lip, then smoothed out the letter to continue reading. Catherine looked on solemnly, but refrained from speaking; now was not the time to intervene.

> '...However, my dear lady, not all my news is bad. We still have reason to be optimistic in that there is

much evidence to support the belief that the expedition may be found eventually. Such is the capricious nature of the ice fields that we cannot say for certain if St John is blocked in a channel and cannot extricate his ships. A channel can be clear one year and blocked for the next several, by way of explanation.

I obviously wish to speak to you personally and at length, possibly at Spilsby, as you suggested before I undertook the mission. However, I would mention that we found evidence on Beechey Island of their presence. Although we found three graves of some unfortunate souls, it is not indicative of any disaster or misfortune. We believe the ships wintered there in 1845/46, but, unfortunately we did not discover any new information regarding Sir John's intentions. The usual procedure is to leave plans and messages within a stone cairn for anyone following on. It is customary to expect them in such circumstances, but we were again disappointed.

I feel at this point, that an in-depth explanation of our search mission will provide some solace and renewed passion for your quest to find Sir John.

I believe Lincolnshire is extremely beautiful at this time of year and would welcome the opportunity to meet with you there, subject to your approval of my suggestion.

I remain, as always, your friend and John's,

John Ross

Lady Jane sat quietly for a few moments before addressing Catherine. 'I must write to John Ross immediately and invite him to stay at Spilsby. He's intimated that he has much information to impart and probably suggestions on continuing our search for Sir John...and your Davy, Catherine.

'This will undoubtedly be the last time that I'll be able to afford the lease on this Manor House, so I intend enjoying our stay this time, but first we must visit Nottingham for some lace and material for dresses. We'll stay at an Inn in Southwell on the way; you'll also be impressed with the Minster, it's quite spectacular, although not as big as the Cathedral at Lincoln. I'm glad you agreed to accompany me to Lincolnshire, I feel closer to Sir John here you see, as it was where he was born. I know you'll miss seeing Marie, but you'll be able to tell her all about your visit on your return.'

'Actually, it was she who persuaded me to go...to take my mind off the daunting prospect that the expedition is lost,' countered Catherine, 'but from what you say, that might not be the case, if John Ross has positive feelings to the contrary.'

'Let's keep our optimism intact then Catherine. Consequently, I'd appreciate you packing for several weeks away in Southwell and Nottingham and inform Jenkins of our plans, I'll write to John Ross inviting him there. We should expect him, in say a week or perhaps ten days, which gives us plenty of time to enjoy ourselves.'

'Of course Lady Jane, I'm really looking forward to it,' said Catherine enthusiastically.

CHAPTER TWO

Return to 'The Jolly Sailor'
1850

The two days passed quickly, but Eve savoured every minute.

'We'll be on our way this afternoon,' Davy announced apologetically. His mother nodded, resigned to the fact that they must leave, at least for now. 'However, I need a favour,' continued Davy.

'Oh and what might that be?' asked Eve.

'Would you look after Mitzi and Fritz for a while?' requested Davy.

'I'd love to son,' said Eve happily, as she'd already grown fond of the mischievous pair in the short time they'd been there. The cats, too, seemed happy with her attention and were enjoying the extra 'tit bits' that Eve constantly provided.

'Good, that's settled then,' sighed a relieved Davy, because his forthcoming travels precluded their presence somewhat.

Midday came relatively quickly, with Eve pressing a small package into each of their hands as they hugged and said goodbye. 'Madeira cake and a small pie each, for your journey,' she explained.

Eve waved them off as the cats played around her skirts, seemingly oblivious to the men's departure.

'I'll see you soon,' she shouted. 'Not another five years this time!' Eve admonished.

Tom and Davy laughed together, blowing a kiss in her direction.

'Yes, mam, see you soon,' he shouted back. They waved until out of sight.

Eve sighed, 'Come on cats, let's see what's in the larder.'

⁂

Tom and Davy retraced their journey back to London, although a problem with the carriage wheels meant they had to walk the last eight miles into the city, along with the many other, muttering and disgruntled passengers. It was almost two in the morning when they eventually turned into the narrow cobbled street and the welcoming façade of *The Jolly Sailor*.

"Ain't that a sight for sore eyes,' exclaimed Tom. "Asn't changed a bit.'

'I'm not so sure of that,' responded Davy, 'but one thing's for sure, they've battened down for the night. The doors are locked and all the lamps are out.'

'Don't worry lad, I've a plan,' said Tom with inspirational optimism.

Davy raised an eyebrow but watched his uncle intently, as he threw down his kitbag and proceeded to look in the gutter. *What an earth is he up to*, thought Davy.

After a few moments, Tom picked up a small stone, whilst encountering a distinct feeling of 'déjà vu'. 'Now which window was Marie's?' he muttered aloud.

'What's that Uncle Tom? Did you say something?'

'Just thinking,' he explained. His motionless frame conveyed just that as he scanned the upper floor windows. 'I reckon that's Marie's window, the one with the bull's eye pane,' stated Tom eventually.

'How do you know that?' asked Davy.

'Long story,' replied Tom. 'Anyway, in for a penny,' he suggested, as he threw the stone, which connected with the window with a loud crack.

A few moments passed before the window was thrown open and a voice penetrated the silence. 'What the 'ell do you think you're on with? Clear off, before I call H-Division!'

'That'ull be Marie,' said Tom matter-of-factly. 'At least she's consistent, even after five years.'

Tom raised himself to his full stature before speaking. He cleared his throat, 'I was hoping you still wanted to marry me?' ventured Tom.

A palpable silence ensued, followed by several happy sobs. Eventually, Marie leant out, rested her chin on the folded arms and observed him through tear-stained sparkling eyes.

'You're not drunk this time and you're real…tell me it's really you Tom,' she managed through a mixture of happiness and undiluted fear.

'Yes, it's really me…and Davy too,' who until then had gone unnoticed by Marie, as he'd stood in the shadows.

'Oh, my,' exclaimed Marie. 'I'm coming down,' she shouted as she reached the stairs in double quick time, to unbolt the barred door to *The Jolly Sailor*.

Marie opened the door and threw herself into his arms, sobbing quietly, then kissing him on the cheeks, then fully on the lips. 'You bastard, Tom, where have you been?' she managed at last.

'Steady on girl, plenty of time for explanations. Can we come in?'

'Yes, yes,' she said excitedly, turning her attention to Davy at last, giving him a huge hug and a kiss too.

She led them into a back parlour, after closing *The Jolly Sailor's* door behind them.

'Sit down boys', she begged and then set to, pouring them a tankard of ale each before producing a large pork pie from the larder. 'I bet you're hungry,' she stated, not waiting for a reply, as she cut the pie in two, serving it on tin plates.

Tom was left in no doubt as to Marie's continued affection. She was deliriously happy as she plonked herself firmly on his knee and placed her arms around him, again kissing him on the cheek.

'I've missed you, Tom, but I would have waited forever... yes of course, I still want to marry you.'

An hour passed in earnest conversation between all three, until Marie took control.

'Davy, there's a spare room upstairs in the attic. I'll make a bed up for you. Now Tom, as soon as that's done, you're with me. We can talk in the morning about Catherine, Davy,' she winked, then turned her attention to Tom, inviting him to follow her upstairs.

The following morning Marie was up early, bright eyed and ecstatically happy. She still had *The Jolly Sailor* to run, but maybe, just maybe, she'd be able to take a few days off, leaving the *Sailor* in the hands of Martha and Albert. They were her 'barmaid' and 'cellar man' but also her friends of many years.

By ten o'clock and before Tom was up and dressed, having had the best night of his life, Marie had already made the arrangements. 'Don't unpack that kitbag Tom,' Marie instructed on entering her bedroom. 'We're off to Colchester. We can stay at my cousin's cottage, while she's away looking after her sick mother in Ireland. Don't worry, she's often said I need some time away from *The Jolly Sailor* and has already offered a few times. She said the cottage shouldn't be left empty anyway, so I'd be doing her a favour.'

Tom rubbed his eyes, 'Whatever you say…where's Colchester?'

'Not far from Harwich,' Marie replied. 'Being a seafarer, you will have heard of that surely?'

'Aye Marie, I have,' said Tom knowledgeably.

'Good, now go and inform Davy, there's a carriage owned by a friend of mine leaving for Chelmsford at two this afternoon, that's about halfway, but we'll have to make our own way from there.'

The speed of their departure both helped and hindered Davy. It seemed a good thing that their presence in London had gone unnoticed, but he did wonder how on earth he was going to make contact with Catherine. However, he was soon assured by Marie that she had a plan on the commencement of their journey to Colchester. 'Catherine's in Spilsby; that's in Lincolnshire Davy,' informed Marie.

'Yes, I know, mam told me, but just how do I get there?'

'Easier than you'd think,' grinned Marie. 'My cousin's husband owns two coastal vessels which run from Harwich to Boston, through the Wash and Boston's only a few miles from Spilsby. They trade between the two ports every week. I'm sure they'll take you on temporarily and it will be quicker than travelling over land.'

'It's obvious that she's got the brains and you've got the brawn,' said Davy, tongue in cheek, as he directed his remark to Tom.

Tom shot friendly daggers at his nephew, pursed his lips but said nothing detrimental, because he knew how important seeing Catherine again meant to him.

Marie continued, 'I'll arrange everything once we reach Colchester. Now tell me everything about the *Erebus*.'

'We don't know where to begin,' said Tom.

'At the beginning, when you left London,' encouraged Marie solemnly, because she knew instinctively that they'd lived through harsh and harrowing times. Several hours later into their journey, she realized just how lucky they'd been to survive.

꒰ঌ꒱

True to her word, Marie arranged Davy's passage on the sixty foot coastal ketch[67], which usually carried a crew of four. Davy's presence would increase that complement, but the skipper was pleased to have an experienced seaman aboard to assist with the sails. The ketch, named after her cousin and herself, was impressive. The *AnnMarie* sat well in the water and, by all accounts, had a good rate of knots. Boston was well within reach.

Before Davy left, Tom and Marie had already reached a decision. They would remain in Colchester and not return to London. *The Jolly Sailor* would survive without Marie and Tom had ideas of his own for a business. He intended using his experience of butchering and his seafaring to start a small concern, supplying cans to ships on the east coast, but first he needed to learn the art of 'canning'.

He'd witnessed first hand, consequences of the calamitous provisions supplied by Goldner, on Franklin's expedition. Now, *he* would learn the trade and ensure that

---

67 Ketch – two masts. Main mast with gaffsail and boom, triangular topsail, two jibs, two staysails; mizzen with spanker and spritsail topsail.

history would not be repeated. He felt he owed his fellow seafarers at least that assurance…what better than to supply canned provisions himself with an assured quality.

'What do you think Davy?' asked Tom.

'I think it's a great idea and will be a fitting tribute to our shipmate's on the *Erebus* and *Terror*, but where's the money coming from?' queried Davy.

'Well, Marie has some savings and her cousin's husband is interested in investing; reckons it will fit nicely into his shipping business as a sideline. Canned food all along the east coast as well as provisions for all vessels visiting the ports. Of course, I may have to do a couple of trips on the 'Clipper' run to Australia…that will be my contribution…but I'm confident,' explained Tom.

'Good luck then, I'm sure you'll succeed,' said Davy with certainty.

'Thanks, Davy, but now you'd better be off. Don't keep Catherine waiting, but make sure you're available for our wedding whenever that might be.'

'Wouldn't miss it,' promised Davy, as he hugged Marie and his Uncle, before leaving for the *AnnMarie* in confident anticipation.

CHAPTER THREE

A Long Overdue Reunion

Apprehensive but excited, Davy threw himself into the exhilaration of the short voyage to Boston. The ketch passed Aldenburgh, Southwold, Lowestoft and Yarmouth in quick succession, driven on by a fresh south easterly. Cromer was sighted the following day and by noon, they entered the Wash. Twilight saw them anchor off the mouth of the Haven, with direct access to Boston.

'We'll berth on the morning tide,' informed the Captain. 'Once we've offloaded our cargo on to the steam driven riverboats, we're back loading a cargo of grain and cereals for London. Might be one of our last cargoes, as we've got competition from that Great Northern Railway; stops at Peterborough, via Boston, Lincoln and Doncaster before continuing on to York apparently. We won't be able to compete with that I'm thinking. Anyway, it's not your problem Davy, which brings me on to my next point.'

'What's that skipper?' enquired Davy.

'Well, Marie says you're on your way to Spilsby...young love eh?'

Davy blushed at the Captain's comment, but nodded.

'Well, it's not far, you can ask for Jed at the *Mucky Duck*... sorry, *Grey Goose*. He's usually there suppin' ale, in between running his horse and cart to and fro' from Boston to Spilsby. He'll give you a ride, but if not, you can always walk, it's about fifteen miles.'

In that fleeting moment, Davy remembered Tom's comment at Whale Cove, directed at Rob and himself…*'Well, what are you waiting for…A horse and cart?'*

'I'd best see Jed then,' Davy said wryly, 'but thanks for helping me reach Boston.'

'You're welcome lad and if you're ever stuck for a berth aboard, you know where to find me,' promised the Captain.

'Thank you, I will,' responded Davy.

༺༒༻

By noon, Davy found himself outside the dusty façade of the *Grey Goose*, its leaded lights obviously not cleaned in a good while. He eased open the oak door, which creaked abominably and stood for a moment until his eyes accustomed to the gloom after the bright sunshine outside. Save for the sullen 'bar-keep', sat on a stool gazing forlornly out of the dusty windows, there was only one other occupant. The unshaven drover was sitting in a booth, both hands cuddling a pewter tankard, the contents of which were long gone.

Davy approached the man, 'Jed?' he enquired.

'Who wants to know?' came the reply.

'Captain of the *AnnMarie,'* said I'd find you here. I'm Davy by the way,' he informed.

'Did he now…assuming I'm Jed, just what did the Captain say I'd be able to do for you?'

At this point, Davy stifled a laugh, but managed to control himself. It was obvious that Jed was in fact, Jed and that he wasn't the brightest of souls, but he seemed genuine enough and he did need his assistance.

'A lift to Spilsby,' was the response. 'I'd be able to offer you something,' continued Davy.

Jed's eyes lit up! 'Thruppence!' he suggested.

'I'll give you sixpence,' stated Davy generously.

Jed's eyes lit up again, 'Done!...Let's go, no time like the present.' He motioned to Davy to precede him out to the yard where his trusted carthorse 'Barney' was waiting patiently for his master, already in harness with a fully loaded cart.

A mixture of ribald country humour and occasional stops at an alehouse or two brought Davy to the hamlet of Spilsby in the early evening. Thanking Jed for the ride and his company, Davy proffered the promised sixpence, which Jed proceeded to bite in age-old tradition. 'Good Luck lad,' was his parting comment, as Barney trundled off to another destination. Davy hoped 'Barney' knew the way better than Jed, because a copious amount of ale had been drunk by his owner on their journey. However, he had other things on his mind, so was not too worried about Jed's welfare. He doubted it was the first time 'Barney' was in sole control of the cart.

Davy walked to the end of a cobbled street before he encountered a neatly dressed woman in a bonnet, blouse and long skirt, hurriedly making her way out of the hamlet on to a country path. 'Excuse me please,' gestured Davy, holding his arm up to indicate he wished to talk to her.

'Yes,' she enquired, eyeing him suspiciously, although partially relieved that he looked presentable and probably wasn't a real threat to her.

'Would Lady Franklin's residence be near here by any chance?' he enquired.

'Why, yes it is,' she smiled. 'I'm on my way there now as it happens. I work in the kitchens. It's about half a mile.'

'Would you mind if I walk with you, as I've come to see my girl...she's Lady Franklin's companion...Catherine?'

Any reservations that the woman had were instantly relieved, as she knew Catherine. 'Such a nice lady,' expressed the woman with genuine warmth. 'Oh I'm Liz by the way, but I'm afraid Catherine or Lady Jane for that matter, aren't in residence at present.'

Davy was crestfallen. He'd come all this way to be told she wasn't here. 'Do you know where she might be, Liz?...I'm Davy,' he volunteered as an afterthought.

'Well, yes I do as a matter of fact, they've gone to Nottingham on a mission to buy dress material and lace. They'll be away for a couple of weeks, so I'm told and may stop off at Southwell...where the great Minster is to be found.'

'I've not heard of it,' said Davy, now somewhat perplexed as to what his next actions must be, 'but no doubt I'll find it.'

'Not tonight you won't, but I'm sure we'll be able to find you a place to sleep at the hall. Follow me,' instructed Liz.

Davy dutifully followed Liz, where, as good as her promise, she found him a bed for the night.

'We'll sort you out in the morning,' Liz announced, before starting her duties.

꽃

The following morning, Davy awoke to the mouth-watering smells of bacon and eggs, being prepared by Liz, whilst her husband cleaned his boots.

'Here,' she said. 'Sit yourself down and enjoy this, you'll be needing a good start today...Alfred,' she shouted, 'come and introduce yourself to Davy, you're taking him back to Boston this morning.'

'Oh, I am, am I,' came the resigned reply. 'Pleased to meet you Davy,' he grinned, knowing that to contradict Liz in any way whatsoever, was futile and pointless. Their many years of marriage had obviously resulted in Alfred's acceptance of the fact that arguing was not worth the effort.

'My husband,' Liz indicated unnecessarily, waving a hand in his direction.

'Pray why am I taking Davy to Boston?' asked Alfred.

'He's catching the *Favourite* to Lincoln of course,' offered Liz. 'That's a paddle steamer Davy,' she continued, turning her attention to the young sailor, still enjoying his breakfast and the exhibition of the almost one-sided encounter performed by the husband and wife. 'Captain Temperton and Alfred went to school together, so there won't be any problem gaining a seat.'

'She's right, Davy...lucky I was going to Boston today eh. Anyway, he'll point you in the right direction for Southwell and Nottingham when you arrive at Lincoln.'

At this point, Davy knew that Liz and Alfred must have colluded the previous evening. How else would Alfred have known where he was heading? It was obvious, despite their dismissive exteriors that theirs was a loving relationship that was destined to continue.

Alfred knew his place in Liz's heart and could be relied upon to act accordingly. Liz usually made decisions; at least that was what Alfred led her to believe. Ultimately, it could be said that they 'rubbed along' nicely together, with understanding and forgiveness; essential qualities in any marriage.

Armed with the information provided by Liz and the ample breakfast in his stomach, Davy was again cheerful and optimistic that he'd soon be reunited with Catherine.

'Ready young man?' prompted Alfred. 'I reckon your return journey to Boston will be a lot quicker in our pony and trap than on Jed's cart.'

'I hope so,' replied Davy, rising to thank Liz for her kindness and hospitality and to pick up his kitbag.

The *Favourite*, built in 1819, seemed a robust steamer, capable of providing many more years of service on the River Witham. She'd built up a head of steam, ready for departure when Davy arrived, only just in time.

'Another passenger for you,' shouted Alfred in some desperation, as they were later than anticipated. Seconds passed before Captain Temperton peered inquisitively over the Bridge guardrail to ascertain the source of the somewhat anguished cry. Recognition dawned instantly.

'I wasn't expecting your company Alfred. Does Liz want something from Lincoln in a hurry?' Temperton jested.

Alfred laughed before answering. 'No, not this time, but I'd be obliged if you could find space for young Davy here, he's on a mission...matter of the heart,' he added.

Davy frowned at Alfred's transparency, especially when his comment was picked up by a mother with two adolescent daughters already aboard. While the mother raised her eyebrows, the daughters giggled uncontrollably.

'Well now, how can I refuse such a plea?' smiled Temperton, not expecting an answer, followed by: 'Jump aboard young man, I'll not be putting the gangway down again for someone obviously as fit as you.'

Davy didn't wait to be asked again. He hurriedly thanked Alfred and leapt aboard, as the Captain gave the order to cast off.

'Hope to see you again sometime,' shouted Alfred, 'with someone else perhaps?'

Lincoln Cathedral towered above them on the hill. Its ageless façade a tribute to the many stonemasons who'd spent their lives steadfastly adding to its overall splendour. Davy stepped ashore at Brayford Pool, weary and slightly perplexed. Temperton had offered his advice for his onward journey to Southwell, but he still needed to locate the coaching inn on Bailgate. *Near the castle and Cathedral*, Temperton had instructed...*ask for Molly Flynn, she'll see you right.*

I can't miss the Cathedral, thought Davy, *it stands out like a 'sore thumb'.*

Fifteen minutes of energetic walking uphill later, Davy stood outside the *White Hart's* main coaching archway, as a team of horses, pulling a well-maintained coach, entered the courtyard. Davy edged around the coach and headed inside to the reception area. Several persons were hovering around the reception desk, but one in particular drew his eye, an attractive lady with black hair, wearing a green dress, who bore an uncanny resemblance to a certain Valerie.

Fortunately, Temperton had forewarned Davy of Molly's obvious appearance and attributes, but he still suffered a queasy feeling in the pit of his stomach as he remembered his last encounter with a lady in a green dress. He hesitated for a second, then realised she was eyeing him expectantly.

'Can I help you, sir?' she enquired, taking in his well-built frame and handsome rugged features at a glance.

'Molly Flynn?' stammered Davy.

'Why yes, but I don't believe I've had the pleasure?'

'Oh, sorry, Davy Young...Captain Temperton mentioned you could help me with a seat on the coach to Newark then on to Southwell.'

'Well, if you're a friend of Temperton's then of course I can. There's one leaving this morning at ten thirty, which goes to Newark then on to Southwell. It's a little more than thirty miles and is expected to arrive there at four o'clock this evening. Unless of course, you'd prefer to stay overnight and catch the early morning coach to Southwell, which goes direct to the *Saracen's Head Inn*?' she winked coquettishly and expectantly.

Now Davy was alarmed, but managed a quick response, 'Thank you, but no, I have to travel today.'

'Are you sure I can't tempt you,' she brazenly enquired, thrusting her ample breasts in his direction, in one last attempt at seduction. 'We have some very comfortable rooms.'

'How much is it on today's coach?' he persisted.

Molly looked him over again before answering, then sighed in reluctant acceptance of his intent. 'Two shillings and fourpence...perhaps you could stay longer when you return,' she added nonchalantly, but provocatively.

Whatever green dresses do for women, I'm uncertain, but it's not good, thought Davy to himself as he gingerly counted out the coins on to the reception desk, not daring to offer the money directly into Molly's hand for fear of actually touching her.

'I'll wait in the yard,' Davy informed Molly.

'As you wish sir,' replied Molly, smiling happily at what she thought was her latest conquest.

The coach left at ten thirty sharp and reached the Castle and Falcon Inn on London Road, Newark at one thirty that afternoon. The driver mentioned to Davy that the horses would be rested before they resumed the journey to Southwell, so he took the opportunity of a quick bite to eat on a grassy bank of the *Trent*. His repast was simple and consisted of an apple, a hunk of bread and a small piece of cheese, all that he needed, as his mind raced to the future, his encounter with Molly already long forgotten.

The clatter of hooves on cobbles announced the departure of the two thirty coach to Southwell, with Davy safely ensconced aboard.

Despite his nervousness at the prospect of a reunion with Catherine in the near future, Davy managed to enjoy the green fields and rolling hills of the Nottinghamshire country-side. The coach passed through several quaint and pictur-esque villages along the way, stopping briefly at Kelham and then Upton to water the horses, as it was a very hot day, with scarcely a cloud in the blue sky.

Eventually, the coach reached the outskirts of Southwell.

'That's the Minster,' one of Davy's fellow passengers indicated, pointing his finger out of the coach window. 'It was more impressive in the past,' he continued, 'but since the fire in 1711, when the bell tower and the organ were destroyed and latterly in 1815 when the unstable twin spires were removed...too dangerous for worshippers it seems...it's lost its magnificence.' In a parting comment, the passenger delivered with some relish his 'Pièce de Résistance', 'Oliver Cromwell used the place for stabling his horses during the civil war.'

'Really,' acknowledged Davy, wondering if the fellow considered himself the local historian.

However, his musing was cut short as the driver indicated their arrival with a loud shout, *'Saracen's Head,'* located a mere hundred yards away from the Minster.

The coach drove through the heavily beamed archway into another cobbled courtyard. Davy noted that it was barely distinguishable from other coaching inns around England, save for the distinctive wooden sign hanging from a wrought iron frame, depicting a twelfth century Arabian warrior's turbaned head and shoulders in garish colours, complete with scimitar.

Davy stepped down from the coach and waited for his kitbag to be thrown down to him. Muttering his thanks to the driver, he skipped up the three stone steps into the dark oak panelled lobby of the *Saracen's Head*. He half expected another 'siren' attired in a green dress, but was plainly relieved to encounter a bespectacled middle aged gentleman dressed immaculately in a dark suit with a white stiff collar shirt, a dark waistcoat and black silk cravat.

'May I be of assistance, sir,' enquired the man, who, if he donned the appropriate hat, could have been mistaken for an 'undertaker'.

He eyed Davy expectantly, looking him up and down from head to toe, as if checking his credentials. Davy knew he was probably not the best dressed man in the establishment, but consoled himself that he probably wasn't the worst either. He just hoped that the 'receptionist' was not hiding a tape measure in his waistcoat pocket. If so, he may well have been an undertaker, or at best, a bespoke tailor, wishing to provide him with a new suit...or a wooden overcoat! Davy laughed out loud at his own afterthought, although the man failed to react and looked on resignedly.

'Do you want a room, sir?' he asked specifically.

Davy composed himself, before replying, 'Yes and some information if you please.'

'And what might that be, sir? I'd be happy to oblige if at all possible.'

Davy thought carefully before he framed his next question. He didn't want the 'receptionist' to become suspicious with regard to his enquiry if he mentioned Lady Jane Franklin, but he did want information. He was hardly the well-dressed gentleman that moved in high-class society, so he needed to couch his question accordingly and gain the man's trust. He decided that a truthful explanation might be the best option, so proceeded to extract the miniature portrait of Catherine from his kitbag, which he placed on the oak counter between them.

'I hope you're not wanting to barter the miniature for a night's stay, sir?' the 'receptionist' said gloomily.

'No, I wouldn't part with this for a hundred rooms,' explained Davy.

'Oh and why's that, sir,' replied 'severe man'.

'She's the girl I hope to marry and I believe she may have stayed here as companion to a lady on their way to Nottingham.'

The 'undertaker's' features softened, almost betraying a smile.

'Well now, happen I may have seen this young lady recently.'

Davy's expression brightened, but was then dashed by the man's following statement, 'They did stay here for one night, a week last Saturday, but left the next day. A bright young person as I recall, talking excitedly about Nottingham lace to her mistress.'

'Thank you,' whispered a deflated Davy, obviously disappointed and wondering what his next move should be, until the unflappable man tapped his fingers on the desk, close to the miniature of Catherine, which drew Davy's attention.

'I reckon you're genuine enough young man, so I'm prepared to take a chance and 'tip you the wink'. Davy hadn't the faintest idea what 'severe man' rapidly becoming 'helpful man' meant, but watched as he retrieved a leather bound book, which he proceeded to open at the point where a thick blue ribbon divided the pages.

'Now, let's see,' he proceeded, running his fingers down the neatly annotated 'cursive' script. 'Appears they'll be returning on the Nottingham coach tomorrow, booked in for a further two days, her and...' before he could continue, Davy interrupted—

'Lady Jane Franklin,' he offered.

'Why, yes. I take it you'll want that room then Mr ?' This time, 'severe man' beamed in complete contrast to his exterior.

'Davy Young and yes, I do, I do,' said Davy.

'Best save that comment for the church Mr Young,' he advised. 'I'm Leonard Whomsley...you can call me Len. Up the stairs to the right, third door on the left...your room.'

'Thanks, Len,' said Davy, struggling to extract some coins from his money belt.

'Put your money away,' advised Len. 'You'll need every penny if you're to be married I can assure you. I remember when I was about your age, it was a struggle to make ends meet, which was before I inherited the Saracen's from my Aunt...only nephew you see. Anyway my good fortune is your good fortune, if you get my meaning.'

'Thanks again, Len,' enthused Davy. 'That's very generous.'

'Just do right by that young lady,' responded Len.

'I will, I will,' Davy promised.

'There you go again,' said Len, laughing heartily.

The morning sun streaked in through a chink in the curtains, as Davy awoke from a fitful sleep, despite the comfortable bed. His mind was in turmoil once again. He'd envisaged his reunion in so many ways during the passage home on the *Rupert*, but he was no nearer to reaching a satisfactory answer as to how he'd handle it.

How would she react? The question still burned in his brain as he completed his daily task of washing and shaving, before laying his shirt and trousers on the bed. Worryingly, they seemed to him to be terribly shabby and not befitting the grandeur of the *Saracen's* for his reunion. *I can hardly don my Inuit suit,* he thought, *so I'll just have to make the best use of what I have.*

A sharp tap on the door interrupted his deliberations. He opened the door sufficiently to find a well-presented, middle-aged lady waiting patiently outside with a number of folded garments over her arm.

'I'm Gladys, Len's wife,' she announced. 'May I come in?"

'Err, I'm not dressed,' said Davy, alarmed at the unexpected intrusion.

'Never mind, nothing I haven't seen before,' insisted Gladys bustling in.

Davy grabbed his jacket, which was hanging on the back of the door and proceeded to hide his modesty, as Gladys laid out some very clean and presentable clothing, next to his own on the bed.

'There you are young man; Len said you might be in need of a change, if you're to meet someone special. They were my son's but he won't need them any more,' she explained, without giving a reason.

A crisp white shirt with detachable collar and cuffs lay on the bed, alongside a neatly pressed pair of black trousers, jacket and black shoes.

'There's socks too,' said Gladys, 'inside the shoes. I'm sure everything will fit, as you appear to be identical in size... Len thought so too,' she emphasised.

Davy was non-plussed, but very grateful, despite the embarrassing pose behind his jacket. 'I don't know how to thank you enough,' said Davy, whilst actually thanking his lucky stars for such providential generosity.

'No need, try them on then. If you're comfortable, come downstairs for some breakfast with us.' Gladys then left, as abruptly as she'd entered, leaving Davy bemused, slightly embarrassed, but quite happy.

A hearty breakfast greeted Davy, now neatly attired. Every garment did fit perfectly, including the shoes. Fortunately, Gladys and Len were not overly inquisitive and allowed Davy to dictate the conversation. This pleased him, in that he was able to be truthful about his life, without being informative. However, his own curiosity prompted him to enquire after their son. After all, he was wearing his clothes. Their subdued response, although matter of fact was disarming, in that he'd been lost at sea on the *William Brown*, some eleven years previously off Newfoundland.

'I'm sorry,' was all he could manage to say at the time.

Alone at last with his thoughts, in a small booth situated in the annex adjacent the reception area, Davy gazed intently at the miniature of Catherine. *Will she have changed? Will I recognise her?*

At breakfast, Len indicated that the coach was expected at midday and, barring any delays, both Catherine and Lady Jane should be on board, which left Davy another two hours of conjecture. Now his collar seemed tighter than when he'd donned it. *I'm not used to these*, he thought, as he ran his forefinger around the inside of the collar. Still, the reflection of himself in the mirror upstairs had impressed him greatly and compensated for his discomfort. 'Not bad at all,' he'd modestly complimented himself out loud.

Noon came and went, which added to Davy's nervousness. It wasn't until twenty past twelve that the clatter of hooves were heard as the coach entered the courtyard. He remained seated at the booth, but in direct sight of the reception desk. Len was awaiting the passengers' arrival, with his accustomed patience. Two male passengers appeared and were directed swiftly and efficiently to previously booked rooms, followed by what Davy believed could only be Lady Jane Franklin. Her bearing and demeanour conveyed authority and prestige. Len spoke quietly to the lady before instructing a boy, who he'd not seen before to carry her luggage to the suite of rooms allocated to her party.

Lady Jane turned to face the entrance, which was obscured to Davy from his position inside the booth. She motioned for someone to join her. Davy's heart was pumping madly in expectation, but even he was totally surprised at the vision of loveliness of Catherine when she eventually joined Lady Jane at the desk. Catherine was unmistakably Catherine, but mature beyond belief, attractively dressed in a blue travelling tunic and matching skirt. It was all he could do to prevent himself rushing over to her. Instead, he sat mesmerised, transfixed to the seat in the shadow of the booth. He watched intently as Len spoke clearly to Catherine, at the same time indicating with his hand, the direction of the booth. This time, he caught the words. 'There's a gentleman sitting over there who wishes to speak with you.'

Catherine peered in his direction, but would not have been able to see him clearly. She approached slowly, intrigued to ascertain who the gentleman might be, simultaneously removing her bonnet, before shaking out her beautiful shoulder length hair. Davy was both stunned and excited; a whole gambit of emotions flowed through his whole being as she glided towards him, swaying her skirts, until suddenly she stopped. Her gloved hand went to her mouth as she instantly recognised the young man, whom she believed might be dead, although she'd never given up hope completely.

'Davy,' she whispered, then 'Davy,' again, not daring to believe that this dreamlike, romantic scene, in which she was the only other participant, was actually real. She moved closer as Davy stood up in the booth, his manly frame filled her vision. Tears formed in her eyes as she ran forward to meet him. 'Davy, Davy, is it really you?' she managed, before he took her in his arms and kissed her on each cheek, then passionately, as only true lovers know how. Words were unnecessary as they embraced, savouring the moment in an eternity of emotional release.

Over at the reception desk, Len, Gladys and Lady Jane looked on, mesmerised by the unmistakable outpouring of long lost love, now found again. All three crying unashamedly as the occasion justly demanded.

CHAPTER FOUR

Mixed Emotions
Autumn 1850

The implications of the scene she had just witnessed were not lost on Lady Jane Franklin. The stark reality of Catherine's beau re-appearing in such an unlikely setting in Nottinghamshire, after five years of silence, was terrifyingly surreal. Her immediate reaction to their reunion was one of overwhelming happiness for Catherine, hence the tears, but she was clearly shaken. The illusion she'd aggressively clung on to, of survivors, had become reality. The question foremost in her mind would soon be answered...*Was John alive?*

Devastatingly, that hope was shattered almost immediately as Catherine approached her with the intention of introducing Davy.

Lady Jane locked eyes with Davy as he neared the reception desk. The imperceptible shake of his head conveyed the finality of all hope lost forever. Her husband had perished in the Arctic. The implicit confirmation was too much and she collapsed with an anguished sigh, before fainting completely.

Catherine and Davy rushed to assist, while a shocked Len still managed to produce a bottle of smelling salts out of nowhere. 'Here, try this,' insisted Len, handing Catherine the salts, but still totally oblivious as to the real reason for the faint. He believed the emotion of the couple's reunion to have been too much for Lady Franklin.

It was only a matter of seconds before Lady Jane regained her consciousness and then her composure. She apologised immediately to Len as she regained her feet with Davy and Catherine's assistance. 'Please have tea for three persons sent to my suite,' she instructed, now seemingly recovered from her ordeal.

'Of course, ma'am,' said Len obligingly.

'Catherine and you young man, please help me up the stairs, I've had a shock and we've much to discuss,' confirmed Lady Jane.

By the time the three reached the suite on the second floor, Lady Jane had recovered sufficiently to open the door herself. She removed her gloves and placed them on the arm of a superior leather chair, before facing them. 'David Young, I presume,' she intonated precisely and positively. 'I've heard a lot about you; please sit down over there with Catherine and tell me everything. Begin at the beginning and leave nothing out. I need to know *everything*,' she repeated.

Catherine was anxious and she looked at Davy with mixed emotions. The joy of seeing him again was inextricably linked with a sense of foreboding. Whatever had happened to the crews of the *Erebus* and *Terror* was obviously bad... very bad.

Before Davy could compose himself, the tea was brought in by Gladys, who, despite her concern, maintained a diplomatic silence throughout.

After Gladys left, Davy cleared his throat and began his story.

'I'm honoured to meet you ma'am,' ventured Davy, 'as I was your husband, he was a great man and I admired him tremendously. I'm sorry I could not hide my knowledge from you when you caught my eye in the lobby; the unspoken word sometimes comes as a complete shock, more than the realisation of what you feared most.'

'You're a very perceptive man, Mr Young and obviously intelligent, but Catherine already knew that in the short time you were together, before the expedition sailed. Please continue Davy...you don't mind if I use the abbreviated form of your Christian name do you?'

'No ma'am,' Davy replied, wondering just how to phrase his next statement before he continued his story of tragedy and despair.

'Apparently,' he began, 'Sir John, your husband, died aboard the Erebus on the 11th June 1847.'

'Apparently?' questioned Lady Jane, raising a feint hope in her mind for a fleeting instance.

'I wasn't there,' explained Davy, 'but it is recorded in the ship's logbook.

'I won't ask why you weren't there at this juncture Davy, but please continue. No doubt all will become clear, as painful as it is for me to contemplate his death, just at this moment.'

Davy took a deep breath and began, while Catherine and Lady Jane listened intently.

❦

Several hours later, Davy completed his story. He'd repeated it several times before of course, but it never became easier in the telling. The sun had long since gone down when Davy finished. Both Lady Jane and Catherine remained silent for several minutes afterward, still absorbing the enormity of the calamities that had befallen the crews.

Lady Jane spoke at last, 'Thank you Davy...you're a very brave man. I'm tired now, but we'll speak again in the morning. Catherine, please advise the proprietor that we'll breakfast downstairs at eight thirty. I have already decided what I must do now by the way, which includes a visit to the Minster to arrange your wedding. In the meantime, I believe you have your own room, Davy,' she said pointedly. Any uncertainty or ambiguity was thereby resolved. Catherine even managed a slight smile as she squeezed Davy's hand.

The following day, Lady Franklin arranged for all three of them to remain at the *Saracen's Head* and, true to her word, sought an audience with the Bishop of Southwell to fulfil her promise of organising Catherine and Davy's wedding.

Whilst the couple spent an idyllic autumn in the splendid countryside surrounding Southwell, which included several visits to Fiskerton beside the River Trent, Lady Jane became extremely productive and wrote several important letters.

Alfred and Liz were invited to the wedding and word was sent to Tom and Marie in Colchester. Davy's mother Eve was delighted to hear the news and travelled by train with Mitzi and Fritz. She informed everyone on her arrival how excited she'd been on her first train ride. Sadly, Catherine's parents had passed away during her formative years, but Eve, during the time Davy was away had formed a strong relationship with the girl, now destined to be her daughter-in-law.

The night before the wedding was due to take place, Tom, who was delighted to have been asked to be best man, arrived with Marie. Catherine too, was ecstatic, as several months had passed since they'd last spoken. They hugged each other before secreting themselves in an inconspicuous corner of the *Saracen's Head*, which offered complete privacy. Marie was amazed at how many 'nooks and crannies' existed in the place, unlike the *Jolly Sailor*. They were soon joined by Eve, carrying a wicker basket. Catherine seemed puzzled, a wedding gift perhaps? Eve proceeded to lift the lid on the basket as Catherine watched intently and expectantly.

'Two more guests,' Eve announced. 'Davy told me you'd be disappointed if they didn't attend.'

Intrigued, Catherine peered into the basket, to be confronted by two purring cats. She couldn't believe her eyes...Mitzi, Fritz,' she cried. They were unmistakably the same kittens, now cats, their distinct markings confirming their identity. With happy tears clouding her eyes, she lifted them out and sat them on her knee; it was though they'd never been separated.

'How wonderful,' she exclaimed, 'two more survivors... and guests. Thank you, Eve.'

Lady Jane Franklin and the two men, Davy and Tom, watched the reunion, beaming their approval at Catherine's reaction, until Lady Jane ushered them aside. 'Please follow me to my suite, where there's complete privacy,' she instructed.

Tom and Davy followed dutifully, wondering just what was on Franklin's widow's mind.

Lady Jane closed the door behind her and gestured for them to sit. 'Gentlemen,' she began, 'We have much to discuss.' She turned to Tom and addressed him directly. 'Incredibly and unbeknown to any of us until Davy appeared, you survived too Mr Terry.'

'Call me Tom,' he replied.

'Well, Tom, you look remarkably well for a dead sailor,' she sympathetically acknowledged. 'Four of you altogether, including the carpenter and engineer; quite remarkable in such dire circumstances,' she stated. 'However, I must explore even the remotest possibility that others may have survived, so I intend continuing with my searches. John would have wanted me to continue and it is my moral duty, while a vestige of survival exists. Of course, my husband's death must remain concealed while I pursue my intentions, otherwise, many will abandon the cause. If only one more survivor is to be found, it will be worthwhile and my conscience will be clear. I hope I can count on you?' she finished sombrely.

'Of course, ma'am,' offered Tom and Davy in unison.

'Thank you gentlemen.'

'You're very welcome ma'am,' smiled Tom knuckling his forehead.

With their commitment assured, Lady Jane moved on, her affinity with the big man growing by the minute. 'I know you are both very proud men, but I wish to make an offer to each of you. I hope you won't refuse, as it would mean so much to me that you accept. Tom, I wish to buy some shares in your new venture, which I feel is distinctly worthwhile.' she emphasised, addressing him directly with serious eye to eye contact. Tom was shocked but allowed her to continue. 'Of course, I would remain anonymous through a broker. I trust that shares will be available on the Stock Exchange? Many of my friends will be interested I can assure you and, therefore, I know you will succeed. The welfare of seafarers is uppermost in my mind. I must ensure, with your help, that such a devastating occurrence will never be repeated.'

'In that case, ma'am, I'm indebted to you...how could I refuse?'

'Good, that's settled then. Have you a name for the Company?'

'Yes,' replied Tom. 'Nothing too fancy...'The Colchester Canning Company,' seems appropriate I think. The 'CCC' for short, rolls off the tongue so to speak.'

'I quite agree,' laughed Lady Jane. 'Anyway, I'll contact you in Colchester after the wedding, when I return to London.'

'As you wish ma'am,' beamed Tom, not quite believing his good fortune.

She turned to Davy. 'You know that Catherine has grown to love this part of England in the short time she's been here. It's the sort of place where you can bring children up in a safe environment...away from the hustle and bustle of London?'

'I am aware ma'am, she has hinted as much.'

'Quite so Davy. Well, Southwell is not that far from Spilsby, my home, so I'll look forward to visiting you on occasion.'

Davy frowned and then followed it with an equally quizzical expression. 'I'm not sure what you are proposing ma'am,' he stated, framing a question in the statement.

'Well,' she hesitated, 'I've a wedding present for Catherine and yourself,' she continued, handing him a bulky manila envelope tied with pink ribbon. 'I've spoken to the Bishop on a number of occasions since we've been here and he advised me of a small but quaint cottage for sale on the *Burgage;* my gift to you both. I won't hear any protestations, as Catherine has been an exceptional companion to me whilst in my employment and you have survived so many hardships aboard my husband's ship that you thoroughly deserve some good fortune. Please enjoy it. Oh, there's a small annex for your mother, Eve, should she wish to live with you in the future.'

Davy was shocked to receive such an extraordinary gift. 'I'm overwhelmed,' he managed. 'Thank you so much. How can we ever repay you?'

'No need, your happiness is all that I require,' she assured him, 'but now we should return to the ladies downstairs, as I also have an item for each, which they will need. She then ushered Davy and Tom out, reaching for her expensively embroidered purse, as she closed the door behind them.

Lady Jane smiled benevolently at the small group seated around an unusual Ash table, although most of the favoured furniture in the *Saracen's* was made of oak. 'I'm so happy to be able to call you all my friends,' she began. 'Of course this is a sad time for me, but I have much to achieve, which gives me hope for the future. The wedding of Davy and Catherine will be a new beginning for them and also one for me.

'I know Marie has been a true friend to you Catherine and that you have supported each other throughout those difficult years, so in appreciation of your steadfast loyalty to each other and to Tom and Davy, I wish you both to have something that I hope you will find extremely, *useful*...as only *we* women can.' She smiled and her eyes twinkled conspiratorially as she produced two rings from her embroidered purse. 'One for Marie,' she announced. A green emerald flanked by two diamonds and one for Catherine, a deep blue sapphire, also flanked by two diamonds. 'Engagement rings,' she explained, as if an explanation was really necessary. 'Now you don't need to delay any longer do you Tom?' she emphasised quite forcefully in the big man's direction.

Marie blushed, but wasn't actually prepared to wait another five years for them to be married, hence her next comment. 'Well, what are you waiting for Tom?' Marie teased. 'Ask me to marry you...again, but this time don't throw any stones at windows.

Everyone laughed, but Tom knew his place and proposed formally once more to the cheers of all.

An hour's illuminating conversation ensued before everyone agreed to retire in preparation for the big day.

⊶⊷

The wedding party proceeded down the large sandstone slabbed pathway to be greeted by the Bishop himself. It was a beautiful sunny day befitting such an occasion. Even the builders downed tools, agreeing to delay their reconstruction of the twin spires, which they'd begun earlier that year, whilst the ceremony was taking place.

The side-chapel was deemed appropriate by the Bishop for such a small congregation of souls, including himself. Liz and Alfred were to be the two witnesses, Tom the Best Man and Marie the Maid of Honour, whilst Gladys and Len from the *Saracen's*, deeply moved to be invited, were welcomed guests. Lady Jane and Eve were the honoured guests.

Davy wore the suit recently given to him by Gladys and Len, while Cathryn wore a very pretty white lace dress bought recently in Nottingham, which would have graced any occasion. Nevertheless, an open-mouthed and speechless Davy conveyed his thoughts to all when his beautiful Catherine walked the isle toward him.

'I bet you're glad you didn't wear your 'Inuit' tunic this time eh Davy?' quipped Tom as she approached. 'Not that it would have been totally inappropriate, as it did save your life,' he whispered as an afterthought...'but perhaps too warm for an English wedding. Anyway, *Tapeesa* would be

344

proud of her adopted son, whatever he chose to wear today.'

A dig in the ribs by Davy indicated to Tom that now would be a good time to keep quiet. He'd noticed the Bishop's warning frown, although what he was really concentrating on was Catherine's radiant smile, which he nervously reciprocated.

No sooner had the service began than it was over and they were outside once again.

Gladys and Len brought small baskets of dried rose petals for everyone to throw over the bride and groom, before they took the short walk to the Saracen's where their reception awaited. A whirlwind of happy memories were generated in the minds of everyone that afternoon and evening.

Much later, Catherine and Davy excused themselves to be alone together in a 'special' room, complete with fresh flowers prepared by Gladys prior to the ceremony. Their life together had begun.

CHAPTER FIVE

Letters
March 1853

The years passed quickly, which saw Tom and Marie's business flourish, after their wedding in Colchester. In addition, Tom's runs to Australia, following a recommendation from Eugene Conlon, which secured him the position of 'mate', raised extra money for the Colchester Canning Company.

Meanwhile, Catherine and Davy, as butler and housemaid, established themselves at a country residence near Southwell.

Early in 1853, Lady Jane received an unusual request from Davy:

1st March 1853
Dear Lady Jane,

I hope you are in good health and that your continuing endeavours, in conjunction with the Admiralty are proceeding well.

However, I must apologise for contacting you again, especially as you have been extremely helpful and generous to both Catherine and myself in securing the cottage and obtaining our positions at the Manor House in Southwell.

Quite fortuitously, I have received some information from my uncle, which provides us with a unique opportunity, one which I must engage with to obtain strong evidence with respect to Stephan Goldner's insufferable canning operations.

Apparently, he has dismissed his present butler and housekeeper, which, if correct, 'opens the door' to other applicants. In short, with your help, I wish to secure those positions, which brings me to my request.

A reference from yourself for both Catherine and me would undoubtedly convince Goldner of our suitability. Of course, we would need to change our names; might I suggest, Stephen and Emily Rorret.

We realise that you may wish to consider our proposal at some length because there is a degree of deception involved, but we believe the risk is worth taking to obtain as much evidence against Goldner as possible, which may take some months.

Our present employers are prepared to accept two weeks notice, which should give us sufficient time to apply for the positions, should you agree.

If you are totally uncomfortable with our proposal, then we completely understand and would not wish to compromise your good name. However, if we are to proceed quickly, a decision from yourself is required at your earliest convenience.

We are, of course, forever in your debt for the kindness shown to us over many years.

Your indebted friends, Catherine and Davy Young

Lady Jane was at first intrigued and then somewhat worried when she realised who the new employer would be...none other than Stephan Goldner. Granted a plausible explanation was given by Davy in that he expressed his intention to gather sufficient information to expose Goldner for what he was...a complete charlatan in her opinion, but she still had misgivings that Davy, but especially Catherine would need to live with Goldner at his residence. However, she placed these misgivings aside and decided to oblige the young couple. After all, was this not the man who'd supplied her husband's expedition with seriously impaired supplies?

Lady Jane re-read the letter once more before reaching for her pen and a single sheet of parchment.

She began her letter to Mr Goldner. Several minutes later, satisfied with her endeavours, she placed the sheet in a Manila envelope and melted sealing wax before embossing her seal on the reverse of the envelope.

Next she penned a letter to Catherine and Davy, stating that she agreed to their request, but warning them to be careful with such a potentially lengthy and dangerous undertaking.

Lastly, she rang the bell to summon her maid. 'Please give these two letters to Jenkins, he'll ensure they reach their destinations.'

'Yes ma'am,' came the respectful reply.

What have we here, thought Goldner, as he opened a manila envelope addressed to him personally and embossed with a crest he failed to identify at first glance. He broke the waxed seal and took out the single sheet of paper. He frowned before adjusting his recently purchased monocle and began reading:

3rd March 1853
Dear Mr Goldner,

Please forgive the imposition of my writing to you 'out of the blue' as it were, but I may be in the position to provide a favour.

A mutual acquaintance mentioned that you might require the services of a new butler and housekeeper. I am reliably informed that the last incumbents of the posts left somewhat 'under a cloud'. If this is in fact the case, then I am only too pleased to recommend two diligent, trustworthy and experienced persons for you to consider.

Their names are Emily and Stephen Rorret who, until recently, were employed by myself. Unfortunately, I am unable to continue their employment due to the temporary closure of one of my country residences.

By way of explanation: To continue the search for survivors of my husband's expedition, I need to raise sufficient funding, hence this particular action.

For your information, we met once, very briefly at the Admiralty. I hoped to convince them to instigate another search expedition, which, you will recall, was successful, in that their agreement was secured.

However, I do wish to find positions for the couple as they provided excellent service in my employ.

I am sure you would find Emily and Stephen extremely suitable and commensurate with your present needs. Consequently, I would be obliged if you would contact me as convenient.

Yours sincerely
Lady Jane Franklin

Goldner 'humphed', *why not,* he thought. None other than such a refined personage as Lady Jane Franklin was recommending the pair. *Couldn't be any worse than the last two!' I'll arrange an interview tomorrow,* he promised himself...*on less pay...I was too generous last time.*

Grinning contentedly, he crumpled the letter in his fist before throwing it on to the fire, housed in an ornate ironwork frame in his living room. The paper crackled furiously as it was consumed by the flames.

CHAPTER SIX

Pay the Ferryman
Shoreditch (Goldner's Residence)
31st March-1st April 1855

Stephan Goldner perused his latest contract for the Admiralty. The profit margin exceeded his wildest expectations, but he did wonder how long the gravy train could last...how many more Arctic Expeditions would the Admiralty authorise? Rumours indicated that the Admiralty were considering their own canning factory, but they would still need him to maintain a consistent supply to supplement the provisions of a vast navy, or so he presumed.

⌘

It was nearly dusk, the last rays of the weak March sun were filtering through the opulent silk curtains of the luxurious abode, Goldner humorously described as his 'country house'; in reality his winter residence, in a less than desirable part of London. He mused that tomorrow would be April 1st. An inconspicuous date in the calendar for himself, but one of profound importance for the ill-fated crews of the *Erebus* and *Terror* and some ten years since their disastrous voyage.

The canning of provisions had come a long way since he stored those ships and a slight twinge of conscience tempered his observation. Oh well, it had driven his business forward and established his credentials in the right quarters, even if most of his claims on canned provisions were suspect.

He yawned, it had been a long day and an early night was a distinct possibility. His wife had died eight years ago in childbirth and his daughter, Susan, born at the time, now lived with adopted parents. He regretted his negligible involvement, but his business fired his imagination and greed. The house was empty, as *Stephen*, the butler and *Emily*, his housekeeper were both visiting elderly relatives...a rare occasion for them to be away together indeed. He comforted himself by pouring a healthy measure of port.

A church bell chimed twice, but did not interfere with Goldner's slumber. The night was still and peaceful, captivated by a full moon. An owl hooted in response to another, thirty yards away...they were hunting together... mice their probable, if not obvious prey.

The latch on the Judas gate made a dull metallic sound as the heavily hinged door inched open. A shadowy figure moved into the cobbled courtyard and headed resolutely for the servants entrance. The man, in his late twenties, was lithe and well built with an agile spring to his step. He eyed the lock with purposeful intent, retrieved a heavy key from his jacket pocket and inserted it into the lock. It clunked satisfactorily as the mechanism released. The robust, iron banded, wooden door swung open with a slight creak, but not enough to disturb the pair of owls, or even a deep sleeper like Goldner.

The intruder proceeded silently up the flight of stairs and along the well-appointed corridor towards Goldner's bedroom. He paused at the bedroom door, retrieved the well worn but very sharp wood handled deck knife from its sheath, which hung from his leather belt and entered the room. The door creaked but failed to waken Goldner. Only when the man sat on the embroidered silk counterpane did Goldner stir, to peer apprehensively at the figure at the foot of his bed.

'Oh, it's you *Stephen*, you gave me a real fright I can tell you...what on earth are you doing here at this hour?'

Stephen stared intently at Goldner's lined, etched face with its sagging jowls and pock marked cheeks. After a prolonged but studied silence, he replied in a soft but vaguely menacing tone. 'I returned earlier than expected Stephan,' using Goldner's first name on this occasion. 'Only it's not *Stephen*...it's Davy.'

Goldner looked perplexed.

'David Young to be precise, ex *Erebus* ship's boy.'

Goldner looked even more bemused, realisation still far off.

'A survivor of Sir John Franklin's ill-fated expedition of 1845.'

'But no one survived!' exclaimed Goldner.

'I did,' replied Davy, with conviction and a slight trace of anger at Goldner's selfish and arrogant assumption.

'But you're *Stephen*, my butler and confidant of two years.

'Not any more I'm afraid,' responded Davy. 'I knew before you appointed me that you would look favourably on the English version of your own name. This, in conjunction with my reference from Lady Jane Franklin, whose reputation preceded her, gained me the position of butler in your household...but we've moved on...haven't we?'

Goldner frowned in exasperation, his sleep dulled brain not yet quite functioning properly, until, momentarily, he caught a glint of steel reflecting in the moonlight. 'What do you want,' demanded Goldner, reverting to his normal and usual domineering manner.

'You,' replied Davy matter of factly, as he sprang at him, inverting the deck knife to deliver a stunning blow to Goldner's temple with its hilt, which rendered him immediately unconscious.

❧

Goldner awoke, bound and gagged, some thirty minutes later as he was hurriedly removed from a small cart by two persons, one male, one female, whose voices sounded familiar. *Emily,* he thought, *my housekeeper...What's happening here?*

Goldner's house was sited a stone's throw away from his cannery and it was to the cannery that Davy and Catherine, had taken him. Although cold outside, beads of sweat formed on Goldner's forehead as he was unceremoniously bundled down a stone staircase to one of the three large cellar rooms used in the canning process.

A faint smell of lead solder mingled with the more vile smells associated with any canning process invaded his nostrils. Cleanliness in the business had not been one of Goldner's priorities and rotting meat, vegetables and other indistinguishable items littered the premises.

Goldner's nerves were jangling as he was laid upon a large stone slab used for cutting and slicing animal carcases, by the team of butchers he employed.

Real fear showed in his eyes as he contemplated the unimaginable, but Davy seemed icy calm and in no hurry, settling himself on a stool, two feet away from the cold slab, directly opposite Goldner's face.

Davy stared coldly into Goldner's eyes and spoke slowly. 'First let me introduce you to Catherine, my wife, who you know as *Emily*.' He did not want a verbal response from Goldner, hence the gag, but he did want to witness his terror as he carried out his long awaited, self-imposed task, not so much for himself, but for the other one hundred and twenty five[68] officers and men who had suffered unimaginably and died in atrocious circumstances in the unforgiving Arctic.

'You must have realised that your provisions contravened most, if not all, the specifications and regulations that the Admiralty required, but this did not deter you one iota. 'Profit'...a small word, but one that motivates the greedy, or possibly the criminally insane. The latter category would arguably be better, but I perceive you have no conscience whatsoever, so greed it has to be in your case. You could not and did not expect anyone to survive even one winter in the Arctic. You condemned the men of the *Erebus* and *Terror* to an horrendous death of bad food and starvation, frozen in time...but, unfortunately for you, not forgotten...by me nor the other three survivors!

Goldner, incredulous and frantic, stared back at Davy. His eyes darted from side to side in the vain hope that there may be some means of escape, or possibly divine intervention.

'What punishment fits the crime in the case, I wonder?' mused Davy. 'Should I be a witness for the prosecution, the jury perhaps, or even the judge?

'No, I think not. There is little time before dawn to arrange such a complex undertaking, especially on April Fool's Day!' You may think that I chose this day as some kind of sick joke...but I assure you that it's not...you will die

---

68 Muster Rolls of H.M.SS. Erebus and Terror

tonight, but not quickly...and you will observe your own demise—'

'...and so will I!' An ethereal voice both interrupted and astonished the small gathering of diverse souls. 'Wouldn't have missed this for a banquet prepared by cannibals!' exclaimed the intruder.

Another second elapsed before relieved recognition dawned on Davy...*but it couldn't be...could it?...not Tom, his beloved Uncle*? However, the unmistakeable cockney accent left him in no doubt, confirmed in no small part by the ferocious bear hug bestowed by way of long overdue greeting. Tom was still as strong as an ox. In his late forties, he'd retained his stature, despite the privations of Franklin's disastrous voyage and the intervening years on the Australian Clipper run and at Colchester.

'Thought you might need a hand,' emphasised Tom pointedly, directing his comment to Goldner, as he produced his own sharp deck knife, the blade glistening in the light from the oil lamp.

'How on earth did you know where to find me?' asked an incredulous Davy.

'Been observing you for a couple of days,' responded Tom, 'and realised what you were up to,' he continued. 'It didn't take me long to fathom what you were planning. Consequently, I couldn't let you go through with this on your own. But enough of talking, we've a task to accomplish and it will be my pleasure to assist.' He glared menacingly in Goldner's direction and this provoked an instant reaction of petrifying fear as the blood drained from his face. Goldner's eyes conveyed the sensation and abject terror of all hope lost forever.

Catherine took this as her opportunity to leave the anteroom, although she was left in no doubt as to their resolve.

The sun was just rising over the rooftops, as Tom and Davy vacated the dimly lit and evil smelling room, locking it securely, before proceeding down the narrow passageway and securing the door at the top of the stone staircase. The unique smell of lead solder followed their retreating steps into the winter sunlight...out into the yard where Catherine waited patiently.

Their eyes met in mutual understanding, as words were unnecessary, but she shivered momentarily in the realisation that life would never be quite the same again.

CHAPTER SEVEN

Post Mortem
3rd April 1855, 11 a.m.
The Jolly Sailor

Marie and Catherine sat opposite Tom and Davy in the secluded booth in one corner of the 'Jolly Sailor'. They exchanged apprehensive glances but remained silent.

An inconspicuous carriage pulled up outside the main entrance. The driver stepped down from his seat, opened the carriage door and escorted a meticulously dressed woman in her late fifties into the building. He glanced around the gloomy interior, not helped by the ethereal mist outside, which had enveloped the building.

His eyes acclimatized to the light and focused on the small group occupying the booth. He noted that only one other person was present in the public house, slouched at the far end of the room at a barrel table and he seemed in no fit state to remember his own name, let alone their presence.

Davy stood and offered their guest a comfortable chair at the end of the booth, while the driver watched the door.

"You have some important news for me?' she enquired matter-of-factly.

Davy nodded, before adding, 'Apparently, there is concern in some quarters that Goldner's disappeared without trace.

'His sins must have caught up with him at last,' she ventured.

'Undoubtedly,' confirmed Davy.

'Well that's not for us to worry about I think, but I suspect that the truth will out some day in the future, although possibly not in our lifetime. Anyway, enough of my conjecture. Thank you once again for coming to me with your story, Davy. It was comforting to know the salient facts, after all those years of searching.'

'You're very welcome,' offered Davy with sadness and compassion.

'It seems a very long time ago in the autumn of 1850 that you, Davy, found Catherine and myself at Southwell. Your story of survival, both fascinated and saddened me, but I will always be indebted to you for providing me with the truth. Your shocking account of the state of the canned provisions provided me with many facts about Mr Goldner, a man with little or no conscience whatsoever. I was glad to supply references to convince him to employ you and Catherine in the roles of butler and housekeeper. A change of names to Stephen and Emily Rorret was all that was required. It did help, of course, that he'd just advertised for new staff. Apparently, he accused the previous incumbents of stealing from him and had them incarcerated...poor souls. However, I rectified that particular miscarriage of justice and arranged for their release later. I have, of course, encouraged others to continue looking for the crews of the *Erebus* and *Terror* in the event that some did survive, however unlikely, but it is still possible even after all this time.

'However your vivid account of what actually happened, was overwhelmingly comprehensive if emotionally disturbing. It is unforgiveable that sailors, whilst attempting a survival trek across the ice, were hampered by inadequate food supplies. Vital nourishment was denied them, due to Goldner's ambitious greed, consequently, their chances were almost non-existent.' She paused while she took out a small, but exquisitely embroidered silk handkerchief to dab away a tear from each eye, then smiled momentarily at the small gathering before continuing...

'You won't ever see me again. I am sure you will agree, it will be prudent for us not to meet, but I will be forever in your debt.

'You must have truly loved him,' remarked Catherine, which was more of a statement than a question.

'Yes I did and will all my days,' she said, clearing her throat. 'Please remember my husband and myself in your future together, as I will remember my friends too.' This last poignant comment signalled the departure of a remarkable lady. She turned determinedly to leave the *Jolly Sailor,* accompanied by her driver.

'There weren't any survivors...were there Jenkins?'

'No, ma'am, sadly they were all lost.' Jenkins replied sombrely and understandingly as he helped her into the carriage.

The group remained motionless for a few minutes after their departure, before Tom broke the silence. 'It's time for us to make ourselves scarce,' stated Tom 'and that includes you two. You can't stay in London and neither can Marie and I; although officially, of course, we don't exist. We intend staying in Colchester, to oversee our canning venture. I don't doubt that 'H' Division will be looking for a reason behind Goldner's disappearance, but with his reputation, they won't be too concerned. However, we need to be cautious.'

'Thanks for the advice Uncle Tom, but we already plan to leave for Nottinghamshire, as soon as possible.'

'It's perfect for us,' interjected Catherine with enthusiasm. 'Lady Jane has given us references again, so I'm sure we will gain employment. Eve's already at our cottage with Mitzi and Fritz,' she explained.

'Well then, let's hope we've tied up all the loose ends, but be careful Davy lad, especially if you return to London for any reason. At least you can now use your own name. Rorret is not one to embrace, especially as we all know it spells 'Terror' backwards. Well I guess this is goodbye for now, but Marie and I will visit when we have the chance.' Davy acknowledged with a nod, before Tom stood to hug his nephew with a compassion born out of tragedy and terrible consequence, but also of camaraderie and ultimate survival.

Marie and Catherine looked on with meaningful and complete understanding. They too hugged until the silence was broken by Tom, 'Something that will bind us together forever Davy...oh and Marie wants you to have this too.'

Davy looked down. In his hand was Tom's treasured deck knife and his compass, a gift from Marie.

'I reckon the inscription is appropriate for all of us now,' said Tom emotionally.

The four left the *Jolly Sailor* shortly afterward; fate would dictate their future.

Innovations
Admiralty Buildings Woolwich –
4th April 1855

Rear Admiral Edward Bell peered over his 'pince-nez'[69] at his much junior subordinate who had just submitted a brief but disturbing report on the state of Goldner's canning facility. 'Disappeared you say and hasn't been seen since 31st March when he left the premises at 5.30 that evening?'

'Yes, sir,' replied the junior officer.

'What's he up to now I wonder? Can't trust the man one inch. I've a mind to wind up his contract immediately and pursue other avenues.'

The officer cringed in his highly polished boots as the Admiral let rip his innermost concerns in a most vehement fashion. He didn't so much as shout, but growled his dissatisfaction. 'I've had my suspicions of that obsequious little Hungarian since Franklin's expedition failed to return. Can't think why we awarded him several more supply contracts, including another two search and rescue expeditions. Will we ever learn? We've been very remiss Andrews, Goldner's

---

69 Pince-nez is a style of spectacles, popular in the 19th century, that are supported without earpieces, by pinching the bridge of the nose. The name comes from French pincer, "to pinch", and nez, "nose". Although pince-nez were used in Europe in the 15th, 16th, and 17th centuries, modern ones appeared in the 1840s.

glaring ineptness as a supplier should have shouted a warning, at least a 'shot across the bows'[70]. We've been very foolish.

'Remember the *Plover* in '53, Andrews? They threw nearly sixteen hundred pounds of canned meat overboard in the Bering Strait. The captain reported the contents to be in a 'pulpy, decayed and putrid state, totally unfit for the men's food...and that's not all, most of our depots have found meat cans in their storage facility to be garbage and in a horrible state. Even the *Illustrated London News* reported some disturbing facts concerning a group of meat inspectors' findings. Apparently, they fished out pieces of heart, rotting tongues of sheep or possibly dog, along with offal, blood, ligaments, tendons and putrid kidney. Some of the organs were reported to have come from diseased animals... God help us! I haven't the faintest who's going to take responsibility for this one, but it certainly won't be me!'

The junior officer raised a quizzical eyebrow but kept silent, as he was totally appalled and shocked with all the Admiral's revelations.

'Send my secretary in!' he motioned in dismissive fashion.

The officer, relieved, hastily vacated the office before forewarning the secretary of the Rear Admiral's foul mood. 'Watch your step in there, he's fuming, wants you to go in now.'

The secretary entered with trepidation, but unexpectedly encountered the Rear Admiral in inspirational agitation. 'I'm

---

70 'Shot across the bows' (originally eighteenth century) – a warning shot (in nautical terms), could be fired towards any ship whose 'colours' (nationality) had to be ascertained. According to the law of the sea, a ship thus hailed had to fly her flag and confirm it with a gunshot.

sending a proposal to the 'big guns' — you know the system well enough. We should explore the possibility of operating our own canning production facility, only then can we be secure in the knowledge that all provisions are of the quality we require and in the quantities needed.'

The secretary nodded.

'Set up a meeting with the key personnel. I'll outline my thoughts then. I'm sure that approval will be granted, as this particular thorn in our side has needed removing for some considerable time.'

'What about Goldner, himself sir?' queried the secretary. 'I'm aware that he's disappeared and that the police's 'H' Division in Whitechapel are currently investigating, but where does that leave us?'

'We'll survive,' replied the Rear Admiral, 'unlike poor Franklin and his men. Let's ensure our own canning facility[71] is up and running as soon as possible...next year seems reasonably optimistic in the circumstances.'

The secretary was impressed, he'd known the Rear Admiral for some years now and acknowledged his determination. If he even jokingly, stated he'd achieve a result, he usually did.

'1856 it is then!' bellowed Bell. The secretary concealed his own knowing smile as he vacated the office to begin his allotted task. *'Ding Dong' was in unusually fine form this morning,* he observed.

---

71 The Admiralty set up its own Canning Factory in 1856

CHAPTER NINE

A 'Crystal Vision'
London – 19th November 2007, 7.30 p.m.

'Come with me and bring that torch.' Seth ordered crisply, then motioned me to follow him. He led me from the office and along a passageway until we came across a stout wooden door, criss-crossed with iron bands and a small square barred grill at eye level.

'What do you make of this?' he remarked as he inserted the smallest of my three keys into the lock, turning it swiftly. The well-oiled mechanism released the sliding bolt and he opened the door, which revealed a stone staircase to a lower passageway.

'Quite astonishing,' I said and followed him down the stairwell, each step worn and bevelled by thousands of footsteps. 'Correct me if I'm wrong, but I'm under the distinct impression that you are also familiar with the other two keys?'

'Not the keys exactly,' replied Seth mysteriously, 'but possibly the locks and doors.'

We continued along another narrow, dimly lit passageway leading from the stairway until we encountered a roughly hewn arched door off the main passage. Odd items, including wooden boxes, chains and iron tools were stacked against it. I helped Seth remove them. He chuckled as he retrieved the two remaining keys from his worn, almost threadbare, grey cardigan pocket. 'Be my guest,' he suggested, proffering the two keys in the palm of his hand.

I chose the large ornate one. 'Go ahead I prompted. You seem to be on a roll and know what you're about. It's not the entrance to Newgate Prison is it?' I laughed jokingly.

'I don't actually know, never had occasion to open it before – no key you see.' He smiled belatedly acknowledging my lame joke. I'm just as puzzled and curious as you are now...here goes!' He attempted to turn the key but the mechanism refused to budge.

'Better try the other key,' I suggested.

He did and this time the lock grumbled begrudgingly into life, releasing its ancient mechanism after some effort. The door, however, seemed even more reluctant to want to open, so I selected a piece of flat ironwork to jolly it along. I inserted the metal to the side and prised it open sufficiently to find leverage for my fingers, then pulled it ajar after a brief struggle. There was just enough space to squeeze through into a dusty, cobweb filled ante-room, lined with shelves stacked with old cans and a very solid looking oak cabinet on one wall. The light from the torch enabled Seth to locate an old and rusty oil lamp, which wouldn't have disgraced the museum upstairs. Remarkably, it still contained oil in the reservoir.

'In for a penny,' joked Seth as he produced a 'Zippo' lighter from his cardigan pocket. 'G.I. gave it to my mother during the Second World War...don't know why,' said Seth, as if an explanation was indeed required.

He fired up the lighter, which in turn ignited the wick of the lamp. The glass funnel, after a quick rub on his cardigan sleeve, was replaced on the lamp and the room came into focus, obviously some kind of store or work room, but evidently not used for decades.

Our attention was drawn to some cans, the style and thick lead soldering indicated their age. The labels on most were indecipherable, but some could be made out...*'Lentil and Bean Broth'*...*'Plums'*...*'Herrings'.*

My attention transferred to the oak cabinet, which I noticed was locked. It carried an ornate escutcheon on the face of the middle door of three. On inspection we discovered it matched the design of the remaining key, which confirmed it was indeed the lock's partner.

Our faces betrayed the excitement we were both feeling. What lay behind the cabinet doors was anybody's guess, but he wasn't waiting to find out as he attacked the lock with gusto. The lock operated smoothly, it was well oiled. The doors swung open to reveal...more tin cans, slightly longer but with much larger diameters and obviously well made, unlike the others in the ante-room. The four largest, which occupied the middle shelf were clearly labelled. One bore the initial 'E', the next the initial 'T', the third 'SG' and the last, the initials 'DY'.

'What do you make of these?' asked Seth.

'Not sure,' I replied, 'but there's only one way to find out.'

'Did you bring along that sharp deck knife that you tipped on to my desk with the other items from your father's 'ditty' box?' enquired Seth.

'Wouldn't be without it,' I laughingly assured him.

'Well then, let's see you make a hole in these cans.' He passed the two marked 'E' and 'T'. 'Try these for starters. Stick them in the wood vice on the edge of that bench.'

I picked up a small iron block from the floor and placed the first can in the vice, then chivvied the deck knife's hard edge around the rim of the well-engineered can using the iron block. I repeated the exercise with the second, then levered the lids open. Driven almost frantic by curiosity, we inspected the strange contents. Both cans contained identical objects. We stared incomprehensibly at two black cylindrical shaped oilskins. We withdrew them from the cans and placed them on the bench.

'What do you think they contain?' I posed the question, but didn't really expect a conclusive answer from Seth.

All he said was, 'Slit them open, light the blue touch paper and stand clear!'

I laughed again but unconvincingly, *who knew what they actually contained?*

I carefully slit the oily fabric, which had been stitched with sail twine and sealed with wax. Contained within were two large bundles of rolled papers. We opened them out simultaneously and gasped in astonishment. On the cover of each were three words— '*Ship's log, Erebus* and '*Ship's log, Terror.* We were left in no doubt as to their importance, but how they came to be here, in the labyrinth below Houndsditch Road eluded us.

It was with some trepidation and nervousness that we now diverted our attention to the third container, marked SG. I picked up the metal block and once more used the deck knife on the lid...I prised it open, looked inside and instantly recoiled, as there before me floated a well preserved pickled human head, its wide open staring eyes silently pleading for a salvation that had obviously not been forthcoming. Whoever had murdered this man had done so with vengeful intent.

A few minutes passed before we recovered from the shock contained in the third can, but eventually, with trembling hands, I reluctantly opened the final can, another oilskin. I raised the deck knife, which glistened in the reflected light from the oil lamp and severed the strands of sail twine. I took out another manuscript— *'A true story'* signed *Davy Young, 1st April 1855.*

I could now be in no doubt as to the circumstances of this man's horrific demise and by whose hands!

⚜

I re-read Davy's document the following morning in the privacy of my hotel room, before reluctantly returning it, along with the logbooks from the Erebus and Terror, to Seth, at the *Copperknob Museum*.

I retraced my steps along the cobbled street to the Judas gate, before ringing the bell once again. Seth opened the gate; no words were exchanged, but we looked at one another in mutual understanding of the commitment we were about to make.

We resealed the documents in the oilskins and secreted them in one larger package, which he locked in his office safe. I was to play no further part in their future. Seth, however, still had a role...he would ensure they reached the appropriate authority after his own death, although he assured me he was not in a hurry to say his goodbyes.

A statement made in his own inimitable way...*'I'm not for 'pushing the daisies up' just yet!'* described his character perfectly.

I never saw Seth again after that gripping and meaningful handshake, which signalled my departure from the museum and London. Our pasts were intertwined irrevocably and, in a sense, our futures were too; although my part was complete, save possibly for a visit to Jane Eley, my father's solicitor, to enlighten her as to the meaning behind the contents of the 'ditty box'.

On reflection, I decided against that particular strategy, some explanations are best left in the past.

CHAPTER TEN

'Mercury' Oil Drilling Vessel
Located to the West of King William Island
September, 2014

Captain Sam Stokes focussed his attention on the drill rig's superintendent with a withering look that was part disdain and part acceptance of what would undoubtedly be another setback. It wouldn't be the first time that he'd reported problems with the drilling operation.

'What is it now?' he asked resignedly.

'Well, Sir, it's unusual in some respects, in that we weren't expecting this one.'

'And what exactly is this 'one'? queried Captain Stokes, 'kindly explain?'

'Certainly, Sir,' answered the Drill Super. 'Well we've suffered another drill malfunction. Our side scan sonar grid did indicate an old wreck some two hundred metres away from our site, but we weren't concerned about its proximity.

'Sounds as though you should have been then?' indicated the Captain, pursing his lips together, which implied fault and made the Drill Super uncomfortable and ill at ease. 'Out with it,' he continued.

'Well,' the Drill Super responded hesitantly, 'I approached Bill Holmes,' Hydrospace's Dive Support superintendent to organise and investigate the drill lock up. You can imagine he wasn't too pleased, as most of his team were out of 'dive time', but he agreed to go himself along with another senior diver.

'Yes, yes,' cajoled Captain Stokes. I'm assuming he found the problem?'

'Of course, Bill's very experienced, used to work in the Arabian Gulf for many years you know. It didn't take him long to fathom out what the problem was.'

'And what was it,' Stokes queried, holding out the palms of his hands to his subordinate in exasperated supplication. 'Time's money you know Drill Super.'

'Well, to cut a long story short,' he hesitated before continuing, 'We'll need to order another drill bit, as the one Bill sighted has suffered some fracturing on a heavy piece of wrecked machinery, apparently some kind of engine. You can still see the maker's name quite clearly, although Bill says it must be over a hundred years' old.'

'What's the maker's name?' queried Stokes, his interest increasing by the second.

'Edmund Bury, Sir,' he replied with enthusiasm.

'Good Lord,' expostulated Stokes. 'You may have stumbled on something that won't cost *us* money this time. Better radio base for a replacement drill by the way, for urgent delivery on the next supply vessel.'

'Will do, Sir, I'll get on to it straight away,' confirmed the Drill Super.

Stokes watched his Super exit, then considered his next move. Head Office would be extremely interested in this latest development. He laughed out loud, rubbed his hands together and said, 'Well, well, well,' before pouring himself a stiff drink, which contravened company regulations. However, on this auspicious occasion, he didn't really care... he was celebrating!

CHAPTER ELEVEN

'Conclusive Evidence'
Admiralty Buildings Chatham – July 20th 2016
Admiral Crabtree's Office

'Package for you, Sir,' announced the pretty but obviously exceedingly efficient 'Wren'. 'Addressed to you personally from a late Mr Seth Terry. The accompanying letter affirms that the contents...documents I believe, will prove to be illuminating and in the National interest!'

'Thank you, Natalie, that sounds intriguing. I'd better examine them immediately. I trust security have cleared the package...can't be too careful these days!' joked Admiral Crabtree with a smile. 'We don't want a 'bombshell' going off at the Admiralty now do we?'

'Certainly not Admiral,' responded Natalie, with a polite grin as she quietly closed his office door.

A few minutes elapsed before several extremely guttural, but obviously concerned expletives emanated from inside the Admiral's office...'Bloody Hell', followed by, the 'proverbial's' certainly hit the fan this time'.

On hearing the Admiral's anguish, Natalie re-entered his office without the courtesy of knocking on this particular occasion.

'Are you all right, Sir?' she queried, concern showing on her face.

He gestured to the open packages atop his desk, before attempting a response, 'Actually, no, I'm not. Ever heard of the *Erebus* and *Terror* and Franklin's lost expedition?'

Vaguely, Sir...what of it?' she questioned. 'I recall that the Erebus was discovered in the September of 2014.'

'Well it looks like we, that's the Admiralty, have some explaining to do. Mr Terry's covering letter doesn't go into any great detail, but the fundamental issue is that there's been a 'cover up', with far reaching implications. There's mention of cannibalism, which Dr John Rae, an overland man, working for the Hudson Bay Company alluded to on his fact-finding search expedition and reported to the Admiralty back in 1853. They, subsequently ignored, then quashed his report. However, there's more...oh, there's much more! Batten down the hatches, Natalie, we're in for rough seas and a prolonged storm.

'Yes, Sir,' she acknowledged, not quite understanding the reasoning behind his last statement. 'I'll fetch my shorthand notepad. I've a feeling my presence is needed urgently.'

'Indeed Natalie, indeed,' responded Crabtree.

CHAPTER TWELVE

Southwell Minster – December 24, 2007

I drew up in the car park located opposite the impressive Minster and switched off the ignition, on that crisp moonlit evening. My father's ditty box, secured by the front passenger's seat belt, seemed to be urging me on. I released the belt and raised the lid of the box. I was, of course, familiar with the contents, but I needed reassurance.

This strange collection of items did indeed tell a story, but each one taken in isolation conveyed relatively nothing. Together, their meaning became exceedingly powerful:

The 'scrimshaw', given by Rob Ellis to Davy, as a parting gift, before Tom and Davy left on the *Prince Rupert*.

The wooden handled deck knife, in a copper sheath, given to Davy by his Uncle Tom, before Catherine and himself left London for Nottingham. An inanimate relic of a failed expedition maybe, but what an improbable tale it would reveal, should it miraculously acquire a voice.

The three iron forged keys returned to me by Seth after securely re-locking the mysterious doors along the passageway beneath the *'Copperknob Museum'*.

The hand brass compass with its inscription given to Catherine and Davy by Tom and Marie 'Harding'…undoubtedly as a keepsake. An assumption of my own of course, but seemingly, highly probable…what other explanation could there be?

And lastly, the exquisite gold ring, which incorporated a sapphire, flanked by two diamonds…Catherine's gift from a loyal nineteenth century lady. All were uniquely important to such a fascinating and intriguing tale.

I reluctantly closed the lid of the ditty box, containing so many memories, relocating the box in the boot of the car for safekeeping, before crossing the festively lit road adjacent the Minster.

～✺～

With significant melancholy I entered the graveyard annex of Southwell Minster's magnificent architectural heritage. A light dusting of snowflakes covered the granite gravestones, for which I was searching.

I took out my copy of the death certificate once more and checked, just as I had checked with the Sexton some twenty minutes previously. He'd directed me to this spot, after generously referring to the records for 1915, on such a busy evening.

I crouched down and brushed away the snow from the inscription, with my gloved hand. It had obviously worn little over the years. One word burned into my soul amidst the simple tribute, which read:

Davy Young
Born June, 9th 1826
Died March, 29th 1915 and
Catherine Young his beloved wife
Born July, 23rd 1826
Died March 30th 1915

Underneath Davy's name, three more letters had been added by the stonemason:

'UKI'

I smiled in understanding, as an uncontrollable tear welled up in the corner of my eye.

In an instant, the centuries merged, as if my father and his ancestors were present, standing close beside me, bonded by the secrets of the ditty box.

His imagined words, *'Now you know too...'* pierced my innermost being in a crystal vision of understanding, at least I thought I'd imagined them.

Map of Franklin's Expedition Route

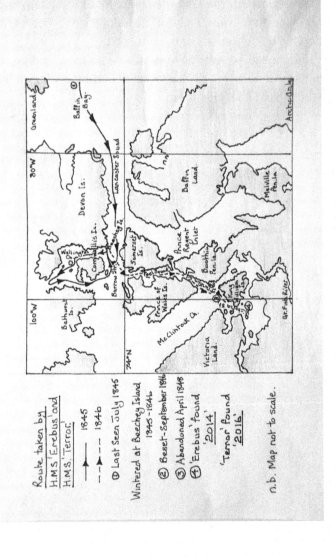

The Yarn of the 'Nancy Bell' –
Sir William Schwenck Gilbert

'Twas on the shores that round our coast
From Deal to Ramsgate span,
That I found alone on a piece of stone
An elderly naval man.

His hair was weedy, his beard was long,
And weedy and long was he,
And I heard this wight on the shore recite,
In a singular minor key:

"Oh, I am a cook and a captain bold,
And the mate of the Nancy brig,
And a bo'sun tight, and a midshipmite,
And the crew of the captain's gig."

And he shook his fists and he tore his hair,
Till I really felt afraid,
For I couldn't help thinking the man had been
drinking,
And so I simply said:

"O, elderly man, it's little I know
Of the duties of men of the sea,
But I'll eat my hand if I understand
How you can possibly be

"At once a cook, and a captain bold,
And the mate of the Nancy brig,
And a bo'sun tight, and a midshipmite,
And the crew of the captain's gig."

Then he gave a hitch to his trousers, which
Is a trick all seamen larn,
And having got rid of a thumping quid,
He spun this painful yarn:

"'Twas in the good ship Nancy Bell
That we sailed to the Indian sea,
And there on a reef we come to grief,
Which has often occurred to me.

"And pretty nigh all o' the crew was drowned
(There was seventy-seven o' soul),
And only ten of the Nancy's men
Said 'Here!' to the muster-roll.

"There was me and the cook and the captain bold,
And the mate of the Nancy brig
And the bo'sun tight, and a midshipmite,
And the crew of the captain's gig.

"For a month we'd neither wittles nor drink,
Till a-hungry we did feel,
So we drawed a lot, and accordin' shot
The captain for our meal.

"The next lot fell to the Nancy's mate,
And a delicate dish he made;
Then our appetite with the midshipmite
We seven survivors stayed.

"And then we murdered the bo'sun tight,
And he much resembled pig,
Then we wittled free, did the cook and me,
On the crew of the captain's gig.

"Then only the cook and me was left,
And the delicate question, 'Which
Of us two goes to the kettle?' arose
And we argued it out as sich.

"For I loved that cook as a brother, I did,
And the cook he worshipped me;
But we'd both be blowed if we'd either be stowed
In the other chap's hold, you see.

"'I'll be eat if you dines off me,' says Tom,
'Yes, that,' says I, 'you'll be,' —
'I'm boiled if I die, my friend,' quoth I,
And 'Exactly so,' quoth he.

"Says he, 'Dear James, to murder me
Were a foolish thing to do,
For don't you see that you can't cook me,
While I can – and will – cook you!'

"So he boils the water, and takes the salt
And the pepper in portions true
(Which he never forgot) and some chopped shalot,
And some sage and parsley too.

"'Come here,' says he, with a proper pride,
Which his smiling features tell,
' 'Twill soothing be if I let you see,
How extremely nice you'll smell.'

"And he stirred it round and round and round,
And he sniffed at the foaming froth;
When I ups with his heels, and smothers his squeals
In the scum of the boiling broth.

"And I eat that cook in a week or less,
And – as I eating be
The last of his chops, why, I almost drops,
For a wessel in sight I see!

"And I never grin, and I never smile,
And I never larf nor play,
But I sit and croak, and a single joke
I have – which is to say:

"Oh, I am a cook and a captain bold,
And the mate of the Nancy brig,
And a bo'sun tight, and a midshipmite,
And the crew of the captain's gig!"

Muster Rolls of H.M.SS. "Erebus" and "Terror"
From Richard J. Cyriax, *Sir John Franklin's
Last Arctic Expedition*,
Collated with the original rolls,
ADM 38/672 and ADM 38/1962, Public Record
Office, London

HMS Erebus

Officers
Sir John Franklin, Captain, Commanding the Expedition
James Fitzjames, Commander
Graham Gore, Lieutenant
H.T.D. Le Vesconte, Lieutenant
James Walter Fairholme, Lieutenant
Robert Orme Sergeant, Mate
Charles Frederick Des Voeux, Mate
Edward Couch, Mate
Henry Foster Collins, Second Master
James Reid, Ice Master
Stephen Samuel Stanley, Surgeon
Harry D.S. Goodsir, Assistant Surgeon
Charles Hamilton Osmer, Purser

Warrant Officers
John Gregory, Engineer
Thomas Terry, Boatswain
John Weekes, Carpenter

Petty Officers
John Murray, Sailmaker, age 43
William Smith, Blacksmith, age 28
Thomas Burt, Armorer, age 22

James W. Brown, Caulker, age 28
Francis Dunn, Caulker's Mate, age 25
Thomas Watson, Carpenter's Mate, age 40
Samuel Brown, Boatswain's Mate, age 27
Richard Wall, Ship's Cook, age 45
James Rigden, Captain's Coxwain, age 32
William Bell, Quartermaster, age 36
Daniel Arthur, Quartermaster, age 35
John Downing, Quartermaster
Robert Sinclair, Captain of the Foretop, age 25
John Sullivan, Captain of the Maintop, age 28
Phillip Reddington, Captain of the Forecastle, age 28
Joseph Andrews, Captain of the Hold, age 35
Edmund Hoar, Captain's Steward, age 23
John Bridgens, Subordinate Officers' Steward, age 26
Richard Aylmore, Gunroom Steward, age 24
William Fowler, Purser's Steward, age 26
John Cowie, Stoker
Thomas Plater, Stoker

Able Seamen
George Thompson, age 27
John Hartnell, age 25
John Stickland, age 24
Thomas Hartnell, age 23
William Orren, age 34
William Closson, age 25
Charles Coombs, age 28
John Morfin, age 25
Charles Best, age 23
Thomas McConvey, age 24
Henry Lloyd, age 26
Thomas Work, age 41

Robert Ferrier, age 29
Josephus Geater, age 32
Thomas Tadman, age 28
Abraham Seeley, age 34
Francis Pocock, age 24
Robert Johns, age 24
William Mark, age 24

Royal Marines
David Bryant, Sergeant, age 31
Alexander Pearson, Corporal, age 30
Robert Hopcraft, Private, age 38
William Pilkington, Private, age 28
William Braine, Private, age 31
Joseph Healey, Private, age 29
William Reed, Private, age 28

Boys
George Chambers, age18
David Young, age 18

HMS Terror

Officers
Francis Rawden Moira Crozier, Captain
Edward Little, Lieutenant
George Henry Hodgson, Lieutenant
John Irving, Lieutenant
Frederick John Hornby, Mate
Robert Thomas, Mate
Giles Alexander McBean, Second Master
Thomas Blanky, Ice Master
John Smart Peddie, Surgeon

Alexander McDonald, Assistant Surgeon
E.J. Helpman, Clerk in Charge

Warrant Officers
James Thompson, Engineer
John Lane, Boatswain
Thomas Honey, Carpenter

Petty Officers
Thomas Johnson, Boatswain's Mate, age 28
Alexander Wilson, Carpenter's Mate, age 27
Reuben Male, Captain of the Forecastle, age 27
David McDonald, Quartermaster, age 45
John Kenley, Quartermaster
William Rhodes, Quartermaster, age 31
Thomas Darlington, Caulker, age 29
Samuel Honey, Blacksmith, age 22
John Torrington, Leading Stoker, age 19
John Diggle, Cook, age 36
John Wilson, Captain's Coxwain, age 33
Thomas R. Farr, Captain of the Maintop, age 32
Harry Peglar, Captain of the Foretop, age 37
William Goddard, Captain of the Hold, age 39
Cornelius Hickey, Caulker's Mate, age 24
Thomas Jopson, Captain's Steward, age 27
Thomas Armitage, Gun-room Steward, age 40
William Gibson, Subordinate Officers' Steward, age 22
Edward Genge, Subordinate Officers' Steward, age 21
Luke Smith, Stoker, age 27
William Johnson, Stoker, age 45

Able Seamen
George J. Cann, age 23
William Strong, age 22

David Sims, age 24
John Bailey, age 21
William Jerry, age 29
Henry Sait, age 23
Alexander Berry, age 32
John Handford, age 28
John Bates, age 24
Samuel Crispe, age 24
Charles Johnson, age 28
William Shanks, age 29
David Leys, age 37
William Sinclair, age 30
Goerge Kinnaird, age23
Edwin Lawrence, age 30
Magnus Manson, age 28
James Walker, age 29
William Wentzall, age 33

Royal Marines
Solomon Tozer, Sergeant, age 34
William Hedges, Corporal, age 30
William Heather, Private, age 37
Henry Wilkes, Private, age 28
John Hammond, Private, age 32
James Daly, Private, age 30

Boys
Robert Golding, age 19
Thomas Evans, age 18

Author's Notes

Sir John Franklin

Sir John Franklin was born in Spilsby, Lincolnshire in 1786 and joined the Royal Navy aged fifteen. Four years later, he participated in the *Battle of Trafalgar* in 1805 aboard *HMS Bellerophon*.

Franklin undertook in total four expeditions to the Arctic. He mapped over 3000 miles of coastline and collected a huge amount of information on the ecology, geology and meteorology of the Arctic and Northern Canada.

In 1828 he married Jane Griffin, a friend of his first wife, Eleanor Anne Porden, who died in 1825 of tuberculosis. In 1829, he was knighted by George IV. In the same year, he was awarded the first Gold Medal of the *The Société de Géographie* (French, 'Geographical Society'). The world's oldest geographical society, founded in 1821.

In 1836 he received two more honours: *Knight Commander of the Royal Guelphic Order* (by King William IV) and *Knight of the Greek Order of the Redeemer.*

That same year, he was appointed Lieutenant Governor of Tasmania (Van Dieman's Land) and served until 1843. During this period and again afterward, his wife, Jane gained a reputation for being extremely liberated for a woman of that period. Her exploits were occasionally 'at odds' with others in polite society circles of the day. She was considered a well travelled lady, who spoke her mind.

In 1845, Franklin agreed to command an expedition to

locate the North West Passage, many years after his last foray into the Arctic. His wife advised against such an enterprise. Nevertheless, his two vessels, the *Erebus* and *Terror*, set course on their fateful journey on 19th May 1845, a voyage expected to last three or more years.

When nothing was heard from the expedition, the Admiralty and Lady Jane Franklin organised a series of search expeditions over several years.

In all, thirty-nine expeditions were launched to ascertain the fate of Franklin's ships, with varying degrees of success. A reward of £20,000 for the rescue of Franklin, £10,000 for finding the ships and £10,000 for finding the North West Passage was offered by the Admiralty. A cynical observer might believe that the Admiralty's prime motivation was to locate the passage by engaging the fervour of the nation in a search for Franklin (a popular figure of his time). Whatever the real reason, many ships were lost in the process, e.g. In 1852 alone, four ships were lost. That same year, Franklin was promoted to Rear Admiral of the Blue, an unintentional posthumous promotion.

Confirmation of Franklin's death was eventually determined by Captain McClintock aboard the *Fox*, a vessel owned by Lady Jane Franklin. A document, 'The Victory Point Letter', found in a cairn (pile of stones where messages were secreted), indicated that Franklin died on 11th June 1847, fourteen years before McClintock found the evidence. NB: three men died on the *Fox* expedition.

Several statues exist today honouring Sir John Franklin: In London, Hobart, Tasmania and Spilsby, Lincolnshire.

The epitaph inscribed on a memorial in Westminster Abbey and the plinth of the Tasmanian Hobart statue probably encapsulates Franklin's determined character:

Not here! The white North hath thy bones; and thou
Heroic sailor-soul,
Art passing on thine happier voyage now
Toward no earthly pole

Alfred, Lord Tennyson (1809–1892)

The actual cost of finding Franklin, both in monetary terms and lives lost was tremendously high. Recent figures (cost equivalent in 2014) suggest that the Admiralty expended £20.5 million, Lady Jane Franklin, £1 million and the U.S. government £3 million. Other investors' also spent huge amounts to ascertain the complete Franklin story.

In September 2014, the wreck of the *Erebus* was located near King William Island, followed by the discovery of the *Terror* in September 2016, which may prove extremely significant.

Many tried to locate the North West Passage before and after Franklin. One such expedition, led by Captain Robert McClure between 1850 and 1855, ostensibly to search for Franklin, succeeded. He progressed in stages, travelling by ship and overland on foot. For his determination and fortitude, he was knighted and received a reward of £5,000. However, his expedition fell short of the aspiration...a navigable sea route from the Atlantic to the Pacific. This feat was eventually achieved by Norwegian, Roald Amundsen many years later.

In 1903, Amundsen commissioned the *Freya*, a vessel with a very shallow draft for the expedition. Although 'frozen in' each winter for five consecutive years, the small crew finally achieved their goal.

In 1911, Amundsen achieved world-wide fame. He reached the South Pole ahead of Scott. However, despite Amundsen's success in the Arctic, a commercial route is, even now, only viable in the warmest of summers for cargo carrying vessels, assisted in part by modern 'Ice breakers', i.e. ships with reinforced bows and hulls. Global warming *may* arguably change the North West's Passage viability in the future.

Stephan Goldner
Stephan Goldner, born in Hungary around 1810, arrived in London as an immigrant in 1837, stating his profession as a merchant.

In the 1841 census, he changed his name to Stephen and in the same year, filed a patent to use a process in his canning factory, which consisted of using brine instead of water as a 'boiling agent' to increase cooking temperatures. Incredibly, the patent for such a process had already been accepted in France two years previously.

His wife, Susan, had one child, also called Susan. She was adopted as an eight year old by another family, according to the Census of 1851, presumably after his wife died.

Known as the 'preserved provisions man' in the 1845 Trade Directory, he succeeded in obtaining the contract to supply the Franklin expedition, against established competition.

Despite rumours as to the fate of the Franklin expedition, he was awarded several more contracts by the Admiralty, but was warned in 1850 that his meat needed to be 'genuine'. To meet demand, he increased the can size, but failed to do the mathematics, which led to the 'genuine' meat not being cooked adequately.

Much of Goldner's produce was inevitably dumped at sea by Admiralty vessels. This prompted the Admiralty to investigate setting up their own operation in 1856, after a Commons Select Committee sat to look into a series of complaints.

Author, Sue Shephard considered the whole 'Goldner debacle' a 'PR disaster for canned food'.

Ultimately and possibly unforgivably, the Admiralty were guilty of being too hasty in awarding the contract to Goldner to supply Franklin's expedition.

He was to supply thousands of cans in a short time span from a suspect Whitechapel factory that hadn't been inspected. If the Admiralty had seen fit to inspect the premises, they would have been appalled to find workers recruited from the poorest London families, where hygiene standards were almost non-existent and where bacteria thrived. Additionally, the 'produce', which consisted mainly of poor meat, rotten vegetables and, occasionally, cartilage and bone provided a damning statement of his overall operation.

Strangely, nothing more was heard of Goldner after 1855. His reputation was most certainly irreversibly damaged by a series of questionable supply contracts. His disappearance may have raised more than a raised eyebrow in some quarters, but I suspect most of his competitors, including, 'Gamble', 'Hogarth' and 'Cooper and Aves' welcomed his demise whether literal or by a planned departure, initiated to extricate himself from future prosecution.

Akaiktcho

Akaitcho, Chief of the Yellowknives was an aggressive but shrewd leader. In 1820, several of the tribe were recruited by the Royal Navy to act as guides and hunters in an overland search for the North West Passage. *Akaitcho* acted as interpreter. Participants in this expedition included Franklin, George Back and John Richardson, a doctor and naturalist. In 1833, George Back once again used *Akaitcho's* knowledge and expertise on another search. He had great respect for the *Yellowknife's* abilities in overcoming difficulties.

Akaitcho had seven wives, but produced just one son. His legacy was honoured with the formation of the 'Akaitcho Territory Government' (A 'First Nations' organisation). *Akaitcho Lake*, between the Great Bear Lake and the Coppermine River is named after him. *Akaitcho's* name translates into 'Big Foot', meaning 'like a wolf, with big paws who can travel long distances over snow'.

NB Akaitcho lived from 1786 to 1838 and would have come into contact with many explorers and been aware of Samuel Hearne. For the purposes of my story, I have extended Akaitcho's lifespan by another twelve plus years.

Finally, my apologies to the 'purists' still engaged with the history of sailing and the Tall Ships that still ply the oceans of the world today. My knowledge is, unfortunately, lacking in the finesse and workings of such magnificent ships and sadly confined to power driven vessels of the twentieth century.

With respect to the *Erebus* and *Terror*, I have introduced some fictional elements in their construction and operation. I hope that these do not detract from the overall storyline.

ABOUT THE AUTHOR

Born in Nottingham. Attended *'Training Ship Mercury'* at Hamble, Southampton, aged 13 to 17, leaving as Cadet Captain of Drake Division. Served in the Merchant Navy (world-wide voyages) as a navigation officer with Ropners (a trampship company), Christian Salvesen, Salén and Reardon Smith, before relocating to the Arabian Gulf as Captain of various vessels engaged in the offshore oil industry: Hydrographic Survey, Dive Support and Oil Rig Supply, based at Dubai and Abu Dhabi.

He spent several years in the Middle East, latterly as Marine Superintendent/Manager of Gulf Pilots, based at Khor Fakkan, Sharjah, U.A.E., where he pursued interests in sailing, scuba diving and tennis; even playing a season for Fujairah Football Club.

On his return to the U.K., Alan secured a position with Nottingham Trent University as Head of Auxiliary Services, with diverse responsibilities. During this period, he participated in Karate with his son, Stephen (both gaining belts along the way). More recently, he achieved success, first as a navigator in *'Extreme Chaos'* and then as driver of *'Alien'* in the Honda Formula Four Stroke Offshore Powerboat race series, completing eight seasons.

Whilst researching Franklin's Expedition, he noted a name on the crew list, which was the same as his father's. This inspired him to write *'Crystal Vision'*.